THE ANTIHEROES

Book One
of
THE ANTIHEROES

by

JACOB PEPPERS

Visit the author website:
www.JacobPeppersAuthor.com

For Norah Alaina Peppers
Right now you're just a bump in your mom's belly
And a blessing in your dad's life
Soon, though, you'll be here and that's a fine thing
After all, Gabriel needs a partner in crime

Sign up for my new releases mailing list to hear about promotions, launches, and, for a limited time, get a FREE copy of *The Silent Blade,* the prequel book to the bestselling epic fantasy series, The Seven Virtues.

Go to JacobPeppersAuthor.com to claim your free book!

CHAPTER ONE

The ale wasn't bad. It wasn't good either, but Dannen knew from experience that a couple of mugs of the stuff and taste wouldn't factor into it anymore. It was one of those little bits of magic even a normal man, without any sorcery, might experience. Like that warm, slightly-sick feeling a man got when a beautiful girl smiled at him, even if that beautiful girl also happened to work at an establishment where beautiful girls were paid good coin for such smiles. And, of course, what would follow.

There was the sound of shouting from the other side of the common room, and Dannen glanced over. A fight, probably, but no way to tell for sure as a crowd had begun to gather, obscuring the source of the shouts. Instead of making his way over like everyone else, Dannen leaned back, propped his feet on a chair and let out a satisfied sigh. The shouting was growing louder, and men and women in the crowd were whispering excitedly to each other, but Dannen paid them no mind. The older he got, the more it seemed there was always some commotion going on, always some sort of trouble of this kind or that. The best a clever man could do was to try his best to avoid it. After all, trouble always found a man soon enough. There wasn't any reason to go hunting for it.

Mind your business. Avoid commotions. Preventatives for misery if ever there were any. Like those spells street wizards sometimes sold to the foolish or desperate—often one in the same—charms and tonics to make a poor man rich or a sick man well. The difference, of course, was that they actually worked. At least, most of the time. And for those times that didn't? For those times a man couldn't hide from trouble no matter how he tried?

1

Well, that was why the gods had invented ale, wasn't it? Another bit of its magic—as far as Dannen was concerned a foaming mug of the stuff was more magical than any sorcerer's potion or healer's prayers. If a man drank enough of it, his troubles vanished as if they'd never been. For a while, anyway, until the potion's effects wore off. Not perfect magic, maybe, but the best on offer.

The price of such magic—there always was one where magic was concerned—was a man got a bit loose around the midsection, and that he had to be a magician himself to fit into his trousers on some days. A price Dannen would pay and pay gladly. He'd given up what little vanity he'd started with long ago, traded it for...well, he wasn't sure for *what* exactly, but he still counted it fair. After all, vanity, like so many other conceits, seemed to inevitably lead to trouble. And if he was anything, Dannen was a man who avoided trouble.

Which was why when the commotion grew louder, when he heard a woman's shout for help, he ignored the small, frail internal voice—not quite dead, no matter how many years he spent trying to drown it in ale—telling him he should go help. Oh, it sounded reasonable enough, that voice, sounded *nice* enough, but Dannen had cause to know that it was a real son of a bitch. Like one of those friends who always pushed a man forward into the fight, telling him he was bound to win, cheering him on, sure, but really just wanting to watch the fool get his ass kicked.

Dannen had been that fool, more than once. He didn't intend on being it again. Better to be a new kind of fool, for the variety of the thing. He sighed as the shouting continued, taking another pull from his ale. Then he noticed a young man, maybe not even in his twenties, rising from a nearby table where he'd been sitting with some of his friends. There was a determined look in his eyes, one Dannen recognized all too well, and he grunted wearily as he watched the man's friends try to pull him back down into his chair.

The man, however—if a youth with a mustache thinner than some women's Dannen had seen could be called a man—knocked his friends' hands away. He rose and gripped the handle of a sword sheathed at his side, a blade which, judging by the ornate, ridiculously-tasseled scabbard, was as useless as the man was terrified. But terrified or not the young man shouted, "Unhand her!" in a voice that might have been more intimidating if it had squeaked a little less. Dannen rubbed at his eyes. *Unhand her.* Who spoke like that, anyway? Nobody. Nobody except those shining, blond-headed heroes in storybooks the young man's mother had probably read him when he was a child...like a week ago.

Dannen took another drink of his ale, watching the boy make his way toward the crowd which began to part for him, opening up a space with indecent haste, those milling men and women eager to see the blood that would inevitably follow.

The crowd's parting revealed three men and one of the tavern's serving women. The woman's back was pressed against a table, and one of the men was pawing at her bodice, trying to undo the laces at her breasts but fumbling them in his haste. The man's two companions, however, had turned to regard the challenger. Big men, each of them, with enough scars on their forearms and faces to show that though they might not have been the best fighters out there, they certainly had far more experience than the would-be hero.

"The fuck you say, boy?" one asked, grinning and revealing a mouth that was missing more teeth than it had, another indication, had one been needed, of the man's experience in brawls.

The young man glanced back at his table as if for help, but his friends all seemed possessed of a suddenly dire need to look anywhere but at him. The hero wilted somewhat, his shoulders slumping at perhaps his first realization—certainly not his last—that the world was no storybook. Dannen had the brief hope that he would leave it. In real life, after all, most of the heroes were dead, and the villains almost always won.

But the young man rallied, calling on what courage—and foolishness—he possessed, squaring his shoulders and meeting the grinning man's gaze as best he could. "I-I sa—" He paused, clearing his throat. "I said, unhand her."

"And if we don't?" the man asked, obviously as eager as the would-be hero was afraid.

The boy's fingers flittered at the hilt of his sword like a moth around a flame, wanting to draw it just as the moth wanted to touch the blaze, never mind that they'd each get burned for their trouble. *Don't, you damned fool,* Dannen thought. Without the sword, the boy would probably walk away with a black eye or two, maybe a few bruises, and one priceless understanding—that he wasn't a hero. That no one was, really. All in all, Dannen thought he'd be the better for it. But if he drew the blade, a black eye would be the least of his problems.

He could see the boy thinking about it, weighing his options, deciding whether his pride could survive backing down. Dannen would have told him, had he asked, that it could survive far more than that. He ought to know; after all, his own pride had long since become little more than a withered husk and he the happier—and healthier—for it.

But the boy, like so many doomed men before him, was committed or at least thought he was, and in the end, there was no difference between the two. The sword didn't ring as it came free of its scabbard the way they did in the books. It didn't come free at all, at least not on the first attempt. Instead, the youth botched the job somehow, only getting it halfway free before he stumbled and nearly fell. He kept his feet though, and the second tug got the blade free.

Shit. Dannen started to take another drink from his ale only to realize that it was empty. With a sigh, he rose and started toward the bar, thinking he wasn't anywhere near as drunk as he ought to be. In the suddenly near-silence of the tavern—save the girl's weeping, at least—he heard the two men exchanging pleasantries as he made his way through the crowd. All common enough words, ones he'd heard thousands of times before and that amounted to little more than—"I'll kill you *this* much." "Oh, yeah? Then I'll kill you *harder.*" All words, threats he'd long since become bored with and that only meant one thing—blood was on the way.

He had to slap the counter before the bartender turned away from the spectacle. "Another ale," Dannen said.

The man frowned, but poured it, likely suspecting—rightly so as far as Dannen was concerned—that he would need the coin to fix the place up after the coming fight.

"*Careful, Claude, he's got a knife!*" one of the lad's friends shouted, though he did so from the safety of his chair. Not a fool like his buddy, then, and that was something. Though, judging by the would-be hero's tense stance, he needn't have bothered with the warning.

Based on his pale expression and wide eyes as he studied the bared blade—no stylish sword this, a blade to impress one's friends with, but one nicked from hard and bloody use—Dannen doubted the young man saw anything else in the world, just then.

Just put the blade down, Dannen thought. *You'll get a beating, sure, but one you'll live to bitch about.* The young man didn't, though. Instead, he squared his slim shoulders, doing his best to look tough and not giving it a good go considering that what he looked like, more than anything, was getting ready to piss himself. "I s-said u-unhand her."

Words from a children's story again. Words the hero spouted pompously before wreaking absolute havoc and mayhem on any unfortunate villain who dared disobey. The problem, of course, was that all of those heroes—and the villains, come to that—were fictional, men whose victory came as easy, quite literally, as the swipe of the author's pen. In fiction the heroes always won. After all, no one wanted to hear a story where the hero was a fool who got himself cut down in a tavern to save a serving maid who'd no doubt seen far worse.

Dannen glanced around the room, thinking surely someone would stop this one-sided nonsense before it went too far—after all the direction it was going was plain enough for anyone to see. No one did though, all of them far too excited at the spectacle to come to consider it except the serving woman, maybe, and she was too preoccupied trying to keep the tattered front of her dress over her breasts—nice ones, Dannen had to admit—to help her would-be hero.

The men started toward the boy, and Dannen bit back a curse, rising himself and moving back toward his table with a drunken swagger that hadn't been noticeable on his way to the bar. Mostly because he *wasn't* drunk—more's the pity—and made it a habit never to swagger. Now though, he did, stumbling into the crowd behind the boy, those who'd fought fiercely to be close to the action. Maybe even close enough, if they were lucky, to get some of the young hero's blood on their shirt or face as he was killed, a story to tell their children, Dannen supposed.

Dannen pushed into them, hiding the disgust he felt behind a drunken, blinking mask. Might have been he pushed them a bit harder than he needed to, but no one challenged him. They cursed and hissed, sure, but that was all. After all, why go looking for a fight when you were about to witness one and probably a killing to boot? Dannen paid them no attention, too busy being drunk and swaggering and all that, until he was finally behind the boy. "Wha's at?" he slurred. He spun as if someone had spoken and anyone watching might have been forgiven for believing it an accident that the movement brought the thick glass of his ale mug into the back of the youth's head.

The boy let out a groan, the sword falling out of his fingers as he collapsed to the ground unconscious. "Aye, fella," Dannen grumbled, turning back, "watch where you're goin, eh?"

The youth didn't answer. Mostly because, just then, he was too busy being unconscious to answer. Too busy being unconscious to get killed too, though, so that was something.

The two men, suddenly robbed of their easy prey, scowled at Dannen, and judging by the way the one in the front held the knife in a white-knuckled grip, considered whether or not to go to work on Dannen with it if for no other reason than he'd ruined their fun. The serving woman—whose harasser had paused to stare at Dannen along with the rest of the common room— hocked and spat a very un-damsel-like glob of spit at his feet. "You drunken son of a bitch."

Well. He'd been called far worse in his time, often by people he liked, so that didn't bother him. He even understood her anger, in a way. After all, her hero was lying unconscious on the floor now, his sword beside him, and if he was the hero, the other men the dragon, that surely cast her as the damsel. Not that damsels went around calling people sons of bitches, at least so far as Dannen knew...but then, the world was an interesting place, that if nothing else.

But he wasn't paying much attention to the woman, not then. Instead, he was looking at the man with the knife, the guy trying to decide if maybe he wanted to cut somebody up so bad that anybody would do, Dannen hoping he would just let it go. But as always, hope was no more than makeup on a cheap whore, pretty enough to look at maybe, but hiding inevitable disappointment underneath.

Dannen watched the man start forward and gave a heavy sigh. No doubt, the man would have been hard pressed, if asked, to explain why he wanted Dannen dead, all of a sudden. The others, too, who'd forgotten all about the serving woman. But if anyone in the common room save Dannen himself had any doubts about their motive, none voiced it, everyone making space around him, eager for the bloodshed that he would have denied them.

"Don't want any trouble," Dannen said, backing away, and holding up his hands, one of which still held the mug of ale.

"Maybe not," the closest man, the one with the knife agreed, "but you got it anyway."

A line that belonged in a play, one uttered by the villain. It seemed to Dannen, now as always, that most people made of themselves actors, not being who they were, not really, but playing a part, their part as they saw it. And Dannen's part, most certainly, was not one of hero. It was, in fact, one of the assholes who was going to try his level best—and by pretty much any means necessary—not to end the day with a few more holes than when he'd started it.

"I'm just going to leave and—"

But the man with the knife was done talking, charging at him with a shout.

Most people, in such a situation, might have grabbed the unconscious youth's sword lying on the floor in easy reach, but not Dannen. He'd learned long ago that swords were as much a danger to the one wielding them as to those they were wielded against. He had promised himself, had promised Val, never to pick one up again. And though he'd broken many promises over the years, that one he had kept. So instead of grasping the blade, he pivoted to the side as the man rushed him.

Years ago, it would have been an easy enough thing to do, but Dannen was older than he'd once been with the first gray hairs of middle age showing in his beard. More to the point, he was fatter, slower, and he didn't manage to get entirely out of the man's way. Instead, the thug's shoulder struck him a glancing blow, hurling Dannen into a table. He tried to catch his balance but stumbled backward, sprawling over the wooden, beer-drenched surface, his face striking an ale mug.

There was a burst of pain in his nose where it hit the hard mug. And there it was. Blood, shining bright red in the lantern light. The best reward a man could hope for when he played at being a hero. He'd thought himself past such arrogant, and almost always fatal notions, thought he'd changed, but life and time loved nothing more than making fools of men. "Son of a bitch," he muttered. It wasn't the first time he'd had his nose bloodied. Truth was, he'd had far worse. Of course, such a thing didn't stop it from hurting like a bastard.

He rose from the table unsteadily, some part of him thinking it still might not be too late to talk his way out of it, a thought that was shot down as soon as he saw the man's face. Saw, too, that he was holding the knife like he meant to use it. Luckily, meaning to do something and knowing *how* to do it were very different, so when he brought the blade down, Dannen, gut and all, rolled off the table, narrowly avoiding the blade but not quite managing to avoid the knee of one of those sitting at the table, apparently too excited about the show to get out of the damned way.

The knee—bony as all shit—struck Dannen in his already tender nose, but, life being what it was, he wasn't surprised. What *did* surprise him after he'd managed to pick himself up off the ground was just how angry he was. That anger was the reason he'd sworn off violence—and swords—years ago. Proof yet again that he was a fool, if anyone was still bothering to keep track. After all, just because a man swore off violence didn't mean violence swore off *him.*

Dannen knew he should relax, take it easy. But knowing changed nothing. Suddenly, he didn't care if the man wanted to talk it out or not, and when the thug rushed at him again, remembering which end of the blade to hold and no more than that, Dannen gave him a bloody smile. The thug swiped at him, telegraphing the blow so much that he may as well have drawn a diagram. Well, he might have been out of shape, might have had aches in his knees and elbows he wouldn't have imagined a man *could* have ten years ago, but Dannen wasn't the type of man to pass up an invitation, not when it was so kindly put. So when the thug extended his front leg and started a spin that looked like it might be finished some time tomorrow, it was an easy enough thing to kick him a good one in the balls.

Another one of the bits of wisdom life had been kind enough to teach Dannen was it didn't much matter how big or strong a man was, how angry either. A well-placed kick in the balls was enough to make him rethink some things—when, that was, he was able to think at all. The thug let out a shriek, dropping the knife and gripping his aching fruits instead.

Dannen felt no small amount of satisfaction as he wiped an arm across his bloody nose, staining his tunic—a new one too, and damn the priests for saying the gods weren't cruel—watching the man writhe for a brief moment. Then, remembering that there were still a couple more of the bastards behind him, he did what any sensible man would do under the circumstances. He kicked the bastard in the face. Best way to keep him out of the fight, that was the reason, had nothing to do with enjoying it. That's what the second kick was for.

With the man thoroughly unconscious, Dannen spun to face the others, and a part of him that wasn't full of anger—an increasingly small part—felt a stab of worry. It wasn't good to get angry, not for anybody. His old swordmaster had told him as much repeatedly a lifetime ago, and on that much, at least, he'd been right. Anger was bad, was dangerous for anybody, but for Dannen most of all, so he took a slow deep breath.

It didn't help. But then, a man had to breathe so there was that. He realized his fists were clenched at his sides and the lunatic, gibberish ravings of fury he'd heard for the last several seconds were coming from him. *Easy,* he told himself, *take it easy, damnit,* but the words made no more sense than the snarlings coming from his mouth. The second man hesitated, suddenly looking unsure, and who wouldn't, when confronted with a raving man with blood pouring down his face, mixing with flecks of spittle in a crimson froth?

The man hesitated, but Dannen did not. He charged, screaming wildly, feeling happy, *really* happy, for the first time in years. It was strange how anger and violence could make him feel that way when all the drinking and whoring in the world didn't come close.

Strange..

It was the last rational, truly understandable thought he had. What followed weren't thoughts so much as shouts of fury inside his head, growls and hisses, the language of violence, a language no man truly understood. Though, it had to be said, that Dannen Ateran, once known as the Bloody Butcher, understood it better than most.

CHAPTER TWO

He woke in a damp alleyway. The first thing he became aware of was the tacky, coppery taste of blood in his mouth. It was a taste he was all too familiar with. Gingerly, he probed along the inside of his cheeks with his tongue to discover, unsurprisingly, that he'd bitten chunks out of both sides. He'd done it before, many times when the battle lust was on him. It was a wonder he had any cheeks left. Still, as annoying as the sharp pain was, he didn't think that was the worst of it.

Gods, but I should know better.

His head was pounding like an anvil beneath the blows of a blacksmith with a cruel streak. He groaned, opening his eyes with a monumental effort. He climbed his way to a sitting position, propped his back against the alley wall, and began to take stock. His mouth and chin were covered in dried blood from where the thug had busted his nose, but not enough to account for the blood staining his once-white tunic—so much that a man could have been forgiven for believing the tailor had used crimson fabric.

Someone, then, had done a lot of bleeding, and it hadn't all been Dannen. Knowing well how he got when the lust came on him, he doubted even most of it was his. A good thing, sure, but bad, too. He sighed heavily. It wasn't the first alleyway he'd woken in, more's the pity, but he'd promised himself years ago that the last time would *be* the last time. A liar, then, as well as a fool.

If the gods had a sense of humor, it was a dark one. The skin on his knuckles was scraped raw from hitting something—what, he didn't remember, but considering that the answer was likely one of the thugs' faces, he'd just as soon not.

Well, he hadn't had a sword on him, so at least that was one vow that was still intact. Probably. Certainly he didn't remember drawing a blade, and if a man couldn't remember breaking a vow, did it even count?

He hocked and spat up a mouthful of blood then swallowed past a dusty throat. He considered just lying there, going back to sleep or at least to an oblivious unconsciousness. Based on how much he hurt, moving would probably be a mistake. The problem, of course, was that hanging around until friends of the person—or, more likely, people—he'd hurt showed up would be worse. He began to rise, a job made more difficult by the incessant throbbing in his head, though whether that came from a blow he'd taken or the drink there was no way of knowing.

He was halfway to his feet when a shout came from the end of the alleyway.

"There he is!" cried a heavy-set woman in a blue dress, pointing at Dannen like he was a piece of cow shit she'd nearly stepped on. Only a glance was enough to tell him that here was the sort of woman who made for a miserable husband. Or, more likely, a dead one, and that no doubt under suspicious circumstances. It was a toss up then, which was more intimidating: the woman or the four uniformed guardsmen standing beside her, all with bared swords in their hands.

"He's the one burned down Pelver's tavern!" the woman exclaimed—he had a feeling she never spoke, this woman, only exclaimed. Her shrieking wasn't doing any favors for Dannen's headache, but he thought that probably the least of his problems, the frowning guardsmen a bit higher on the list.

"That true, stranger?" one of the guards asked, the tight grip he had on his sword showing he had little doubt.

How the shit should I know? Dannen thought. But since he figured there were probably better ways to die than being hacked to pieces by four offended guardsmen, he shrugged. "Doesn't sound much like me."

"Of *course* he did it!" the shrew screeched, and Dannen felt another twinge of pity for her husband. If the poor bastard wasn't dead yet, he was damn sure trying to be. "He's wearing the gods-blasted *sign* around his gods-blasted *neck!*"

Dannen followed her pointing finger—wielded it like a sword, that one—and was as surprised as the guardsmen to find that the woman was right. A thick wooden sign sat at his chest, hanging there by a chain around his neck which at least went a little way toward explaining the ache he'd been having. *Pelver's Tavern*, it read, *NO Fighting.*

There was a bit of blood staining the sign—more than a bit, in truth—enough to nearly obscure the word "fighting." Blame it on the drink or the ridiculousness of it all, but something about that struck Dannen as funny, and he started to laugh. He regretted it immediately, of course, for it sent a fresh wave of pain through his fragile head. More concerning, however, was that the laughter did a pretty good job of ridding the guards of any lingering doubts they might have had that he'd been up to mischief. They marched toward him then, their blades at the ready, looking like they were waiting on an excuse to start chopping.

Dannen sighed. Maybe he could have outrun them—certainly there was plenty of alley between him and them, but why bother? His whole body hurt, and he thought maybe a night in the dungeons—or a couple of them—might not be such a bad thing. Of course, if he'd actually killed any of those poor bastards back at the tavern it might be a bit more than that, but he thought he'd probably remember a murder or two.

"Look, fellas," he said, trying his best to be reasonable—it was important, being reasonable, kept a man from killing or getting killed...except for when it didn't, of course. "I'll come along quietly, alright? There's no need for the blades."

Which was true enough. If he'd had a mind to fight just then— something just about as far from Dannen's mind as anything could have been—he thought he could have been conquered pretty damned thoroughly by another shout or two from the woman.

"Put the weapon down!" one of the guards barked. "Slowly."

Weapon? Dannen thought, what in the name—that was when he noticed the stick in his hands. Probably, he should have noticed it sooner, but circumstances being what they were, he'd been a bit distracted. The stick was a foot and a half long, but judging by the jagged edge it had been decidedly longer at some point. An edge that, as it happened, was stained with dried blood.

Well, he thought. *Bastard no doubt had it coming.* Not that he could remember that nor, if he was being honest, could he strictly remember who the bastard in question had been. Whoever it was though, stabbed with a length of broken off wood or not, he doubted his day was looking as shitty as Dannen's own. He tossed the broken piece of wood away. There was nothing else to do.

The two guardsmen approached warily despite his words, and considering his appearance, he couldn't really blame them. The woman was right behind them, actually gripping the jerkin of one of the guardsmen, and between them, he figured her to be the scariest.

"Look," he said, holding up his hands, "I don't want any trouble." The guards didn't believe him, that much was obvious, approaching like he was a wild man—a wild man who attacked people with brooms and passed out with a tavern sign hung around his neck. Which, of course, he was. Likely, the blood staining his hands didn't help matters, but at some point it just became gratuitous anyway.

"Put these on," one of the men said, producing a pair of manacles from where they hung on his belt and tossing them at Dannen's feet.

Dannen stared at the hateful metal cuffs, lying there in a coil like some snake about to strike and felt his jaw tense as a flood of memories threatened to beat down the wall he'd built around it, a wall which was always eroding, always in need of repair. "No."

"The fuck did you say?" another guard asked.

"*Kill him!*" the shrew screamed.

"Listen," Dannen said softly, doing his best to quell his rapidly-beating heart. "I'll come with you, and if it turns out I've earned some time in the dungeons, I'll take it without a word of complaint." He glanced down at the manacles again lying a foot away. Had they been so close before? Or had they moved closer when he wasn't looking, eager to find a home clasped around his flesh, stealing his freedom? *Never again,* he told himself.

"I'll come with you," he said again, his mouth as dry as if he'd swallowed glass. Which, considering how the night had gone, he supposed was possible. "But I'm not putting those damned things on."

The second guard grunted, scowling and opening his mouth, no doubt to utter some threat or another, but the shrew beat him to it.

"You're a criminal, that's what you are! I saw what you did—I saw." Saying the last like he was some sneak thief caught with his hand in her pocket. Ridiculous, of course. Dannen was no thief, and he wouldn't have dared reach into the woman's pockets even if he had been. Probably full of snakes and vinegar.

"Look," the first guard said, clearly struggling to keep his patience, "I don't know what all this is about, but it's our job to figure it out, savvy? So why don't you just take it easy, huh?"

Dannen glanced down at himself, covered in blood and spilled beer and the gods alone knew what else. "This is me taking it easy, and I get it. You've got a job to do. Fact is, I did a lot of drinking last night, and I'm not really sure what happened."

And that was true enough, at least the part about the drinking. No need to go any further than that, to talk about the other thing. "Well, sure, sure," the guard said, nodding repeatedly in a way Dannen thought people usually reserved for the very old or very insane. Considering how many aches and minor pains he was feeling just then, he thought he would have traded places with any of the former quickly enough. As for the latter...well, sane men didn't wake up in alleyways with tavern signs around their necks clutching bloody lengths of wood.

"I get it," the guard went on, trying for a laugh. "Shit, I've been there. We all have. One ale leads to another, so on and so forth. My wife, the gods bless her, I guess I've lost count of the times she's had to wake me up when I passed out on our floor, not quite making it to the bed, understand? We're all reasonable men here," he said, gesturing to himself and the other guards but not, Dannen noted, to the woman. "So's how's about you just put on the manacles, eh? Then we'll take you to the guard office, figure this whole thing out. You haven't done nothin', why, you'll be gone in an hour and can get back to..." He hesitated, looking Dannen up and down. "Well, whatever it was you were doing."

Dannen didn't *feel* reasonable, not then, not with him wearing the world's heaviest tavern-sign necklace, and not with those steel manacles so close, seeming to hiss at him with deadly promise. "You want to go to the guard house," Dannen said softly, "I'll go to

14

the guardhouse. If there's a cell needs an ass in it I'll be that a—"
He cleared his throat. "What I mean is, I'll go to the dungeon if I
need to, answer what questions you have also. But I'll say it one
more time—I won't be bound."

"Fuck this," the second guard said, shouting as he charged
forward, his sword leading. A young guardsman, this one, eager to
prove himself *to* himself. Dannen saw a bit of the man he'd once
been in the scowling face as it rushed toward him. A far younger,
far dumber version, if such a thing were possible. It might have
been the Dannen of twenty years ago charging forward, hungry to
show his skill. The difference, though, was that the younger
version of him might have been a dumb asshole, but he *had* known
how to fight, and he never would have overextended the reach of
his sword.

Not hard, then, to step to the side of the wild swing, to grab a
handful of the man's hair, and give it a good yank before burying
the guard's head in the alley wall. There was a crunching sound as
the guard's nose broke—Dannen sympathized—then he let out a
soft groan and fell to the ground unconscious.

Shit. Well, that had been foolish. Breaking tavern signs was
one thing but assaulting a city guardsman was quite another. Men
didn't do time in the dungeon for something like that—they were
hung for it. It was the damned manacles, sitting there, making him
unreasonable. "Hey," he said slowly, holding his hands up again as
he looked at the other guardsmen who were staring at their
unconscious companion in shock as if still trying to piece together
what had happened. There, too, Dannen sympathized. "Look, he
had that coming, huh? The man seemed like a bit of a dick. Me and
you, though," he said, meeting the nicer guard's eyes, "we can work
something out, right?"

Whatever sympathy the guardsman had had a moment ago—
real or feigned—it was nowhere in evidence now as he met
Dannen's gaze with a look he recognized all too well. Be hard not
to, as many times as he'd seen it. It was a look that said the talking
was over and any questions the guardsman might have had, he
wanted them answered in blood.

An unconscious guard, another with the battle lust in his eyes,
shared by his two companions, and a woman whose screams
echoed in his head like the end of the world. Dannen did the only

thing he could do, the only thing any sensible man would do, under the circumstances.

He ran.

It felt awkward, running, not least because he'd lost his belt somewhere only the gods alone could guess, and his trousers kept trying to fall around his ankles. Still, that didn't account for just how damned difficult it was. That question, though, was answered a second later when he noticed that he was only wearing one shoe. Maybe the other one had conspired with the belt, made off in search of a better life. Dannen would have wished both of them luck, but in his experience, a better life was something other people had.

He managed to make it to the end of the alley without getting spitted so that was something, and he glanced back to see that the guards were actually some distance behind, the woman screaming words of encouragement or—and this was more likely—curses at their backs as they ran toward him.

Grinning and feeling finer than he had since he'd woken—not saying much maybe, but he'd take what he could get—Dannen rounded the corner of the alley, falling trousers and all, confident that, if he could make it to the main street, he'd be able to lose his pursuers easily enough, becoming just one more asshole in a city full of them. He was already making plans for what he would do once he'd escaped—plans largely centered around having an ale, because if any man ever needed a drink it was him. Then he saw four more guardsmen waiting for him in the street.

"Well, shit," Dannen muttered because, honestly, given the circumstances, there didn't seem much point of saying anything else.

"Stop there, criminal!" one of the men shouted.

Dannen took a bit of issue with being called a criminal. Oh, he'd been called worse, but it wasn't so much what the guard had said as the *way* he'd said it, in a rude tone Dannen would have liked to have stopped and discussed with him. Assuming, of course, that the man in question hadn't been flanked by three other guys who, though they hadn't spoken yet, just *looked* like assholes. And there was the sword he held, of course, and who was to say? He might be the one city guardsman in the world who actually knew how to use the damned thing. So, Dannen did what any sane man would do.

He ran. Or, at least, he tried to.

It didn't take him long to find three possible avenues of escape. Three options, which wasn't so bad. What *was*, though, was the city guardsmen standing in all of them. Damned inconsiderate, but not as inconsiderate as they had a mind to be judging by the sharp looks and sharper swords aimed in his direction.

There was a shop entrance a few feet away, turned out when he looked at the sign that it was a brothel which went a long way toward explaining the topless women hanging out of the windows shouting encouragement into the street—though whether at him or the guards he didn't know, wasn't sure *they* knew, come to that. Would have been a happy enough turn of luck to find his wild ramblings bringing him so close to a brothel if there wasn't the whole getting executed thing to worry about. Not exactly spoiled for choice, Dannen charged toward the brothel.

He barged through the door, some part of his mind—the dumb part, of which he'd always had more than his fair share—thought it would surely have to be locked. It was this part which took over just for long enough to decide him that charging the wooden portal would be the best way in, that convinced him that only a fool would stop and try the latch. Well, turned out that the brothel— like every other brothel *ever*—was still open. This, of course, meant that Dannen's heroic ramming of the door quickly turned into him stumbling as it swung easily aside, and then he wasn't stumbling at all but falling, falling, fallen on an ass that was, thank you gods one and all, quite bare.

By happy chance—or the gods' cruelty, and wasn't it really just one and the same?—he fell in what he *hoped* was spilled ale. No time to check, though, as he could hear the guards rushing the door from outside, could see them too since his blow to it had knocked it off one of its hinges, though it had to be said that he thought the door had still gotten the better of the exchange.

He was up in a moment, one hand tugging his trousers back up to his waist, the other pushing away a shirtless fat man who had decided—the world really was full of fools—that a half-naked man being chased by a dozen city guardsmen was something he just had to investigate.

Dannen gave him a good shove, and the fat man let out a squawk, tumbling over a chair and a very pissed-off prostitute. Dannen wanted to take a minute, tell the man only a fool would come up and try to have a conversation with a clear fugitive when there was a woman, bought and paid for, that would prove far better company, but he didn't have the time.

The guards were only seconds away now, so he charged for the stairs leading to the brothel's second—and no doubt far more entertaining—floor. He took the steps two at a time, the shouts of the angry prostitute ringing behind him.

He reached the second-floor landing and sprinted past rooms and some women plying their trade right there in the hall, like maybe there was a shortage of space. They screamed as he passed, though whether those screams were screams of fear or the sort of screams the men who came to places like this enjoyed paying for, Dannen didn't know and didn't have time to find out. He ran to the end of the hall, hoping for a window he might dive out of, but since he was just about as far from an acrobat as you could get and still be breathing, it was likely that diving out of one would just be dying on his own terms instead of the guards'.

Of course, there *wasn't* one, so he didn't have the chance either way and was left with the options of diving at the wall, at the guards behind him, or walking—by the gods *walking* not charging—through the closed door to his left. He glanced back and saw the guards gaining the second-floor landing.

Well, there was still the off-chance he might stumble in on a free show, a nice image to take with him to the guillotine. But as he entered the room, slamming the door shut behind him, he saw it was empty. Dannen turned back to the door, setting the latch. Not that it would make much difference, of course. The latch was a weak, frail thing that seemed ready to give way to a stern look, and he figured a good kick from one of the guardsmen would do for it easily enough.

He looked around, hoping for something he might use, though unless there was an army hiding under the bed—or an ogre, he wasn't picky—he was probably well and truly screwed. Screwed in a brothel. There was a song there, maybe, but not one he'd be around to sing, so there was no real point worrying about it.

There was a wardrobe sitting in the corner of the room, though why the rooms of a brothel would need one he couldn't imagine. It seemed to him that they were in the business of taking clothes off and part of the charm was that those clothes, when they were taken off, ended up scattered about the floor or draped on the bed posts, not hung up neatly in a closet.

He considered hiding in it, anyway, hoping all the guards would be struck dumb by the time they made it to his room, maybe would overlook him altogether, but decided against it. For one, what little chances he had would be non-existent if they came on him hiding in a closet. And perhaps more importantly, if he was going to die, he'd just as soon keep what little dignity was left to him.

Alright then, he told himself as he heard the guards shouting, clearing the room next to his own, *alright.* He was at peace about dying mostly. The gods knew he'd earned his death more than a few times. It was coming, that was all. It had been coming for a long time now. He just wished he knew what he'd done the night before. Likely, he'd done far worse on any number of occasions and either by luck or blind chance had walked away without a scratch, but then a man couldn't count on luck or chance forever.

A door creaked open, and he spun, expecting to see the guards pouring into the room from the hallway. But the door to the hallway was still closed. Then there was another creak, and he caught movement out of the corner of his eye. One of the guards must have made it inside somehow, been waiting for him in the closet. It ought to have been impossible, but then Dannen had traveled the world a lot in his younger years, and he'd seen men killed by creatures and things most people thought were impossible myths more than a few times. How they would have known he'd come here he couldn't guess, and there wasn't time to think about it anyway. He spun, raising his fists, but the figure he saw stepping calmly out of the closet wasn't one of the guards.

The first thing he noticed about the man was that he *was* a man. The second, though, was far more interesting. The stranger was glowing. A golden glow that was accompanied by a melodic humming filling the air as if someone were playing the harp. The figure was smiling, but Dannen could make out little else before the glow began to intensify, and he was forced to raise a hand, shielding his eyes.

The figure waved a golden-limned hand and for a brief, terrifying moment, Dannen felt the air grow thick all around him, so thick he felt as if he'd be crushed. A moment later, there was a *pop* in the air and the incredible pressure vanished as quickly as it had come. But things felt...different, somehow. At first, Dannen couldn't figure out what had changed, but then he knew.

He could still hear the soldiers shouting, but now those shouts sounded as if they came from far away, sounded, too, as if they were in a language he did not know. After a moment, Dannen realized that it wasn't a different language after all. Instead, the guards seemed to be shouting in slow motion, their words coming out so slowly as to be near incomprehensible.

Dannen thought probably he was having a fit. He'd heard of such things before, usually when someone had suffered a terrible blow to the head or was under an extreme amount of stress. He didn't remember suffering such a blow, but considering that he didn't remember anything of the last eight hours or so, that didn't mean a whole lot. As for stress, well, if imminent death didn't cause a man anxiety, he was dead already.

"Ah, Dannen Ateran," the figure said. His voice, at least, sounded normal, perhaps even amused, which might have been explained by Dannen's appearance. "Or should I call you the Bloody Butcher?"

Dannen didn't know how most people would react to a glowing figure emerging from an empty closet, accompanied by an unexplainable hum and smirking like he knew a thousand things no one else could hope to know. Maybe, most people would have wanted to run or beg for their lives. Dannen, though, didn't want either of those things. What he wanted, more than anything, was to punch the figure in the face, to wipe some of the smugness off his expression.

"Seems a bit creepy, doesn't it?" he asked instead. "A grown man hanging out in a brothel closet?" He glanced over the man's shoulder at the small closet. "Couldn't have been comfortable."

The man looked back at the closet and gave a soft grunt. "Ah. I hadn't realized." He turned back to Dannen, watching him, the arrogant smile back in place. Begging for a punching, this one. "Though, you are wrong, Dannen."

"You're right," Dannen said. "Not just a bit creepy. Damned creepy."

The man rolled his eyes, not amused. "That is not what I mean. I am not a grown man, Dannen. In fact, I'm not a man at all."

Dannen squinted. "Huh. Sure, sort of feminine features...yeah, I can see it. A woman, then, though the gods could have been a bit kinder when they made you."

"What?" the figure asked, the hum and the glow faltering. "No, wait. No, I'm *not* a woman. I'm a man or—" He trailed off, and it was Dannen's turn to smirk. The figure took a slow, deep breath as if to gather his patience. "What I mean, Dannen Ateran," he intoned, reassuming the sonorous, officious tone he'd used when he first spoke, "is that I am no man. *I am a god.*"

Dannen grunted, thinking the guards must have caught him after all. Maybe he'd knocked himself unconscious, probably when slamming into the brothel door like a damned fool, and the figure before him was nothing more than a figment of his mind as it expired. "A god who spends his time hiding out in closets then?" Dannen said, figuring that if he was dying he might as well have a little bit of fun. "No wonder the world's screwed up."

The figure sputtered, and this time the hum and glow didn't falter, they vanished altogether. "I'll have you know, Dannen, that I am indeed a god and—" He cut off abruptly, letting out a squawk as Dannen poked him in the nose. "*Excuse me?*" the figure said in a shocked voice.

Dannen grunted. "Feel awfully real for a figment of my imagination." He shrugged. "Well. I've heard healers say that a man's mind is what makes him feel, so I suppose it isn't completely unreasonable to imagine you'd feel real. Anyhow," he went on, glancing around the room, "if this is the land of the dead, and you're to be my company, I was more of a bastard than I realized."

The figure pinched the bridge of his nose, shaking his head in frustration. "It'll be easy, they said," he murmured, "it's your *turn*, they said. That bastard Hephaestus has got a lot of answering to do."

"Hephaestus," Dannen said, frowning. "That name sounds familiar." Then it hit him, and he laughed. "You mean *the* Hephaestus? As in the God of Smiths?"

"God of some other things, too," the figure muttered, then paused before he could say more, dismissing whatever he'd planned to say with a wave of his hand. "That is a matter that might be dealt with later. For now, let us get back to business." He closed his eyes and took a slow, deep breath, as if gathering himself. When he opened them again, the soft, golden nimbus of light had returned, as had that damned humming. Dannen decided if he had to listen to that for the rest of his afterlife, he'd likely go insane before the week was out. Not that he was all that certain the afterlife *had* weeks as such. It was a new thing, being dead.

"Dannen Ateran," the stranger said in that deep, resonant voice that reminded Dannen of the officious priests who sometimes took it on themselves to stand on street corners and tell all the heathens of the city—a population that generally included everyone but themselves—just how heathen they were. "Son of Fildius and Margaret, *I* am Perandius, and I have come to summon you to your duties for—"

"Why are you talking like that?" Dannen interrupted.

The figure frowned. "Talking like what?"

"Come on, you know what I mean," Dannen said. "Why are you talking like you're some messenger reading a king's proclamation for an entire city? Gods, man, it's just you and me here."

The figure's mouth opened and closed several times as if he was having difficulty figuring out what to say. Then, finally, he scowled. "It may surprise you to know most mortals *like* it when I talk that way."

Dannen gave the stranger a dubious look. "Tell you that, did they?"

The stranger shifted, clearly uncomfortable. "Well, no...not as such but..." He shook his head, clearly frustrated. "You know, I am accustomed to getting considerably more respect than this. Awe, you might even say."

"You keep talking like that," Dannen said, "I'm going to consider *awing* myself into that wall a few times, see if I can't respectfully knock myself out."

The figure studied him thoughtfully. "You really are a bit of a bastard, aren't you?" he said dryly.

Dannen grunted. "Been called worse by worse, though to be fair, none of the ones saying it were ever hiding in closets, at least to my recollection."

The stranger's face turned red, and he pinched the bridge of his nose again. "Very well, I will speak normally. Even if it does ruin the experience," he finished, muttering the last.

"Oh, I wouldn't worry about it," Dannen said. "You ask me, the experience is well and truly ruined already. I would've thought that the one thing dying had going for it was some damned peace for a change."

"Yes," the figure said sourly, "at any rate, best get on with it. You, Dannen Ataran, have been called to service, enacting the vow you accepted when you came of age to defend the world against its enemies, should the need arise. Will you answer these summons and, thereby, fulfill your vow?"

The figure was looking at him expectantly, and Dannen grunted. "You know, I haven't been having much luck with vows lately. Anyway, what is this? Some sort of joke? Pretty sure if I made a vow to defend the *world* I'd remember it."

The stranger took a slow, deep breath. "I assure you; it is no joke." He produced a scroll, seemingly from thin air, and held it up in front of Dannen. There was a bunch of writing in a tight hand telling him the author could do with a few drinks to loosen up a bit, too much writing by far for Dannen to spend time reading it, though he did notice the signature at the bottom. *His* signature and written in his own hand, or at least it appeared to be.

"Well, that's a damned fine trick," he said. "Someone's forged my signature, eh? Well. It's a wonder the sorts of things people get up to. You know, I saw a man once, this fella, he filed all his teeth down to a bunch of sharp points, opened his mouth he looked like a damn shark. Must have made it a trial to kiss a girl..." He trailed off, thinking on that. "Then again, I doubt he had to worry about that much, come to it. Seems like the sort of problem that solves itself."

"Err...nevertheless," the figure said after a moment, "the vow was made, and you are, by your own hand, bound. I, Perandius, Messenger of the Gods, have spoken. Now, will you accompany me?" He gestured toward the closet and suddenly it wasn't a closet anymore. Instead of the rack for clothes that had been there a moment ago, now there was a shining golden oval portal, fluttering and shifting as if it were swayed by some unfelt breeze.

Dannen peered at the circle, thinking that dying, if nothing else, was interesting. "What in the name of the gods is that?"

"Which?"

"What's that?" Dannen asked.

"Which god?"

He frowned. "What I *mean* is, what is that big glowing circle?"

"That, Dannen Ateran," the figure began in that resonant voice then seemed to give it up. "Well. It's a portal to the land of the gods. We're supposed to walk through it now."

Dannen frowned. "And if I don't?"

The figure gave him a smug look and shrugged. "Well. I suppose you can always take your chances with the guards. In my presence, their progress has been...*slowed* somewhat, but I am leaving and, when I do, they will return to their normal speed. A speed that, in moments, will bring them here to this room in which you have sought shelter."

"I see," Dannen said. "They got ale there?"

The smug look slowly faded from the stranger's face. "What?"

"In that land of the gods you're talking about? They got any ale? Come to that, can a dead man even get drunk?"

The figure let out an angry hiss. "You're not d—you know what? Never mind. Follow or do not—it's up to you. I, Perandius, have spoken." Then, with that, the figure turned and started toward the golden portal.

"So, you mean to tell me," Dannen said, "that you're Perandius? As in, Messenger of the Gods, Communicator of Their Will and all that?"

The figure turned back at the edge of the portal, looking over his shoulder. "That is correct, Dannen Ateran," he said in a formal voice.

"Dannen's fine. No need to go saying my whole name all the time. Anyhow, if you're telling the truth, where are your wings?"

"What's that?"

"You know, your wings. According to all the stories, Perandius has wings, little ones, you know, though, thinking on it, I imagine he'd have to flap those bastards like mad to keep himself upright."

The figure scowled, turning and walking into the golden portal. As he disappeared through it, Dannen heard him mutter, "You lose *one* bet..."

Then he was alone in the room and as good as the stranger's words, there seemed to be an audible *click* in the air, and sound—time itself, in fact—seemed to suddenly reassert itself. He heard the guards stomping out in the hall, right outside the door now. A metallic noise drew his attention, and he glanced at the latch to see it move as one of the guardsmen tried it only to find it locked. In another moment, maybe two, they'd break it open and find Dannen standing here like a fool.

He peered back into the portal, weighing his options, but he could see nothing through it, the entirety of it filled with a golden haze. Stay and be killed or go through a glowing portal and probably be killed? Not the best options, maybe, but about as good as they ever were. Dannen took a slow, deep breath, and stepped into the closet.

CHAPTER THREE

The first thing he saw as he emerged from the other side of the portal was a beautiful city. Otherworldly architecture loomed everywhere, buildings with great, sweeping balustrades and towers, all of them made of something white, perhaps marble, so bright it seemed to shine, dazzling his eyes, everything—even the streets themselves—enamored in gold. The second thing he noticed—this seeming a bit more urgent than the first—was that he was falling.

He had just enough time to begin a shout of surprise, but not enough time to finish it before he struck the ground hard. Groaning, he rubbed at his head where it had struck and looked around to see that he had fallen in the center of a white circle crafted from marble that shined just as impossibly as the rest of the city. The golden road, like a dozen or so others, branched off from the circle like the spoke of some great wheel.

Still rubbing his aching head, Dannen rose to his feet and grunted, impressed despite himself. "Well," he said. "Either this is the longest death dream I've ever heard of, or you really are the Messenger God."

"I said as much, I believe," Perandius answered with a raised eyebrow.

Dannen looked behind him to see the golden portal hovering in the air a good three or four feet off the ground. A moment later, it winked out as if it had never been. Gods, but he hated magic. Oh, in theory it was great. Don't feel like pouring your own beer? No worries, let the magic do the heavy lifting. Don't feel like having to drink so much to get well and truly sloshed? No worries, magic can do that too. In practice, though, anytime he'd been around the stuff—more than most people did in their lives and far more than he wanted—it inevitably ended badly.

"Couldn't you have put the damned portal a bit closer to the ground?" he groused.

"Strictly speaking?" Perandius asked, giving him a small smile. "Yes, yes, I suppose I could have."

"Might be you ought to do that next time," Dannen muttered. "Not much of a welcome for your visitors, coming to the land of the gods only to fall on their asses."

"Or their heads," the god said, clearly enjoying Dannen's discomfort, "as the case may be."

Dannen decided he still wanted to punch the man in the face, god or no god. And if he *was* a god—a fact seeming to become more and more likely by the minute—Dannen figured he probably deserved it for letting the world become the absolute shit show that it was. Still, it probably wasn't the healthiest thing, punching a god in the face, particularly since, if there were any more portals to go through soon, there wasn't anything keeping the bastard from making sure they didn't open onto a pool full of sharks. Dannen had never met a shark, not personally, but he thought it safe to say he hated them anyway.

"Well," he said, deciding it best to change the subject and maybe find a way to distract himself from his aching head, "we're here. What now?"

The god frowned. "Most of those fortunate enough to visit the land of the gods are a little bit more...well, amazed."

"Sure, I'm amazed right enough," Dannen agreed. "But I've got to tell you, Perd—can I call you Perd?

The god frowned. "No, you cannot. That doesn't even make se—"

"Anyway, Perd," Dannen went on, "I've seen some pretty amazing things in my life, so forgive me if I'm not suitably impressed. Did I tell you about the guy with the shark teeth?"

The god blinked. "You may have mentioned it."

"Well," Dannen said, nodding. "There you go. Still, you seem a bit upset. I suppose, if it means that much to you, I can pretend to be impressed. Give you a few 'oohs' and 'aahs,' that sort of thing, maybe even throw in a blush or two, how'd that be?"

"I am beginning to think you're more than just a bit of a bastard," the god said.

Dannen grunted. "Well, if that's the case, and you're really a god, and you gods are the ones who made all people—me included—then that's kind of on you, isn't it?"

Perandius stared at him for several seconds before finally blinking. "This way."

Before Dannen could say anything more, the god turned on his heel and started down the golden streets. Now that he wasn't being watched, Dannen took the opportunity as he followed behind the god to stare in awe at his surroundings. He was no carpenter, but the buildings around him were like nothing he'd ever seen before as were the people—or, he supposed, gods—who walked the streets, some lazing about or talking in quiet conversation. Even the sky here was different. Instead of the nice, simple blue one he was used to, it was tinged with vibrant oranges and reds and yellows. It was more than a little disconcerting, and Dannen pulled his gaze away from it with an effort, deciding to stare at the buildings and the city's denizens instead.

To say those traveling the streets were unusual would have been a drastic understatement. Here, Dannen saw a god with shoulders as wide as he was tall which had to be a good seven feet, speaking to a female whose beauty was literally painful to look upon as she seemed to shine like the sun. They were both eating something from golden plates, though what it was Dannen couldn't tell from this distance, and he didn't much care in any case. He'd never considered the fact that gods would eat like men did, though whether by necessity or just because they enjoyed it he supposed there was no telling.

They passed another in a white tunic who was levitating several feet above the street in a sitting position, playing a harp more beautifully than anything Dannen had ever heard. He stopped following Perandius to listen.

For several seconds, Dannen wasn't aware of anything except that music, except each strum of the harp which seemed to reach directly to his heart. Then he felt a hand on his shoulder and turned to see Perandius frowning at him. "Well? We don't have all day, you know."

"It's…it's amazing," Dannen breathed.

The god grunted. "Give it a few thousand years, and you'll want to pull your hair out. Or someone else's," he muttered, the scowl he shot the harpist god making it all too clear who he meant. "Now, come on."

Dannen reluctantly allowed himself to be pulled away, some part of him thinking that, if he could listen to music like that all the time, maybe he really would be able to swear off violence. There was so much to look at, so much beauty, it was almost overwhelming.

The next few minutes passed in a blur of white and gold buildings until finally Dannen grunted. "You ask me, you all might need to think about hiring a decorator. I mean, white and gold are fine enough, but it's a bit painful on the eyes, isn't it?"

"Not so loud," Perandius hissed, turning on him, then glancing around as if expecting an army to come charging out from one of the nearby buildings.

Dannen frowned. "Why? You gods take your buildings that seriously, eh?"

Perandius raised an eyebrow, "Some more than others. If Feralest heard you say as much, I'd never hear the end of it."

"Wait a minute," Dannen said, unable to keep the awe from his voice, "you mean the God of Death? He's here?"

Perandius rolled his eyes. "Oh, he's skulking somewhere, I'm sure. If he had it his way, the whole place would be black and crimson. He brings it up at every council meeting, has for the last few thousand years or more. He is quite stubborn."

Dannen thought if Perandius believed it a surprise that the God of Death was stubborn he was out of touch, but he shrugged. "Whatever you say."

The god studied him for a moment then turned and started down the street again. Dannen followed him—there wasn't much else to do—but they'd only taken a few steps when a woman walked out of an alleyway, interposing herself directly in front of Dannen, so he was forced to stop.

"Hi there," the woman said, and Dannen was surprised to see that her face looked drawn, her hands shaking, reminding him of those addicted to one of the herbs which were intoxicating but, inevitably as all good things did, led to pain or death.

"Hi," he managed.

"W-would you like to know how to be happy for the rest of your life? To experience real joy without consequence a—"

"Enough of that," Perandius said sternly, coming to stand beside them.

"Oh, Perandius," the woman said, giving him a nervous grin and studying him with eyes that were slightly too wide and more than a little wild. "I-it's good, you know, to see you. I...well. I was just telling your friend here—"

The messenger god sighed. "Later, Elaria, please, okay?"

"I-I've got an idea," the woman pressed, "for the next council meeting. I thought, maybe, we could talk about it and—"

"I promise, I'll listen, just not now, alright? I'm quite busy and...you understand, of course?"

"Of course, of course," the woman blurted, nodding her head so roughly that it looked in danger of coming off. "B-but you will come see me? Soon?"

Perandius nodded. "I will. I promise."

"Okay then," she said, flashing Dannen a smile that was beautiful despite her strange appearance and one that engendered in him a feeling of tranquility before she scurried back into the alleyway.

He watched her go then turned to Perandius. "Wait a minute...you said that was Elaria? As in the Goddess of Peace?"

Perandius winced, nodding. "Yes. She means well, but she'll talk your ear off if you let her and if you're fool enough to answer your door without checking, there's an afternoon—or a year—gone before you know it. My father says she was magnificent once, but..." He shrugged.

Dannen stared after the quickly departing goddess. "What's uh...what's wrong with her?"

Perandius looked at him as if he was daft. "She's the Goddess of Peace."

"Right," Dannen said slowly, "but what does that have to do with anything?"

The god sighed. "Does the world feel particularly peaceful to you, just now?"

"Well," Dannen said, "I've heard of some troubles up north, but...well, no," he finished lamely under the god's annoyed gaze. "No, I guess not."

"Exactly," Perandius said. "Not a lot for the Goddess of Peace to do, if there isn't any *peace* is there? And you mortals, while fond of many things, cannot count peace among them." He glanced off in the direction she'd vanished. "One sympathizes, but that doesn't make it any easier to endure one of her lectures. Now, come on. We're late as it is."

Dannen meant to ask the god what exactly they were late *for,* but before he had a chance Perandius turned on his heel and started off again. He was left with no choice but to follow or hang around where he was and since he had no idea *where* he was, he hurried after the god.

In time, they came to a house considerably smaller than any of the others they had passed. He was just about to ask Perandius what poor fool lived in what amounted to be little more than a shack. Then the god walked inside, answering his question for him.

Dannen followed. He wasn't sure what he had expected when entering a god's home, but if it was something magical, a horse with wings, maybe, then he was doomed to disappointment. The god's house wasn't magical, wasn't extravagant. What it was, more than anything, was boring. The walls were lined with bookshelves packed near to bursting with all manner of scrolls and tomes. The room had a single table and chair. The only other piece of furniture in the main room was what Dannen took for a desk, though he couldn't be sure as it was so covered in scrolls and parchments as to be nearly invisible.

"Eh...nice place," Dannen said, because it was the type of thing a person said when walking into a god's house. Or maybe not. If he was being honest, Dannen had done a pretty shit job so far in his life of getting on with normal people. The gods only knew how a man was supposed to treat the...he paused, laughing.

"Something funny?" Perandius asked, and god or not there was a very human-like defensiveness in his tone.

"Ah, no, nothing," Dannen said. And that, at least, was true. There wasn't anything funny about the god's home, though home didn't feel like the right word. Hovel, maybe. Or cave. Certainly, what little bit of the strange light from the sky would have made it into the home was largely blocked by row after row of documents stacked nearly as high as the top of the home's only window.

31

The god watched him for another moment then apparently decided to take his words at face value, which was just as well as Dannen figured he probably already had enough problems in his life without incurring the wrath of a god.

Perandius moved to a shelf and began rummaging through the stacks of documents there, though how he thought to find anything in those haphazard towers of paper, Dannen couldn't imagine. "Now, I know it was here somewhere," the god muttered.

"You must be a blast at parties," Dannen said, but the god appeared too distracted by whatever task he'd set himself to pay the mortal in his midst any mind.

"Got anything to drink in this du—" Dannen cut himself off before he could finish. "That is, anything to drink in this place?"

"There's a fountain outside, the water will be the purest you have ever tasted. Some mortals have—"

"I mean a man's drink."

Perandius looked at him, and after a moment a decidedly mischievous look came over his face, and he nodded. "Of course. It's just there, a golden bottle on the desk." He motioned vaguely at the pile of parchments at the far end of the room.

Dannen considered whether or not it was worth the trouble, but considering the fact that his head was pounding from a night of drinking he didn't remember, he'd barely escaped death at least once today, and was meeting a god for the first time in his life—a decidedly anticlimactic experience—he thought he deserved it. He walked to the vaguely desk-shaped pile of parchments and began shoving them aside. He was just about to give up the search altogether when he saw a glimmer in the stack and pulled out a golden bottle.

"Ha!" He popped the cork from the top of the bottle and was about to turn it up when the god spoke.

"I would proceed with caution, Dannen Ateran. The gods' ambrosia is not a drink for mortals."

Dannen snorted. "If I've got some reading needs doing, Perandius, I'll ask for your advice. But when it comes to drinking, I'm a bit of an expert, so don't be offended if I don't listen to the god version of a clerk."

The god opened his mouth as if to object then gave a faint shrug, the ghost of a smile on his face. "As you wish. I suppose losing a day will not be so terrible."

Dannen wasn't sure what the god meant by that, and it didn't matter much in any case, for he was already drinking. He didn't know what the god's water tasted like—didn't much care—but the alcohol was damned fine. Tart sweetness filled his mouth, and he was immediately suffused with a pleasant warmth that made his toes and fingertips tingle.

"I'm supposed to be scared of this?" Dannen barked a laugh. "Shit, Perandius, I've had water with more of a ki..." He trailed off, suddenly forgetting what he'd intended to say. Well, that was weird, maybe even something he ought to be concerned about, but the warmth was continuing to spread through his extremities, and he couldn't find it in him to care.

The drink of the gods themselves and wasn't that a fine thing? Dannen thought it always important to be reasonable—thought it was, by and large, why he was still alive when so many of his former companions were dead—and so he did what any reasonable man would when offered such a beverage. He drank some more.

The next thing he knew, he was sitting in the single chair by the table. He didn't remember walking to it, but that was okay, nothing to worry about, surely. He'd never cared much for walking anyway but sitting, now that was a fine thing. He was still sitting that way, his feet propped up, when the door opened, and a large man walked in, having to ease in sideways to fit his bulk through the doorframe. The man seemed to be made entirely of muscle, without an ounce of fat. He was tall, too, with long white hair past his shoulders, despite which his face had a youthful appearance, and had he not obviously been a god—no doubting it, not with this one—Dannen might have put him in his early forties.

Dannen thought that *this* was what a god should look like, a far cry from the Messenger God in clothes that looked slightly rumpled and appeared to not quite fit, looking too small in some places and too large in others. Even the god's voice, when he spoke, was what a man thought of when he prayed to the gods, deep and resonant and seeming to fill the room like thunder. "Ah, Perandius. You have returned."

Perandius spun, and Dannen noticed his eyes go slightly wide. He bowed his head, "Yes, si—" he began, but was interrupted by a second newcomer walking through the door. "Though late, it seems." The newcomer said in a sneering, arrogant tone. "As always, *younger* brother."

There was a noticeable emphasis on 'younger' which, judging by the annoyance that flitted briefly across Perandius's face, was clearly meant as a jab. "The situation was a bit more...complicated, than I expected," he said, speaking to the larger of the two and pointedly ignoring the second.

"Oh, Perandius," yet another new voice said, and a third stranger sauntered in.

The newcomer was a woman, and though she was undeniably beautiful, there was something about her Dannen immediately took a disliking to, though what it was he couldn't have said. She appeared to have dark hair, though he couldn't be sure as it was brushed back and looked decidedly wet. She gave a smirk as she glanced at the Messenger God.

"You do always have a way of needlessly complicating things, don't you?" she purred as she glanced around the house, her nose high in the air, a faint look of disgust on her perfect features. "Always writing, always reading, chronicling the great deeds of others, god and mortal alike. How you live in this dusty old tomb I'll never know."

Perandius's face flushed with embarrassment or anger, probably both. Dannen frowned. Moments ago, he'd been thinking similar thoughts, but hearing them in the woman's arrogant, sneering voice made him angry.

"I'm no expert," Dannen said, "but it seems to me that someone ought to do it. I'm not a big fan of history myself, but only a fool would act as if it's unimportant." He glanced between the woman and the smaller male god. "Or fools, maybe."

The two turned to him, staring at him in disbelief as if a mongrel dog had just approached them on the street and struck up a conversation. A moment later, the disbelief turned to anger which plastered itself across their faces.

"How *dare* you, you insolent whelp," the male began, starting forward.

Dannen had a brief thought that maybe antagonizing gods wasn't the best idea, but the warm contentment of the ambrosia soothed it quickly, and he raised his fists. There was suddenly an inexplicable breeze in the house despite the closed door. He was watching the god approach, feeling the breeze and wondering if a man could give a god a black eye, getting ready to give it a shot, when a voice spoke.

"Enough."

This from the largest and oldest of the three. He did not raise his voice, yet his words filled the room, rumbling like an avalanche, and sending a thrill of terror past Dannen's pleasant drunkenness. If there was a voice able to level mountains, this was it. And he was clearly not the only one who felt so. The other gods, Perandius included, winced, avoiding the god's stern gaze and studying their feet instead.

"Forgive us, Father," the two newcomers muttered in unison, all traces of their former arrogance vanishing in an instant, replaced with obsequious humility.

The god studied them for several seconds, then, apparently satisfied that they were cowed, turned to Dannen. He stepped closer, looking Dannen over like a farmer might a cow he was considering purchasing. Dannen fidgeted under the god's scrutiny, feeling, for reasons he couldn't explain, ashamed, as if all of his darkest desires, his worst acts were being laid bare. A lifetime of regret and pain he'd spent years trying to bury suddenly unearthed, opened like a book for anyone to read, if they had a mind.

Finding themselves in such a situation, some people, probably most, would have been frozen with fear, and any with good sense would have stood terrified at what the god might see. But Dannen, more's the pity, had never been known for his good sense. What he *had* been known for though was his anger, a constant, if unwanted companion. And he was angry now—not just angry. Furious. He felt the cloud of that anger seeping into his mind as it had so many times before, threatening to drown out the voice of good sense—admittedly weak and malnourished from years of being ignored—that was trying to convince him to not say or do anything particularly stupid.

Just when Dannen was thinking he was destined to punch a god in the face—and no doubt be turned into a pile of ash for his trouble, the large god grunted. "This is the one you spoke of, Perandius?"

"Yes, sir."

"He doesn't look like much," the god said, his gaze coming to rest on Dannen's paunch. Dannen's first thought—that he really needed to lay off the ale and sweet tarts—was quickly eclipsed by a far more urgent and dangerous observation, that the god was an incredibly muscular, imposingly threatening prick.

"Let me guess," he said, the words coming out of his mouth despite his strenuous, if inevitably doomed efforts to the contrary. "You the God of Assholes, that it?" He glanced behind the massive god at the younger male and female. "And what, a whole two followers? Well, at least if anything happens to you, they both seem more than ready to step in and take up the mantle."

There was a sharp intake of breath, and Dannen saw that Perandius's face had taken on a decidedly pale, sickly look, his eyes so wide they appeared as if they might pop out of his head at any moment. His mouth worked as if he meant to say something, but the female beat him to it.

"The *insolence,*" she said, stepping forward, "let me strike him down, Father, ple—"

She cut off as the massive god held up a hand, forestalling her, his face unreadable. Dannen tensed while he waited to die horribly, putting a brave face on the thing because there wasn't much else he could do.

But instead of turning him into a toad or ripping his heart out through his chest, the hulking god grinned widely. "Got some fire to him, though. A spark. That's fine. He'll need it."

Dannen didn't know what *that* meant, but he wasn't about to show his ignorance, not with the two smaller gods eyeing him like he was a meal they were eager to dig into, so he shrugged. "I've got enough for what needs doing," he said with far more confidence than he felt.

The god eyed him critically for a moment then nodded. "I believe you just might, no matter the others who failed before you." He turned to the Messenger God, and it was all Dannen could do to keep from breathing a sigh of relief as the god's regard left him. "Very well, Perandius. I admit to having some doubt when you presented this plan to the Council, but I see I was perhaps wrong to do so. I wish you and your champion here luck. Should you need anything, let me know." With that, he turned on his heel, his two cronies scattering before him like leaves before a high wind, and walked out the door as abruptly as he had come.

As he did, the air, which had seemed so thick and suffocating a moment ago, seemed to thin, and Dannen took a slow, deep breath. The god's two toadies, however, remained.

"You will fail, brother," the male said, his arrogant sneer back in place, "and when you do, I will be there to see it."

"Yes," the female said, favoring Perandius and Dannen with a wintry smile, "I have always enjoyed a good show."

Their threats and parting words were ruined somewhat by the way they hurriedly scampered off after the larger god after they'd uttered them. In another moment, Dannen and Perandius stood alone in the house.

Perandius let loose a shuddering sigh, wiping an arm across his brow. "Tell me, truly, Dannen Ateran," he said, glancing at him, "do you wish to die?"

Dannen frowned. That wasn't the sort of thing you asked a man, was it? Damned impolite, is what it was, and if either of the two of them looked like death might be an improvement, he thought it must surely be the god whose house looked like a library had thrown up inside of it, no signs of life except the chronicles of the lives others had lived.

"What's the big deal?" he asked. "They were a couple of assholes—not the first I've met, and I don't imagine they'll be the last either."

The messenger god pinched his nose between a thumb and forefinger. "Those *assholes,* as you so eloquently put it, are my brother and sister." He scowled at the doorway as if he could still see them standing there. "My *older* brother and sister as it just so happens, though how they can be so arrogant over a single millennia's difference I'll never know."

Dannen blinked. The more he saw of the land of the gods, the more he realized that they had just as many problems as the land of mortals, though there was no denying their problems were prettier. If he were a priest, perhaps he would have been able to extract some great wisdom from that. If he were a scholar, he likely would have been able to distill the last hour or so into a treatise to change the course of humanity. But Dannen was no priest, and he was no scholar. He was simply a man. And, more than that, he was becoming increasingly sure that he was a drunk one. Very drunk, in fact, though he was suffering none of the ill effects that would often indicate that was so, namely, puking his guts out all over his boots.

"And the last one?" he asked. "The big bastard? Another pain in the ass sibling, I'm guessing?"

Perandius's face took on a decidedly green cast. "Um...no. That was my father."

Dannen grunted, vaguely remembering something about the woman and the man calling the big one "Father," so he supposed it would stand to reason that, if they were siblings, the hulking god would also be Perandius's father. "Tell me, they always follow him around like that?"

"Like what?" the messenger god asked, though it seemed clear enough to Dannen that he knew exactly what he was talking about.

Dannen snorted. "Like what? Like a couple of dogs tailing their master, hoping he drops them some scraps, that's what."

"Wind and rain must surely follow thunder," Perandius said in a mocking tone, scrunching up his face in disgust to make it clear he was repeating a phrase he'd heard often.

To Dannen, though, the man might as well have been speaking another language. "What in the name of the gods do—" He paused, grunting a laugh. "What in the name of *you* do you mean by that?"

Perandius rolled his eyes. "Just something my brother and sister love to say, their way of explaining what you refer to as them following father around like a couple of dogs, though indeed you are not far off the mark. They follow him in hopes he will show them favor."

"Wind and rain and thunder." Dannen shrugged. "Doesn't make any sense, you ask me."

"It does," Perandius said slowly, "if you consider who they are. You see, my brother—the one who so pointedly insists on being older—is the God of the Wind."

Dannen blinked. "Your brother—the asshole that was just in here—is Sahael?"

"Unfortunately," Perandius muttered.

Dannen's thoughts were sluggish, incredibly so, in fact, but he concentrated hard enough that his head began to pound. "Which would make your sister the Goddess of Rain."

"Just so," the Messenger God said, inclining his head. "Hydrallia."

Dannen thought back over the sentence Perandius had said. "Wind...rain." There was something he felt as if he was missing, then it struck him, and his breath caught in his chest. "Your father—the big god that was here. You mean...that was—"

"Feladandrius," Perandius agreed, "God of Thunder and Lightning, and Father of all the Major Gods. And you called him an a..." He trailed off, shaking his head, an expression on his face somewhere between disbelief and awe.

Suddenly, Dannen felt lightheaded, and not the pleasant, *I'm feeling fine, so who cares if my toes and fingers are numb* kind. Instead, it was more along the lines of the *I just spilled my beer on a professional bruiser looking for something to bruise* kind. Only *this* bruiser just so happened to be the most powerful of all the gods.

"Shit," Dannen breathed.

"My sentiments exactly," Perandius said.

Or, at least, that's what Dannen thought he heard before he passed out. Or fainted, maybe, depending on how honest a man wanted to be.

CHAPTER FOUR

"Ah," Perandius said, "you're awake."

Dannen opened his eyes gingerly, expecting the throbbing pain that nearly always followed a night of drink and debauchery. Not that there'd *been* any debauchery, of course, just him picking a fight with the most powerful of all the gods. Then again, Dannen had been accused of a lot of things in his life—most of them probably true—but none, so far as he recalled, had been being too smart. Foolish, though, that one he'd heard and more than once.

He was surprised, however, to discover that he felt good. Maybe even great. "How long have I been asleep?" he asked, his words sounding slurred even to his own ears as his tongue felt two sizes too thick.

The god glanced up from a tome at least six inches thick and gave a small shrug. "Six hours, or so? Give or take."

Six hours. "Damn," Dannen said. "That drink's incredible. You could have warned me."

Perandius raised an eyebrow. "I seem to recall doing just that."

Dannen couldn't remember—it all seemed a bit fuzzy at this point—but he didn't see much point in arguing, so he shrugged. "Well," he said, taking in the massive book. "Been doing some light reading while I was out, have you?"

Either the god didn't catch the sarcasm or he chose to ignore it. "Yes, though rare are the times I've heard the Epistles of Echenwold referred to as light reading."

Dannen was no historian—he had plenty enough problems in his life, most happening *right now* and quite a few looking like they had some definite plans on seeing him dead to ever bother—but in his younger days he'd been saddled with one or two, all of them thinking that following him would give them some great story to tell. If they ever got their story, Dannen had never heard of it—not that he would have read such a thing as he was fairly sure he'd end up hating himself even more if he had, and that was no small trick—but as an unfortunate by-product, he had learned, mostly against his own wishes, quite a bit of history. Scholars and historians both, in his experience, on those rare instances when they didn't have their noses stuck in a book, were incapable of shutting up, as if they intended to get all the talking a normal person might do in a year done in as brief a time as possible, hit their quota, and get back to reading.

So it was with some surprise that he realized he'd never heard of the book the god referred to. "What did you call it again?"

Perandius sighed, putting the book down. "Oh, you wouldn't know it."

Something about the way the god said it struck a defensive note in Dannen, and he frowned. "Maybe I do."

"It is a fairly old work," Perandius said in the tone of voice one usually reserved for those times it was necessary to warn a fool that he was doing or saying something particularly foolish.

Fool I might be, Dannen thought angrily, *but I'm not the foolish foo...foolishest?* He grunted. "Oh? So all mortals are idiots, that it?"

Perandius blinked, surprised by his anger. "Of course not. I meant no offense, Dannen Ateran. I only intended to tell you this one is..." He smirked in a way that made Dannen want to punch him again. "Let us say, a bit before your time."

"Might be I'm older than you think," Dannen countered. "Just aged well, is all. Clean-living, mostly."

"It would have to be very clean indeed," Perandius said in an amused voice. "For the Epistles are over eight centuries old."

He stared at Dannen, waiting for a reaction, but Dannen would be damned if he was going to give him one. "Probably a dumb book anyway," he said finally, aware he was sour about the whole exchange but not caring.

Perandius gave a thoughtful expression as if seriously considering the idea. "Admittedly, some believe the tenets Echenwold expounds upon originate from a faulty premise and, thereby, are doomed to be incorrect, but there are whole tribes who..." He trailed off. "Well, there *were* whole tribes which considered the Epistles a holy work."

"Were?"

Perandius winced. "All dead now, I'm afraid. My but time does fly."

"Well, since those who thought it holy are all dead," Dannen said dryly, "you'll forgive me if I don't start praying."

"Of course," Perandius agreed. Dannen was starting to think the god was incapable of detecting sarcasm, something he would have thought important for the god of messengers, but then he awoke this morning missing a shoe and a belt and had gone on to poke fun at the God of Thunder and Lightning, so who was he to judge?

"Reckon he was sore about the asshole joke?"

"I'm sorry?" Perandius asked, clearly confused by the abrupt change of topic.

"Your father, I mean," Dannen said. "From all the stories, he isn't exactly the most patient fella. They say Zeu—"

"*No,*" Perandius interrupted, a horrified expression on his face.

"No what?" Dannen said. "Gods, man or...man, god, you look like somebody walked all over your grave."

"It's not *my* grave I'm worried about," the god answered, glancing at the door as if expecting someone to come charging through it wielding a bloody axe any moment. "That name—the one you meant to say. I would not utter it, were I you. Father does...not like that name. Not at all."

Dannen grunted. "Why's that? It's a damned sight easier to say that Feledandrius."

"Irrelevant," Perandius said, still looking at the door. "You will not be able to say either if you are dead. You have been lucky so far, but as you say my father is not known for his patience."

Dannen frowned. "Seems a bit much, doesn't it? To get that angry over a name?"

Perandius winced. "It is not a name, not as such. You see that word is, in truth, a derogatory term, one that the Banthinians, in their hate of the gods and my father in particular gave him. It means..." He shook his head. "Never mind. It does not matter what it means. Only understand it is not flattering, not at all."

"Banthinians?" Dannen asked doubtfully, beginning to think the god was putting him on, something he would have thought the god incapable of up until that moment. Although if he *was* making a joke at Dannen's expense, he was doing a damn fine job of acting terrified. "Never heard of them."

"Nor would you have," Perandius said. "No one has, in fact, not for many, many years."

"Oh?" Dannen asked. "What happened to them?" The god didn't answer, only met his eyes with a grim expression, and he supposed that was answer enough. Thought, too, that maybe careless neglect was about the best a man could hope for from the gods.

He decided it would be best—and probably safest—to change the subject. "Anyway, what now?"

"Ah, right," the god said, nodding and equally relieved to be moving on to another topic. "Well, you expressed some disbelief before, about the validity of the summation contract I showed you."

Dannen rubbed at his temples. "Do all gods talk like that?"

"Like what?"

"Like they're making a game of dancing around the point without ever touching it, using fancy words like a garnish on food a man never gets to eat."

Perandius cocked his head then gave a small smile. "Interesting. Anyway, I apologize. Let me attempt, then, to be more forthright." He retrieved a scroll from his desk, and the next thing Dannen knew, the scroll unfurled as if by magic, a dozen or more feet long, unrolling across the floor until it fetched up against the far wall.

"What in the name of the gods is that?" Dannen asked.

The messenger god smirked. "That, Dannen Ateran, is your contract, one which you agreed to and one which I witnessed myself."

Dannen glanced at foot after foot of the long parchment, hardly any blank space, all of it covered in writing so tiny and cramped he got a headache just looking at it. He tried to imagine reading it but decided that, given a choice, he'd rather take his chances insulting the father of the gods again. "Say I take your word for it."

"You are quite sure?" Perandius asked as if surprised. "It is no small thing, the duty you are called to perform, one that quite possibly may end in your death, I'm afraid to say. I would think that in your circumstances, I would want to verify the contract."

What *Dannen* thought was that if he tried to read through every word in the contract he'd likely die of boredom before dying whatever way the god seemed to have in store for him, so he nodded. "I'm sure. Now, how about you tell me why you interrupted my morning." At least, he thought it had been morning when he'd woken in the alley, though he couldn't be sure. Furthermore, had the god *not* interrupted him, he'd quite likely be dead by now, but there was no point in saying as much and showing the bastard his hand.

Perandius gave a small smile that showed he knew well enough just how much his interruption had contributed to keeping Dannen's head on his shoulders, but he didn't press the issue. "Very well. Tell me, have you heard about the..." He paused, fidgeting, clearly uncomfortable, "...Erm...present *difficulties* in the north?"

Dannen laughed. "Sure, I've heard about them. Assuming the 'difficulties' you mean are the dead rising from their graves, eating human flesh and all that." Then, because he couldn't resist prodding the god a bit more, "Seems to me some of the priests there have been quite a bit put out by it. The king of the north too. I guess corpses rising and chewing on your subjects have a way of putting a damper on commerce."

The god looked decidedly green at that, and he took a slow, deep breath, the expression on his face one of a man who has an unpleasant job ahead of him and means to get it over with as quickly as possible. "Just so, though unnecessarily crass, if you'd like my opinion."

"I wouldn't."

Perandius frowned. "Very well. Anyway, on to the reason you are here. These undead are, in point of fact, not a natural occurrence."

"You don't say," Dannen answered dryly.

A man—or a god—would have had to have been blind to have missed the sarcasm that time. Perandius's face turned red, and he took a moment, clearly gathering his patience. "What I *mean* is their reanimation has not happened on its own but has instead been caused by an individual. *Two* individuals, in fact."

"Well, go on," Dannen said. "You've got me all in a lather. Don't keep me waiting."

Perandius sighed heavily. "These two men, you see, are brothers. One, it must be said, is the most powerful necromancer of this age, perhaps of *any* age. The other is a warrior without equal. It is these two who seek to bend the north, and eventually, the entire world to their will. And it is they who are behind the curse which now causes the dead of that place to rise from their graves to seek the flesh of the living."

"Wait a minute," Dannen interrupted, "you mean to tell me that you've summoned me here to go on a...I don't know, let's call it a *quest* to defeat a powerful wizard, a mighty warrior, to fight off the living dead, and to break a *curse?*"

"Yes," Perandius said, eyeing Dannen as if he'd gone mad. "Yes, that sums it up, though there are a few details which—"

"And just how many dragons are there?"

The god blinked. "I'm sorry?"

"Oh, come on," Dannen said, rolling his eyes. "Wizards, warriors, zombies and curses. Surely there have got to be some dragons in this story."

Perandius frowned. "Forgive me, Dannen Ateran, but you don't appear to be taking this seriously. And no, to answer your question, there are no dragons. This isn't that kind of *story.*"

Dannen grunted. "Just as well, I suppose. Never thought I'd get on with those bastards."

"Yes," Perandius said dismissively. "Anyway, I must point out that the brother is not a *wizard* but a necromancer."

"Casts spells, does he?" Dannen asked.

"Yes."

"And does he wear a robe?"

Perandius narrowed his eyes. "According to our latest reports...he does."

"Probably a black one," Dannen said, holding up a hand to forestall the god that appeared ready to speak. "What about a staff. This asshole, he got a staff?"

The messenger god gritted his teeth. "I really don't see the point of—"

"All I'm saying," Dannen interrupted, "he sounds like a wizard to me. But go on telling me your bedtime story—I could do with a good nap." Especially considering that his last few "naps" had been the result of passing out. Certainly not fainting because he'd insulted the God of Thunder. Dannen Ateran was a lot of things, but he was *not* the type of man to pass out from fear. Or so he told himself.

"I assure you," Perandius managed through gritted teeth, "this is no bedtime story, and the foes of whom I speak are quite real."

"Fine, fine, take it easy, will you?" Dannen said. "So, anyway, I'm supposed to what? Track this wizard"—he paused, smirking as the god shifted, clearly fighting back the urge to correct him—"and this warrior down, these two bastard brothers, and kill them, thereby breaking the curse and releasing the land's people from this unholy magic?" he finished, smiling widely. Never let it be said of Dannen Ateran that he could not enjoy a joke as much as anyone.

The god, though, only looked surprised. "Well...yes. In essence, that is the task before you."

Dannen waited for the god to laugh, but he did not. In fact, he looked as if, just then, he couldn't have said what laughter was. Still, he gave it a moment, then another, waiting for the god to tell him it was only a prank, one in poor taste, maybe, but then what was life if not a cosmic joke, one in decidedly poor taste? When the god didn't respond, Dannen grunted. "You're serious."

"Yes."

"Well, sure," Dannen said dryly. "And why not? How about, I just go to the north, slay a few zombies, kill a wizard and a warrior, and make it back before supper, how'd that be?"

Perandius frowned. "The trip to the north will take considerably longer than—"

"Not for me it won't," Dannen interrupted, "because I'm not going."

Perandius blinked as if he'd never expected this, as if it were every man's dream to go and pick a fight with a couple of insane brothers powerful enough to put the whole northern kingdom at risk. "You're...not going?" the god asked as if speaking in a different language and unsure of what the words meant.

"That's right," Dannen agreed. Then he rose from his chair—carefully, for whatever had been in the golden bottle had been powerful stuff, and his feet still felt unsteady beneath him. "Still, I appreciate the offer. I appreciate you saving me from getting executed too, but I think it's time I got on with my life, don't you?"

"What life?"

Dannen froze from where he'd turned toward the door at that then looked back at the god, frowning. "What's that?"

"I said," the messenger god answered, meeting his eyes, "what life? You were a noble warrior once, Dannen Ateran, a man who fought for the weak, who was willing to sacrifice himself, if necessary, to stand up for what he believed in. A man feared by evil's greatest champions. What happened?"

Memories, thousands of them and nearly all bad, pushed at Dannen's mind then, and he gave his head a furious shake, forcing them back. They went, this time—there were other times, many others, when they did not.

"I grew up," he answered. "That's what happened. Finally got a bit of wisdom in me—maybe it was on the tips of several blades my *heroics* got me stabbed with, who knows? But I can tell you this much, Perandius, no matter how much evil a man defeats, there's always more to take its place. And when it does, it's always the weak who get trampled underfoot. And no one, neither god nor man, can change that."

Perandius's look of disappointment might have hurt Dannen's feelings, if he hadn't weathered a thousand such before it. If Dannen Ateran was good at anything, it was at disappointing people. "Perhaps not," the god said finally, "but is the honor not in the attempt?"

Dannen snorted. "Gods, but you need to get out more. The world, Perandius, is a runaway cart, the horses carrying it mad with fear or rage—maybe both, it doesn't matter. Either way, sooner or later, that cart is going to roll over everyone and everything a man has come to care about. It will destroy everything in its path not because it's evil or full of malice but simply because that's what it does. And these innocents you talk about, those who need saving, who even *expect* to be saved, are positioned square in that cart's path. What good does it do them, or anyone, to jump forward just to get crushed right along beside them? Tell me, Perandius, where's the distinction, where's the *honor* in that?" When Dannen finished, his throat was hoarse, and he realized he'd been shouting.

"You surprise me," the god said, and Dannen supposed that one benefit of being an immortal being was not having to show any particular concern about pissing someone off. "Perhaps...perhaps you are right. Perhaps you are not the man I thought you to be."

"Here's another bit of free wisdom for you, Perandius," Dannen said. "*None* of us are the men people think us to be—particularly ourselves."

"But...people are dying," the god said, displaying a naiveté that would have been more at home on a child than a being who had lived thousands of years. "People you might save."

Dannen sighed. He wasn't angry now, or at least not mostly. Mostly, he was just tired. "You may not have much experience with this, Perandius, being an immortal and all, but people are *always* dying. In fact, I'd go so far as to say it's what we're best at. Why, there's folks dedicate their whole lives looking for new ways to kill themselves or kill others."

"Death comes for all men, sooner or later. What defines them, then, is not their ends, but how they meet those ends."

"A pretty quote," Dannen said. "Too bad it's a damn fool who said it."

"My father," Perandius answered.

Dannen grunted. "Anyway, death comes for everybody, but just so long as there's ale and whores left in the world I don't see any reason to get in line and wait my turn. When that bastard comes, I'd just as soon he had to do a bit of searching."

"What has made you so callous?" Perandius asked softly. "You stood for something, once. It is why you accepted the contract in the first place. Is it...did the loss of your wife—"

"Not another fucking word," Dannen growled, surprised to find that his face was only inches from the god's. "You leave her out of this, Perandius, you understand? Or we'll be putting that immortality of yours to the test, that much I can promise you."

The god looked taken aback at that. Not scared, which would have been nice, but then it wasn't easy, threatening a being who, as Dannen understood it, couldn't be killed. "I meant no offense,

Dannen Ateran," he said, sounding sincere, "and I apologize for any hurt my words caused, of course, for that is not my intention. It is only...these people. Their prayers have reached us. Morning, day, and night they pray, asking for help."

Dannen unclenched his fists, working his sore fingers. Suddenly, as was often the case once his anger had gotten the better of him, he felt ashamed, and it was an effort to meet the god's eyes, to sound nonchalant. "So answer them."

Perandius met his eyes. "I am trying to."

At first, Dannen didn't understand what he meant. Then, when he did, he snorted. "What's the big deal, anyway? Can't you just go down there, wave your hand and kill all the bad guys? Or send your brother—I've seen a few that enjoy causing pain in my day, and that bastard fits the bill sure enough."

"I cannot," the messenger god said. "None of us can. Long ago, it was decided that the gods would never directly interfere in mortal affairs, either to help or hurt."

Dannen grunted. "Kind of makes you all useless, doesn't it?"

"Not useless, Dannen Ateran, or at least not entirely. Although we cannot impose our will directly, we still have ways in which we might help. But believe me when I tell you it is better this way, far better. Once, there were no such restrictions, and the world was a wild, dangerous place."

"As opposed to now when it's all puppy dogs and rainbows?"

Perandius shook his head, clearly frustrated. "You do not understand. You see, Dannen Ateran, all gods have their roles, yes? That quality or facet of life which they exemplify. Are you following me?"

Dannen was a fool—no one would likely argue any different, him least of all—but he wasn't stupid. "Like the Goddess of Rain," he said, "that sister of yours."

"Exactly so," Perandius answered, inclining his head. "But for each god or goddess who represents one thing, so, too, is there an opposite, one who opposes them. For the Goddess of Peace, a God of War, for the Goddess of Wealth, the God of the Poor."

"A nice theology lesson," Dannen said, "but that doesn't explain why it would be so bad to get up off your collective asses from time to time and lend us a hand. Maybe you haven't looked in the last few millennia, Perandius, but damn if we couldn't use one."

"But it *does* explain it," Perandius persisted, "only you choose not to listen. There was a time, long ago, when no such strictures existed, and the gods were free to roam the earth as they chose, exercising their will on any man or woman they wished. The world, Dannen, was not better for it. It was not a perfect world, not a utopia. It was chaos. For you see, each god, as I have told you, has his or her diametric opposite, that which opposes them by their very *nature.* Opposition leads to conflict which, inevitably leads to war. Many wars, in fact, ones in which mortals, those men and women who sided with one god or the other, suffered most. For while gods might be weakened—as you saw my aunt, the Goddess of Peace, earlier—they may never be killed, may never *truly* be defeated except in the destruction of those who follow them."

Dannen tried to imagine what that world might have looked like, gods walking among men, bending—or breaking—them to their cause as a man might train a dog. The man might even be fond of the dog, as much as a man could be. But in the end, it was still just a beast to be tamed, one expected to obey without question in the hopes of receiving what scraps it could, one no one ever expected—or wanted—to think for itself. Reluctantly, he was forced to nod. "I think I catch your point. So, you all decided to leave off, then?"

"My father, in his wisdom, decided it," Perandius corrected.

"So, what? All us poor mortals are just on our own, is that it?"

"No, Dannen. We gods must now choose our champions, those who will do what we cannot, who will protect the world against the many evils which arise against it."

Dannen grunted. "And who was the damned fool who chose me, eh?"

Perandius blinked. "Forgive me, but I thought that much was clear. I did."

He laughed, then. "I'm guessing you're not much of a card player. Anyway, even if I do believe all you're telling me, even if I *wanted* to help, surely there's got to be others better suited to deal with this problem of yours."

"There were," Perandius agreed, apparently not even considering that saying as much might offend Dannen. "Unfortunately, they are no longer…available."

Dannen frowned deeply at that, not liking the way the god said it. "No longer available?"

Perandius sighed. "Dead, I'm afraid. All those heroes, those champions on whom we, the gods, might normally rely, have been...defeated."

"Well." Dannen said after a moment, "guess I wasn't your first choice. Suppose I can live with that."

"You were, in fact, our hundred and third."

Dannen barked a harsh laugh. "Not much for sparing a fella's feelings, are you?"

Perandius shrugged. "Forgive me if I am blunt, Dannen, but there is little time. You see, after so many of the gods' champions were vanquished, many among the gods began to believe there were none left who might oppose the necromancer and his brother, who might stand any chance against the hordes of undead which they are even now amassing as their own personal army. There are even those on the Council who seek the removal of my father's decree of no direct interference with the world of men altogether, using the plight of the north as their reason. It is, thankfully, a minority right now, but one which grows with each day that the brothers' evil is left unchecked."

"Which..." Dannen said, struggling to process everything the god was telling him, "wouldn't be a good thing."

"It would not be good," Perandius said, eyeing him, "if I were to return you to the tavern and those guards eagerly seeking your death. This, Dannen Ateran, would be unmitigated chaos."

Dannen grunted. "I catch your point. But if it's as bad as all that, why didn't you call on me sooner? And if I am part of this, I don't know, champion reserve or whatever you call it, why haven't I been summoned before?"

The messenger god winced then looked him up and down as if it were obvious. "Well. You're not exactly the heroic type, are you?"

Dannen looked down, wiggling the toes of the foot still missing a shoe, noting the way the waistband of his trousers was obscured somewhat by the paunch hanging over them, then grunted. Gods, but he needed to get in shape. He told himself—not for the first time over the last few years—he was going to give up drinking and start doing his combat forms again. And, not for the first time, he knew the thought to be a lie even as he had it.

"Harsh," he said finally, "but probably fair. Thing is, Perandius, even if I *wanted* to help those people—and I'm not saying I do—I'm not the man I once was. And even if I *were* still that man, I couldn't do what you're asking. A necromancer, a master warrior, and an army of the dead? It's a suicide mission. No man could do it."

"You're right, of course," Perandius said. "No single man could hope to do such a thing. Not alone."

Dannen frowned, not much liking the sound of that. He'd had partners over the years, of course, had worked with a few groups, and he'd always come off worse for the experience. From what he'd seen, a man did best on his own. After all, the ones most able to stab a man in the back were the ones he trusted to watch it. "Look, I don't know if you've noticed this yet or not, but I don't exactly play well with others. Besides, who would I even work with, anyway? According to you, all the heroes are already dead."

Perandius winced. "That isn't...*exactly* true. You see, when choosing our champions, we gods take into account all manner of factors. The individual's life—and abilities—are reviewed in depth by all members of the council. Then, once all have had an opportunity to look over the candidate, the matter is put to a vote in the next council meeting. Once a possible champion has been accepted, he—or she—is then brought to the land of the gods where they are presented with a contract identical to the one you signed so long ago."

"And I'm betting they're just jumping at the chance, the fools," Dannen said, ignoring, as best he could, that he had apparently been one of those fools in his youth.

"None have ever refused the honor," Perandius agreed. "Though, to be fair, no one expects they will. After all, one of the qualities we look for in a champion is the willingness to sacrifice for the good of others."

"Kind of a rigged game then, isn't it?"

Perandius shrugged. "If you choose to see it that way, I suppose. But it is a system that has worked for millennia."

"Until now."

The god frowned. "Yes. Until now."

"So what? You just forgot you had a few extra heroes lying around, and now you want me to team up with them, that it?"

"Not...exactly. You see, all those who I propose to comprise your team are...let us say that, for one reason or another, they did not quite pass the vote to become champions of the gods."

"Failures, then," Dannen said, having seen enough of life in all its shitty glory to not be all that surprised. "You're wanting to saddle me with a bunch of failures to take on a couple of badasses who—by your own admission—have killed all of the actual heroes you sent against them."

"I do not think of them as failures," Perandius said. "I prefer to think of them as those who have not quite reached their potential."

"Potential failures then."

"We are all potential failures, Dannen Ateran," Perandius answered in a somber tone as he walked to his desk and sat and began to study a parchment seemingly chosen at random out of the haphazard stacks. "God and man alike."

"That sounds like it comes from experience," Dannen chided. "What is it, Perandius? All the other little boy and girl gods got better things to do than hang out and read books with you? Or is it that your dad would rather spend time with the asshole twins than—"

"That's *enough!*" Perandius roared, springing out of his seat. Suddenly, his eyes, which had been some nondescript, boring color moments ago, were blazing gold, almost painful to look at.

For the first time since Dannen had met him, the messenger god actually *seemed* like a god, one that, as it happened, was pretty well pissed-off.

"Woah, take it easy," he said, holding up his hands. "I'm just messing with you, alright?"

Perandius's chest was heaving but slowly, the fire in his eyes dimming down until they glimmered like the dying embers of a campfire and then did not glimmer at all. "Excuse my...outburst," he said, "but as you have asked me not to speak of your family, so, too, shall I ask you not to speak of mine. Rivalries and jealousies are, I fear, not exclusive to mortals. The difference is that, most often, the hatreds of mortals die with them, but that of gods lives an eternity, an eternity in which they might nurse their offenses and grievances, in which their hatred festers and grows."

Dannen sighed. "Okay, Perandius. I'll take a look at this failure team of yours—a look," he said, noting the god's hopeful expression, "that's all. Fact is, I've got better things to do than risk my life trying to save a bunch of strangers that—in my experience—won't thank me for it."

"Really?" the god asked, his face a mask of innocence. "And during these last years of your life, Dannen Ateran, those which you have frittered away in one tavern after another, waking in one alley after another and being chased by one guard after another, have you done any of these 'better things'?'"

Dannen grunted. A direct hit, no mistake, and judging by the smug look on the god's face, the bastard knew it. "Well," Dannen said, because it was never in his nature to say nothing when he could keep talking and get himself into more trouble, "all that frittering, all that running for your life, it keeps a man pretty busy."

"I see," Perandius answered, a tone in his voice that said he saw a damn sight more clearly than Dannen would have liked.

"Anyway," Dannen said, clearing his throat, "guess we'd best be getting on with it. World to save and all that."

"Of course," Perandius agreed, a small smile on his face as he rose. "As I believe I mentioned, your team has already been chosen for you. I have a list of names somewhere..." he rifled through the seemingly endless pile of scrolls and tomes until he finally produced a small parchment and offered it to Dannen.

Dannen took it, glancing over the names. Two he didn't recognize. The third, though, he only wished he didn't. Val, his late wife, had always told him that a man's sins followed him, finding him out, sooner or later. It seemed she was right. "No way," he said, shaking his head. "No damn way."

"Ah," Perandius said, nodding. "I seem to recall that you have had some acquaintance with Fedder Firemaker."

Dannen barked a harsh laugh, but there was no humor in it. "All that mad bastard's acquaintances are dead or wishing they were."

"Interesting," the god mused. "I had understood that you and the Firemaker worked together on several successful missions. The ogre incursion in Baldeah comes to mind."

"Worked together," Dannen repeated. "And successful? Well, that's one way to put it. A better way, maybe, is that we just happened to be the last ones still alive at the end of it, despite that crazy wizard's best efforts, I might add."

"Still," Perandius persisted, "his talents will be quite necessary, I believe, to the mission's success. He is a High Mage, after all."

Dannen grunted. "If this is the type of person you gods are down to for champions, I'm thinking the world is well and truly fucked. What the man is, mostly, is a high pain in my ass, and his talents, such as they are, mostly consist of being insane enough to take on any challenge and mad enough to somehow come out the other end still breathing, something that can't be said for a lot of those unfortunate souls who have worked with him."

"Yet, many believe him to be the most powerful mage of this era and certainly he is far more capable than any alternatives."

"I've made a lot of mistakes in my life, Perandius. I've pretty much made a career out of it. But if any of the myriad of my blunders could be counted the greatest, it was my relatively brief—and incredibly painful—association with the mage." He waved his hand to silence Perandius's objections. "Just tell me about the others. You're on a roll—why stop now?"

"Both quite powerful individuals in their own right," Perandius said in a voice he obviously intended to be reassuring. "One may well be the world's best assassin, and the other an individual of vast talents...you might call a druid."

Well. Dannen had to admit the assassin thing sounded damned fine. With any luck, the bastard could sneak in and kill the two brothers, they'd all get some cheers and go back home.

"A druid, huh?" he asked. "Don't see many of them around anymore." Which was a state of affairs Dannen didn't mind in the least, if he was being honest. He hadn't met many of the nature-lovers, for most tended to spend their time in the woods, hugging trees and kissing sloths. But those he had met hadn't impressed him overly much. One had claimed to possess the ability to speak to plants, though it had never come in handy, and Dannen had never been able to imagine a situation where it could. Plants, as far as he knew, were content to sit and do a lot of nothing. In any event, the man had died most gruesomely—a common trait among many would-be heroes—and if the flowers had tried to save him they had failed miserably. The other had been a man who had been able to turn into a bear. Quite impressive, that, though a bit less so when he showed the trick and then proceeded, like any bear would, Dannen supposed, to attack the rest of the squad, chewing a man's arm damn near clean off before he was, ultimately, put down.

Still, if this was all some great joke, the god wasn't giving anything away. Maybe Val had been right and he did have a suicidal streak, or maybe it was the lingering effects of whatever potent drink had been in the golden bottle—perhaps even some combination of the two—but either way, Dannen shrugged.

"Fine. I can think of worse ways to die, I guess, than being butchered by some badass warrior and being turned into a zombie by his insane brother." In fact, he couldn't, and he thought he could think of some damn fine better ways—being smothered beneath the voluptuous bosom of a particularly eager lady of the night came to mind—but saying so wouldn't do any good.

It was his signature on the contract, of that much he was sure, but it wasn't his only motivation for his acquiescence. Nor was it that his life seemed to stretch on before him in depressing monotony, one tavern after another, one alleyway after another. About that much, at least, Perandius had been right.

Mostly, he hadn't liked the way Perandius's brother and sister had looked at him like he was trash. Maybe he *was* trash. He certainly wasn't the man he'd once been, and even he had to admit he wouldn't want to look at a statue of himself as he now was. But he mostly just wanted to prove to the gods that even trash could get the job done sometimes. And who knew? If he was lucky, he might even get to show them that trash could be dangerous, too, when it walked and punched you in your arrogant face.

It was his pride, then, the same pride Val had told him would get him killed on more than one occasion. Also, the chivalrous part of him—weak, dying, surely, but not quite dead—railed at the injustice of the tyrant brothers. The dead should not be brought back to be slaves, doing the bidding of a cruel master, just as they should not haunt a man's dreams, reminding him of what he'd lost, of the happiness he could never have again. He understood, logically, that defeating the necromancer would not stop the dreams, but neither had copious amounts of ale—he'd tried enough to know it—so why not give something else a shot?

"We all done here then?" he asked, suddenly eager to get on with it. "Because if you could teleport me to the bastards' bedchamber, that might settle all this a bit quicker."

"Unfortunately," Perandius said, "it doesn't work like that."

Dannen sighed. "No, no, I don't suppose I thought it would. Your father's rules, I'm guessing?"

"Just so."

"Well. Where am I going then?"

"You must travel to the town of Berridan."

In his younger days, Dannen had traveled damn near the width and breadth of the country of Ebenfall, and more than a few places beyond, so he was surprised that he didn't recognize the name.

When he said as much, Perandius winced.

"Nor would you. It's a small village, I'm afraid, no more than a few hundred souls all told, but it is where you will find Firemaker, the first of your companions. Still, Berridan is a quaint place, a friendly place."

"Quaint and friendly, eh? Well, if Firemaker's there, I wouldn't bet on it staying that way for long. So, what? You need to wave your hands or something? Do I need to close my eyes?"

The god smiled. "Nothing so theatrical as that. Still, there is one more small bit of help I would give you, if you will accompany me."

Dannen shrugged, following the god out of the hovel. After so long spent in the small house, the wide, sprawling vista of the city of the gods felt overwhelming, and Dannen took the first breath he'd had in many hours which didn't taste of stale books and dusty parchments, thinking maybe the tree-hugging druids weren't so far off the mark, after all.

Perandius led him down the streets without a word until they reached an ornate golden gate. Dannen followed him into a massive, luscious garden the likes of which he had never seen. Flowers bloomed everywhere, a vista of colors brighter and more vibrant than he ever imagined existed. Great, elaborate fountains spewed water into the air, and golden statues stood majestic and proud. Dannen wasn't much a man for art or beauty, but even he had to admit the gardens were the most beautiful thing he'd ever seen. He suspected any of the world's artists would have killed for the opportunity to paint some of the brightly colored plants and flowers.

But Dannen was no artist, so he only followed as the god walked down a cobbled lane, leading him to the base of one of the fountains—this one a statue of the God of Thunder. At the base of the fountain, beneath the water, were hundreds of perfectly rounded stones, all of which, incongruously with what he'd so far seen of the land of the gods, were perfectly black, a black so profound each seemed to suck in the light around it.

"Damn," Dannen said, unable to pull his gaze away from the endless depths of the stones. "What are they?"

"These," Perandius said, reaching in and withdrawing one of the stones, "are Divining Stones. Their purposes may vary, but..." He hesitated, closing his eyes. It seemed to Dannen an invisible force gathered only to dissipate a moment later. "There. This one will alert you when you have found the other members of your team."

Dannen grunted, taking the proffered stone. "That's handy, though it seems to me asking their names might save some trouble."

"Perhaps," Perandius admitted, "but the enemies you face are not fools. In truth, they have shown an uncanny ability, thus far, to possess knowledge which is largely unexplainable, seeming to know every move our champions make before they make it, and it is this prescience that has allowed them to so thoroughly defeat those we have sent against them."

Dannen thought that type of thing should have been mentioned before he signed on for the job, but there was no point making a fuss, not now, so he shoved the stone into his pocket. "What else do you have for me?"

Perandius frowned. "Um...oh, right. My best wishes for your and your team's success, of course."

"You're kidding, right?" Dannen asked. "I was thinking more along the lines of, shit, I don't know, a magic sword or a horse with wings, that sort of thing."

"Ah. Well, I regret to inform you that we are...well, that is, we are currently out of magic swords. Those we had were given to those who came before you. As for the horse with wings...believe me when I tell you that though beautiful, Pegasi are, without fail, far more trouble than they're worth. Stubborn, obstinate beasts at the best of times," he said with obvious distaste. "Besides, I was given to understand that you vowed off using swords."

"I did," Dannen said, and that, at least, was a vow he intended to stick to. "But that's not the point. Surely there's some sort of help you can give us instead of just a pat on the back and a 'good luck.'"

Perandius huffed. "Look, it isn't exactly as if magic swords grow on trees, okay? Besides—" He paused, following Dannen's gaze to a massive tree in the distance one from which hung what looked like daggers, but the proportions were all wrong, the blades far too thick and wide for their length, the handles, too, seeming smooshed and misshapen.

"Fine," Perandius said. "They *do* grow on trees, but in any event none are ripe, so it makes no difference. I am only able to give you the Divining Stone to aid you in your quest."

Dannen didn't much like the sound of that, "quest." He'd been on a few quests in his time, had spoken to others before they went on their own. Rare, though, were the times in which he spoke with them *after*, for those heading out on quests generally ended dead in one fashion or another. Usually that fashion being a pissed off ogre, an evil wizard or, for those particularly discerning and lucky questers, a short trip down the gullet of a dragon. None of which appealed to him. "Thanks, I guess."

"You are welcome," the messenger god said, once again displaying his obliviousness to sarcasm. "And I need not tell you that, should you and your team fail, those voices in the Council who wish to withdraw my father's edict will be far louder and far more influential. What is at risk, then, is no less than the survival of the world as you know it."

That was another damned thing about quests. It always seemed that the stakes were the world. Dannen wondered where all the smaller quests were, the ones where failure resulted in nothing worse than a puppy getting kicked, or a child's tears. He thought he could have handled those well enough. "Well, if we fail, that'll be somebody else's problem as I'll most likely be dead."

"That is true," the god said, agreeing far too readily for Dannen's comfort. Then Perandius cleared his throat and stood straighter, as a golden glow began to appear around him as it had in the tavern. "Dannen Ateran," he intoned, "you have accepted this quest"—*there was that damned word again*—"this burden, and for that, you have my thanks. In the coming trials you will face, both gods and mortals alike will watch you and witness your sacrifice."

Oh, the gods might watch, but if what Perandius had said was true, they'd do no more than that, not bothering to lift a finger if a zombie decided to make Dannen its next meal. He was just about to say as much when, suddenly, the god was no longer there. The world blurred around him, seemed to *shift,* and the next thing he knew, he was falling.

He had just enough time to shout in surprise before he hit the ground with a grunt, stumbling and falling on his ass. "Bastard enjoys it," Dannen muttered. He rose, dusting himself off and rubbing his tailbone. He stood on a dirt trail flanked on either side by fields.

Men and women crouched in the fields, harvesting their crops. Or, at least, they had been. Now, all of them were busy studying the suspicious man who had appeared out of thin air. With no other course left him, Dannen waved, thinking maybe he shouldn't have teased the Messenger God quite so much. Still, if a sore ass was the worst he suffered in the next few weeks, he'd count it a win.

A town lay ahead, a short distance down the road, and Dannen suspected this was where Perandius had told him he'd find the Firemaker. He couldn't remember the town's name, too distracted by the ache in his hindquarters, but it didn't matter in any case, for if the crazy bastard mage hung around much longer, "charred ruins" would be as good a name as any.

If anything, the farmers seemed even more hostile for his waving, so Dannen sighed and started toward the village, weathering the disapproving scowls of the men and women as he did. After all, he'd weathered far worse than that in his life and had the scars to prove it.

He was more than a little surprised, upon entering the town in which the mage supposedly resided, to see no corpses on the ground. Not that it was much of a town to begin with. The road, such as it was, was little more than a tightly-packed dirt trail with weeds sprouting here and there, and the few people he saw were dressed in the functional, nearly always dirty clothes of physical laborers. There was a small stable in which he could see several horses, nags if he was any judge, and several chickens bounded across the path chased by dirty, laughing children.

Dannen paused, breathing in the cool air. He'd spent the last years in one city or the other, and it had been some time since he'd traveled to a village as small as this one. Such villages, in his experience, had poor selections of drink and even worse of prostitutes. Still, there was something relaxing, peaceful, somehow *honest* about it, something he hadn't realized he'd missed until experiencing it again. In fact, the village seemed *so* peaceful he was beginning to think Perandius had got the mage's whereabouts wrong after all. That was when the quiet was shattered by a familiar roar from a nearby building. The shout was followed seconds later by a loud *crash* and the sound of something breaking—a table, a chair, maybe a person. Dannen rubbed his temples.

Only a damn fool would sign up for this, he thought. Necromancers and powerful warriors, not to mention an army of the undead was bad enough. But on top of that, one of the members of his "team" was as likely to kill him as any of the enemies he faced. A fool's errand, for certain. Perhaps, he shouldn't have been surprised, then, to find himself moving toward the distant shouts—screams, really—and the mage's deep, unmistakable bellow.

There was no sign hanging over the place. Perhaps it was unnecessary in so small a village where any visitor would only be passing through. Still, it *was* a tavern, of that much there was no doubt. The proof of that, mostly, was that the mage was there at all.

The door creaked loudly, perhaps because whoever had built the place had done a poor job of it, or perhaps it was simply to serve as a way to alert the tavernkeeper of customers' arrival. Clever, if it was the second, but just then, it had the dubious effect of making all of those in the tavern—the conscious ones, at any rate—turn to regard him.

This included the massive mage, a man Dannen had not seen in nearly ten years, but one whom he recognized instantly. Mainly because now, as the last time he'd seen him—nearly every time, in point of fact—the man had some unfortunate soul's neck tucked up under his armpit and was doing his level best to choke him out.

In the other hand, he held a foaming mug of ale that looked like a child's teacup in his platter-sized hands, one which he took a long pull from and promptly spewed out when he noticed Dannen. *"By the gods!"* he roared—the Firemaker never spoke or uttered, certainly never whispered, but he roared often enough—"If it ain't the Bloody Butcher himself!"

"Fedder," Dannen replied, inclining his head. "How have you been?"

The mage's expression split into a wide grin that was, in many ways, even more terrifying than his usual angry snarl. This, because it did a fine job of showing off the gaps in his teeth where one of his unfortunate opponents in his all too common fights got in a lucky blow before promptly getting the shit kicked out of him. Or her. Or it. The Firemaker was many things, but particular could not be listed among them.

"Oh, I've been damn fine, lad, damn fine." He glanced down at the man he had tucked under one arm whose face had turned an alarming shade of blue. "You see that fella there?" he asked the semi-conscious man. "Why, that's the Bloody Butcher, man! You lucky bastards," he said, sweeping the room with his gaze, though Dannen thought the poor soul tucked under his arm might have argued about that lucky bit. Not that he was likely to be saying anything for some time. "You're in the presence of *greatness,* don't you understand?" the mage roared. "Why, this man here's put more fools in the dirt than entire armies!"

Dannen doubted that, or at least he wanted to, but he wouldn't have argued with the mage, either way. For one, he'd learned long ago that it was at best useless and at worst dangerous, for Fedder tended to either ignore or—as now, choke the life out of—anything or anyone who challenged his view of the world.

"So," the mage said, still grinning that mad grin, "what brings you to this shithole, eh?"

Dannen sighed. "That's a bit of a story. How about we get a drink? I'll tell you all about it."

"Why that sounds damn fine," Fedder agreed. "Two ales," he roared, "on the double." Then he glanced back at Dannen, "What about you, lad? Want anything to drink?"

Dannen laughed despite himself. It had just been that kind of day. "An ale is fine," he told the wide-eyed barkeep, though whether or not he heard it was hard to tell as the barkeep was staring at Fedder as if he were some wild beast ready to kill them all at any moment. Which, it turns out, wasn't that far from the truth.

Dannen started toward the bar and paused, raising an eyebrow at Fedder. "You going to bring your friend along?"

The hulking figure frowned, looking down at the man, his long red beard—mostly red, at least, though some of it, Dannen saw, shot through with gray—bristling. "Made fun of my robe. He and his friends." Six or so, Dannen counted, all of whom were decorating the floor just then, and none of whom looked like making fun of anything—or being conscious—for quite some time.

Dannen wouldn't have ever said as much to the mage—he preferred his head uncrushed—but he understood why the lads had thought to make fun of the robe. It was made of a light blue fabric which stretched across the mage's massive frame, and on which had been sewn the shapes of moons and constellations. What he *didn't* understand was why any fool would look at the mage and think mocking him—or his garments—could end any way but badly. "Well," Dannen said, looking at the man who the mage was still strangling while carrying on a conversation. "I'm sure he's sorry."

Fedder gave the guy a brisk—which, for him, no doubt meant incredibly painful—shake. "That right? You sorry, boy?"

The man's head lolled in what might have been a nod or, more likely, was just an involuntary spasm as the lack of air took its toll. Thankfully, Fedder seemed satisfied. He released the man who proceeded to collapse like a man who...well, like a man who'd just had the shit strangled out of him by what amounted to little less than a giant. Dannen had never been particularly fond of—or particularly good at—analogies, but he thought this one held up well enough.

"Now then," Fedder said, plopping onto one of the stools and ignoring its creak of protest, just as he didn't notice the way the terrified bartender set the two beers in front of him and practically leapt back out of the way. The bartender then retreated into the kitchen to see to some no doubt pressing matter—like not getting strangled.

"What's it been, Butcher?" Fedder asked. "Eight, nine years?"

Dannen didn't get his beer, but then he wasn't surprised and couldn't honestly blame the barkeep. He'd wanted to run from the insane mage more than a few times himself, and Fedder *liked* him. Or, at least, he hadn't strangled him half to death yet at any rate. He tossed a few coins onto the counter anyway, figuring that, judging by several broken tables and shattered chairs strewn about the place, the man would likely need it, not to mention the several fresh, suspiciously head-sized dents in the walls.

"Ten," Dannen said, pulling his gaze back to the mage. *And not nearly long enough.*

"That long?" Fedder asked, then grunted, rubbing at his ale-sodden beard. "Shit. And how you been?" He looked Dannen up and down appraisingly, taking in his clothes and smirking at his one bare foot before grinning. "No offense, but you got damn fat, didn't you?"

Dannen scowled. "It's a baggy shirt."

"Sure it is," the mage said, barking a laugh which might have come from a lion. "Anyway, least you ain't been starvin'. Now we got all the pleasantries out of the way, you kissed my ass a bit and me yours, what's brought you here? Lookin' for some bloodlettin' are ya?"

Dannen frowned. "I've never been much for bloodletting," he said, doing his best to ignore the huge grin splayed across Fedder's face. "Anyway, there's...a job."

The mage didn't just smirk at that, he leaned back in his stool—which gave another tortured groan—and bellowed a laugh loud and deep enough to shake the walls, spraying ale out of his mouth. "You hear that, lad?" rhe mage asked of the man lying on the ground who, if Dannen was any judge, wasn't in any condition to hear much of anything as he was fairly certain the poor fool had passed out. That didn't stop Fedder, though, who balled some more laughter, clapping Dannen on the shoulder and nearly knocking him out of his chair. "Never been much on bloodlettin' but he's got a job he needs poor old Fedder for. Let me tell you something, boyo," he said, turning to the unconscious man on the floor then pausing as he finally realized he was unlikely to get an answer from that quarter. "You know somethin', Butcher?" he asked in a contemplative voice, "I think the bastard passed out. Shit himself too, by the smell. Though, suppose maybe he always smells like that."

"Some folks have no manners," Dannen said.

"Anyway," Fedder went on, turning to the bartender who had made the foolish mistake of thinking to step into the common room of his tavern once more, "you ever heard of the Bloody Butcher?"

The man stood as if frozen to the spot. "I...yes. E-everyone has heard of the Butcher. It's said he's possessed b-by a demon with a heart as black as p-pitch. Some say he isn't even human, n-not completely."

Fedder laughed. "Oh, he's human alright, though I can understand them bein' confused, if'n they ever found themselves at the business end of his sword..." He made a thoughtful sound, rubbing a hand at his filthy beard. "Not that many of those are still around to be much confused about anything. Anyway, you got the privilege—no, the gods-blasted *honor*—of having that very same Butcher in your shitty little tavern, now how's that?"

The barkeep turned a bit red at that, but decided—proof the man was no fool—not to be offended. After a moment, he turned to Dannen, his eyes wide. "Y-you're...you're the Butcher?"

Dannen frowned at Fedder. "I was, once. That...it was a long time ago."

The mage bellowed a laugh. "Oh, not that long, lad. Why, there's widows weeping over the graves of their dead husbands would say it ain't been no time at all. Anyway, here you are, talking about a job and tryin' to act like you ain't thrilled at the prospect of spillin' a bit of blood. Ten years and ain't a damned thing changed, but I wouldn't have it any other way."

The mage said the part about widows as if it was a compliment which, to his insane mind, it probably was. Dannen, though, winced as he felt the familiar guilt—guilt that, it seemed, had been following him all his life—begin to take hold.

"I-I'm s-s-sorry," the barkeep said, his wide eyes locked on Dannen and looking, if anything, even more terrified now that he knew the Bloody Butcher—a fool nickname if Dannen had ever heard one—was in his midst. "I-I didn't know."

The bartender wasn't looking at Fedder, not now, but at Dannen. Dannen had seen such looks before, often plastered across the faces of those he saved when the killing was done or, as his exploits became more well-known, many of the villagers of the places he visited. Fear or hate. He should have been accustomed to such looks, for he had weathered them often enough, but that look, that fear, wasn't something a man got used to.

"It's fine," Dannen muttered. "Really."

"The Bloody damn Butcher!" Fedder roared, either unaware or unconcerned with the mood of the others in the room. He lifted his ale in a toast, not bothering to see if anyone else was drinking before finishing his ale in a single pull, though whether more made it into his mouth or splattered down his beard was anyone's guess.

"If you're finished," Dannen said, "maybe we can get back to business."

"Oh, sure, sure, 'course we can, Butcher. Whatever you say, lad."

Dannen pinched his nose between his thumb and forefinger before remembering Perandius doing much the same while dealing with him and stopped. "Anyway, what brought you here?"

The mage winced, the question making him uncomfortable in a way a common room full of men wanting to kill him never could. "Well. It's a bit of a story, that. One there ain't no sense in goin' into."

Seeing the mage avoiding the question aroused Dannen's curiosity. "Oh, come on now, what is it?"

"Well," Fedder answered slowly, "it uh...it's a bit of a secret mission, you might call it."

Dannen blinked. "A secret," he said dryly, for whatever else the mage was, he was the least subtle person Dannen had ever met. A thought struck him, and he grunted. "Wait a minute. Don't tell me you're still doing jobs for that bastard Seladrius."

"What?" Fedder said, confused. "Oh, no, no, that ain't it. Gods, I ain't got no time at all for that backstabbing bastard, even if he were still alive."

"Wait," Dannen said, surprised, "Seladrius is dead?"

The mage nodded. "Goin' on five years now. I tell ya, Dannen, it's a bitch—gettin' older, I mean. But what can you do? Lady Time takes us all, in the end."

Seladrius, who had served as their manager of sorts. He had been old, it was true, but the thought of him being dead now struck Dannen harder than he would have expected. It brought home his own mortality in a way that waking up half-naked and confused in an alleyway had not. Seladrius had been a sketchy bastard, and Dannen was fairly certain he'd skimmed some of his reward money on more than a few occasions, but he was still sad at the thought. And it wasn't *just* sad he felt. Mostly, he just felt old.

He was a relic, that's what he was. Some might have said legend—Fedder, who'd always had an unnatural appetite for violence certainly would have—but Dannen thought relic was closer to the mark. Legends were in storybooks, the sort of men and women parents told their kids about, hoping to make them see how good they could be. Legends rode on shining horses in shining armor and swung shiny swords at particularly *unshiny* trolls, doing good everywhere they went. It wasn't even as if they *chose* to be good in such stories; more like they couldn't have done anything else if they'd tried. Stab a random person in the street, on account of they felt like doing so and no other reason, like as not the bastard would turn out to be some mass murderer.

No, Dannen didn't fit the part of a hero or a legend, that much Perandius had been right about. Probably he was closer to the troll. Certainly he sympathized with the dumb beast. People believed trolls to be evil, but they just wanted to be left alone under their bridges. Sure, maybe they ate the odd visitor, but another word for an unwanted visitor was *trespasser,* and Dannen figured he'd have some choice words to say to someone who came stomping into—or, in the case of trolls and bridges, on *top* of—his house. And that was before he stopped to consider their dietary needs. Dannen had never had a good long talk with a troll—had killed a few in his time, though, that had to be said—but as far as he knew, man-flesh was a necessary staple of a troll's diet. Sort of like vegetables for a man. Or beer.

"Yeah," Fedder said gruffly, perhaps mistaking the sudden fatalistic streak likely visible in Dannen's expression as grief over the dead old crook. "Well, what can you do? Seladrius was a funny bastard, and I always liked him. Figured the money he skimmed was a small enough price to pay for listening to his jokes—that fella could tell some of the finest jokes I ever heard, that's sure." He shrugged his shoulders, and Dannen could hear the blue fabric tearing as it stretched across his massive frame. "Anyway, hope you weren't countin' on him figurin' out all the details for you on this one."

The first thing to pop into Dannen's head was, *But he was so young.* Thing was, that wasn't true. Seladrius had been an old, ornery bastard with one foot in the grave when Dannen had known him, and that had been ten years ago. "Well," he said finally, "as you said. Time's a bitch, and she gets us all in the end."

Fedder's thick red eyebrows furrowed at that, his face scrunching up as if deep in thought, even went so far as to tug at his thick red beard. "Sure, I reckon that's so. Guess the joke's on her then, this time, at least." He grinned, displaying teeth as big and wide as some gravemarkers Dannen had seen.

He frowned. "What do you mean? I thought you said he died of old age."

Fedder nodded thoughtfully. "I'm sure he would have, given the chance. He was old, true enough, though I'm fairly sure it was the dagger in the back did him in."

Dannen blinked. "Dagger?"

Fedder grunted. "Seems some folks didn't appreciate the grumpy old bastard's humor as much as we did, Butcher. Anyway." He shrugged as if folks dying was an everyday occurrence—which, of course, it was, particularly if they had the unfortunate luck to wind up in Fedder's line of sight. "What can you do? Shit happens."

As far as Dannen was concerned that summed up the human condition pretty nicely, so he hoisted his cup. "To Seladrius."

"Aye," the mage said, and if Dannen hadn't known better he would have thought he saw a tear in the man's eye before he rubbed the arm of his soiled robe roughly across his face, no doubt leaving both dirtier than they had been. "Here's to the grumpy old bastard. May the God of the Dead have some whores waitin' on him, and may he remember what to do with 'em when he gets there."

Left with nothing else to do, Dannen drank his own ale, taking a long pull. No god's nectar, this, that was for damned sure, but at least he had a relatively good idea how much of it was likely to get him in trouble. "Anyway, what have you been up to?" he said after a time.

The mage winced, refusing to meet his eyes, an expression on his face that Dannen would have taken as embarrassment on another man. "Oh, you know. This and that."

Normally, Dannen operated on the belief that a man's shit should stay *his* shit, but the typically lugubrious mage's odd behavior was interesting. "What sort of this and that?"

Fedder grunted, turning up his ale again only to realize it was empty. He scowled at the mug with a dark, menacing expression that would have sent any man either running or begging—and likely both—for his life. Alas, the mug was just a mug and didn't have the sense to be suitably terrified, so the mage slammed it on the counter, disgusted at the personal affront of it daring to be empty in his presence. "There was a troupe goin' around to towns," he said in the tone of voice of a man confessing some terrible secret. "Mummers, you know, actin' out the histories, doin' tricks, that sort of thing. I took up work with 'em, little enchantments, sparks and fireworks mostly. Simple shit a first-year apprentice could do, but the locals eat it up."

Dannen tried to imagine the fiery—both in hair color and temperament—mage performing for a heckling crowd and laughed. "Sounds...fun."

Fedder grunted sourly. "Damned shame is what it is. It's the reason I'm wearin' this damned get-up," he growled, waving a disgusted hand at the light-blue robe with its sewn-on constellations. "Makes me look like a sissy."

Dannen thought that, given the amount of blood staining the garment, he doubted anyone would think its wearer a sissy. But he didn't get a chance to say as much before Fedder went on, roaring in his usual manner, "*A damn shame!* I'm a gods-blasted *hero*, Butcher. And now, look at me, doing parlor tricks so kiddies can have a story to tell their friends, the little shits. We are *both* heroes. I miss the old times, hunting down folks as needed killin' and gettin' it done. Best days of my life and that's a fact."

Dannen remembered those days well enough—too well, truth be told—though not with quite the same nostalgia as the Firemaker. Mostly, he remembered being shit-himself scared most of the time, running—or, when that failed, fighting—for his life. Still, there was such a look of morose depression on the mage's face that it was all he could do to keep the grin off his own. "Well. I was going to ask you about joining me for a job, but if you're previously engaged..."

"Eh," Fedder grunted after a time. "Don't reckon it was goin' to work out with the troupe anyway."

"Oh?" Dannen asked as innocently as he could manage. "Why's that?"

The mage shrugged his massive shoulders. "Me and some of 'em, well, we didn't see eye to eye on a few things. Most things, really. Particularly that bastard as runs the show. Real asshole, that one, thinks he can talk to a man any way he wants on account of his brother's the captain of what this little shithole considers its guards."

Dannen didn't bother asking what things. In his experience, few people saw eye to eye with the Firemaker on much of anything, and that was just how the violent bastard liked it. "Well," he pressed. "Still, might be best that we speak to him before you sign on for the job. It'd be the polite thing to do."

Fedder frowned. "Maybe, but I think I've pretty well tendered my resignation on that little venture already, Butcher. Besides, we'd have to wake 'em up, and that just seems like more trouble than it's worth, you want to know the truth."

"Wake him up?" Dannen asked, suddenly getting a sinking feeling in his stomach, one that was confirmed a moment later when the mage glanced over at one of the unconscious men littering the common room floor.

"Sure," the Firemaker said, "assumin' he's alive." He snorted. "I tell you, Butcher, folks can't take a hit anymore, not like they used to."

"Wait a minute," Dannen said carefully, "do you mean to say that the guy there"—he pointed, indicating the unconscious man—*please, gods, let him just be unconscious*—"is the troupe leader?"

"That's right."

"The same troop leader," Dannen said, "who happens to be the brother of this town's guard captain?"

"That'd be the one," the red-haired giant agreed, and if he was at all concerned by that fact, he hid it well. Which, knowing him as he did, Dannen thought it likely that the man hadn't even considered it.

"Anyway," the mage went on, turning back around and holding a sausage-sized finger up to the barkeep to order another beer, "what were you sayin', about this job and all?"

Gods help me. "I'll tell you about it," Dannen said, "but let's do it on the road, eh?"

"You sure?" The mage asked curiously. "I'll admit this swill ain't the best drink I've had, but you look like you could use one, anyway. Might do you some good to take a load off."

Dannen was quite sure that hanging around long enough for the unconscious or dead fellow's guard-captain brother to catch wind that he'd had the shit kicked out of him wouldn't do him any good at all, but he knew saying as much would do nothing to motivate the mage, so he decided to try a different tack. "Yeah, we're behind schedule already."

Fedder snorted. "Behind schedule. I like that. Well," He shrugged. "I guess these folks of yours need killin' done need it quick." He glanced at the barkeep, rising from his stool. "How much do I owe ya, fella?"

The barkeep reminded Dannen of a frightened rabbit, ready to flee at any moment, but he gave the giant a sickly smile. "I-it's on...the house, of course."

Fedder grunted as if surprised that a man who wanted to go on living, faced with an insane mage, would do anything so crazy as not dare to charge him. "Well, that's damned fine of you, sport, damned fine. Makes me feel bad for what I did—talkin' about the ale and all. It helps, I've had plenty worse and that's a fact."

Sorry about the ale, but apparently feeling nothing about the half a dozen unconscious men lying around, ones he'd put there, nor about the furniture—not all of it was broken, not quite, but Dannen thought the mage had given it a good effort just the same. But then, that was Fedder Firemaker. Only a fool would intentionally put himself in the giant's path. Dannen had heard folks say it plenty of times, back in the day, and he had been one of them. *So you're a fool then,* he thought sourly. *What exactly, up to this point in your life, has made you think any different?* Nothing. Nothing at all, that was the damn truth of it. "Come on," he said with a sigh, "we'll talk on the way."

CHAPTER FIVE

An hour later, they were riding away from Berridan on two horses which Fedder had "purchased" from a terrified stablemaster for the unsurprising price of free. Dannen glanced back down the path behind them, surprised to find it empty instead of populated by an angry mob carrying torches and pitchforks. Surprised, but not exactly comforted. After all, not seeing the mob didn't mean it didn't exist, and where one man—or two, in this case—might get horses, so might others.

He'd finished telling the Firemaker everything that had happened only moments ago, and the giant's face was scrunched up nearly as much as the back of the poor beast struggling beneath his massive frame as he thought it over like it was a puzzle he might solve.

"Champions of the gods," the giant said finally, hocking and spitting on the dusty trail. "Ain't that a damned fine thing."

"It's *some*thing, for sure," Dannen said. Thinking that, by and large—saving the possible exception of Perandius, he still wasn't sure on that count—the gods struck him as a bunch of assholes. Best not to say as much to the mage though, for the man was always looking for someone to fight, but seemed to look to Dannen to guide his way. It was all too likely, then, that if he said what he really thought about the situation—that it was pretty well fucked—the mage would take it on himself to start up a war with the gods which, like most of the big bastard's pursuits, would likely to end in horrible deaths for the both of them.

"And this pebble the letter god gave you," Firemaker said, "it's s'pose to what, talk to you, tell you which way to go?"

Dannen grunted. "I don't think it talks. At least, Perandius never said as much."

"I see," Firemaker said, nodding. "So how's it work then?"

Dannen realized that he had no damned idea how the "pebble" worked. And that made him angry. Maybe angrier than it should have. His day had been pretty well shit so far—his *life* had been pretty much shit, come to it. If it wasn't bad enough that he was on his way to gather up a team of what Perandius himself had admitted were failed heroes to go fight some villains who had killed all the *real* ones, now he realized he didn't even know *how* he was going to find them in the first place. He sighed heavily, rubbing at his temple where a headache was beginning to form. "I have no idea."

Fedder studied him for several seconds with a blank expression, before he turned his head up and roared with laughter, the sound of it echoing through the trees surrounding the path like thunder and sending a pack of birds fleeing into the sky. The Firemaker, in his mirth, slapped his horse's side with a good-natured *whap* which, good-natured or not, made the beast skitter-step to the side, nearly tipping over and just managing to right itself. But if he even so much as noticed his mount's dismay, the mage gave no sign, wiping at tears of mirth with his calloused, grubby fingers. "Gods, Butcher, but you ain't changed a bit. Too worried about the killin' to come to think on how we're gonna get to it."

Dannen *was* worried about the killing to come—or the dying, which seemed all the more likely—just not in the way the mage thought. He was just getting ready to say as much when he felt an uncomfortable heat in his pocket. He reached inside his trousers and pulled out the stone. It wasn't hot, not exactly, but though it looked exactly as it had when the god had given it to him, there was no denying it was unnaturally warm. "Well, I'll be."

"That it, then?" Fedder asked, leaning forward—an abrupt movement which almost toppled his tortured mount once more—to peer at the stone.

"This is it," Dannen agreed.

"Doesn't look like much, does it?" the mage said. "'Course, neither do we, I reckon." He roared with laughter again at that, but Dannen was barely listening, too distracted by the feel of the stone

73

in his hands. There was the warmth, that was part of it, but not all. There was the knowing. Suddenly, without explanation, he knew—beyond any shadow of a doubt—that they needed to head west. And then it wasn't just the direction in his head, but a name. *Talinseh.*

It was the place where he would find the next member of their team, of that much he was certain. It was also, as it happened, a name he was familiar with, a name which, he was just as certain, he wished would have been any other.

"Felt somethin' just then," Fedder grunted. No matter how much he might disdain the use of magic—largely thinking it was for sissies and preferring to drink and bash skulls over reading dusty old tomes any day—Dannen was reminded of just how powerful the man's gift was.

He sighed heavily, slipping the stone back into his pocket. "I know where we have to go. Talinseh."

Fedder laughed again, grinning widely. "The Assassin City, eh? Well, sure, why not. And here I was thinkin' we might have to do quite a bit of walkin' before we got a taste of blood."

Dannen didn't share the mage's excitement at the prospect of bloodshed. He thought it unlikely things could get any worse. But he pushed the thought away, feared that the universe would take it as a challenge.

"Hey, Butcher," Fedder said.

Dannen fought back a sigh. "Yes, Fedder?"

"Did you know you were missin' a boot?"

CHAPTER SIX

The city of Talinseh, known as the Crimson Jewel and, less poetically but, in Dannen's experience, far more accurately, the Assassin City, was not the sort of place a man might travel to with his family to see the sights. In fact, it wasn't the type of place any man would go, if he could help it, excepting, of course, if that man just so happened to be a thief or a murderer.

But for all the danger in it, there was no denying the city's beauty. Now, as every time he'd visited the place, Dannen stared in awe at the massive white walls rising all around it, their surfaces shining in the sunlight as if embedded with millions of diamonds. There were no such diamonds, of course, and if there had been they would have long since been pilfered by the city's denizens, but that didn't change the arresting quality of the city when he and the mage guided their weary mounts over a hilltop and it came into sight.

And despite all the dangers he knew lurked within the walls, Dannen was glad to see them just the same. He'd spent the last two weeks with the giant of a mage, traveling on the road, sleeping in abandoned barns when they could and on the side of the road when they could not. He had passed more than a few nights sodden and miserable as the rain fell on them, the mage—who would have been more than capable of casting a spell to ward off the rain—not deigning to do so, no doubt believing it would make him less of a man.

But the rain wasn't the worst of it, nor were the Firemaker's snores which, if Dannen was any judge, sounded more like the roar of a particularly pissed-off dragon. Instead, the longer they'd been on the road, the worse the mage's mood had become. An interesting facet of the mage's personality that Dannen had forgotten—or likely *chosen* to forget—was that the man didn't do well on the road. Largely, Dannen suspected, because when he was alone with only himself and his traveling companions, the chances of the mage finding someone to fight—his favorite activity—were pretty remote. Excepting, of course, those times when he'd decided to take out his frustrations on his traveling companions themselves, some few—very few—of whom lived to complain about.

Dannen had never found himself on the wrong end of the mage's ire, but he preferred not to risk it anymore than he had to. So while trepidation filled him at the sight of the city, so too did no small amount of relief. "Beautiful," he said.

"It'll do," Fedder growled, but Dannen didn't miss the slow grin spreading across the mage's face, and why not? Fedder was a man who would have been far more at home on some great battlefield of old, covered in the blood and viscera of his enemies. Now that they were back among civilization, it was a craving he would have an opportunity to satisfy, and what better place to do just that than an entire city full of thieves and murderers?

Dannen sighed, thinking that if he survived the next few hours in the mage's company it would be a miracle in itself. Still, there was nothing to be done for it. There was no denying the knowledge the stone had given him as much as he might have wanted to, so he clucked at his horse, giving its flanks a kick, and started toward the Assassin City. Outside the gate, they were forced to wait in line while the four guards stationed there looked over the wagons and goods of any wishing entry, going so far as to search them. Dannen was familiar with the practice, for he'd undergone it the last time he'd visited the city. He knew that, should any of those seeking entry be carrying a weapon, the guards would seize it, giving them in return a small slip of paper to present to the clerks when leaving the city and, for a small fee, pay for holding their weapon while in the city.

Somebody visiting Talinseh for the first time might have thought the measures a good thing and in some ways, they would have been correct. That same new visitor might have thought the city's ruler—a council of seven supposedly chosen by the populace and known as the Tribunal—were concerned with the safety of the city's people, might think this the reason for the armed searches, might have taken the heavy guard presence at the gate as a deterrent for crimes. But in this, the visitor would have been very wrong.

It was not that the ruling council of Talinseh sought to keep weapons out of the city—its members only sought to make sure that those who carried weapons worked for *them*. And none of them, the last time Dannen had been given occasion to speak with them, had expressed overmuch concern about crimes being perpetrated in the city. Just so long, of course, as they got their cut.

Still, the guards—as guilty and corrupt as any criminal in the city—made a good show of it, wearing stern expressions, standing in what Dannen thought they must have imagined was a professional way, bellowing everything instead of speaking normally. Of course, their professionalism was belied somewhat by the covert exchanging of a coin pouch from one of the visitors to one of the guardsmen. For the most part, though, the act continued, not just for the guards but for the visitors as well. All of them, even a fool could have seen at a glance, were criminals of some kind or another, men used to lurking in the shadows of alleyways trying for open, honest smiles, most managing no better than menacing sneers. All of it a show, one he had seen before. The only real question Dannen wasn't able to answer was who the show was *for*. Everyone in the city—up to and including the council—was corrupt, so why pretend at anything else?

But pretend they did, doing such a thorough job of wasting their time at it that Dannen began to grow frustrated. He kept glancing warily at the giant mage, expecting the man to go mad and attack one of the guards if for no other reason than that he was bored. He didn't, though. It seemed, now they'd reached civilization—or at least a reasonable facsimile thereof—the mage seemed content to wait, likely under the unfortunately accurate belief he would get the chance to punch somebody's face in soon enough.

Finally, they reached the front of the line, and the guards scowled at them. "State your business in Talinseh, stranger."

"Well," Fedder said, grinning, "to find an assassin, you can believe it, and take on a bleedin' *necroma*—"

77

"Our business is our own," Dannen managed in a choked voice.

The guard frowned, glancing between the two of them, trying to decide whether to pursue Fedder's explanation further or take offense at Dannen's statement. The man, unsurprisingly, chose to focus his scowl on Dannen. "Your business is what I say it is, you want to come through this gate and into my city," the guard growled.

Dannen cursed himself underneath his breath. There was no need to piss the man off. After all, how was he supposed to go and get murdered by a necromancer and his badass brother, if he ended up locked in a jail cell? Not that he expected such a visit would last long. He—and the Firemaker, too, for that matter—were known in Talinseh. Like most places, they were known, but not well-loved. So instead of arguing more with the guard, he bowed his head in acquiescence. "Of course, you're right, sir. I meant no offense."

The guard studied him suspiciously, and Dannen did his best to appear contrite and apologetic, a thing made more difficult by the way Fedder was staring at him as if Dannen had started to tell a joke, and he was only waiting for the punchline.

"Well," the guard said after a moment, apparently satisfied. "Now, why don't you tell me what you're both doin' here. I don't want to have to ask again."

"I already told you, you damned f—" Fedder began, but Dannen spoke over him, determined to make it at least a few hours more without somebody trying to kill them.

"Got a cousin lives here," he said, blurting the words out over. "An uncle, too. They tell me there's good, honest work for a man who isn't afraid of breaking a sweat." Rubbish, of course. The only honest thing about Talinseh was its nickname as Assassin City. Still, if the guards were anything like those of the city Dannen had met before—a theory which seemed to be supported by the thorough show of complete bullshit he'd watched them perform like actors in a play for the last half hour—then they'd eat up anything coloring the city in a light opposite of what it was.

Sure enough, the man was nodding, a grin on his face. "Well, stranger, your cousin and uncle told you right. There's not a place the length or breadth of the world where a good, hardworking man might prosper as much as Talinseh."

"Of course not," Dannen agreed, holding up his hand to silence Fedder who looked in deliberate danger of speaking at any moment, a thing which would at best end them up in a fight and, at worse—and far more likely—end up with them both dead or wishing they were.

The guard nodded. "Well, I believe you—course I do, right?—you just got a trustworthy face. Still, orders are orders, and I'm afraid we've got to check you for weapons."

Sure, Dannen thought, *weapons or anything worth stealing.* "Of course," he said.

"Either of you got anything on you might be construed as a weapon," the guard went on, "best say so now. Save us all some time, and it'll be a lot better than if we find it, do you understand?"

"I have nothing," Dannen said honestly. He'd stopped at a small village they passed and gotten fresh clothes and boots, as well as a belt, solving *that* problem at least, but he still had no weapon. There had been a few swords for sale—he knew because the Firemaker had taken it on himself to check, the bastard—but Dannen had promised Val he'd never pick up a sword again, and it was a promise he meant to keep. But instead of telling the mage and listening to his roaring laughter, Dannen had managed to find something wrong with each sword on offer. One with a blade that was too nicked, another with a blade too small, a third with an uncomfortable handle—the older he got the more Dannen was concerned with comfort—and so on and so on until there were none left. Then he'd sighed, shrugging and telling the mage something about how they'd find a better blade in Talinseh. Which, of course, *could* be true, if he wanted it to be. After all, in the Assassin City finding a blade was never a problem—keeping it from being sheathed in your back, though, was a separate issue.

The guard glanced at Fedder who gave an offended look. "I'm a mage, lad," he said, gesturing at the light blue robe which he still wore despite the several opportunities he'd had to find something else. Of course, there was only a hint of light blue left, for days of hard travel had done little for the patina of dried blood, grease, and beer staining the fabric a muddied brown color. "What use have I for such primitive tools?"

"You got any weapons on you or not, old man?" the guard demanded, and Dannen tensed, glancing carefully at the mage.

"Old man?" Fedder sputtered, a vein as thick as a shipping cable popping out on his neck, its cousin snaking down his forehead. He turned to Dannen a look of incredulous, building fury on his face.

Shit. *Let it go,* Dannen thought, not daring to say anything, knowing that, just then, with the mage's hands, the size of dinner plates, squeezing into fists at his sides, that anything he said would inevitably be the wrong thing. *Just let it go, you bastard,* he thought.

And to his absolute astonishment, the mage did. The veins—which, for a moment there, had looked in imminent danger of popping right out from his skin—receded, and he grunted a laugh, slapping the guard on the shoulder. Judging by the way the man's knees threatened to buckle under the blow, he did it a bit harder than necessary, but Dannen was impressed for all that. Age, it seemed, could temper even the sharpest of blades.

The guard, though, didn't seem as impressed by the mage's show of restraint, and he frowned, an expression that nearly managed to hide his pained wince, gesturing one of the others forward. "Check him."

The guard looked hesitant—and who in the name of the gods wouldn't, when ordered to frisk a man wholly half again as tall and wide as he was?—but he moved forward. Fedder rolled his eyes, holding his arms out to his sides. After a moment's searching, the guard froze and glanced up at the Firemaker who gave what might have been an embarrassed wince before withdrawing a long knife and its leather sheath from inside his robe. For the giant, it might have been a knife, though most people would have labeled it a sword.

"No weapons, huh?" the spokesperson of the guards asked, narrowing his eyes.

"What, that?" Fedder said, glancing at the blade. "Just a buttering knife for my bread, is all. Nothin' a tough guy like you need concern himself with."

"Uh-huh. Anything else?"

"'Course not," Fedder answered. "I said there wasn't, didn't I?"

Dannen glanced around for a place to sit or maybe be buried in, thinking it likely he'd be needing one or the other before too much longer. Sure enough, the guard had barely resumed his search of Fedder's person before he paused again. With a glance back at his commander, he withdrew a hatchet.

"And that?" the commander asked, narrowing his eyes.

Fedder scoffed. "Don't be ridiculous. Just a travelin' hatchet, is all, used for cuttin' kindling for fires. My, but you're some jumpy bastards, aren't you?"

"Keep searching," the guard growled at companion, the words barely understandable, spoken as they were through gritted teeth, and Dannen thought it was looking more and more like burying and not sitting by the minute.

Dannen blinked, amazed despite his growing certainty they were about to die. He had traveled with the mage for weeks, yet he had never seen any of the weapons. He was wondering if the man had slept with them when the guard searching him—a man in need of a salary bump if Dannen had ever seen one—withdrew a club from Fedder's robe.

"And this one, old man?" the guard captain asked. "This not a weapon either or are you just too old and addled to remember? Let me guess." He paused, grinning, satisfied by his own cleverness. "It's a walking stick, helps you get around in your infirmity, that it?"

The guard looked positively smug as Fedder's face grew a bright shade of crimson to match his fiery red hair and beard, clearly satisfied that his jape had struck home. But the satisfaction—and the look of smugness—vanished a moment later when the giant mage moved with a speed most wouldn't have credited in a man of his size, snatching the club back from the startled searcher and knocking the captain over the head with it.

A *mew* of surprise escaped the guard captain's throat and, a moment later, he collapsed in a heap at their feet. "Not a walking stick, not this one," the mage said, flashing a humorless smile at the guards who were still conscious. "This is a club I use to knock some sense into fools."

A moment later, the air was filled with a metallic *hiss* as the remaining guards drew their blades.

"Hold on," Dannen said, "let's talk about th—"

The guards, though, were done talking. With a shout, one charged at Fedder, his sword leading.

The mage roared with laughter, stepping to the side of the blade and lifting the unfortunate searcher off the ground with one hand and hurling him at one of his companions. The two collided and went sprawling on the ground.

The remaining guard cursed, easing toward the mage, his sword grasped in a shaking hand. Fedder produced a wicked-looking dagger from somewhere inside his robe and the mad grin was back in place as he watched the man come.

Shit.

Knocking a couple of guards unconscious was one thing, but killing a few wasn't something likely to be ignored, even in the Assassin City, so Dannen did the only thing he could do, the only *reasonable* thing. As the remaining guard moved past, all his attention focused on the giant mage—and who could blame him?—Dannen grabbed the hatchet from where it had landed on the ground and hit the man over the head with the flat-side of it.

The guard's whole body tensed as if he'd been struck by lightning, he uttered some unintelligible word and collapsed. Dannen glanced among the four guards sprawled on the ground, two of which were—no, make that three, as the mage chose that moment to help one along with the club he still held—unconscious, and he remembered, at that moment, why he had given up the hero business altogether, leaving it to younger, bigger fools. A moment after *that* he remembered they were standing at a busy city gate, a line of people behind them—yep, still there when he checked—staring at them as if they were insane. Which, he supposed, was only fair.

"We've got to get out of here," he said. Fedder didn't respond, and Dannen turned to him to see a look of inarguable disappointment on his face as he scowled at the four men, angry, it seemed, that they hadn't put up more of a fight.

"Fedder!" Dannen snapped.

The mage turned to him and blinked. "What's that?"

"I said we have to go, damnit. Now."

The giant grunted. "Fine, fine. Ain't no cause to go yellin' like that, Butcher, I'm with you."

"No cause to," Dannen began, then decided he didn't have the effort—or the time—to argue. "Just come on, you loon."

Dannen started into the city at a run, not looking to see—and not much caring—whether the mage was following him. He heard the still-conscious guard give a shout from behind and glanced back to see the man getting to his feet but choosing, it seemed, to focus on waking his friends instead of giving chase.

Fedder was keeping pace with him, a mad grin on his face as if he were a child caught up in an exciting game of tag instead of a fool getting ready to get his fool head lopped off his fool shoulders. Dannen bit back a curse, saving his breath for gasping—years spent drinking in taverns, he was discovering, weren't the best training for running for your life—as he turned off the main concourse down a shadowy alleyway.

A figure stepped in front of him as he did, seeming to materialize out of the shadows. *"Hey, there,"* the figure said, brandishing a knife, *"what's the hu—"*

"Get the fuck out of my way!" Dannen roared, barely slowing as he grabbed the would-be mugger's head and slammed it into the alley wall.

Fedder roared with mad laughter—the only laughter of which the crazy bastard was capable—and followed Dannen out into the street.

They ran that way for fifteen minutes until Dannen finally began to believe they had put enough distance between themselves and the gate to be safe. A belief largely grounded in the suspicion, the absolute *certainty* that if he ran any more, he'd die right here and cheat the headsman his due. He propped his back against a street wall, his hands on his knees, and struggled to get his breath back. Once he felt that he wasn't in imminent danger of passing out, he spun on the mage. "What in the name of all the gods were you *thinking?*"

Fedder scowled, studying his feet like a child being called out for bad behavior. "He was rude."

Dannen stared at him, blinking. *"What?"*

The mage risked a glance at him. "He was rude, I said. You ought to go to a healer, Butcher, if you're havin' problems with your hearin'. It's amazin' the sort of—"

"Shut up," Dannen said, not caring, for the moment, if he roused the mage's temper. "Just shut up."

"Don't know why you're actin' angry at me," the Firemaker mumbled. "Somebody needed to teach that fella a lesson, that's all. Respect for his elders."

Dannen hissed in frustration, pinching the bridge of his nose and trying to rein in his temper, his head throbbing the way it often did before one of his spells. It was never wise for a man to lose himself in his anger, foolish at the best of times, but losing it with the Firemaker would likely be deadly. "Maybe," he said, "but that somebody didn't need to be *us*, did it? Damnit, Fedder, we came here for a reason, and that reason isn't to get killed." Not that such a thing wasn't likely considering what they'd set out to do, but that wasn't the point.

"Findin' the team, you mean," the mage said, "with that stone of yours."

"That's right," Dannen said, "we have to find them and—"

"Dannen, the stone," Fedder said.

"I *know* the damned stone, Fedder," Dannen said, "now, why don't you just listen for a second and—"

"No, Butcher," Fedder said, pointing, "I mean, the stone, it...I think your leg might be on fire."

Dannen rolled his eyes, ignoring the Firemaker's terrible attempt at changing the subject. At least, he meant to, but he suddenly became aware of an uncomfortable heat against his leg, spared a moment in his anger to glance down, and saw that there was smoke coming from his pocket. Then the uncomfortable heat wasn't just uncomfortable, not anymore, but burning.

He yelped, reaching into his pocket and hissing as he withdrew the stone. As soon as he grasped it, the heat faded as if it had never been, leaving nothing but a tingly thigh to show it had ever been there at all.

Smoke still roiled up from the stone as if it were a piece of charcoal picked from a campfire, and Fedder studied it curiously. "Reckon the god gave you a bad rock?"

"How in the name of the gods should I know?" Dannen demanded, but then, suddenly, knowledge exploded in his mind much as the knowledge that had led him to Talinseh. "The woman we've come for," he said, "she's this way."

"You sure?" Fedder asked. "How can you—"

Dannen sighed, exasperated, turning back from where he'd started down the street. "Magic god-rock, remember?"

"Ah," the mage said, nodding. "Right. Well, lead on then."

Dannen decided he would lecture Fedder about not committing suicide by guard later, assuming he was alive to do it. For now, he felt an unexplainable sense of urgency to find the woman, felt as if they were running out of time. *The magic of the stone?* he wondered, *Or just well-deserved paranoia?*

He suspected it was the latter, but that didn't stop him from hurrying down the street at a fast clip, trusting the mage would stay behind him as he was far too unlucky to lose the Firemaker now. They had only traveled for a few minutes when he heard voices raised in anger. Dannen shot a look behind him thinking the guards must have found them, but the street was empty. Once his heart had stopped the worst of its hammering, Dannen realized that the shouting wasn't coming from behind them but from somewhere ahead.

He frowned, sharing a troubled look with the mage. At least, *his* look was troubled—the mage looked more than a little excited. "Come on," Dannen growled. He led the way out of the alley toward the city square where several dozen people were gathered.

The crowd was facing the other way and none of those standing in the street noticed his and the mage's approach, too focused, it seemed, on whatever had roused their anger. Dannen was unable to make out much in that storm of yelling, but he thought he heard someone shout "Murderer!" Enough then to make any reasonable man walk the other way. But, then, a reasonable man wouldn't have traveled to the Assassin City on a god-given quest the objective of which, it seemed, could only be a terrible death. And what was worse was the knowledge given to him by the stone which told him the woman they had come for was somewhere among that crowd.

Still, Dannen hesitated. He had seen mobs before, far too many, in fact, and this one's mood was worsening by the moment, building to a frenetic pitch which meant that they soon they would take their collective anger out on something or some*one*. Usually, such a release came in the form of burning buildings or someone dying and since none of those present carried torches, Dannen thought he knew all too well which it would be. "Fedder?" he said finally.

"Yeah, Butcher?"

"We need to get to the front of this crowd."

The mage grinned, like Dannen supposed a hound might if its owner let it off its leash and told it that, right then, the most important thing in the world was for it to chase down rabbits. Or maybe shit on the floor where he was bound to step on it. He was still grinning as he began to push his way into the crowd, shoving those unfortunate or foolish enough to remain in his path to the side like rag dolls where they sprawled and flopped onto those also unfortunate enough to have been standing beside them.

And then, as if by magic—though it wasn't the mage's supernatural talents so much as his size and menace which had cleared the way—they were standing at the front of the crowd where two men, both scowling as if they were competing to see who was the best at it, held a small figure between them.

The girl, for surely based on her size, she couldn't have been any more than fifteen, maybe sixteen years old, didn't struggle, standing with an almost bored expression on her face as if a murderous mob hurling curses—seemingly in her direction—was a common occurrence.

"*Well?*" one of the men holding her demanded, giving her a shake. "What 'ave you got to say for yourself, girl?"

Perhaps those in the crowd were eager to hear the girl's answer or they all simply decided to choose that moment to take a collective breath after all the shouting. Either way, there was a sudden, abrupt silence as the girl answered, one which Dannen was glad of—his ears were practically ringing from all the noise—until he heard the exact content and flippancy of that answer.

"Me?" the girl said thoughtfully, nodding slowly as if really giving it a think. "Well, my name's Mariana Vendaria, but you can call me, 'sir,'" she went on, giving the guard a wink. "As for what I have to say for myself, well, I like dogs—who doesn't, am I right? Also, long walks on the—"

"*Enough of that!*" the man holding her shouted, giving her a shake.

Fedder raised an eyebrow at Dannen as if to ask if the girl was the one they'd come for, now that she'd said her name. Which, of course she was. Because the world, like always, thought the best time to kick a man was when he was already down. "Just hang back for a second," he muttered to Firemaker, thinking the last thing he needed was the mage getting antsy and lighting someone on fire or punching someone that didn't need punching, thereby getting them put on the mob's list.

One of the men holding the girl went for a knife, and Dannen decided that it was either now or never. He stepped forward. "Excuse me." The crowd grew silent. The two men turned their scowls on him, and Dannen could feel the gazes of the mob on his back.

"Best move on, stranger," one growled. "Only thing you'll find here is trouble."

"Story of my life," Dannen muttered. "Sorry to interrupt," he said, raising his voice. "It seems, I mean, that you all have a lot going on, no doubt have a schedule to keep and all that."

The man's eyes narrowed. "What do you want, aye?"

How about a puppy dog, Dannen thought, *or a good lay?* But instead of saying that—it would have been funny, probably, but not for long—he gave a slight shrug as if it didn't matter much to him one way or the other. "I just thought I'd check on what's going on here, you know, as a concerned citizen."

There was some angry muttering from the crowd at that, and the man's scowl deepened. "A concerned citizen," he said flatly.

"That's right," Dannen agreed. "After all, once you kill her— leastways, that's what you're lookin' to do, isn't it?—are you going to clean up the body? And the blood, too?"

The man's brow furrowed, and Dannen imagined he could practically see the smoke coming out of his head. "What are you talking about?"

"Well," Dannen said as if it was obvious, "*somebody* has to do those things, don't they? Can't just leave bodies lyin' about everywhere, wreak havoc on cartwheels and horse hooves, and that's before you even start talking about the stink."

The man hesitated, suddenly unsure, and Dannen leaned forward, speaking in the confidential tones of a man passing on some great secret. "And I don't mean to tell you your business, but you know how the Tribunal is—they frown on folks messing up their city."

At the mention of Taliinseh's ruling council, the man's face, crimson a moment before with his anger, paled, and he swallowed hard, glancing at his companion. Dannen was just beginning to think they might make it out of the square with all their proper parts in all their proper places, feeling better than he had in some time. That was when Fedder chose to speak.

"And anyway," the mage said, ignoring the look Dannen was giving him—the one that was unmistakably telling him to shut up—"she ain't nothin' but a kid. What trouble can a little thing like her cause?"

And then, reminded once more of the girl and his grievances with her, the man's expression changed, as if by magic, from stricken terror to sullen anger. *And for his next trick,* Dannen thought, seriously considering stabbing Fedder just as soon as he got something to stab him *with, he'll turn two living, breathing men into corpses.* The man holding the girl grunted, opening his mouth to respond to the mage's question, but the "little thing" in question beat him to it, her voice angry. "I'll have you know I can cause *plenty* of trouble, you old bastard," she snapped at Fedder. "As for my age, I look younger than I am, not that it's any of your business."

"That so?" the Firemage asked, grinning. "I only ask because you look like you're twelve, and I imagine the most trouble you know how to get in is kissin' a boy your ma don't like."

The girl's face turned crimson. "I'm *nineteen,*" she hissed. "And I'll have you know that I'm one of the world's best assassins, capable of..." She cut off, finally seeming to remember where she was, and Dannen stared at the two of them, wondering if this was just some intricate way of committing suicide, and they'd forgotten to tell him.

"Look," he interjected, thinking it best to redirect the mob's attention to him, "what's she done? That's all I'm asking."

The mob's spoke person snorted. "What's she done? I'll *tell* you what she's done, first of all, she tried to *kill* me."

"Run off with my dog!" another from the crowd shouted.

"Told me she'd a contract to kill me, said she'd pay me half of it if I killed myself!"

There were more shouts from the crowd, and Dannen bit back a curse as he turned to the girl. "Is that true?" he asked. This part, he believed, would be simple enough. All the girl had to do was say no, and then Dannen could make a point that the case needed to be tried in front of the Tribunal. Even in the Assassin City, the government—stricter here than most places, from what Dannen had seen—after all, how could the people in power trust the citizens when they knew the citizens were murderers and thieves?—would have its say, and you couldn't just go slaughtering people in the street. Not without the proper permits, anyway.

The girl, though, didn't say no. She glanced disdainfully at the man who held her. "If I'd tried to kill you, you'd be well and truly killed, alright? And as for offering you half," she shouted at the man from the crowd, "that seemed more than a fair price, considerin' I was doin' all the work, sneakin' in your house and all that, makin' it past your guards. What did you have to do except die? Gods, it's so easy even a fool can do it."

There were angry mutterings from the mob at that, enough for Dannen to gather that the man who'd shouted that particular accusation wasn't the only one who shared such a grievance. "And how are we s'pose to *use* that money, if'n we're dead?" someone else from the crowd demanded.

The girl grunted, glancing at Dannen, then winced as she gave a small shrug. "To be honest, I hadn't thought of that."

Dannen pinched the bridge of his nose with his thumb and forefinger, thinking that he'd have been better off if Perandius would have left him to take his chances with the guards. "And the dog?" he asked, fearing the answer.

The girl smiled. "Ah, Herbert. He's the sweetest hound you'll ever—"

"*His name is Axel!*" a heavyset merchant shouted.

That started up a fresh wave of angry accusations from the crowd, and Dannen didn't need to be a prophet to see that the near-future included at least one murder, likely several as once a mob got started at it they tended to warm to the idea. He thought desperately, looking for a way out, then had an idea. "So the Tribunal's signed off on her execution then?" he asked, this time loud enough to be heard in the crowd. "That's good, though I've got to admit I'm a bit surprised. Last I heard, they usually liked to have stonings and impromptu executions held in designated locations. Or has that changed?"

The man who'd spoken up to this point said nothing, only winced, and Dannen glanced at the crowd, giving any of them a chance to speak. He was pleased, at least, to notice more than a few of them shifting uncomfortably at the mention of the Tribunal. Which just went to show that a man could get angry without being a complete fool, a skill the Firemaker would do well to learn.

"Well, now," he said in a shocked voice, "surely, you don't mean to tell me that you all intended on sentencing and passing judgment on this woman here without the due course of a fair trial?" Ridiculous, of course. Dannen had never seen or heard of a fair trial in his life and if any such proceeding was guaranteed to be as crooked as a witch's hat it would be one held in a city where criminals ruled, and the only innocent people were those who could afford to pay enough to make all the witnesses blind, deaf, or if they were particularly stubborn, dead.

But ridiculous or not, it had the desired effect. The people in the crowd began to look even more unsure, gazing at each other with barely restrained panic, and who could blame them? It had been years since Dannen had been to the Assassin City, but he'd had reason—far more than he'd liked—to learn, then, that it wasn't the sort of place where the governing body was known for its compassion. And to make matters worse, a man couldn't even use the expedient of paying off the guards since they'd already been paid and by someone with far deeper pockets than the criminal in question could hope to have. After all, that wealth— and the requisite lack of hesitation in torturing or killing anyone that got in one's way—was how a person became a member of the ruling body in a city of criminals in the first place.

"We don't want no trouble with the Tribunal, of course," the man said, a desperate note in his voice.

Dannen smiled. "Well, of course not, so best—"

"Besides," the girl interrupted, "I don't know why *you're* complaining about a *dog* of all things, Merchant Hubbard. At least Banker Clause," she went on, gesturing to someone else in the crowd, "actually has a legitimate complaint. I mean you took out a contract to have him *killed.* Which would be damned inconvenient for him, wouldn't it? Here I am, just trying to do my job, and I get accosted in the street like....well," She frowned, folding her arms. "Like a criminal, that's what."

The two men were staring at each other then, shock on their features, but the girl didn't seem to notice, speaking on. "And you, Archibald, how would you like it if I constantly bothered you while you were working at your bakery? Yet here I am, doing my best to do my job and do it well, and you're giving me grief about it. Do you think it's *easy* being a secret member of the Assassin's Guild, is that it? Well, it's most certainly not. Tell them, Sloan," she said, gesturing to another man in the crowd who, up to that point, hadn't spoken.

The man shifted uncomfortably as the people nearest him backed away, leaving him standing alone. "I don't know what you—"

"Oh, come off it!" the girl said. "You've been the Guild's top assassin for, what? Five years? Which," she went on, grudgingly, "considering the turnover, is damned impressive. But that's not the point, the point is, you know more than anybody how hard it is to kill somebody. Like what about the job you pulled on Lord Everett last year? Couldn't have been easy that, what with—"

"Lord Everett was my cousin, you son of a bitch!" someone else from the crowd shouted, then Dannen heard the unmistakable sound of steel being drawn, lots of it, as seemingly everyone— including a thin, bespectacled man who could only be a clerk and a woman who looked old enough to be spending her spare time picking out grave plots—drew a knife or sword they'd had secreted about their person and began doing their level best to kill each other.

Dannen was still standing there, stunned, staring in disbelief at the girl who, unaccountably, looked decidedly pleased with herself.

"Might be we ought to get out of here, Butcher."

He turned, blinking, to see Fedder standing beside him. He still could hardly believe what had happened, was so stunned that he would have likely stood there while the mob killed off their former allies and decided to give him a go, if not for one thing. There was an almost concerned look on the mage's face, an expression completely out of place there. The incongruity was enough to spur him into action, for anything concerning the Firemaker ought to be enough to send anyone with any sense running for the hills.

"Come on," he said, tugging his eyes away from the mob of fighting people and moving toward the girl and the two men still holding her, blades in their free hands now, but looking unsure of what to do with them as they regarded the embattled crowd.

The fight had broken into a full-on free-for-all at this point with blood, blades, and curses flying everywhere. Rushing toward the girl, Dannen was forced to dodge a man who, judging by the knife sticking out of his stomach, was having a decidedly bad day. He shouldered aside a woman in an apron holding a mace of all things.

He didn't have much of a plan, not really, consisting as it did largely of not dying in the next few seconds. He had no idea of how he was going to get the girl free of the two men holding her before they killed her or—and this would be far worse—him.

That was when the girl solved the problem for him.

She spun, lightning-quick, and her foot lashed out like a striking serpent, hitting one of the men in the temple, delivering a pressing invitation to unconsciousness which he accepted with alacrity, collapsing in a heap at her feet.

The second man shouted something, but what it was could have been anyone's guess for Dannen couldn't hear it over the sounds of mass murder taking place all around him.

The girl, though, seemed to hear it and judging by the angry expression on her face, it wasn't a compliment about her hair—which, to be fair, was lank and sweaty. In any event, she leapt into the air, spinning like a dervish and planting both her feet in the man's stomach. To say he bent over the blow wouldn't cover it. More accurate to say he folded over it the way a a sheet folded over a clothesline. Dannen was fairly certain he saw the man's lips touch the tops of his boots before he went flying backward.

"Damn," Fedder said, coming to stand beside Dannen who had only just realized he'd stopped in shock. "The girl's got a violent streak, don't she?" he asked in hushed admiration.

Dannen clenched his jaw in frustration then charged forward, starting to grab the girl—still admiring her handiwork with a smug expression—by the arm then regarding the handiwork himself, chose to clear his throat instead. "My name's Dannen," he said, "and I've come to get you out of here." The words sounded ridiculous, the sort of thing one of the actors from Fedder's erstwhile mummer troupe might have declared pompously. He wished he could take them back.

The girl though, smiled, which made her look young and innocent, nothing like an assassin who spent her time kicking the shit out of people trying to kill her. "My hero," she said, batting her eyelashes in an exaggerated manner. "So, where are we going?"

Dannen had to wait a second to answer, for one of the members of the mob chose that moment to charge at him, yelling angrily, though over what Dannen couldn't imagine since he'd never met the man before. The man brandished a knife, and Dannen caught his wrist, burying his other fist in his attacker's stomach then following up with a hook that busted his lip.

Well, a solid punch to the face had a way of taking the fight out of a man, and Dannen shoved his erstwhile attacker stumbling into several of the nearest mob members before turning back to the girl who no longer looked smug but instead looked decidedly nauseated. "I reckon anywhere will do," he said.

The girl nodded, a hand on her mouth as if afraid she might throw up. "Lead on."

Dannen glanced once more at the crowd, saw that the men and women in it were far too busy killing each other to worry about him and the others, then nodded toward a nearby alley. "Come on—this way."

***

They ran far enough for Dannen to be pretty sure they hadn't been tracked and absolutely sure that a minute's more running, and he'd die on the spot, save the growing list of people interested in seeing what he'd look like as a corpse a lot of trouble. Then, since it was really between him stopping or his heart stopping, he came to a halt, wheezing and spitting and cursing—or would have been if he'd had the breath to spare.

"So," the girl said, studying him, hardly out of breath at all, "what's the contract?"

Dannen couldn't decide whether he was angrier at the girl for not being tired or nearly getting them killed, it was simply too close to call, but he settled on a scowl. "What...makes you think...we have a contract?"

She shrugged, looking almost bored. "Just a guess, I reckon. My experience, folks don't go confronting angry mobs to save assassins on the verge of attending their own impromptu execution 'less they've got some killin' needs doing."

"Got a lot of experience with those types of situations have you?" he asked dryly.

She winced. "More'n you'd guess. Anyhow, time's money and all that, so if it's all the same to you, I'd just as soon forego the pleasantries where you kiss my ass—though deserved—and I kiss yours—no doubt less so."

For a moment, Dannen was so shocked—angry too, but mostly too shocked to be angry—at the girl's casual manner, as if she hadn't just about gotten them both killed by an angry mob, that he couldn't speak. Instead, he turned to stare at Firemaker, to share with a glance some of his incredulity. The Firemaker, though, didn't look incredulous or angry. Instead, he was grinning.

"A bit of a firecracker, ain't she, Butcher?"

"Really?" Dannen asked. "She just about gets us killed—at least twice by my count, though I'll admit I was a bit distracted at the time—and all you've got to say is she's a *firecracker?*"

"Well," the mage said, clearing his throat. "She didn't, though, did she?"

"Didn't *what?*" Dannen demanded.

"You know, get us killed and all that," Fedder muttered.

Dannen sighed. "Give her time. We only just met, after all."

"Well," the girl said, "fun chatting with you both and all that, but I guess maybe I was wrong and there isn't a job after all in which case I'd best be getting on. You know, victims to victimize, people to kill and all that."

She started away, all smug and full of herself, and Dannen considered strangling her, considered it very seriously. The problem, of course, was then there'd be a corpse to deal with and likely someone else would want to kill *him*, an inevitable product of waking up, it seemed, but there wasn't much point in going looking for trouble. So, instead of committing murder, Dannen decided to do the next best thing. "Oh, there's a job, alright, and if I'm any judge there'll be killing enough"—*and likely dying*—"for anybody. Come on—let's get a drink."

It didn't take them long to track down the nearest tavern. Dannen had always had a talent for that particular sort of thing, but he didn't get the chance to use it this time as the Firemaker, in Firemaker fashion, chose the expedient of lifting the first person they ran into off the ground by the front of his shirt and demanding to know the location of the closest tavern.

Less than fifteen minutes later they were seated at the back table of a common room, listening to the energetic—if painfully off-key—singing of a man who, in a city full of assassins, either had a contract out on his life already or soon would. Dannen, though, could pay the man little mind. He was too busy relaying to the girl the events since he'd woken up beltless with only one shoe.

When he was finished, the girl leaned back, propping her feet up on the table and giving a low whistle. "My but that's a story, isn't it? I mean, you've got what? Necromancers, warriors, the undead, and gods, to boot." She frowned. "Could use some dragons though."

"Sorry to disappoint you," Dannen said, taking a long pull of his ale. Since picking a fight with the father of all the gods, he'd told himself it would probably be wise to lay off the drinking for a bit. But then dealing with the girl and Firemaker together, coupled with the fact that half the city wanted to kill them, he figured he had far bigger problems to worry about than a hangover.

"Well, life's a disappointment," the girl said, shrugging, "or so my mother always told me." She frowned. "Or maybe it was *I'm* a disappointment. Anyway, I'm in."

Dannen studied her. He'd been expecting her to respond to the ridiculous offer like anyone would—namely, running away as fast as her legs would carry her, though, considering how she'd acted with the mob he realized that maybe he shouldn't have. While he'd been talking, telling her everything, in the back of his mind, he'd been working on a motivational speech, one to overcome her objections easily. But considering that he hadn't made it past 'listen,' it was probably just as well that she hadn't voiced any. Still, her quick acceptance for what appeared to be a suicide mission was a little disconcerting, so he couldn't help asking, "Why?"

"What's that?" she said.

"Why would you come with us?"

"You know," the girl said, suddenly seeming evasive and refusing to meet his eyes, "to save the world and all that. Someone's got to kill the undea...wait a minute, can you kill the undead? I mean, they've already *been* killed, haven't they?" She frowned. "It's sort of a cheat, if you think about it. Like a redo."

"I...don't know," Dannen said. "I suppose, when we meet one, we can ask him." *Assuming we're not getting chewed on.* "Anyway, what's the real reason?"

The girl sighed. "Well, you remember back there when I told the crowd about Sloan, about him, you know, being an assassin and all that?"

"Sure," Fedder said, "clever, too, makin' up a story and distracting 'em, makin' 'em worry about him instead of about you."

"Yeah," she said, clearing her throat, "right. Only, the thing is, not *all* of it was made up."

Dannen was getting that sinking feeling in his stomach again. "What do you mean? Which part?"

She winced. "Well, all of it, really. See, the thing is, Sloan really *does* work for the Guild, the Guild that, incidentally, probably won't be too keen on the fact I just outed their best assassin to half of Talinseh. So, I was thinkin', you know, all things considered, maybe it might not be the worst time to take a bit of a holiday. See the world."

"He's an assassin," Dannen muttered. "Of course he is." He'd been thinking, hoping, really, up to that point that she'd just been bluffing, trying to direct attention away from herself. Certainly, he hadn't wanted to think someone had done anything quite so suicidal as revealing the identity of a member of the Assassin's Guild in the *Assassin City.* But then, he was beginning to think that the girl, if not courting suicide, certainly didn't mind exchanging pleasantries with it. His only source of solace was that, between her and Fedder, he'd probably be dead long before he needed to worry about the necromancer or his swordsman brother.

Firemaker barked a laugh. "My, but the balls on you, girl."

"Yeah," she said, smiling, looking *pleased* for the gods' sake.

Dannen was trying to decide what to do, wondering what a deer would do if it decided to stumble into a hunters' camp—if not his exact situation, near enough to make no difference—when, as if on cue, he heard several chairs slide out from the tables somewhere behind them. He also didn't miss the concerned look the bartender gave the room.

"You're payin' for any damages," the man said to the people behind them.

"Sure," a voice growled.

Dannen shared a look with Fedder then sighed, standing up from his chair and turning. A moment later, the mage and the girl did the same. Half a dozen men had gathered and were studying them with hard looks, some holding swords, others daggers that, while short, looked plenty sharp enough to ruin a man's day without much effort.

"Hey, fellas," Dannen said, "how about I buy you a drink? How'd that be?"

"How about," one said, grinning and displaying black teeth, "we kill you, take your coin and buy *ourselves* a drink, maybe a few of 'em, considerin' the price the Guild's got out on your heads?"

Well, it had been worth a try. "That quick?" Dannen asked. "You have to hand it to them—that's damned efficient." But he wasn't really paying much attention. In truth, he was busy staring at the six men who, it looked like, he was going to be fighting to the death in just a few moments. All of them were dressed in leather jerkins, enough scars between them that, if a god happened to get hold of all that missing flesh, Dannen figured he could shape another whole person with some to spare. They all grinned evilly back at him, like maybe they'd entered a contest and all of them were going for first place.

"You're sure about this?" he asked, giving it one more go.

"Oh, we're sure, alright," the spokesperson for the group said. "I'm gonna gut you first, old man."

Fedder let out a growl at that, and Dannen raised his hand, not liking the thought of the mage going into one of his rages with him standing so close. "I'd be careful with that thing there, *young* man," he said, nodding his head at the sword, "might be you'll cut yourself."

The man laughed. "Or something."

Dannen sighed again. "Or something."

The other patrons in the common room wisely began to move toward the edges of the room, close enough to see the blood to come but not so close to risk it being their own. Dannen was wishing he was among them, was wondering if it was his curse to always be the one others watched bleed or that made someone else bleed.

"How many you got, girly?" Fedder asked.

"*Girly?*" she demanded, turning and scowling at him past Dannen, as if this was the best time to be offended.

"*Hoy!*" another of the would-be killers said. "Why, she's a fine one, ain't she? Might be we can have some fun with you first before the Guild gets its due, *girly.*"

Dannen wasn't quite sure what changed in the woman. He knew only that, in the space of a moment, she went from being a strange, likely suicidal girl to exuding an air of menace that was palpable. "That one's mine," she said, "him and his smiling friend there," she jerked her chin at the one standing nearest the one who'd spoken.

Dannen decided he would avoid using the term "girly" in the future and opt for something a little less likely to get him knifed instead. Assuming, of course—a big assumption, right up there with maybe he'd never drink again—that he ended up having a future at all.

"Alright then," Fedder said, grinning like a madman now that bloodshed seemed inevitable, the same expression on his face as might crop up on a homeless child finding a coin—or, in the Assassin City, more likely a knife—lying in an alleyway. "That'll do fine then. Butcher, you good to take the ugly one?"

Dannen frowned. "Which is the ugly one?"

Firemaker barked a laugh as if he had just told a joke. "Sure." Then he lifted the heavy wooden chair he'd been sitting in moments before, slapping it on the ground almost casually. The chair shattered and he was left holding a stout length of wood in a big hand that made it look like a twig. "*Alright then, lads,*" he roared, "*if we're goin' to fight, let's get it done. I'm gettin' bored.*"

The six hesitated at the Firemaker's bellow—as any sensible man would—then one, perhaps having heard that bullshit line about the importance of a man facing his fears, brandished a sword and, roaring a battlecry, charged the mage. A battle cry that abruptly turned into a panicked squeal as Fedder dodged to the side with his surprising speed, hefted the man as if he weighed no more than a child, and launched him across the room. Battlecry turned to squeal, and squeal turned to a decidedly unpleasant *crunching* sound. Then silence.

A silence which was broken a moment later by one of the other men's shout. *"Kill the bastards!"*

Beside Dannen, the girl suddenly had what he at first took to be two knives, one in either hand, but after peering closer he realized they weren't knives after all. Instead, they were thin steel rods a little over a foot long each. He had time to wonder at that, then a little more time to realize that he, of course, was the only asshole walking into a life or death struggle without a weapon. Then there was no time at all, for one of the men was on him, swinging his sword in an overhand blow like a lumberjack chopping wood.

Dannen might not have had a weapon, but he still had feet, and he used them to launch himself forward, tackling his opponent. They both flew backward into a table which, predictably given the course of Dannen's life to date, gave way under their combined weight, spilling them both on the floor. As they struggled, Dannen was pleased to see his opponent had dropped his sword when he'd struck him, though he was slightly less thrilled at the knife the man drew from his belt. Dannen grunted as the blade dug a shallow furrow across his upper arm and tried to roll away, but he was too slow. The man lunged on top of him, bringing the blade down in a two-handed grip, and Dannen caught his wrists, stopping the steel inches away from his eye.

They hissed and spat, Dannen trying his best to end the day with the same number of eyes he'd started with, but no matter how hard he strained, Dannen couldn't knock his opponent off. The man bore down harder, putting all his body weight into it, his lips bared in a strained grin that put his rank breath and black teeth on full display.

Dannen had faced some terrible odds in his career as a would-be hero and still-was fool. Ogres, trolls, mad hedge-wizards and homicidal pixies, a thousand others besides, yet he'd managed to walk away from all of them, if not completely intact, then still breathing, and he'd be *damned* if he let himself die to some thug with shit-stained teeth. So instead of continuing to struggle in a fight he could only lose as his opponent had all the leverage, he pretended to commit to one side, throwing his weight. He did so just long enough for his opponent—his grin widening now as he grew assured of his victory—to compensate then by leaning in that direction. Then, with a growl and savage twist he was sure he'd feel in the morning, he pivoted in the other direction, throwing the man off.

They rolled across the ground in a mass of limbs and just when the man was gaining the top again, Dannen bit the wrist of his knife hand hard. Not the most sporting move, maybe, particularly judging by the offended look of pain on his opponent's face as he dropped his knife, but Dannen had been in enough scraps to know it was rarely the noblest who won. So he didn't hesitate, catching the blade and bracing the handle in the crack between two slats of the wooden floor before grabbing a fistful of his attacker's dark hair and slamming his face down into the waiting blade.

He couldn't see exactly where the knife went, but when a person caught a blade through the face, he didn't think it mattered much. His opponent gave a series of spasms and then was still. Dannen lay there gasping for breath, surprised, as he seemed to be pretty much every day of his life, that he was still alive. Then he realized—easy enough considering the shout of rage from nearby—that if he didn't move, he'd never have to worry about being surprised by it or anything else ever again.

His would-be murderer apparently decided then that shouting wasn't going to kill Dannen after all, and that maybe he'd try his sword instead, swinging it down at Dannen who let out a decidedly unmanly shout as he skittered out of the way in the nick of time, sitting on his butt and pushing away with his hands. The nicked edge of the sword buried itself in the floor between his legs, and the man's untrained attack had the added benefit of putting him and, more importantly, his shins, directly in front of Dannen.

There were plenty of women in the world—well, maybe not plenty but some anyway—who would have attested that Dannen had never turned down an invitation before, and he didn't plan on starting now. He reared his foot back and gave the man's shin as hard of a kick as he could manage. Not the most heroic thing he'd ever done maybe, but it certainly wasn't the least, and he didn't think being a corpse would be particularly heroic either. Either way, he couldn't argue with the results as his attacker became particularly distracted by the terrible, unique pain a well-delivered kick to the shin could elicit—like most pains, Dannen had more than enough experience to qualify as an expert.

The thug promptly let go of his sword, screaming in pain, and Dannen took advantage of his distraction to stand up—carefully, as the sword was still embedded in the floor only inches away from ruining his day—and get his bearings. He shot a glance around to check on his friends and saw they were faring far better than he was.

Fedder was holding two men up in the air by the front of their shirts, one in either hand and playing a game—Dannen knew it was a game by the way the man was keeping a shouted count—of seeing how many times he could slam the two men's heads into each other. The men, mercifully, were both either unconscious or dead with all the blood it was impossible for Dannen to tell which, but the giant mage was clearly determined not to let that ruin his fun.

The girl, on the other hand, was playing a very different sort of game, wielding the two steel batons or whatever they were with skill and speed shocking even to Dannen who had spent his life seeing some of the best killers in the world working earnestly at their trade. Not that she *was* killing her two opponents or, at least, not quickly. She, like the Firemaker, was grinning, but instead of making a game of seeing just how dead she could make the two men, she seemed to be intent on taking them apart piece by piece, striking them in the chest and shoulder and back with blows almost too fast for the eye to follow. She seemed to be everywhere at once, dodging out of the way of her opponent's attacks far before they had any chance of hitting her. Dannen didn't envy the poor bastards, for he'd been outclassed in a fight more times than he could count, and it was only luck that he was still alive to complain about it.

"*You son of a bitch,*" someone growled in front of him, and it got his attention—threatening growls nearly always did. He spun back to see that the man had recovered enough from the kick in the shin to draw a knife from his belt.

The sword was still stuck in the tavern floor, easily within Dannen's reach, and it would have been a small enough thing to pull it out, but he did not. He had held such a blade before, countless times in countless fights, and it never ended well. Instead, he braced himself, slightly widening his stance and holding his hands out in front of him as his opponent charged forward.

The man was furious, but all the anger in the world didn't grant a man skill he didn't have, and he couldn't have telegraphed the overhanded stab more if he'd written Dannen a letter about it beforehand. Dannen dodged the knife as it plunged toward him, giving the man a solid punch in the side followed quickly by another. His attacker shouted in pain but managed to keep hold of the blade, spinning and lashing out with a blow Dannen only just managed to scramble away from.

"Die, you fucker," the man growled, and Dannen realized for the first time that it was the same man who'd spoken for the group.

In the end, he decided to deny the man's polite request, catching the wrist of his hand as he swiped again and changing its direction so that the blade plunged into his attacker's stomach. Warm blood spilled out, coating Dannen's hands, and his attacker stared at him in surprise, as if he'd never imagined that someone might end up getting stabbed in a knife fight.

"I said you'd end up cutting yourself," Dannen told the dying man. He gave him a shove, and the man fell to the ground, writhing and pawing at the knife protruding from his stomach. Dannen watched the man for a second, making sure he wasn't going to attack again, but he seemed content to scream and moan and paw.

Satisfied there would be no more trouble from that quarter, Dannen glanced around and saw the Firemaker had finished playing his game. Judging by the smashed features of the two corpses lying at his feet, Dannen assumed he'd won. The girl's two opponents were still alive, but judging by their piteous cries as they lay on the ground, more of them broken than not, Dannen thought they might have preferred not to be.

He eyed the other common room patrons warily, but no one moved to join the fight, which was just as well as his breath was rasping in his chest, and he didn't fancy his chances against a pissed-off bunny just then.

"Well, that was a fine row, wasn't it, Butcher?" Fedder asked, grinning like they were children reminiscing over a pleasant game of hide and seek.

Still, Dannen couldn't disagree, as he'd long ago decided the only satisfaction a man could expect from a fight was to still be breathing at the end of it. He glanced at the girl who was staring up at the ceiling with a sickly expression on her face. "Are you okay?" he asked curiously.

She didn't respond, didn't seem to notice that he'd spoken, so he stepped forward again, putting a hand on her shoulder. "Hey. Girl. I said, are you okay?"

"My name's not *girl*," she said, though there seemed no force behind it, and she was still staring at the ceiling as if the secrets to the universe might be divined there. "Nor girly. It's Mariana."

"Fine," Dannen said. "Sorry. Anyway, are you hurt?"

"By those two louts?" she said in a tone that tried for offended but mostly just sounded sickly. "Of course not, but I think it best we find somewhere else to chat, if it's all the same to you."

Well, that was the first sensible thing he'd heard her say, so Dannen glanced over at Fedder only to see the mage had taken a seat in one of the few unbroken chairs and was currently expressing his own concern about the danger they were in by kicking his feet up on the table and taking a long pull from an ale which had previously belonged to one of their now unconscious—or dead, hard to be sure—attackers.

"Fedder," Dannen said, "it's time to go."

The mage sighed. "It's always go, go, go with you, Butcher." He finished the ale in one long drink then slammed it down on the table before rising and moving toward them.

Dannen bit back a caustic remark and led them toward the door, struggling to come up with some plan to get them out of the city with their heads still on their shoulders. Problem was, he'd never been much for planning, a fact brought home a moment later when he stepped outside the tavern to find at least twenty men and women surrounding the entrance, all of them holding weapons of varying sorts, and all of them looking intent on putting them to use sooner rather than later.

"Well, shit," Dannen said. He thought it a damned shame when a man got to a place in his life where he was no longer even surprised to find that someone—or a lot of someones, in this case—wanted him dead.

His eyes caught on the girl who looked even more sick than before, and he was just about to ask her if she was alright before she answered the question thoroughly by bending over and throwing up on his boots. Dannen blinked, and she looked up at him guiltily, wiping an arm across her mouth. "I'm...that is...sorry about that."

Dannen stared down at his boots which were less than a month old. "Had eggs, did you?"

She cleared her throat. "I uh...I like eggs."

"Yeah," he said. "I used to."

He expected to hear Fedder's roaring laughter—the man always had possessed a sick sense of humor—and when there was only silence he glanced up at him and was surprised to find that even the Firemaker seemed put-off as he stared at the people waiting in the street. Not scared—Dannen didn't figure the man would be scared if the God of Death decided to pay him a personal visit. Instead, he seemed thoughtful, the blunt features of his face twisted as if in concentration, no doubt trying to do the math of how many that meant for each of them, if they split the opponents equally. Dannen could have told him easily enough—too many.

Dannen was trying to decide what to do next—die, most likely—when there was movement in the alleyway and the street was suddenly flooded with at least forty armed city guardsmen. Under normal circumstances, he would have been glad to see them. But in the Assassin City, the guardsmen were just as crooked as anyone else, except maybe paid better, and given what had transpired at the gate, he thought the best thing he could hope for would be for the two groups to get into a fight over who got to kill them first.

Just when he was deciding that they couldn't be any more screwed, the guards—who showed an almost perverse eagerness to use their bludgeons on members of the crowd—pushed the would-be killers aside creating an avenue through which walked a beautiful woman, though walked might not have been the best word for it. Sashayed, maybe. The woman was shockingly beautiful, her face and curves—curves which the snug-fitting dress she wore served to accentuate—the stuff of most men's dreams. Assuming they had strong imaginations, anyway.

Unfortunately, Dannen knew the woman all too well, and though she alone in the street held no weapon—save for him, and that was because he was beginning to think he was a complete and utter moron—she was by far the most dangerous of the lot. "Shit," he said again.

"Hey," Firemaker said, thoughtfully, "that's Clarissa, isn't it?"

"Yes, it is," Dannen whispered. "Gods help us."

"Huh." the mage said thoughtfully. "Didn't you and her—"

"Later, Firemaker," Dannen snapped.

The mage grinned widely but thankfully, chose to let it go.

The woman marched down the street as if she owned it without so much as a glance at those armed people around her. Which, assuming she hadn't changed, she most likely did. She stopped a few feet away from the tavern door, eyeing Dannen and the others. "Well, my, my," she said. "A friend of mine came to me only a few hours ago, told me an interesting story about a bit of a tussle at the city gate. He described the two men involved, but I thought surely he must be mistaken or, at most, that the men he described bore a resemblance to you two out of coincidence and nothing more. I must admit to some surprise to find you both here."

"You and me both," Dannen said, knowing full well the "friend" she spoke of would be one of the army of agents making sure Clarissa was the most well-informed person in the city.

The woman smiled languidly, a smile that had gotten Dannen into trouble more than once, but one that his body, too stupid to know any better, responded to just the same. Her eyes danced as if she knew full well what reaction she had caused before turning to the mage.

"Fedder the Firemaker," she said, nodding her head affably, and if she was at all put-off by the blood covering him she did a good job of hiding it. "How have you been?"

The mage shrugged as if they hadn't just been—and still were, if Dannen was any judge—in mortal danger. "Good to see you, Clare," he said, grinning widely as if the damned fool actually meant it. "And you know, just tryin' to stay busy."

She gave a soft laugh, glancing through the opened tavern door through which some small bit of the devastation could be seen. "I see that." She turned back to Dannen then. "It's good to see you, Danny."

As a general rule, Dannen hated being called "Danny." When he had been young, he'd even gone so far as to get in fights over it. But as always, when it came from her mouth, it seemed like just about the best thing he'd ever heard. Of course, he'd also heard that some poisons could be sweet—that didn't stop them from killing a man. "It's a pleasure, Clarissa," he said, thinking that, if given a choice between seeing her again and a clean death at an executioner's hands, he'd choose the axe every time.

Her smile widened as if she knew exactly what he was thinking, then she glanced around at the would-be murderers still lingering in the street as if surprised they were still there. "Well?" she said, and though she spoke softly, there was no mistaking the menace in her tone.

Suddenly, those people who, drawn by the scent of a hefty reward, had come out with blood on their minds, decided that they had more important things to be about—namely, not dying horribly—and all began to vanish into whatever alleyway was nearest them. In moments, Dannen and the others were left standing in the streets alone except for the guardsmen and Clarissa.

"Now then," she said with satisfaction, as if she had just squashed a bug instead of ordered away some of the city's best killers, "where was I? Oh yes, it is very good to see you both. And...your friend here?"

"Name's Mariana," the girl said, frowning at Clarissa in a way that said she wouldn't have minded pulling out her weapons again.

But if Clarissa noticed the girl's sullen regard, she chose to ignore it. "Pleasure to make your acquaintance, Mariana," she said, though Dannen would have bet all the coin in his pocket—not much, admittedly—that the woman knew just who the girl was, probably knew her entire life story.

"Funny," she said, turning back to Dannen, "I had thought you'd given up the adventuring life long ago. I seem to remember you saying as much before you left rather abruptly."

Dannen winced, hearing the barb in her words even if no one else did. "They say bad habits are the hardest to break."

"So they do," she said, smiling again, but not quite as pleasantly this time. "Well, I am still astonished to see you both. Astonished and, I must admit, pleased. It has been so long since I've talked with any of those from the old days."

That much, at least, Dannen believed. After all, most of those from the old days had died in the old days. "It's good to see you too, Clare," he said, and despite everything, despite the fact that he was now conversing with whom many would have said—with no argument from Dannen—was the most dangerous woman on the planet, he found that it was true.

"Well," she said, "you all really must follow me back to my home for a drink. It's humble, I'll admit, but"—she paused, winking—"I can at least guarantee no one will try to kill you."

Except for you, Dannen thought, *if you see a reason for it.* And he knew Clarissa well enough to know she never needed much of one. "I'd love to," he said, "only, I'm afraid that we're a bit pressed for time. Perhaps, we could reschedule..."

"Pressed for time?" She said. "Ah, I see. No doubt, you've monsters to slay, villains to vanquish and all that."

Dannen winced. "Something like that."

"Still," she said, her full lips shifting into a pout, "surely, you wouldn't begrudge a few minutes of your time, not for an old...friend."

Dannen blushed at the way she said it, and Firemaker must have seen it too, for he barked a laugh that Dannen did his best to ignore. "I'm sorry, Clare, seriously, but...as I said, we're in a bit of a hurry. Besides, we wouldn't want to put you out. I'm sure you've got things to do." *People to murder.* Not that he suspected Clarissa went through the trouble of murdering those she deemed worthy of it much anymore. He thought it likely that she paid good money to have others do such grunt work for her.

"Oh, Dannen," she said, smiling again, "it is so sweet of you to concern yourself with my affairs. But..." She paused for a moment, and though Dannen couldn't have said what changed, her smile suddenly had an edge to it, one sharp enough to cut. "I'm afraid I must insist."

Dannen fought back a sigh and, considering that he liked all his body parts in the exact places they currently occupied, did the only reasonable thing. He smiled back. "In that case, Clare," he said, "we'd be honored."

She laughed softly, the same melodic, entrancing sound he remembered from so many years before, then offered him her arm. "I thought you might be."

***

In Dannen's position, most people might have thought their situation improved, might even have been thankful for the escort of so many guards around them as they made their way down the street. Certainly no mobs or assassins appeared from the alleyways to claim the not inconsiderable bounty the Guild had placed on their heads. Which didn't mean the assassins weren't *there*, of course. It only meant that so many armed guards were enough to dissuade them from trying to collect their reward, at least for the moment. And *had* an assassin been brave enough to show himself, Dannen didn't doubt the guards surrounding them would defend them with alacrity, jumping to follow Clarissa's orders. Dannen, though, wasn't comforted.

After all, those same guards would demonstrate the same eagerness to chop him and his companions to pieces, if the woman striding beside him asked them to, and thank her for the opportunity.

Suddenly the collar of Dannen's jerkin felt impossibly tight, and he cleared his throat, wincing as he stretched his neck to loosen the constricting fabric. "So uh..." he said finally, glancing at the woman walking at his side with a satisfied smile. "How are things, Clare?"

She glanced over at him, her brown eyes, so dark as to be almost black—he'd forgotten just how dark those eyes were, deep enough to get lost in—dancing with amusement. "Oh, you know how it is. Things are things, some pleasant, some less so, and each morning I wake a little older, a little more tired."

Later, Dannen would think of this moment and try to decide if the streak of suicidal tendencies he'd always seemed to have— why else would a man go in for being a hero?—decided to make itself known, or if he was simply too distracted thinking about all those guards around him and, more importantly, all those swords they carried. He would think of it and shake his head, for it, like so many other things in his life, was proof of his own foolishness and the fact that he still *had* a life after, proof only that the gods had a sense of humor.

"How old are you now, anyway?" he muttered, doing his best not to glance over at the guard walking beside him whose sullen gaze he could feel piercing his back like a dagger. "Forty...two, is it?"

Suddenly, Clarissa came to an abrupt halt beside him. The guards did the same in a rattling of armor, and the air was suddenly split with the sound of forty swords leaving forty scabbards. Clarissa studied him with a raised eyebrow. One of the men—the same guard who'd been staring at him like Dannen was a bug he'd love to squish—took a step toward him. He raised his sword and the nearest guards followed, all of them freezing in place as if gripped by some invisible force when Clarissa raised her hand. All, that was, save for the man who'd been eyeing Dannen, who took another step.

"Enough, Palder," Clarissa said, and though she did not raise her voice, there was an unmistakable note of command in her tone.

The man's face flushed an angry red, and he turned to her with a hurt look on his face. He was young, probably in his mid-twenties, obviously with something to prove and, just as obviously, madly in love with Clarissa. The poor bastard.

"B-but he insulted you, ma'am," the guard said incredulous, "the snake doesn't deserve—"

"Do you believe, Palder," Clarissa said slowly, an edge to her voice, "that I need you or anyone else to defend my honor, or"—she glanced sidelong at Dannen with a small smile—"at least what's left of it?"

The other guards slowly backed away from the young man as if as if they expected him to be struck down by Clarissa's wrath and didn't intend to be collateral damage.

Palder glanced around and saw that none of the guardsmen supported him, then stared at his feet like a child being called out. "Of course not, Mistress. I'm...I'm sorry."

"Oh, I am no delicate flower to be so easily bruised, Palder," Clarissa said. "Still, I think it only right you apologize to my friend here. He is far softer than I."

The man tensed as if struck, his eyes going wide. For a moment, Dannen prepared himself, sure the guard was going to launch into an attack no matter what Clarissa said. In the end, though, the younger man took a deep, shuddering breath, and raised his gaze to Dannen. "I am sorry, sir, if I gave offense."

A self-important asshole, that was obvious, but Dannen gave him the best smile he could, deciding that it was always nice to make a new friend, particularly when that friend was holding a bared blade in his hand.

"Oh, that's alright, fella," Dannen said. "We all make mistakes. Besides, I knew Clarissa years ago," he said, quieter, leaning in, "and I know better'n most that she's a handful." He could tell, at once, that it had been the wrong thing to say. The man's visage darkened, and his jaw clenched so hard it was a wonder he didn't crack a tooth.

"It is my pleasure to serve my mistress," the man said tightly, and if looks could kill, Dannen reckoned he and anyone unlucky enough to be standing behind him in a mile-radius or so would have been giving the undertaker some work.

Dannen held back the sigh that threatened to come, telling himself that it was fine. If there was a man in the world able to get along with everybody he met, it certainly wasn't him, and that was no news.

"Let us continue," Clarissa said in a tone that brooked no argument. The man named Palder stared directly at Dannen as he put his sword back in its scabbard, a look that made it clear he'd far rather be sheathing it in Dannen's chest, and in seconds they were moving again.

"That one's a barrel of laughs," he muttered to Fedder who grinned widely but, shockingly, said nothing, and Dannen suddenly remembered that the Firemaker was nearly always speechless in Clarissa's company. The man had never told him why, and Dannen had never bothered asking.

"Palder is loyal," Clarissa said in a slightly scolding tone, "and that is a rare thing in Talinseh."

"Rare meaning expensive?" Dannen asked.

"Rare meaning priceless," Clarissa returned.

Oh, the man had a price, alright, no matter what she might think. He was paid in something, even if nothing more than the sound of her sultry voice or the occasional glance at her swaying hips as she walked in that alluring, rhythmic way of hers. But he saw no reason to say so, doubted Clarissa would have been surprised by it even if he had. Likely, she took the guard's adoration as nothing more than her due and would have been surprised had he felt any other way.

"But never mind Palder," she said, dismissing the man so quickly as irrelevant that Dannen himself felt some of the pain of that dismissal and never mind that it wasn't directed at him. The guard clearly heard her, for his face grew noticeably paler, and he winced before scowling at Dannen as if he were somehow responsible, then trying—and failing—to look unbothered. "It seems," Clarissa went on, either completely unaware of or unconcerned with the effect her words had, "that I was right, Dannen. The years do not seem to have changed you." She glanced down at his midsection, thinner than it had been from days spent on the road with the Firemaker, but still a little thicker than he would have liked. "At least, not emotionally. You never were much for smalltalk, and now, like then, it seems that you enjoy inviting death."

"My experience," Dannen said, "the bastard never needs much of an invitation."

She smiled as if she knew something he didn't—no doubt, she did—and they made their way through the city in silence for a time. Soon, they left the poor district behind, coming to a far better maintained road with no signs of the beggars which had been so prominent in the poor district. The wide street was flanked by large, gated houses, some of which even had a guard posted. Dannen couldn't help but stare, impressed despite himself. When he had known Clarissa ten years ago, he had always thought her bound for great things, but it seemed that even he might have underestimated her. Assuming one of the houses along the street was hers, it was obvious she had not been idle in the last ten years.

Yet the procession of guards did not stop at one of the houses as he thought they would, and as they pressed on, the houses got even fancier, the gates bigger and more imposing until, finally, they came to a shining silver gate at which four guardsmen were posted. The men scanned the street attentively as if expecting murderers to come dashing out of one of the alleys at any moment, the confident looks on their faces and the way they fingered their sword hilts indicating they hoped for such an occurrence.

To Dannen's surprise, the young angry guard spoke to them in hushed tones and a moment later, the silver gates swung open. Dannen stared about him in shock as he and the others were led through the gate and down a cobbled lane with lush gardens filled with flowers and plants of every possible shape and hue.

Had he not so recently traveled the land of the gods, Dannen might have thought he'd walked through some mage's portal, so beautiful were the gardens, the bushes and plants so tall a man might believe he was no longer in a city at all but at some nobleman's country estate. "Damn," he breathed, the word coming out without him intending it to.

Yet, as fine as the gardens were, the house at the end of the cobbled walk was better. Not that "house" really did it justice. In truth, it was nothing short of a castle, one any ruler might have been proud to call his home. Yet here, Clarissa had foregone the usual thick gray stones used in such construction, choosing instead to make use of marble so pristine and white that Dannen fancied he could see his reflection in its surface. "Damn," he said again with feeling.

"So Dannen," Clarissa said, "what do you think of my home?"

Dannen looked at the sprawling gardens, took in, once more, the towering castle, one large enough that a hundred people could have lived in it without ever seeing each other. He grunted. "It's fine, I guess. A bit small though, isn't it?"

Firemaker barked a laugh at that, and Clarissa smiled. "Yes, but then I suppose I focused less on size than beauty. What can I say? I am a woman who does love a thing of beauty."

The castle and the grounds certainly *were* beautiful, but a closer look showed that they were not only that. Dannen didn't miss the turrets rising up on either side, manned by guardsmen with bows. Nor did he fail to notice the reinforced door and reinforced gate they had just passed through. And although the gardens were lush and thick, they were not quite lush or thick enough to completely hide the man crouched in the plants less than ten feet off the path or the tip of his crossbow, ready to make sure any uninvited guests had a bad day. Dannen let his gaze fix on the man just for a moment, long enough to let Clarissa know he saw him, then looked up at the manned battlements...but said nothing. It would be rude, he thought, maybe even considered crass to comment on the hidden guard. Not quite as rude, probably, as guessing at a woman's age, but rude nonetheless, so he smiled and followed Clarissa as she moved toward the door.

The guardsman in front knocked on the door and a concealed slot slid open to reveal eyes peering out along with a crossbow bolt. A moment later, the crossbow was withdrawn, the door slid open, and Dannen and his companions were ushered inside.

The grounds and outside of the castle had set high expectations for what the interior might look like, and it did not disappoint. Paintings and busts decorated the wide hall, and a grand staircase curved up to the second floor. All around were the obvious and undeniable signs of a wealth Dannen, knowing little of such finery, could only guess at.

"What now?" he asked Clarissa, hoping she didn't have a torture room somewhere on the premises—unlikely—and hoping, too, that if she did, she didn't intend on using it just now—a touch more likely.

Clarissa gave him a knowing smile again as if she could read his thoughts as easily as another might read a book. "Fedder," she said, holding Dannen's gaze for a second longer before turning to the mage, "I seem to recall that you appreciate a good ale. I have a barman on the premises. Why don't you and your new friend"—she paused, indicating Mariana with a nod—"go and avail yourselves of his services? Everything, of course, is on the house."

Saying that the Firemaker "appreciated a good ale" was like saying water could sometimes be a bit wet, and Dannen was unsurprised when the giant mage grinned widely.

"Just show me the way, darlin'."

Clarissa returned the smile, nodding to one of the guardsmen who started away, the Firemaker following, only to pause when the girl, Mariana, didn't move.

"Don't care for a drink, if I'm honest," she said. "Had my fill, just now. If, that is," she went on, glancing at Clarissa, "it's all the same to you."

Clarissa smiled. "Mariana Vanderia, isn't it?"

The girl grunted, clearly surprised. "Yes, that's my name. But how do you—"

"Never mind that," Clarissa said, waving her hand dismissively. "Your reputation precedes you, nothing more—all good things, I'm sure. Yet, I'm afraid, Mariana, that it *isn't* all the same to me, and that I must insist you relax with Fedder and take your ease. I am quite sure the day has been trying enough for you already."

The menacing, dangerous note was back in Clarissa's voice, and Dannen stared at Mariana, willing her not to be stupid. The girl hesitated, glancing at him, and she must have seen some of his thoughts in his gaze, for she sighed, shrugging. "Well, if you insist and all, I suppose I might have a drink or two."

"Come on with you," the guard said, grabbing her by the arm. The girl looked down at the offending hand before meeting his gaze.

"I wouldn't," she said simply.

The guard hesitated, suddenly unsure, and Clarissa spoke, "Oh, let her go, Claude, that's no way to treat our guests, is it?"

Guests, not prisoners. Not much, maybe, but Dannen breathed a sigh of relief just the same as the mage and girl were led down the hallway. Clarissa looked after them for a moment, deep in thoughts no doubt far too complex for Dannen to have understood even had she voiced them, which she did not. After a moment, her intense look of concentration abruptly broke, and she turned to him with a smile. "Would you like to have a drink in my study? I feel like I haven't seen you in ages. We've got some catching up to do."

"Sure," Dannen said, allowing them both to continue the fiction that he had any choice in the matter.

"Come, Dannen," she said, giving him a wink his body responded to despite his mind's warnings.

She started up the stairs and Dannen followed. Despite how dangerous a situation he knew he was in, despite the two guards walking behind him—one of whom was the young man who was making little effort to disguise his hatred—Dannen could think of little else at that moment but the way the tight dress Clarissa wore clung to her like a second skin.

She led him up the stairs and down the hall to a door which she opened. She turned to the guards. "You will remain here," she said, then turned to Dannen, beckoning him inside. "Please," she said, smiling a wicked smile that he knew all too well, for it had got him into trouble more than once in the past, "guests first."

"Ma'am," the young guard said incredulously, "you can't—"

"Yes, Palder?" Clarissa asked, a warning clear in her icy voice.

One which, as it happened, the guard decided to ignore. "Let us accompany you. I do not trust this man and—"

"You both will remain outside," Clarissa said coldly. "I will let you know if I require you."

The man should have left it then, certainly Dannen would have, and he was far from the most reasonable person in the world. But love makes fools of all men, and the guard was shaking his head before she was finished. "Forgive me, my lady, but I don't trust him. What...what if he has indecent intentions?" he finished, blushing a deep shade of crimson.

Dannen started to speak, meaning to assure the guard that he had no such intentions, that his only intention was making it out of the castle alive. Unfortunately, Clarissa beat him to it. "I can only hope he does," she said, and Dannen thought that, this time, she was all too aware of the pain her words caused the guardsman, pain evident on his stricken expression before she closed the door in his face.

That done, Clarissa sighed, moving to a well-equipped bar and withdrawing a bottle of wine. "Would you like a drink, Dannen?" she asked as if nothing had happened.

Dannen, though, was staring at the door. "You've made him angry," he said, "but worse yet, you embarrassed him."

She shrugged one shapely shoulder. "In my experience, Dannen, it does a man good to be embarrassed, sometimes, helps him remember he isn't as clever as he thinks. And as for angry, who can control that? For all men's talk about women and their emotions, it seems to me you all spend more than half your time angry at one thing or another, always looking for something to hit to make yourselves feel better."

Dannen would have argued that, if he could, but he knew enough about men—knew enough about himself—that he chose to remain silent, taking the offered goblet of wine.

Clarissa walked to a cushioned divan at one side of the room, sitting before waving a hand at the space beside her. "Please, Dannen, sit. Relax."

Left with little choice, Dannen sat. He didn't relax, however, knowing that to do so, right then, would have been foolishness of the greatest sort. Though he had decided long ago that he *was* a fool, even he had his limits.

"So, Danny, tell me, how have you been?"

And there was that name again. No one had called him Danny in a long time, but Clarissa once had, many years ago, when they had been far closer. Dannen didn't miss it, just as he didn't miss her hand on his thigh. "Oh, I've been surviving," he said, glancing at the door and half-expecting the young guardsman to come charging in any moment with blood on his mind.

Clarissa, though, seemed to have put the guard out of her mind altogether. "Yes? And how is that woman of yours—Valerie, wasn't it?"

Dannen felt a familiar pang of sadness as he thought of his late wife. Despite the years since her death, the sadness, the pain of his loss, always surprised him, often driving him to taverns to order the biggest glass—or glasses—of ale he could find. He swallowed hard. "She died," he said, not trusting himself to say any more.

"Oh gods, Dannen," Clarissa said, "I'm so sorry." Gone was the affected, sultry tone Clarissa usually used to great effect. The person who spoke to him now wasn't the vixen over whom there had been at least two fights to the death, but the actual Clarissa, the woman who despite their history and the years that he'd known her, Dannen had seen on only a few occasions.

"Thank you," he said, meaning it and not trusting himself to say much else, for the memories, the pain of what he'd lost, were close now. He could feel them hovering at his shoulder, breathing their chill breath on the back of his neck, wanting to be noticed.

The next few minutes passed in silence, and Dannen was grateful to her for that, for giving him time. Then, when he felt the specter of his loss recede once more into the shadows of his mind, he took a slow, deep breath. "Anyway, it seems you've been busy," he remarked, glancing around at the rich furnishings of the room.

She smiled, and there was a compassion to it that threatened to bring the shadows back. "Yes, I have."

He cleared his throat. "Plenty of guards, too. Looks like you have your own little army out front. You expecting to be invaded anytime soon?"

She smiled. "In my experience, Danny, carrying the sharpest blade often means one does not have to use it."

Dannen couldn't argue with that, though he wondered what it meant for a once-renowned fighter who had taken a vow against ever wielding a blade in battle again. Probably nothing good. "And the hidden crossbowman? Surely, you don't intend for him to be part of the blade you show to keep the muggers away."

She gave a soft laugh, reclining in her seat and folding one shapely leg over the other. "Well, a bared blade might keep most of the jackals away, but the world has no shortage of fools, does it, Danny?"

Considering that he thought himself one of the biggest, he couldn't argue with that either. "No, I don't suppose it does," he said, glancing again at the door, wondering what the guard on the other side was thinking, wondering if he was fingering the handle of his sword even now and thinking he probably was.

"Oh, would you stop eyeing the door like you expect a troll to burst through it any moment meaning to chew on your bones? You're safe here."

Dannen grunted. "Maybe, but I think that if your man Palder had his way just now, safe is the last thing I'd be."

She rolled her eyes, as if his concerns were ridiculous. "Palder's harmless. Just a bit...well, let's call it overprotective, that's all."

Dannen could have told her it was obvious the man had other things on his mind than protecting her. "He seems ready for violence to me, damn near bent on it, and a chip on his shoulder in want of being knocked off."

She laughed again. "Reminds me of another man I once knew, some years ago."

"Still," Dannen persisted, not willing to be put off so easily, "I'd think with all the money you've got you could do better than him. The man's a bloody mistake waiting to happen."

"How dare you?" she said, sudden anger in her voice, her eyes flashing dangerously. "Palder is *loyal,* as I believe I told you. Loyal in a way you never were, at least not to me."

Dannen was so surprised it took him a minute to speak. "What do you mean, Clare?"

"*Clare,*" she hissed. "It is a name I have not been called in some years, Danny, not since you left me without so much as a goodbye."

Dannen could hardly believe what he was hearing. Yes, he and Clarissa had a history, had, from time to time and on one drunken night or another, found themselves sharing a bed, but he had never thought it any more than that. She had been, likely still was, the most ambitious woman he had ever met, and he'd never considered their occasional dalliances anything to her but a way to pass the time—a decidedly pleasant way no question, but of no real consequence. "Clare," he said slowly, "I mean, I didn't...I'm sorry."

"*Damn* your sorry," she snapped back. "Oh, they were just fun little trysts to you, weren't they, Danny? Just the next story to share with your friends, the Firemaker chief among them. But they weren't just that to m—"

"You're wrong, Clare," he said. "I never talked to Fedder about...about us."

"*Us,*" she said, then snorted. "Sure, and why would you, right? After all, a man doesn't feel the need to go around bragging about every whore he beds, does he, Dannen?"

He recoiled as if slapped at that, her words hitting him like a physical blow. "Clare, I never thought of you like, like that. I mean...I thought—"

"Thought *what*?" she demanded. "That I'm a woman too hungry for money and power to *have* feelings, is that it, Dannen? That I'm too selfish to ever care for another, that I can only care for myself?"

Dannen waited before he spoke, partly because everything he said seemed to be the wrong thing and mostly because he was left feeling guilty by her words, by how near they came to the truth of how he had thought of her years ago. Very near, in fact, to how he had thought of her only a moment ago. But people, it seemed, were always more complex than you thought.

He was still considering what to say when Clarissa spoke. "I looked up to you, do you know that?" she said in a bitter voice. "I thought myself *lucky* you even so much as noticed me. Oh, don't look at me like that, why wouldn't I have? After all, you were the

Bloody Butcher, the greatest hero of the age, some said, a man unstoppable on a battlefield, who bathed in the blood of his enemies and so on and so forth. I was young then, far younger than I am now, as you so gracefully pointed out, and I felt privileged when you so much as spoke to me, more the fool I. Oh, but that wasn't enough for you, was it, Danny? No, you spent time with me, using me as your whore whenever it was convenient, and me imagining that each tumble in the sheets was more than that, that you felt some of what I did. And just when I was sure it was real, that I meant as much to you as you did to me, you up and run off with some...some *woman* you just met without so much as a tip to the whore you gave up."

"She wasn't just some woman, Clare," he said softly. "I married her. And you were never a whore. You were...you were the finest thing I knew during those days, before I met Val. So fine I would have never thought you could be mine, thought..." He shook his head, frustrated that he couldn't seem to say what he meant to. "I'm sorry, Clare," he said finally. "Truly."

She stared at him, her expression unreadable, and Dannen began to sweat, started wondering if maybe she would call for the loyal Palder and have him come and deal with the man who had so wronged her. In the end, though, she only let out a heavy sigh, shaking her head. "No, I'm sorry, Dannen. It...perhaps it wasn't fair of me to expect so much of you, then or now."

He didn't like the sound of that, not at all, and he frowned. "What do you mean, 'then or now?'"

"Hm?" she said, and a trace of what might have been annoyance flashed across her face for a moment. Only a moment, then it was gone, covered once more by the confident, alluring expression that came so easily to her. "Sorry, I must have misspoken. All I meant to say, Danny, is it's okay. You loved her, that's all, and I truly am sorry for your loss. As I told you, I'm older than I was, and I like to think I'm wiser, too."

Dannen nodded. "Thank you. Now, Clare, why don't you tell me why I'm here."

She frowned. "I'm not sure what you—"

"Please, Clare," he sighed. "I have had a trying couple of days. I've already lost count of the number of people who have tried to kill me this week, so if it's all the same to you, can we just get on with it?"

She gave him a pouty face, and Dannen thought it was damn indecent that the woman could make even that look sexy. When he didn't give way to it—a near thing, truth be told—she sighed. "Look, Danny, why don't you relax, alright? After all, unless I'm very much mistaken, I saved you and your friends' asses back there. Some people, in your position, might even be moved to say 'thank you.'"

Dannen winced. "Thanks, Clare."

"See?" she said. "It's not so hard, being nice to me, is it? There was a time where I seem to recall you enjoyed it quite a bit."

He smiled. "Yes."

She returned the smile, clearly satisfied. "Now then, I'll make you a deal, Danny, how would that be? How about, you tell me what it is that brought you to Talinseh, and I'll tell you why I wanted to speak with you."

"And here I thought it was because you enjoyed my company."

"Oh, I do," she said, grinning wickedly, "and with any luck, I'll be enjoying it even more soon. But business before pleasure."

Dannen considered how much to tell her. Just then, he couldn't see any real reason not to tell her everything. After all, he couldn't imagine what she might use such information for, even if she decided she wanted to use it against him. At worst, she'd likely think him insane. At best, she'd let him go with her good wishes. The problem, of course, was although he might not be able to see a way she could use the information to her advantage, Clarissa had made a career—a *life*—of doing just that sort of thing, of seeing the angle when nobody else could. However, if he told her nothing he risked offending her, and he thought that, considering that she'd almost certainly saved his and the others' lives barely an hour ago, he owed her something.

In the end, he shrugged. "We've got a job, Fedder and me."

She nodded slowly. "A job, you say. That's interesting. Fedder, of course, doesn't surprise me as he's always been more than willing to fight for free and being paid coin for it's just a bonus. You, though…well, I was under the impression you gave up being a hero years ago. So…what's changed?"

Dannen thought it was more what hadn't changed, namely, him. Oh, he'd tried to be good for years while Val was still alive, but the truth was he'd never been very good at *being* good. It seemed easy enough, on the surface. Just move through life keeping your head down and your mouth shut, a recipe for avoiding trouble. But in practice, he'd always found it difficult, if not impossible to do. "I...don't know," he said finally.

"I see," she said. "And who, then, is this anonymous employer who has somehow managed to draw the Butcher back into the fray?"

He winced. "Please, Clare. You know how I hate that."

"Yes, I do," she said, "but if a man doesn't want to be called a butcher, he shouldn't spend his days cutting meat, Dannen." She leaned forward, meeting his eyes. "Do you want to know something? When you left, I was hurt. Of course I was, hurt and angry, but I was also glad. I was glad you were giving it up, glad you'd found something better than killing to pass the time, someone better to pass it with than corpses, even if it wasn't me. But now, it seems my relief was premature. Is it the glory, then, Danny? Is that it? Do you miss the killing or having harlots and townsfolk cheer when you walk by?"

He felt the barb in her words almost like physical pain. "It's different this time."

"Really? I've got to be honest with you, Danny, it doesn't look different, not from this side of things. From this side, it looks like you're up to just about the same sort of stuff you always were, hurt and surrounded by strangers who want to kill you. Oh, don't give me that look. You might be able to fool other people, but not me—I know the face you get when you're nursing a hurt and trying to hide it, no doubt out of some foolish idea that to do so is to be a man. Is it your back again?"

"It's nothing," he lied.

She rolled her eyes. "Nothing, is it? As I recall, that 'nothing' was a nine-foot troll who decided to squeeze you like a lemon and see what came out." She arched a perfectly shaped eyebrow. "One can only imagine, considering what I sometimes suspect you're full of."

Dannen grunted, remembering the encounter all too well, for it had been the stuff of his nightmares—and his curses when the back pain was particularly bad in the morning—on more occasions than he would care to admit. "I don't remember him asking me my thoughts on the matter."

"It's the most damning thing about monsters and villains," she said dryly, "they so rarely take into account other people's wants or needs."

"Yeah. Villainous of them."

She gave him a frown, clearly not amused. "Don't try to be clever, Danny. You have your talents, and that's not one of them. Better leave it to us professionals, and we'll leave the getting beaten half to death by a troll to you and your ilk."

Dannen was surprised by the amount of anger in her voice. "You should see the troll," he said, trying to sound lighthearted, but Clarissa only stared at him as if he were the world's biggest fool.

"Oh, I saw it as you well know. Or at least, part of it. A person'd have to be blind not to see the way those villagers paraded its head around on a pike for near a week until the thing rotted and fell off. If I'm not mistaken, the mayor of that shitty little town has the skull mounted on his wall, so if you ever happen through again, maybe you can take a moment to say hello to your old friend. But tell me, Danny, does knowing the troll is dead ease the pain?"

Dannen grunted. "Certainly doesn't hurt it."

She rolled her eyes. "Gods, but men are fools. You get your back hurt acting tough and would walk around hurting to keep people thinking it, because apparently killing a troll isn't enough. And what's worse is that somehow, that pain doesn't remind you of how stupid doing something like picking a fight with troll is."

Dannen grunted. "Oh, it reminds me all the time, Clare."

"Does it?" she said, then leaned forward. "*Does it?* I only ask, Dannen, because it seems it didn't remind you well enough for you to say no to whoever came calling, offering you a job. After all, you're here, aren't you? You and Fedder both, and if that doesn't bring back memories I don't know what does. And very, very few of those memories are good ones, Danny. Mostly, I just remember having to patch you up when you traded a little more flesh for a little more coin."

She was angry again, that much was obvious, though why she might be so aggravated Dannen couldn't guess. "I know, Clare," he said, "and I appreciate it. Really. You were...you *are* a good friend."

"A good friend," she said thoughtfully, as if she'd never heard the words before. "A good friend would throw you in a dungeon, lock you up at least long enough for you to come to your senses, to realize you're far too old to be running around playing at being a hero. This time, Dannen, it's likely you won't get hurt—probably, you'll get killed."

"Damn, Clare," Dannen said, shaking his head in frustration. "I didn't hear you giving Fedder all this shit, and he's several years older than me."

"And what of it?" she demanded. "Fedder's a different breed, and you know it. The man's built for this sort of thing, belongs on some sprawling battlefield, shouting that war-cry of his like some demi-god of destruction. He was made for hurting, for killing, and I couldn't ask him to stop it any more than I could ask the sun to stop shining on assholes and people who owe me money."

Dannen wanted to argue with that. The problem was, she had only voiced a thought he'd had for a long time about Fedder, and as much as he wanted to think he could do anything the mage could, he had to admit he'd never once heard the man complain about the many scars he'd accumulated over the years. And if he was plagued with any of the aches and pains that were Dannen's constant companions, Dannen had never once heard him utter a single word of complaint. If anything, the years seemed to work in reverse on the mage, making him stronger and giving him more energy. Meanwhile, each day, Dannen found it a little harder to get out of bed, found it a little more difficult to think of reasons worth doing so.

"Fine," he admitted grudgingly, "I'll admit I'm no Firemaker. That bastard was made for battle, that much is true."

She studied him for a moment, finally shaking her head. "And I think, Dannen, that somewhere, deep down, you're fool enough to envy him that."

"What do you want, Clare? To give me a hard time, is that it? To make me feel like a fool? Well, you needn't bother. Fact is, I feel like a fool most of the time anyway."

"What do I want?" she repeated. She rolled her eyes. "What I *want,* Dannen, is for every orphan to have a home, every child a meal when they want it, and for the world to up and decide it needs a queen and none better for the job than me. A bit of a tall order, I'll admit, and while the gods are working on it, maybe I'll content myself with trying to keep your fool head attached to your fool shoulders, though I doubt anyone will thank me for it."

"No offense, Clare," he said, "but why do you care? As you said, it's been a long time, and I wronged you, without meaning to, understand. So what difference to you what happens to me and my head?"

She frowned at that. "Ten years isn't so long a time, Danny. Not so long at all, really." There seemed to him to be another meaning to her words, something buried in them, but Dannen had always been far better at wrestling trolls than understanding women and now was no different. "Anyway," she went on while he was still puzzling over it, "it's a pretty enough head. Not prize-worthy or anything, but worth saving." She gave a smile she obviously didn't feel.

"Clare…" he said slowly, "about when I left. I…that is, I—"

"Leave it, Danny," she said, and though she was still smiling, something in her expression changed, turning it into a warning. "Just leave it. The past is the past, that's all. We can't change it, and to try is only to waste time, a thing I have always loathed to do. Anyway," she went on, "if you don't want to tell me the details, that's fine. Probably, I'd just as soon not know. Still, it must be something. Are you getting all the old gang back together or just Firemaker?"

He grunted. "Most of the old gang's dead, as you well know. Anyway, I wouldn't be partnering up with Firemaker except the g…the employer who hired me made it a condition of the job." Not exactly true, but close enough, and getting any closer would mean him having to explain that his employer was, in fact, the Messenger God, and that they were on a holy, god-entrusted mission to slay a necromancer and rescue a kingdom. He thought she would have gotten a kick out of that, but the woman was already too capable of making him feel like a fool, no need to give her that sort of invitation.

She snorted. "Maybe other people might believe that. Maybe you even believe it, but I know better, Danny. As much as you like to pretend, I'd gamble Fedder is the best friend you've ever had. Maybe even the only one, considering you've got an unfortunate tendency of stabbing most of those whose acquaintance you make. The girl, though, this Mariana—about her, I must admit I'm intrigued. What is she about?"

He glanced down at his boots, frowning. They'd been new, an occurrence that, for him, was rare enough he'd been enjoying it, but that feeling was gone now. He'd done the best he could to wipe them off on their way here, but though he could not see any of the foulness the girl had thrown up onto them, he could remember it well enough. *She's about ruining a good pair of boots, that's what,* he thought. *Oh, and suicide, that too.* "I...don't really know her that well." Clarissa raised an eyebrow at him, and he grunted. "Fine. I don't know her at all. Still, from what I've seen so far, she's good in a scrap. If I can somehow manage to convince her to keep her mouth shut, she might even be an asset."

Clarissa's full lips writhed on her face as if she was fighting the urge to smile. Finally, she cleared her throat. "Oh yes, Mariana Vanderia is known throughout all of Talinseh. Certainly, the Guild once hailed her as their best pupil and those who keep track of such things reckoned she would become the fiercest assassin the city had seen in a hundred years. Nobody could have ever predicted..." She paused, glancing at Dannen, a malicious amusement gleaming in her eyes. "Well, never mind."

Dannen frowned. "Predicted what? What is it, Clare? What about her?"

The woman considered for several seconds then finally shook her head. "No. No, Danny. You'll have to discover that little tidbit on your own. Call it payback, if you'd like, for a ten year-overdue apology."

"Clare—" he began, but she shook her head.

"No, Danny, not this time. If this secret might endanger your life, I would tell, but it does not. Instead, it might only endanger your patience or perhaps your pride, and that much you—and I—can live with."

Dannen wanted to protest, not loving the idea of teaming up with the girl, Mariana, when clearly there was something he didn't know, something which Clarissa, while she might not bear him any ill will, certainly enjoyed the thought of. In the end, though, he didn't bother, knowing that once Clarissa had made her mind up about something, a man had a better chance of convincing a river to flow backward than talk her into changing it. "Alright. So now that that's out of the way, will you tell me why you brought me here?"

She sighed. "Very well, though as I believe I've said, I brought you here for two reasons, Dannen. Let us, I suppose, begin with the first." She sat forward then, and suddenly the flirtatious woman was gone, replaced by a woman who had made of her keen mind a weapon, a woman who, though she had no magic like Fedder or natural talent with the sword like Dannen, had surpassed both of them in nearly every way one might measure success. "Tell me, Danny, how familiar are you with the ruling body of Talinseh?"

Dannen grunted. "As little as I can be." A fact he credited as one of the reasons why he was still walking around breathing. In his experience, criminals rarely enjoyed the prospect of someone poking into their affairs, would do something about it—something decidedly unpleasant—if they could, and the type of criminals powerful enough to attain a spot on the Assassin City's ruling council most certainly could.

Clarissa smiled. "Well. It is enough for you to know that the Tribunal is led by the High Justice—" She paused, frowning as Dannen barked a laugh before going on. "And six other men and women, all of whom, including the Justice, are elected by popular vote by the citizens of Talinseh."

Dannen suspected—outright knew, in fact—that in this case, the 'popular' vote went to those most popular for their ability to make any who didn't vote for them suffer terribly before they died, but he nodded. "Go on."

"That it?" she said, her eyes narrowing. "No clever quip?"

"Too many to choose from," Dannen said, shrugging. "Anyway, you were saying?"

"As I was saying," she went on frowning, "it is these seven men and women who determine policies affecting all those who live in the city. Well, men and woman, I suppose, as there's only the one, currently."

"Doesn't seem that hard to guess who that one might be," Dannen offered.

She smiled. "Yes, I am fortunate enough," *read dangerous enough,* Dannen thought, "to have been elected to sit on the Tribunal by my peers," *of which there are none,* "who have trusted their fate into my hands." *Trusted, at least, that should they become obstacles in her path to ascension, they would soon be very miserable, very dead obstacles.*

"So what's the problem?" Dannen asked. "It sounds ideal, if you ask me. I ought to congratulate you. I never doubted you would succeed, of course, but still. A member of the Tribunal—that's impressive."

"Quite," she said, waving a hand, "but you can tell me how amazing I am later, and I'll listen eagerly. For now, though, let's try to stick to the matter at hand."

"That matter being..."

She sighed. "Normally, the Tribunal is relatively unbiased, when any issue comes before them." Dannen grunted another laugh, and she frowned. "Very well, we are not unbiased. We are all terribly biased. However, since our biases and our agendas rarely coincide, it is typical that any decision reached is bound to make none of us happy or unhappy which, in most cases, is for the best, believe me. Any matter is discussed at length and then voted on with the High Justice serving as the final arbiter in these matters, breaking any ties."

"The perfect system," Dannen said, doing his best to keep his expression under control, thinking that, in truth, the system was only perfect so long as you were one of those criminals rich enough and dangerous enough to be a part of it.

She frowned, studying him suspiciously. "No system is perfect, of course, but while many cities and kingdoms have fallen to revolution and bloody wars which enveloped the whole of their populace over the years, Talinseh has remained, relatively speaking, peaceful."

No, not peaceful, but Dannen knew enough about criminals and assassins to know they didn't form up in lines and meet in the open. Instead, their bloody wars were fought in bedrooms and taverns, and their soldiers did not march in ranks but crept through windows with picked locks, their weapons of choice not swords and cavalry horses, but poison and an untended cups of ale. Still, he saw no reason to mention as much to her, and plenty of reasons—the guards stationed outside her study came to mind—not to. "But no longer?" he asked.

"But no longer," she agreed. "Lately, some of the council members have begun to side—indiscriminately—with another of its members, one Histarial Lanesh."

Dannen frowned. "Wait a minute, I've heard that name...do you mean Lord Lanesh?"

Clarissa rolled her eyes. "Hisser is about as much of a lord as I am a troll."

He opened his mouth to answer, but she raised a warning finger. "Careful, Danny. I like you, and the gods know we've got history, but all histories end, sooner or later, and I'm not in the mood for cleverness just now."

Dannen grunted, swallowing the comment he'd been about to make and choosing a different one. "Hisser?" he repeated.

"It's what we call him." She shrugged. "Well, it's what *I* call him at any rate. After all, snakes hiss, don't they? And if there's a bigger snake than Histarial slinking around, I've never met him."

"So you mean to tell me a tribunal of criminals is...corruptible? Gods, is there no decency left in the world?

"You're assuming there was decency to begin with," she countered. "Anyway, *yes* it's true that some members of the council have been accused of being involved in criminal activities in the past. The problem, though, as I believe I've already told you, is that normally such people act solely in their own interests, and therein lies the balance. Now though, what were once selfish, vainglorious men who only ever cared about themselves and their ambitions, have begun to follow Hisser's lead instead."

"All of them?"

"No," she said slowly, "not all of them. Two, so far."

"Two," Dannen echoed. "Well, that's not too bad then, is it? Even assuming you're not reading more into it than there is, that's only half."

"Only half," she said. "First, let me be clear, Danny, we six, as a rule, never agree on anything without hours spent in useless debate until coming to a consensus which no one is happy with. However, on the last three votes—all relatively minor, setting new trade tariffs mostly—the two other councilmen have immediately deferred to Hisser. Perhaps that means that at least half of the council is uncorrupted. But the way things are going, it seems only a matter of time before Hisser gets the others on his side. And with a majority vote on the council in his pocket, he will be king of Talinseh in all but name, at least."

"Forgive me, Clare. I don't mean any offense," Dannen said, "but isn't this sort of thing expected when you make a governing body up of criminals? I mean, it can't be the first time someone's tried to strong-arm one of the other members into agreeing with him...or her."

She raised an eyebrow. "No, you are correct, it is not the first time. But you have to understand, the men who have risen to the Tribunal are not easily intimidated. They, like me, regularly receive death threats and assassination attempts—it's simply the consequence of power. In my estimation, no amount of death threats, no bribes, no matter how large, could sway them."

And if Dannen knew Clarissa and her ambition at all, she had certainly tried the latter, likely the former, so she could no doubt say as much with a large degree of confidence.

"Besides which," she went on, "such matters are policed regularly by the High Justice, the most powerful of us. And should anything be discovered, whether an attempt at bribery, blackmail, or coercion, the offender would be prosecuted...let us say irrevocably. It has happened before, when one councilmember thought to manipulate the others, to threaten them. The High Justice heard of this tampering, and, as far as I know, that was the last thing ever heard about or from that councilmember. The next day, there was an empty spot on the Tribunal."

"That's very...efficient," Dannen said, meaning terrifying.

She inclined her head in a nod. "The High Justice is a powerful man, Dannen, and though his past is...similar, I should say, to the other members of the council, he has very particular ideas about balance, ones which he defends vigorously."

"Well," Dannen said, "if manipulating others' votes is as unlikely as you say, then perhaps these other two men simply happen to agree with Histarial. It isn't impossible, after all, right? There's a first time for everything."

"No," she said simply, "there isn't. Pigs do not fly, Danny, and they never will fly. It is an impossibility and so there can never be a first."

"Sure," Dannen agreed slowly, "but this isn't exactly pigs flying, is it? I mean—"

"There has been an investigation on the matter already, one led by the High Justice himself. If there had been a direct means of manipulation to be found, Dannen, then he would have found it. Nothing was discovered."

Dannen nodded. "Assuming you're right—don't look at me like that, Clare, if you say it's so, I believe you—then isn't the most likely thing that the High Justice himself is corrupt?"

"No."

"But, Clare," he pressed, "surely you—"

"No, Danny," she said forcefully. "No. I am telling you that the High Justice is not corrupt. Or, at least, that he is far less corrupt than the rest of us."

"But how can you be sure? After all, you said yourself—"

"Leave it, Danny," she interrupted, an unmistakable warning in her tone. "Please. I know without doubt the High Justice is not involved. You must trust me on this."

Her jaw was set, and there was a look in her eyes he remembered well, one saying she had made up her mind and would not be swayed, so Dannen shrugged. "Alright, fine. But even if something going on, I can't imagine what you want me to do about it. After all, I don't know any of these people we're talking about and, even if I did, unlike you, I don't have an army ready to do my bidding. If this Hisser is as powerful as I suspect, I wouldn't be able to get within a hundred feet of him without being cut down."

"True," she said slowly, "if you were seen."

It was Dannen's turn to frown. "What is it you're asking me to do, Clare? Because I'll tell you now, history or not, I'm no assassin, no matter what the fool bards claim in their songs, and blood is a damn sight harder to wash out of clothes than ale."

"I'm not asking you to kill anyone, Dannen," she said, acting offended, "I've got men who would do that for me, if that's what I needed. I'm just asking you to...well, to look into it for me. Think of it as a favor for an old friend."

"And this Histarial, I'm assuming he probably wouldn't be happy to learn someone was looking into him. A favor's one thing, Clare, but I told you I'm on a job right now, and my employers would no doubt frown on me getting myself killed before I saw it through. I'd frown too, come to it."

"Yes," she said, "you're right, of course, Dannen. A favor *is* one thing, like the sort of thing that prompts me to save you from a mob of assassins looking to cash in. That sort of thing. And though you may not know it, I put myself at more risk than I care to contemplate by doing so."

He frowned. "What do you mean by that?"

"There have been...some attempts on my life recently."

"Can't imagine it's the first time."

"That's it?" she asked. "No chivalrous vow to protect my virtue? No offer to save me from my persecutors in some heroic manner?"

Dannen cleared his throat, suddenly unsure how to respond, was still struggling to figure it out when Clarissa laughed. "Oh, relax, Danny. I'm no blushing maiden to faint at the sound of a mean word. And to answer your question, no, it is not the first time. Any person in my position—particularly a *woman* who many fools believe has no place on the Tribunal, or anywhere for that matter, besides the kitchen—has to expect a certain degree of...shall we say angst, from those around them. And sometimes—I won't bore you with the details of just how often—something triggers a response in those men and women who would normally be satisfied to wile away their spare hours in one tavern or another, drinking and complaining about me, the Tribunal, and, likely, the world itself. And once that response is triggered, those men and women will not be satisfied with anything less than my death, begin to hold me personally responsible for all their many grievances. They are angry, looking for someone to blame, and even more important to them than their anger is to make their anger known, to be, in some way, understood. And so they plot and they scheme—neither very well, as anger, I find, is a terrible muse when it comes to plotting and scheming—and sooner or later, they make their attempt."

"The way you talk about it," Dannen said, "it seems like it happens often. That's...that's terrible." And that much, at least, he meant, for though he'd had people try to kill him before, they usually had a very personal reason for wanting him dead, one that, had he not been the potential victim in question, he might have even agreed with.

Clarissa gave a shrug which did interesting things with her dress. "It is simply a consequence of being in the position I'm in. One learns not to take it personally. Farmers with pitchforks, mostly, or their equivalent at least."

She was trying for nonchalance, but Dannen didn't buy it. Partly because he'd had plenty of people try to kill him over the years—some of them coming close enough he thought they probably deserved a consolation prize at least—and every time, without fail, it had felt pretty damned personal to him. Mostly, though, it was something in her eyes, a look that, had he not once known her so well, he might not have noticed. But he *had* known her well once, so he *did* notice, and that look was enough to show what she wished to hide—fear.

"Farmers with pitchforks," Dannen repeated, letting some of his doubt come out in the words. "Well, then why concern yourself? Such as those surely have no chance against you."

Clarissa looked at him sharply and, for a moment, rage simmered in her eyes. He was suddenly certain she would call for her guards after all. But in another moment, the look, the anger, was gone as quickly as it had come, and she took a slow, deep breath. "Perhaps I was underplaying the would-be assassins."

"Oh?" Dannen asked, swallowing the mocking remark that came to his mind, deciding he'd rather be alive than clever any day.

She winced. "Well. Suffice to say that many attempts have been made on my life since I came to the Assassin City. Attempts which I have learned to cope with, at least as much as anyone can, taking measures to ensure my safety like those you pointed out when we arrived. Further, I have made a point of responding to such threats in a way to...*dissuade* the aggrieved individuals from trying again. And, until recently, it has worked well."

Knowing Clarissa as he did, he doubted if the individuals in question would be able, after having failed and been discovered, to try anything again. Save, perhaps, the thrilling activity of decomposing in some shallow, unmarked grave. "Until recently," he echoed. "So what's changed?"

"It is enough to say that the latest two attempts have been far closer than any before. And, though it pains me to admit it—and should you repeat this to anyone else I will deny it before making sure something painful happens to you in return—it was not planning or cleverness which saved me either time. It was simply dumb luck. No doubt, when you first saw the men with whom I traveled, the soldiers, I mean, you suspected they were no more than me rubbing my power in the faces of the city, of showing off my strength the way a king might use gold silverware which is softer and less reliable than other kinds only to show off his wealth."

Dannen frowned, feeling a spike of shame, and not bothering trying to argue for, in truth, she could not have been closer to the mark. "I'm listening," he said finally.

She gave a small, knowing smile then inclined her head. "The first time, I was sitting in my study at my desk, going over some accounts of those who owe me by the sunlight filtering through the open window, when, by chance, my foot began to itch and so, as anyone might, I leaned forward in my chair to scratch it. Imagine my surprise, then, when I heard a noise and sat back up only to see a crossbow bolt embedded in the back of my chair."

"Damn," Dannen said. "Still, an open window sort of invites—"

"Let us accept, Danny, that I know as much about such things as you. It will save us some time." She looked at him and sighed. "Forgive me, I am only...distraught. I do not mean to lash out at you. Anyway, back to the point. The window in question faces the back of my property, property extending far enough that no crossbowman could make such a shot without entering my property, a nearly impossible task considering the ten-foot-tall iron fence surrounding the grounds, not to mention the presence of no fewer than six armed guardsmen. It is impossible, understand me, for an assailant to come close without being spotted by at least two of my guards."

"And yet..."

"And yet they *did* manage it, according to my guards. Which, of course, can only mean one thing."

"You believe someone among your guards or staff is a traitor."

133

"No, Danny," she said. "I believe *several* someones are."

He frowned. "How so?"

She waved it away. "The *second* such attempt came while I was seated for dinner. I was on the final course, dessert, which happened to be a sweet cake that I sometimes prefer. One of my newest servants—Tilda, a young woman who, less than a year ago, was living on the streets and who I chose to take into my service—brought it to me."

"Nice of you," Dannen remarked.

"Not so nice, as it turned out," she said, tensing her jaw, and there was no mistaking the anger now. "For, you see, Tilda gazed at that cake, expertly prepared by a pastry chef I keep employed—in so hard and cruel a world, I find something sweet takes the worst of its bite away—as if it were the finest thing she had ever seen. Perhaps it was." She shrugged. "Who can say? All I know is I liked her—oh yes, Dannen, despite what you suspect are my ambitious, malicious intentions, I *am* capable of liking someone—and was moved, when seeing her expression, to offer her the cake." She paused, taking a slow, angry breath. "It took some convincing to get her to try it but finally, embarrassed and pleased at once, she did."

Dannen saw the fury dancing in her eyes, fury and sadness both, and he felt ashamed for thinking of her only as ambitious. "It was poisoned," he said softly.

It was several seconds before Clarissa spoke. When she finally did, her tone was sharp enough to cut. "Yes," she said, "it was. A most vile poison. I am no poisoner, but I know enough to understand that the person who chose it was not satisfied to seek my death, but instead wanted to know that I would suffer terribly before I died, would be carried into the lands of the dead on a wave of agony the likes of which few have ever experienced. As for Tilda, Danny, she died. She died terribly, a death in which she was allowed to maintain none of her dignity, died because I sought to do her a kindness."

Clarissa was one of the toughest women Dannen had ever known, one of the most dangerous, yet he knew a soft heart hid beneath her thick armor, stowed away so that it might not be easily crushed. Now, though, some of that heart made its way past those armored plates and into her eyes, taking the form of tears spilling down her cheeks.

"Clare," Dannen said softly, "I'm sorry. You...she...did not deserve that."

She sniffed, wiping a finger across her eyes. "Oh, don't be ridiculous, Dannen. I deserve such a death and then some, I suspect." Her face writhed with anger. "Tilda, though, was innocent, and I intend to make sure the man or woman in my employ responsible for her death will suffer even more than Tilda did in my stead."

"Did you do an investigation?" Dannen asked curiously. "I mean, to figure out who it was?"

"An investigation?" she said, her eyes going wide in clear mockery. "What a clever idea. My, but I'm glad you are here, Danny." She rolled her eyes. "Of *course* I conducted an investigation. I will not bore you with the actions taken, the blood and tears spilled in the endeavor, for I cannot be bothered recounting it, and we do not have the time in any case. In the end, I am short three of my personal chefs and still have no idea who might have dared poison my food."

Dannen cleared his throat. "I see."

"You don't," she countered, "not yet. But you may, in time. Danny, you have to understand that all this is worrying, and I am certainly concerned with my safety, but this is not my only concern. You see, a question has been brought before the Tribunal, brought, in point of fact, by Histarial himself. A question which should have been dismissed immediately as ridiculous and out of the question. The problem, though, was that it wasn't."

"What question?" Dannen asked.

"Tell me," she said, and for a moment Dannen was pleasantly distracted by the way her dress clung to her body as she rose and walked past him to pour herself another drink, "how informed are you regarding the situation in the north?"

Dannen suddenly had a sinking feeling in his stomach. "A little," he hedged, as unprepared now as he had been before to divulge his conversation with Perandius.

She glanced up from where she was refilling her wine, meeting his eyes. "A little," she echoed. "Does that include knowing about rumors of the dead rising from their graves and attacking villages?"

Dannen grunted. "I might have heard something like that. Hard to believe, isn't it?"

"Not so hard," Clarissa said darkly. "The Tribunal has agents in place that assure us it is true. At least, those few agents who have reported at all...the fate of the others, considering the situation, seems all too certain."

"I don't mean to sound uncaring," Dannen said slowly, "but what difference does any of that make? After all, the north is far, far away."

"It matters," she answered, "because Talinseh, like so many of the cities and kingdoms of the south, relies heavily on the exports of the northern kingdoms. Chief among those exports are furs and salt. These along with dozens of other commodities, commodities which, since the recent troubles began, are a large source of profit and, more than that, survival for the cities and kingdoms of the south, Talinseh included. Already, this city—including each member of the Tribunal—is feeling the pinch of their lack, a lack which coincided with the troubles in the north. Ufrith, the king, is currently far too troubled trying to save his kingdom from the threat these undead pose to concern himself with trade. Yet, for all his efforts, several villages have already fallen to the undead scourge. They say traveling roads between villages and cities at night is growing more and more dangerous. To that end, King Ufrith has written to us, asking for aid."

Dannen grunted. "Aid from the Assassin City?"

She raised an eyebrow. "Try not to look so surprised, Dannen. True, the city might have originated from criminals, but even criminals will act in their own interests, and the economic drain the north's troubles have put on us is very real. Besides which, when the city was first formed, many kingdoms and rulers resisted recognizing us as a separate power. It was the king of the north at the time—Ufrith's grandfather—who first did so, beginning trade with us which allowed us to survive. If you are not willing to believe we would help him out of answer to that kindness, then you must at least allow that we would still do so, if only for selfish reasons. As I've said, Talinseh survives, in large part, due to trade with the northern kingdoms."

Dannen's head felt as if it was spinning. Though he didn't exactly miss the days when he spent his time battling ogres and trolls, dealing with mischievous pixies and do-good dryads, he found that he *did* miss the simplicity of it. Someone—or several someones—trying to kill you might prove damned inconvenient, but it had a way of simplifying a man's thoughts. "So what's all this got to do with Histarial?" he asked.

"As I told you, Ufrith has sent to us asking for aid. Normally, the answer would of course be yes, for I have already explained how reliant we are on trade with him and his kingdom. Now, though, Histarial and his two lackeys are advocating we do nothing."

"Which...would be bad?" Dannen ventured.

"Yes," she said dryly. "That would be bad. Such a decision might well spell the end of the north and certainly, should Ufrith survive the coming days, he will not forget such a refusal. Either way, Talinseh would, at the least, lose trade with the north, trade we desperately rely on to survive. Even now, with trade interrupted, members of the council have begun to feel it in dwindled profits. All, that is, save for Histarial who seems to be doing better than ever."

"This all sounds terrible, Clare, really," Dannen said. "But I don't see what I'm supposed to do about it."

"Even though the High Justice's investigations turned up with nothing," she answered, "it's clear Histarial is being manipulated, though by who or what I cannot say. Quite simply, I need you to sneak into his house and figure out what he's up to."

Dannen laughed. "Oh, is that all? Sure, why not? While I'm at it, maybe I'll solve that whole world peace problem." When she only stared at him, her expression unchanging, Dannen blinked. "Wait a minute. You're serious."

"I am," she agreed.

"Look, Clare," he said, "I'd like to help you, really, but I'm not a thief or an assassin; I've got no talent for sneaking around, and somehow I doubt Histarial's going to be okay with me sneaking into his house, even if I did somehow manage to get in there."

"I imagine he'd torture you and eventually kill you," she agreed.

Dannen grunted. "You're not exactly selling me on it, Clare. Anyway, why don't you just send one of your men? The gods know you've got enough of them."

"I can't," she said. "The truth, Dannen, is that I can't trust them. After all, *someone* in my household is a traitor. Otherwise, the two assassination attempts never would have gotten as close as they did. I can't make you help, obviously, and I wouldn't even if I could. But Dannen...if Historial isn't stopped, it could spell the end of Talinseh. Not to mention that I'll be dead long before then. I've been lucky twice—I don't like my chances at being so a third time."

Dannen sighed. He had told himself so many times that being a hero was a thankless, often painful job—he had plenty of scars that went a good way toward proving it. His initial urge was to say no immediately, to tell Clare to find someone else, *anyone* else. The problem though, was that, if she was telling the truth, there *was* no one else. Yet even that wasn't what stopped his refusal. Instead, it was the fear in her eyes, fear he could never remember having seen before. "I'll think about it, alright? I'll go out tomorrow and take a look at this Historial's place, see if I can find a way in." A pretty much hopeless proposition as he knew nothing of sneaking into anywhere, but he'd do what he could.

"It has to be tonight," she said.

"What?"

She winced. "The Tribunal votes on whether or not to help Ufrith tomorrow. If that vote takes place, I fear Historial will win, and if he does..."

Dannen sighed again. "Calamity and ruin."

She gave a slight smile. "Yes."

"Clare, I—"

"I know what you're thinking, Dannen, and I know what I'm asking you to do sounds impossible, but listen, I have found a way in. That much I have been able to do. One of the guards at Historial's manor has a very particular condition, one which, with enough coin, makes him quite blind. He's your way in."

She said it as if he should be comforted, but Dannen was not. After all, he'd never had much of a problem finding his way into trouble. It was getting out that proved difficult. "I'm not—"

"For your trouble," she said, "I'm willing to pay you a thousand gold coins."

Dannen blinked. That was a lot of money. Far more than he'd ever been offered for a job before. Enough that he could live the rest of his life in relative, drunken comfort, if he so chose. Of course, it would be difficult to spend it from the grave.

"I would offer you more," she said, "but I simply don't have it. As I said, the recent trade troubles have been...problematic."

Dannen thought long and hard then. He wanted to help her, but there was no reasonable way he could say yes. After all, he already had one impossible task ahead of him. The last thing he needed was to take on another. Surely there would be some other way he could help her, could protect her, though he would never say as much, for Clare was far too proud, far too capable to ever feel as if she was being saved. It would have to be a no, the only reasonable response.

"Okay, Clare. I'll help you."

The words were out of his mouth before he realized it, making him wonder—not for the first time in his life—what sort of condition he had that made him take on jobs only a fool would accept. It seemed the only cure for this condition was an inevitable—and inevitably painful—death.

Her eyes widened in surprise. "You mean it?"

No. "Yes," he said again, consoling himself with the notion that at least his death wouldn't be at the hands of a necromancer who was all too likely to summon him back from the grave to become a zombie.

"Oh, Danny," she said softly, and there were tears in her eyes again, but this time tears of relief. "Thank you."

Now that the decision had been made, Dannen didn't bother fighting it or worrying over it. He only nodded. "My pleasure, Clare." He rose. "I'll go get Fedder and—"

She winced. "It's better if you don't."

"Eh?" he asked. Fedder might drive him insane at the best of times, but he had been counting on the mage and his abilities—both physical as well as magical—to give him an edge and, more importantly, to keep such edges from his own throat.

"Well," she said, clearing her throat, "as I told you, this has to be kept quiet. We have to be subtle, for whether he agrees with Historial or not, the High Justice will not condone anyone making a move on a member of the Tribunal. He would be forced to act and, forgive me, Fedder is many things, but subtle is not among them."

Dannen sighed. There was no arguing with that. Fedder was about as subtle as an executioner's axe. "Alright." He rose, stretching. "When do I leave?"

"Everything should be ready in a few hours. There are just one or two things I want to see to first. In the meantime, you're welcome to meet up with Fedder and your new friend, relax and have a drink or two, on the house, of course. Or maybe get some rest, if you'd rather."

Just then, rest was just about the furthest thing from Dannen's mind, and he knew from experience that even had he an entire night to sleep, he'd only spend it tossing and turning, going over, in his mind, the thousands of ways the next day could see him dead. But he only nodded. "Very well." He met her eyes then. "It was good to see you again, Clare," he said. Maybe he would change his mind about that if he ended up with a sword in his guts in the next few hours, but just then, he meant it.

"It was good to be seen, Danny," she said, smiling.

He nodded, started to turn away then glanced back. "If something happens to me, could you...I mean, I dragged Fedder here and without someone to talk some sense into him, he's liable to—"

She smiled. "I'll look after him, Danny. You have my word."

He grunted. "Thanks, Clare." He turned away again then paused as she spoke.

"Danny? Remember, how I said I asked you here for two reasons?"

"I remember," he said, wondering what other terrible thing she might have brought him here for.

"Well," she said, and there was a seductive quality to her voice that sent a tingle up his spine, "I think it's time we talked about the second one. Why don't you turn around?"

His heart hammering in his chest, he did. The dress, which had so elegantly and temptingly hugged Clarissa's curves, wasn't doing so any longer. Instead, it lay puddled at her feet, and she stood completely naked, eyeing him meaningfully before glancing at the divan on which they'd sat. Whatever else the years had done to them both, they had taken away none of her beauty, a beauty which had always left him a little breathless, feeling dizzy and lightheaded.

She smiled, beckoning him with a finger, and he did the only thing he could do, the only reasonable thing. He went to her.

CHAPTER SEVEN

An hour later, Dannen found himself following one of Clarissa's men down a dark city street. At least it wasn't the same young man who had taken such an instant dislike to him. This man was older with a beard shot through with gray and seemed content to walk in silence, answering all of Dannen's questions with monosyllables that either meant he had no interest in talking, or that he wasn't much of a conversationalist. Normally, Dannen would have been glad for that. After all, everyone dealt with danger differently, and Dannen had watched its approach enough to know he was of the sort who liked silence when he felt death near. He would have liked to think it was because he had a stoic outlook, but the truth was he'd always been far too concentrated on not shitting himself to carry on a normal conversation like some he had known.

Now, though, he felt differently. True, he was going into mortal danger, would likely end the day dead or wishing he was, but he had spent the last hour or so in pleasant company with Clarissa, eagerly renewing an acquaintance from his past, and he felt good. Despite everything he had been through in the last few days and everything he was preparing to face, his mind was filled with a sort of soft, comfortable muzziness, his body feeling light and lethargic and numb all at the same time, and he wanted to talk, wanted to share those feelings with someone else.

Clarissa's man was having none of it though, and while he didn't scowl or say anything insulting like the other guard had, after the fourth or fifth time the man shut down Dannen's attempts at conversation he began to get the impression that the guard hated him just as much, in his own way, as the other. Not exactly a comfort, that, considering that he had plenty of things to worry about without having to concern himself with the trustworthiness of those meant to be his allies.

Walking in silence, he was surprised to realize he missed Fedder. The man might be a death sentence in boots, might enjoy fighting to a degree that was unhealthy for anybody except maybe himself, but Dannen had to admit he was a damn fine guy to have a drink with. *He* would have seen quickly enough what Dannen had been about, would have made some comment just funny and just crass enough for Dannen to be forced to pretend wasn't funny for fear laughing would give Fedder permission to be even worse in the future.

But it wasn't just the Firemaker's way of understanding him at a glance, wasn't just their history as, if not friends, certainly regular companions, that made him miss the man's company. Whatever else he was, the Firemaker was a powerful mage, and Dannen had long since lost count of the number of times he had saved his life. Of course, more often than not, the mage had also been the one who put it in danger in the first place, usually by challenging whoever happened by to a fight for no other reason than that he enjoyed it, so maybe that balanced out in the end.

But the Firemaker was not with him, nor was the girl, Mariana, who based on what Dannen had seen would have been far more suited to a task such as this than he would ever be. They were both still safely ensconced in Clarissa's personal tavern, their feet propped up on the table, each with a foaming ale in hand. At least, that was where they had been when Dannen left, and if the mage had his way, Dannen suspected they wouldn't be roused from their spots until long after his own funeral had come and gone.

Mostly, though, these were just distracted thoughts, flitting through his mind before it returned to thinking about Clarissa's divan, soft and warm, of how she had looked in the candlelight, how she had *felt*. Beautiful, soft and yielding, but at the same time, firm, challenging.

Focus, he told himself. As nice as it would be to get lost in the memory, in the smell of her—lavender—he knew he had more pressing concerns, concerns which, should he not give them his full attention, might well make themselves known by ripping a hole in him. At least the streets were quiet...or appeared to be. Which, of course, would have been a dubious comfort in any city as empty streets, in Dannen's opinion, often meant no one else was foolish enough to go traveling down them, likely because criminals lurked in the shadowed alleyways. But if any city was built to put a man at unease, surely it must be Talinseh, the Assassin City. After all, just because a man didn't see the knife didn't mean it wasn't sharp. Assassins, as a general rule, didn't challenge a man face to face before they killed him, preferring to take him by surprise so that one step he was still on the street, and the next he was strolling into the land of the dead without ever noticing the passage between.

"How much farther?" Dannen asked, glancing at his silent companion and realizing the pleasant feeling he'd left Clarissa's with was well and truly gone now, banished by his own morbid thoughts.

"Not long," the man grunted back, the most he'd said in one go since they'd left.

Dannen was about to ask him what exactly *that* was supposed to mean when his escort lifted his head a fraction, indicating a fifteen-foot-high wall surrounding a massive house. "There."

Unlike Clarissa's, this structure *did* look like a house and not a castle, though admittedly it was the largest house Dannen had ever seen, dwarfing even the giant homes around it. They had come at it from the side, so the property's gate was not visible from where they stood—probably just as well as they might have grown suspicious had they seen Dannen gazing at the tall walls in quiet panic, wondering why an innocent man would look as if he expected those walls to stretch out and swallow him whole.

"That's the place?" he whispered.

The man grunted. "That's it. Good luck." He started down the street, and Dannen grabbed his arm.

"What do you mean, 'good luck'? How am I supposed to get in there?"

His escort blinked at him as if he was insane. "You'll have to climb the wall."

"Climb the—" Dannen cut off, struggling to keep himself calm. He wasn't sure what he'd expected when Clarissa had told him she had a way inside, but this hadn't been it. He took a slow, deep breath, pinching the bridge of his nose between a thumb and forefinger. "And what if someone comes down the street while I'm at it?" he asked.

"Well…" the man said slowly, "then they'll probably see you. Oh, and best go in about midway on the side there."

"Why is that?"

The man shrugged. "Well, on account of that's where the guard Lady Clarissa paid is stationed. The others'd probably be a mite upset, they see you climbin' over. Liable to hurt you."

"Your concern for my welfare is heartening," Dannen said, feeling decidedly lightheaded.

The guard nodded, apparently incapable of discerning sarcasm. He turned, starting away, before pausing again. "Oh, I almost forgot. Before you go over the wall, you need to make a nightingale call."

"Wait, what?"

"You know," the man said, "so he'll know it's you climbin' over the wall. Just make a call like a nightingale. That's the signal."

Dannen could only stare at the man. *"What?"*

"What is it, you mean?" his escort asked. "A bird, I think."

"Okay," Dannen said, gritting his teeth. "So what the fuck does a nightingale sound like?

The guard shrugged. "I have no idea."

Dannen stared at him for several seconds, feeling as if he were in a dream, but no, that couldn't be it. The sort of wild shit-yourself terror he felt now would have woken him long ago. His escort, though, only nodded, seemingly unaware of Dannen's incredulity.

"Well?" he demanded. *"Shouldn't* you?"

The soldier looked at him puzzled. "Why? I'm not the one climbing over the wall."

Dannen didn't think of himself as a violent man. True, there were forty or so years of his life that could argue that point, probably win it too, but *he'd* never thought it, and as much violence as he'd taken part in, he'd rarely, if ever, enjoyed it. But he was considering violence just then. Considered it for quite a bit of time, long enough for the guard to clear his throat. "Well," the man said, "guess I'll be off then."

Dannen watched him go, his hands working at his sides, hands that, just then, would have been happy to be wrapped around the guard's throat. But in a few more seconds the man was gone, and Dannen was alone, trying to think of how a nightingale sounded. He knew a lot of calls. He knew just what sort of timbre was in a troll's voice when it was intent on crushing a man to a bloody pulp. Knew, too, what an ogre sounded like when it charged. He knew the sound just about every creature made when it had killing on its mind. The problem, then, was that so far as he knew, nightingales were rarely homicidal.

He turned back to the wall. It had appeared fifteen feet tall when first he'd looked at it, but just then, it looked about as high as a mountain. "Fuck," he said, meaning it. He glanced around the street, making sure no one was coming—not that it would make a difference, for just like a turtle looking both ways before crossing a busy street, such a precaution was largely useless. Even assuming, of course, that he somehow, despite all odds, managed to haul his ass up the wall in the first place.

He walked toward the wall, considering whether he should pretend to be doing something else, in case one of the guard patrols he'd seen happened by, but didn't bother. He was drenched in sweat, nervous, and he supposed probably looking just about as guilty as any man *could* look. Still, he made it to the wall without incident and stared up at it.

Despite the danger of being discovered, he stood that way for several seconds, thinking. Bad thoughts mostly. But when the wall refused to shrink to accommodate him, he sighed, bit back a curse, and grabbed onto some small indentions where the stone had crumbled away. He thought—and in many ways, *hoped*—he'd never be able to make it up the wall. Then, through no fault of his own, he would be forced to go back to Clarissa and tell her that he had tried and failed. Unfortunately, he *could* manage it, just so long as he didn't mind scraping his fingers raw on the rough stone, not to mention chafing his unfortunately protruding stomach where it pressed against the wall.

After an interminable time spent gasping and hissing and sweating, he made it to the top of the wall. He lay there hanging over the top, his chest heaving, his arms and legs—not accustomed to such abuse for several years—aching and throbbing. Then, when the thought of moving another inch became slightly more appealing than lying there until guards found him and executed him for attempting to break into the home of a member of the Tribunal, he started to climb over. He had one leg draped over the wall and hesitated as he realized that, in his exertions, he'd completely forgotten about the nightingale's call.

"Shit," he muttered quietly. He peered into the shadowed grounds on the inside of the wall but could see little in the darkness save for the vague outlines of plants and bushes. The guard—or guards—could have been stationed anywhere, and he would have had no chance of seeing them while they, aided by the pale light of the moon, would have been hard-pressed not to notice him sitting on the wall like a fool currently engaged in an elaborate form of suicide.

He cleared his throat. *"Coo-coo,"* he hissed. *"Coo-coo."* Then, for good measure, *"Nightingale."*

He waited for several seconds, expecting a crossbow bolt to flit out of the darkness and make a day already gone to shit just a little bit worse. When none did, he took a deep, ragged breath and began climbing down the other side of the wall. Or, at least, he meant to. What happened instead was that his foot—which he had carefully placed on the inside of the wall with the intent of working his way down—slipped. He had time enough to grunt in surprise and dismay—mostly dismay—before he fell to the earth below.

He lay there for some time, panting and hurting and expecting a crossbow bolt to lodge itself in some part of his anatomy. When none did, he sat up with a groan, and by the pale light of the moon saw that, for his troubles, he'd cut up his left hand fairly good, enough to set it bleeding.

Surprisingly, this made him feel a little better. After all, if this was as bad as it got, he could manage well enough. Losing a little bit of blood wasn't a big deal. Of course, losing a lot of it *was*, but there wasn't much point in worrying about that. Slowly, he rose to his feet, looking around, but could make out little except the shadowy outline of the garden's plants. He hesitated, suddenly unsure of what to do. Making it over the wall, after all, had been the first obstacle, one he had never really expected to conquer. Now, he had to find some way into the massive house, and if his escort had known what he was meant to do, the man had decided not to share it.

It wasn't as if he could just walk up to the front door and knock. He was still thinking about it when a shadow separated itself from the others. He couldn't make out much of the man's features. Partly, that was because of the darkness, but mostly it was because his eyes were trained on the iron tip of the crossbow bolt pointed at him, glinting with deadly promise. He tensed, preparing to dodge should he hear the release, knowing he'd be too slow, and thinking that out of all the things he'd survived, it was a damn shame that, in the end, he was doomed to die because of not knowing what a nightingale sounded like.

But instead of pulling the crossbow's release, the man grunted. "Took you long enough," he said in a whisper. "You're late."

There was a lot Dannen could have said to that, a lot he wanted to say, but since the man still held the crossbow trained on him, he thought politeness was the way to go. "Yeah, sorry about that. Been a little while since I climbed a wall and broke into someone's house. Bit out of practice." Well. Maybe not politeness, but his hand was smarting, his back aching, and it was the best he could manage just then.

The man grunted again. "This way and hurry. Won't be long 'til one of the patrols comes through."

Dannen didn't relish the idea of following a stranger with a crossbow into the darkness, but since he didn't much relish the idea of hanging around and getting a few new holes poked in him, he followed.

Torches were mounted in brackets around the house's perimeter, and as they drew closer, some of the gardens were revealed. Dannen knew little of the finer things, a bit cruel for a man who'd spent his life battling monsters, but like Clarissa, Tribune Histarial had chosen to flaunt his wealth, using it as a sort of weapon. There, though, the similarities ended, for while Dannen didn't know much about statues and fountains and all the rest, Clarissa's gardens—and home—had seemed somehow elegant, graceful, and if they were wealth used as a weapon, then it was a slim, sharp dagger. Meanwhile, Histarial used his wealth like a bludgeon, crude and gaudy but getting its point across as effectively as...well, a hammer to the head.

He thought about all of this but, mostly, he wondered how he ended up in these sorts of situations. Certainly, he didn't wake up every morning and start planning ways to die horribly. He'd heard people refer to others, sometimes, as "god-touched." The simple meaning was things always seemed to work out to their benefit. The kind of people who won more at dice or cards—or life, for that matter—than anyone could reasonably expect. He had decided long ago that he wasn't such a person, and nothing since then had changed his opinion. At least, if Dannen *was* god-touched, then he thought the god, whoever it was, must be a real bastard.

After a few minutes, the guard escorting him stepped out of the relative cover the gardens provided to one of the many torches bracketed against the house's wall. Dannen hesitated, knowing that the moment he moved into the torchlight he'd be visible to anybody happening to look in the direction of the house, and the guard turned back. "Come on."

Dannen didn't want to, but then his life had largely been made up of him doing things he didn't want—wrestling with a troll for the prize of continuing to breathe came to mind—so he did. Once he was beside him, the guard turned back to the torch and pulled it down with an audible *click*. Suddenly, part of the wall began to slide soundlessly away, revealing a small doorway.

"That's a damn fine trick," Dannen said.

"Hurry through," the guard said. "We're running out of time."

Dannen glanced through the doorway, but he could make out only darkness, thick and oppressive. With a sigh, he stepped through. "What's this here for, anyway?" he asked.

"Lord Historial deals with many people," the guard hissed, looking around, "and some of those people aren't the kind he wants to be seen walking out his front door, understand? Now, enough questions. I got paid good coin for this, but all the coin in the world ain't gonna stop Historial if he learns of it. Look here, it's Historial's study you'll be wantin'. If there's any dirt to be had, you'll find it there. He don't allow anybody in there, even cleans it himself. So what you'll do, you're gonna keep goin' straight for about a hunnerd feet. You'll come to an intersection then, listen close 'cause this is important. You're gonna want to—"

"*Bron!*" came a shout from nearby, somewhere within the gardens.

The guard tensed, his eyes going wide in the torchlight. "Shit on it, we're out of time. Make sure, you get caught, you don't know m—"

"*Bron, where are you, damnit!?*"

"Damn it all. You've got an hour, no more, understand? Any longer, you're on your own," he said, reaching for the torch.

"Wait a minute," Dannen said, "at the interse—" He cut off as the door slid shut in front of him, pitching him into absolute darkness.

"You've got to be shitting me," Dannen hissed, promising himself that, if he somehow managed to survive this, he was going to give Clarissa a piece of his mind.

"Just relax," he whispered to himself and that imagined self who would have likely suffered even worse if he'd shared his anger with Clarissa. He immediately regretted it, though, as his voice echoed hauntingly in the gloom. Sweat was beading on his forehead now, and Dannen squinted into the darkness. It did him no good, of course—pitch black was pitch black no matter how much squinting a man did—and creeping fingers of dread began to scrape up Dannen's spine. He wasn't afraid of the dark, not exactly, but anybody who'd seen the sorts of things he had, ghouls and the undead and worse, knew that it wasn't the dark that killed you. It was the things that lurked inside it.

With no other options, he started forward, trailing one hand along the hard-packed earthen wall while holding the other in front of him. It was silent in the tunnels, the only sound that of his ragged breaths. The darkness felt thick and oppressive, so heavy he fancied he might choke on it. It seemed he traveled that way for a lifetime, but could only have been a few minutes before the hand that had been trailing the wall touched nothing, and his leading hand fell on a wall in front of him.

It had to be the intersection the guard had spoken of, then. Not that such knowledge helped him overly much since the man hadn't managed to spare the second it would have taken him to tell Dannen which direction to go. He glanced in both directions, trying to find some indication of where he should go, but there was nothing. Only the darkness and the stillness and his ragged breaths.

Others, in such a situation, might have spent interminable minutes in that darkness, thinking, trying to imagine what the guard—apparently by the name of Bron—might have been about to say, thinking, likely rightly so, that their life depended on them getting it right. Dannen, though, had been in such situations before, more than he liked to consider sober, and he was alive today largely due to luck. And if those experiences had taught him anything, it was that often the ones who survived weren't the ones who made the right choice, just the ones who made the first one. He took the right path.

He walked on for several minutes. Then, he thought he detected what might have been the glow of firelight in the distance down the tunnel. It was hard to be sure, and he thought it just as likely that his mind was playing tricks on him.

But after another minute or two, the presence of the light could not be questioned any longer, for he could see the sullen red glow of a torch or a fire casting shadows on the wall. Shadows which seemed to dance and caper at his approach. Did a guard stand there with a torch in hand, a last line of defense should any intruder get into the tunnels? There was no way to know, no way to loop around behind him, if indeed that's where the light came from. There was no way but forward. So Dannen walked.

As he drew nearer to the light, he saw that the tunnel opened up into a large room, and he put his back up against the tunnel wall near the corner, peering inside, and realized immediately that he had taken the wrong path, after all. Dannen hadn't seen a lot of studies in his time, never having been the type of man—or having spent much time with such a man—who owned a study or would have known what to do with one, if he had. But he *had* seen a lot of dungeons, and so it was no difficult task to recognize the room he stared on as such, an endeavor aided in no small degree by the cell sitting in one corner of the room, a cell in which a figure in rags knelt. His hands were held in front of him in what might have been prayer, but Dannen couldn't tell for sure, for the figure's back was to him.

Dannen didn't move, remaining crouched low, listening for any sound that might betray a guard. He shot a glance around the corner, taking in the room. It didn't take long. There were three cells against one wall, all of which were empty save for the one holding the praying man. In the middle of the room was a wooden table, its surface covered with several suspicious, crimson stains. Several metallic tools lay on a leather roll atop the table. On the other side of the room opposite the cells was a bookshelf containing—perhaps unsurprisingly—a few books, but mostly jars of transparent liquid in which floated fleshy bits Dannen did his best not to identify.

Not just a dungeon then, but a torture chamber and one any self-respecting crime boss would have been happy to have. *Five bedrooms, three kitchens, oh, and a thinking man's torture room, the smell of piss and despair already included for the discerning master criminal.*

Dannen had never met Historial before, wouldn't have known him if he'd passed him in the street, save for the description Clarissa had given him before he'd left, but he didn't like the man, anyway. The room was enough to tell the story that "Hisser," as Clarissa called him, was one of those individuals who wasn't satisfied with simply killing his enemies, but who, instead, made a game of seeing just how much pain, emotional and physical, he could inflict on them before they were allowed to die. A man hungry for power then, and such a man, Dannen knew from experience, would do anything, would sacrifice anyone, to get it.

Staring at that room, smelling the stale odors of despair and blood, Dannen started to believe maybe Clare wasn't just being paranoid, after all. Maybe Historial was up to something, after all. Certainly, such a man who would have a room like this wouldn't be opposed to crossing any line to get what he wanted. In fact, from the looks of things, it was a line he'd crossed before, many times with many unfortunate souls like the man still kneeling in the cage.

Dannen felt for the prisoner, but he made no move to release him. After all, even if he had, what would they have done? It wasn't as if the man could just traipse out of the house. How far would he—and Dannen—make it before they were cut down? Or, more likely, brought back here to be educated on the precise use of some of the instruments lying on the table? No, better for both of them if he pretended he'd never seen him and, with any luck, the man would remain too engrossed in his prayers—if that's what they were—to notice Dannen crouched at the corner of the room.

He frowned, considering his options. He had chosen the wrong direction. He could backtrack through the tunnels, taking the other path, but the guard, Bron, had warned him that he only had an hour window in which to accomplish the impossible task he had signed on for. Once again, Dannen was left wondering why he had signed on for the damn thing at all, thinking that the way Clarissa's dress had looked on her—and the way it had looked *off* her— might have had more than a little to do with that.

Focus, he told himself.

Yes, he could backtrack, but he would waste precious time in doing so and he didn't see how that would improve his situation much. After all, Bron had been less than forthcoming with what Dannen might expect anyway, so either way, he would be traveling blind. The difference being that, should he backtrack, it would take a big bite out of the forty-five minutes or so he reckoned he had left, further increasing his chances of ending the night as a corpse.

No, it was better to push on. After all, the dungeon would have an exit too, and there didn't appear to be any guard inside the room, at least. There was a staircase leading up to a door, which was good. What was slightly less good was that, as a general rule, people didn't leave dungeons unguarded. If those tasked with making sure its prisoners stayed prisoners weren't inside the dungeons themselves, then it was all too likely they were posted outside the closed door.

They would no doubt be shocked—and then murderous—to discover someone trying to sneak out of the dungeons they were intended to guard, might even be moved to draw the weapons they no doubt carried sheathed at their sides and make their displeasure known so that there could be no mistaking it.

Still, Dannen thought it was also possible there would only be a single guard, and even if there *were* two, he wasn't exactly spoiled for choice. If he moved quickly, he could deal with such men.

Or so he told himself as he took a slow, deep breath and stepped into the room.

"She said you'd come," a voice said, and so unexpected was the sound of it as it shattered the silence that Dannen let out a decidedly unmanly squeak of shock, his right hand, guided by years of instincts honed in countless fights for his life, reaching up and behind his shoulder only to be reminded that the sword hilt it sought was not there.

He spun, scanning the dungeon for the speaker, checking the stairs, and then the tunnel behind him, for the voice had echoed in the stillness of the dungeon, had seemed to come from all around him, and he could not pinpoint its origin. But despite his sudden certainty that he had stumbled into a trap like a hungry hare and that he was surrounded, there was no one there. Frowning, his heart hammering in his chest, he glanced at the cell. The figure kneeling there didn't seem to have moved.

"What's that?" Dannen asked in a whisper.

The figure glanced over his shoulder, revealing a youthful face that Dannen would have guessed was less than twenty-five years old, at least before he saw the man's eyes. The irises were pale gray, so pale as to appear almost white, as if he had no pupils at all. Yet there was something in them that spoke of wisdom and suffering and an understanding that usually only came as a product of that suffering. They were the eyes of an old man, one who had seen the worst and best the world had to offer, and who expected to see more of both.

"She said you would come," the man repeated, and although his face was bruised where he had been beaten and he was stuck in a cell, he did not sound afraid. If anything, the prisoner sounded annoyed. "I didn't believe her and now she gloats."

Dannen didn't like the sound of that at all. "Who said I'd come?"

The man rose slowly as if he were in no hurry, which considering that there were iron bars between him and anywhere he might be in a hurry *to,* made sense. What didn't though, was that he apparently hadn't been praying after all. Instead, his cupped hands held some sort of rodent.

"She did," the man said, raising his hands the slightest amount.

Dannen frowned, deciding that while Historial might be an evil, ambitious bastard, he might have been right to lock this man up. "The rat?"

There followed a steady stream of un-rat-like chittering from the cell, and the young man cleared his throat, looking slightly embarrassed. "*Relax,*" he whispered, "and no, there'll be no smiting today. I told you about that. You can't just go around—"

"Wait a minute," Dannen said, "are you talking to it?"

The man glanced away from the creature and back up at Dannen. "Yes," he said as if there were nothing unusual at all about a man talking to a rodent.

Dannen had seen a few druids in his day—not many, more enough to know that they were, without fail, pompous old bastards, fond of the color green, who spent most of their time hugging trees or kissing dirt. He had never once, truth be told, seen a druid that didn't have gray hair and dressed in what were little better than rags, and it was unlikely that he was seeing one now. More likely, the man was just crazy. "Sure," Dannen said, "anyway..."

"She's a squirrel," the man said as if in answer to a question Dannen hadn't—and had never intended—on asking. There was another bout of chittering, and the man sighed long-sufferingly. "Well. A squirrel god, anyway."

"A...squirrel god," Dannen said slowly.

The man smiled. "That's right." The creature left his hand, scampering up his arm to rest on his shoulder, and the light struck it better, revealing that it was, at least, a squirrel as the man had claimed. A squirrel that, had Dannen not known better, seemed to be scowling at him. The stranger reached a grimy hand through the slits in the bars, offering it to Dannen. "Her name is Maela. I'm Tesler."

"And I'm leaving," Dannen said. "Good luck with..." He paused, gesturing vaguely at the torture instruments on the table. "You know. Everything."

The man beamed as if he didn't have a care in the world. "Kind of you to say so."

Yup, Dannen thought, *crazy as a loon, no doubt of that.* Still, he had more important things to worry about than a madman locked in a dungeon and a squirrel he pretended was a god. Very real things that were most certainly *not* pretend, things like how his chances of surviving the night diminished with each second he squandered talking.

He started toward the stairs.

"It's locked," said a voice from behind him.

Dannen ignored the prisoner, trying the latch to find that indeed it was locked. Still, that wasn't the end of the world. While he'd been telling the truth when he told Clarissa he wasn't a thief or an assassin, he had spent some fair amount of time around both—never by choice—and had picked up a few useful things along the way. Things like how to pick a lock. He examined it carefully. He was by no means an expert, but it seemed simple enough. Histarial or whoever had commissioned the door to be made on his behalf had been satisfied—rightly so, as far as Dannen could see—that the iron cages would be more than enough to keep whatever prisoners he took from escaping. Bad luck for the prisoners, maybe, but good luck for Dannen.

The problem, of course, was that since he *wasn't* a thief, he also wasn't in the habit of carrying around the tools necessary to pick such a lock. He stood there for a moment, frowning, then an idea struck him and he hurried back to the table and the torture implements waiting there. He took two with sharp, pointed ends—the purpose of which he pointedly tried not to think about—and made his way back to the door, slipping the tool into the latch.

It had been a long time since he'd tried to pick a lock, and he was out of practice. He'd never been good at it in the first place, and he was still working on it when the prisoner cleared his throat behind him.

Dannen ignored it just as he tried to ignore the ache in his left hand as he continued to manipulate the metal tools. He found the locking mechanism with the tip of the tool and was trying to move it when the prisoner cleared his throat again, loud enough to startle him, and he lost it. "Damnit," Dannen growled, turning to glare at the cell and its occupant. "Look, man, I get it, alright? Maybe you didn't see being locked in a cage as the way your day would turn out. Well, if it helps, I didn't plan on being here either, but here we are, each of us with what appears to be busy nights ahead, so if it's all the same to you, I'd like to get on with it in silence."

"That wasn't me," the man said.

Dannen frowned. "Really? Who was it then? Let me guess—the squirrel."

The man got a curious look on his face. "As a general rule, squirrels don't clear their throats and when they do, it's certainly not so loud. No, it was them." He pointed.

Dannen rolled his eyes, following the man's finger to the tunnel entrance, then froze as he saw two men standing there. One was cloaked in shadow and so Dannen could make out nothing of his features, but the second moved forward into the light. The newcomer appeared to be in his fifties, and he wore expensive dark blue silk trousers and shirt, but it wasn't his clothes or the small smirk on his face which struck Dannen the most. It was his bearing. He stood confidently, arrogantly, as if he owned the place. Then, it struck Dannen that the man did, in fact, own the place. "Tribune Histarial."

"Ah," the man said, "it seems that you, stranger, know my name. Or, I suppose, stranger might not be the correct term. After all, I know you as well, Dannen Ateran."

Dannen felt a sinking feeling in his stomach. Up to this point, he'd been nurturing the hope of barreling past the newcomers—one of whom still lurked in the shadows—and escaping, leaving them thinking they had interrupted some sneak thief at his work. Admittedly, it would have had to have been the world's worst or most desperate thief as it was unlikely a man would hide his valuables in his already hidden dungeon. Now, though, it was clear the man knew who he was, so even if Dannen *did* escape, he and his companions would only be hunted down by an army of assassins, and whatever else the ostentatious gardens had done, they'd been proof the man could hire as many as needed to finish the job without making even a small dent in his fortune.

"How do you know my name?"

"Oh, you might be surprised about the things I know, Dannen Ateran. I know that you were once a hero famous for his savagery in battle." He paused, eyeing Dannen up and down. "Admittedly, that one I find a little difficult to believe. Still, I suppose age is kinder to some than others."

Dannen frowned, feeling defensive. "I had a big breakfast."

"No doubt," the stranger answered dryly.

Dannen cleared his throat. "Alright, look, Histarial. I'm sure you've got important things to be about, and so do I"—*not dying mostly.* "I haven't taken anything, so how about I leave, you get on with..." He paused, glancing at the prisoner in the cell. "Well, whatever you've got planned for your evening, and we can call it square, how'd that be? Sorry, fella," he muttered to the prisoner.

"I completely understand," the prisoner answered—crazy enough, it seemed to Dannen, that the man still must not realize what awaited him. Which, Dannen supposed, wasn't the worst thing. If the man was lucky, maybe he still wouldn't know what was happening until the torturer started doing his work.

"Wait," Historial said, "you want to *leave?* Oh, tut, tut," he went on, shaking his head, "but you just got here. I'm sorry to say that I insist that you stay. Besides..." He smiled widely, "Another of my guests has been dying to have a...conversation with you."

The second figure chose that moment to step from the shadows, and Dannen was treated to a sight of the scowling man from Clarissa's home, Palder. Though, it had to be said that he was not scowling now but smiling, an expression that held no humor, only malicious content and expectation.

"*You,*" Dannen said, surprised despite himself. He had never doubted, of course, that Palder would have happily chopped him apart, limb by limb, but from what little he'd seen of the man he'd seemed to have demonstrated a fervent loyalty to Clarissa.

"Surprised?" the man said.

"B-but," Dannen said, "Clarissa—"

"Don't you speak her name," the man sneered. "You are not worthy of it."

"And you are?" Dannen countered. "Look, I don't know what this guy has promised you, Palder, but it seems pretty clear to me you've betrayed your mistress by being here."

The guardsman's face twisted in a wild mixture of hate and rage, and Dannen realized, at that moment, that whatever else he was, Palder was insane. "*She* betrayed *me,*" he growled in a voice trembling with rage. "I-I would have done *anything* for her, would have completed any task, killed anybody she wished."

"Well, sure," Dannen said, "nothing more romantic than a good murder, is there?"

Palder bared his teeth. "I would have given her anything," he snarled, "but she chose *you* instead. A man who, it's clear, is far past his prime and the stories told about him. Even though, having met you, I do not doubt that all those stories are lies, ones you likely concocted to demand a higher price for your *help. You* are a charlatan."

"And you're a traitor," Dannen said, anger working its way past his fear. "Gods, man, Clare *trusted* you."

Palder's face twisted again, his lips and nose seeming to writhe as if alive. "T-this is *your* fault. Before you showed up, she was beginning to understand, beginning to appreciate me, the things I do. Then, you came along, and she...she..."

"Enough," Historial said in a bored tone. "Time is slipping away, and there is much to be done. By the time this night is over," he went on, favoring Dannen with an arrogant smile, "the Tribunal will, I'm afraid, be forced to replace one of its dearly departed members."

Up to this point, Dannen's thoughts had been jumbled and confused as his mind tried to catch up to what was happening, but now he understood. Palder, out of jealousy, had betrayed Clarissa to her rival, and with his help, Historial would have little problem sneaking his way past her defenses. And Clarissa, for all her intelligence and wisdom, for all her cleverness, would never see it coming, not from the guardsman.

The thought of it, of these two conspiring against Clarissa, of Palder betraying her trust, made Dannen angry. A deep well of anger surged inside him, anger at this man who would, out of jealousy, conspire to kill one of the finest people Dannen had ever known. His anger, his fury was a wild beast raging inside of him, one which he had spent his entire life trying to leash. Sometimes, the beast was content to pretend the leash was too strong and it was well and truly contained, but times like these reminded him it was just a fiction, just a lie he told himself to get from one day to the next.

Dannen could feel that beast, its anger, now, could feel it rising from its slumber and baring its teeth, its nose catching the scent of something it did not like. "Shit—" he began. He had time enough to utter the word, but no more than that, no time to try to talk the beast down, and even if he had it would have been useless, for the beast, once roused, could be put down again only with blood. The beast roared, lunging forward and snapping the chain with which Dannen had sought to bind it, and Dannen, as always, was carried along with it.

***

When he came back to himself, he was standing at the mouth of the tunnel leading out of the dungeon, his chest heaving. He tasted blood in his mouth. His hands, currently clenched into fists, ached terribly, and it took him several painstaking seconds to unfurl his fingers, so tight had they been clenched. He was standing over a pile of soiled rags.

He stared at those rags confused, feeling as if they were a puzzle he might figure out if only he looked enough. Then, the sound of running from farther down the tunnel drew his attention, snapping him out of the numb, confused haze that often came over him after his anger had its way. Footsteps, somewhere in the darkness, and suddenly Dannen remembered where he was, remembered *who* he was. Footsteps, but they were not coming closer, as he would have expected had the guards been called. Instead, they were dwindling farther away down the tunnel.

Dannen still gazed at the pile of clothes at his feet, barely visible in the orange glow of the lantern on the table deeper in the dungeon, and the light moved in such a way that, for a moment, that pile was revealed. He felt his stomach crawl into his throat, threatening to spew its contents out, and he fought it down with a will. Not clothes, after all. The pile before him, hardly distinguishable as once having been a man, had shown him that much. Blood and bone and a face. One he recognized as Clarissa's man, Palder. Which, he supposed, made it obvious who the footsteps receding down the tunnel must belong to.

Histarial. The man must have taken off while Dannen dealt with the traitor, fleeing down the tunnels instead of facing the beast inside Dannen, the one which had chosen to relax once more, slipping its neck into the waiting leash and pretending it might be bound, might be controlled.

Dannen had seen the results of his anger before, so he was unsurprised the man had chosen to run. Dannen, too, would have chosen to flee from his anger long ago, had he been able. But the Tribune would cause him problems just the same. For one, he would most certainly call more guards to him, guards tasked with the job of rooting out the intruder and putting an end to the threat he represented. And what then? When Dannen was nothing more than a cooling corpse lying on the ground? Well, then Dannen knew Historial would get on with the other activities he'd planned for the night, namely killing Clarissa and thereby ridding himself of his strongest opposition on the Tribunal and ensuring that King Ufrith of the North would not receive the aid he sought.

An occurrence which could likely doom all the north, and that just the beginning, for the north was a powerful country, and if it had been so thoroughly brought low as Clarissa had seemed to indicate, then the south must also fear. So many possibilities...an entire world could be doomed, and Dannen realized that, for the moment at least, all of those untold thousands who might perish in the future, all those northerners fighting for their lives, men and women he had never met and likely never would, were depending on him, though they knew it not. And the sounds of the Tribune's receding footsteps were the doleful ringing of carrion bells announcing the death of those unknown men and women.

Dannen could have forgotten it, could have found his way out of the house and tried to make a run for it. Certainly it would have been the safest thing, likely the smartest thing. In the end, though, he made his decision and ran after those receding footsteps, meaning to stop him—not for the world and the thousands which populated it. That was too big a thing for a man to lift and examine and understand. No, he chased after Historial not for thousands, but for one, for Clarissa. The woman who had, according to her own words, loved him, though he had not deserved it, the woman who had always been there for him, even though he'd been too foolish to realize it at the time. She had helped him, done so without complaint, and he knew, would do so again if she could. And so, he would help her, or he would die trying. He could not be a hero, as Perandius wanted, wasn't cut out for it—he'd learned that long ago. He could not be a savior who might save the world but maybe, just maybe, he could be a friend, one who might save a single woman.

So he charged down the tunnel, feeling a momentary pang for the prisoner he was abandoning to his fate, but no more than that. After all, Clare was a friend, had once been more than that, and the stranger was just a stranger, a crazy man who he had never met and likely never would again—hopefully, in truth, considering that the man was clearly insane.

The Tribune, who had appeared to be at least in his fifties, was surprisingly fast, and Dannen still had not managed to gain any ground by the time he reached the intersection. He hesitated, listening intently, but he could hear no sounds to indicate where the Tribune had gone. "*Shit,*" Dannen said. He would have to guess, that was all, and considering where his last guess in this exact intersection had taken him, he wasn't keen on it.

He was still trying to decide what to do when there was the sound of flint being struck and light bloomed in the tunnel. After several minutes spent in darkness, Dannen winced, covering his eyes, and when he looked again he wished he'd kept them covered. Soldiers stood in both other tunnel entrances, three at each side. He knew they were soldiers for the same reason he knew they weren't his biggest fans—the swords they all held at the ready— and like children with new toys they all looked thrilled at the prospect of putting them to use.

One group separated, opening up a space in the middle through which Historial walked. The man looked calm and collected, as if he hadn't spent the last few minutes sprinting full-out. Meanwhile, Dannen's breath was rasping in his lungs like it had a personal vendetta it was meaning to address, and he took the opportunity to lean his back against the wall, putting his hands on his knees.

"You should not have followed me, Mister Ateran," the Tribune said. Had Dannen not known better he would have had a difficult time reconciling the arrogant, pompous looking man in front of him with the same one who'd been sprinting in fear only moments ago. "Now, it seems, you have gotten yourself into trouble."

"Yeah, maybe you're right, maybe I shouldn't have followed you," Dannen agreed. "But truth be told, I'm not sure I've ever been out of trouble enough to be able to get into it."

The older man gave him a small smile. "Quite. Anyway, there are things I must be about tonight—rivals to deal with and all that. I hope you'll understand if I cut this short."

Six armed men standing in the hallway, and judging by the Tribune's eyes which twinkled with malicious amusement, he didn't think it a coincidence that the man had chosen to use the word "cut." He considered turning and fleeing through the tunnel he'd come down but decided against it. He was already out of breath, a painful stitch in his side. If he ran, the men would catch him, there was no question of that. Dannen didn't have much pride left—a youth spent trying to be a hero had done a pretty fine job of beating it out of him—but he didn't like the idea of being cut down from behind.

So, he did not run, only widened his legs into a fighting stance. Not that it would matter. There had been a time, once, when he might have taken on six men and won, assuming they were conveniently lazy, unskilled guardsmen, but that time was long ago. He was older now, fatter, and if he was going to die—which seemed pretty well certain—he'd just as soon catch his breath first.

"I must admit," the Tribune went on despite his words about keeping it short, "the violence you demonstrated on poor Palder was...effective. And more than a little unfortunate. He was not an easy resource to cultivate, and I had planned on making use of him in the future. You spoiled that for me, and I will make sure you suffer for that."

"I can see you're all tore up about it," Dannen said, because it wasn't as if the man could kill him twice.

"Not very," the Tribune said, giving him a smirk. "Not as much, at least, as I imagine you might be at what I intend to do to your friend...what is it you call her? Ah yes, Clare. How quaint. Oh, I intend to have an *extremely* good time with her, Dannen Ateran. Of course, you won't be there to see it. But then, perhaps I might bring parts of you, your head, or your eyes, maybe. I think I would enjoy seeing her face when she saw what accepting her request for help cost you."

Dannen was angry at that, but it was only normal anger, the kind felt all around the world by all the injustices that crowded in around them, refusing to be ignored. He would have been okay, then, to lose himself in the rage that sometimes overtook him, but the beast, it seemed, was weary from its activities of the day, and refused his prompting. It was too bad, he thought. It would have been good to have that anger for this last part.

"Well, come on then, you fuckers," he said. "Let's get it done."

The soldiers glanced at their boss, waiting for permission, and Historial smiled. "Kill him quickly—we have a busy night ahead.

Palder might be dead, but the information he gave me regarding one Lady Clarissa is still very much alive."

The swordsmen didn't need any more permission than that. They started forward, clearly eager to carry out their orders. It was about that time that what sounded like the roar of a pissed-off bear shook the tunnel walls. Something barreled down the tunnel behind three of the soldiers, hitting them like a runaway carriage with a mean streak, and the men were sent hurtling through the air like dolls. Except, of course, that dolls didn't have bones to snap and break as they struck the hard-packed earthen walls as if hurtled by the vengeful swipe of a god. There were screams but not for long. A man didn't take the kind of hit those three did and still have the extra breath to scream. More likely, they didn't have any breath at all, because their limbs were splayed at angles nobody could endure without letting everyone in the world know about it. If, that was, they were alive to do so.

Two were completely still, but the third was moving, wriggling across the ground with the one arm that wasn't broken scraping at the dirt. Dannen couldn't imagine where the man thought to go, doubted he knew himself, and it didn't matter in any case, for the runaway carriage which had struck him—a carriage named, and this was the happiest Dannen had ever been to see him, Fedder the Firemaker—stepped over him and, without so much as a grunt, lifted him off the ground by the back of his shirt. The man let out what might have been the beginnings of a scream, but it was hard to tell for sure because the sound—and his face—were buried in the earthen wall a moment later.

The man, understandably, was still. Firemaker slung him into it once more for good measure then, apparently satisfied that his now nearly faceless opponent—or perhaps victim would have been more accurate—was no longer a threat, tossed him to the ground. He turned to Dannen, beaming a smile that, by some trick of the torchlight—or maybe just his personality—looked demonic. "It's rude to have a party without invitin' your friends, Butcher."

Dannen was having a hard time answering, was too busy looking at the three corpses, three corpses who, only seconds before, had been alive. He cleared his throat. "Hope you'll forgive me."

Firemaker's grin somehow managed to get even wider. "Well?" he said, turning to the remaining three soldiers who were now standing in front of Histarial. "Are we doing this or what?"

The soldiers all looked startled, though whether it was because they were only just recovering from the shock of seeing three of their number taken out of commission so quickly or at the realization that the man responsible for it was looking to pick a fight with them, Dannen couldn't have said. Not that it mattered much in either case, for the three remaining soldiers shared a glance, then as if on cue, turned and fled down the tunnel, apparently deciding that whatever the Tribune was paying them wasn't enough to cover getting in a life or death—likely death— fight with a giant who comes barreling out of the darkness and takes three of their companions apart the way another might take off his boots.

Dannen caught a momentary glimpse of Histarial baring his teeth in anger in the darkness, heard the man growling like some beast, then the torch, along with the soldier carrying it, disappeared around a corner of the tunnel at a run.

"You will suffer, Dannen Ateran," the Tribune said from somewhere in the pitch black, but Dannen couldn't have said where, for it seemed to him the voice came from all around him. "You will suffer as *she* will suffer. You have made an enemy of me, and there are few left alive who can claim as much. One, of course, I will deal with tonight, then I will make it my personal mission to—"

"Fedder," Dannen interrupted, tired of listening to the man drone on, "light."

"But Dannen," the giant said in a voice that was both embarrassed and reluctant at the same time, "surely there's anoth—"

"Now, Fedder."

The giant heaved a heavy sigh, and a moment later a bright white light bloomed in the darkness, suffusing their surroundings with a soft glow. The light revealed two things of note—one was that Firemaker had his hand raised in the air, palm up, and inside his hand was nestled what looked like a sphere of shifting light. The mage studied it with a slightly-disgusted expression on his face, clearly unhappy, as always, to have to cast his magic, magic that he had somehow decided long ago wasn't manly. But Fedder's complaints would have to wait, for the second thing Dannen noticed was more pressing, and it was the twisted, angry expression of the Tribune before he turned and fled down the tunnel.

Or, at least, tried to. No sooner had Historial taken a step than he—and Dannen—were surprised by a figure seeming to appear out of the edge of Firemaker's magical light, blocking Historial's path. At first, Dannen could make out none of the figure's features, cloaked as they were in darkness, but a moment later the newcomer stepped forward and was revealed to be Mariana. "Hi there," she said, and though she gave the Tribune a sweet smile, neither Dannen nor Historial missed the fact that she held the two short iron rods in her hands that he'd seen her use to such great effect in the tavern.

"Well, Historial," Dannen said, stepping forward, taking his time, giving the man a moment to realize just how desperate his situation was, "I'd say you're in some trouble here. A younger man—type of man I used to be—might choose this moment to be offended by all that talk of yours before, might choose to be angry, maybe even to get revenge for what you were thinking of doing to Clare." He paused, giving the man a grim smile and was satisfied to see the Tribune swallowing hard, his face noticeably paler than it had been moments ago.

Dannen hesitated as if thinking it over, gave the man a minute to sweat. "But I'm not that man," he said finally, "not anymore. I'm too old for vengeance. I've seen enough blood and death to last a lifetime, some killed for being 'villains,' some killed for being 'heroes,' and, my experience, the world just keeps rollin' on like a wagon whose driver's asleep and doesn't care about those he leaves flattened in his wake. Killed a lot of bad people in my day, saw some good ones killed, too, and it doesn't seem to have made much of a difference to me. So here's what I'm going to do, Historial. I'm going to give you a chance. To come clean. I came here looking for evidence of whatever you're involved in, what you've been using to blackmail the other members of the Tribunal, and I figure a confession ought to do just fine."

"A confession," the Tribune repeated, his voice and expression unreadable now, seeming to be blank.

"That's right," Dannen said, "and if you're thinking maybe I'm asking too much, just remember that talking is always easier than bleeding. And if you give me your confession, tell me how you've been manipulating the other Tribunes, I promise I'll give you at least an hour's head start to get out of the city before I tell Clarissa and the High Justice what you've been doing."

"An hour," the man said, his face and tone still blank, reflecting nothing of how he felt about Dannen's proposal. "Is that all?"

Dannen shrugged. "Maybe you'd like a few more, pack up all your goodies, maybe put some face paint on, but an hour's more than most'd give you, Tribune. But as for your question, no, that's not all. You leave this place, Historial, and you never come back to Talinseh. But more than that—you leave Clare alone." He let some of the anger, anger which had roiled through him since the Tribune had threatened Clarissa, color his voice. "And if I ever hear that something happens to her, if I think you were somehow involved, then I swear to you, Historial, by all the gods and devils in the world, that I'll hunt you down and show you that while old soldiers might abhor violence, that doesn't mean they're bad at it. You understand?"

"And if I don't?" Historial asked. "If I don't confess to anything? Or if I don't promise to leave *Clare* alone?"

There was a strange, rasping quality to the Tribune's voice, but Dannen chalked it up to the man's fear and anger. "If you don't confess? Pain. It'll be pain, Historial. And as for Clare, well, I'm leaving here feeling assured that she won't have to worry about any threat from you anymore. A promise and an understanding would do me well enough in that regard, but if neither of those is forthcoming, well, dead men can't hurt anybody...can they?"

Historial stood there for several moments until, finally, Firemaker started forward with a growl, apparently impatient to get back to the violence. Dannen stopped him with a hand on his shoulder, shaking his head. The giant sighed forlornly, but made no move to break away, nor did the girl, Mariana.

Despite both the overt and implied threats in Dannen's statement, despite the fact that he was surrounded on either side with nowhere left to go, the Tribune did not seem afraid, and he studied Dannen with steady, somehow dead eyes. "You think that you have won," he said, that odd rasp back in his throat.

Dannen didn't bother answering that, for it was the sort of thing that answered itself, but Historial nodded slowly, as if he had. "Yes, you believe that you have beaten me, that you have cornered me, but beware, Dannen Ateran. Men, like beasts, are never more dangerous than when cornered."

The man had balls, Dannen had to give him that much, sitting there threatening him after seeing what Fedder was capable of, but Dannen had faced far scarier things in his life than fifty-year-old Tribunes dressed in silk. "I want to start with you telling me about how you got the other members of the Tribunal to follow your lead," Dannen said, choosing to ignore the man's threat. "After that, I want to hear about why you're so adamantly opposed to helping King Ufrith with his troubles."

Historial gave a small smile, and Dannen, who knew that kind of smile, had seen its sort on plenty of dead heroes and villains, sighed. "If he tries to run," he said to Mariana, "knock him over the head. I don't want to torture a man, if I don't have to, but at least I've already found the tools for it."

The Tribune met Dannen's eyes for another moment. Then he smiled and turned away, taking a step directly at Mariana as if the girl weren't there. For her part, the assassin moved with shocking quickness, one of the iron rods she held little more than a blur as it flashed toward the Tribune's head in a strike sure to knock the man unconscious, if not kill him outright.

But instead of hitting Historial, the rod stopped inches from his head as if it had hit a wall. Mariana stared at the rod, seemingly frozen in the air, reflecting the same kind of surprise Dannen felt. What had stopped her strike had not been a wall, after all. The Tribune had, somehow, managed to catch her wrist in mid-blow. But their surprise quickly turned to shock as the old man released his grip on her wrist, grabbed the front of her shirt with his other hand, and lifted her as if she weighed nothing.

Mariana had time to make a surprised sound before Historial gave Dannen a lazy, humorless smile and flung Mariana away in a casual shove. Yet, as casual as it looked, the woman hurtled backward, disappearing beyond the circle of illumination cast by Firemaker's magic light.

A moment later, Dannen heard what sounded like a grunt as something struck the ground followed by a pained moan.

Impossible. Dannen had seen Mariana fight, and he knew she was incredibly fast. In fact, he doubted if he would have been able to stop such a blow, yet the elderly Tribune had seemed to have no difficulty doing it. Neither had he seemed to display the least bit of strain at throwing the girl through the air as if she weighed nothing.

But impossible or not, the man *had,* and Dannen was left staring at him, stunned. He was still standing there stunned when a faint smell of decay wafted into his nose. There was something familiar in that smell, something that made him uneasy, but his thoughts were scrambled and confused by the spectacle of Historial's impossible speed and strength.

Fedder let out a growl and started forward, a dark expression on his face that Dannen had seen plenty of times before, one which usually presaged a lot of blood and criminal charges. He grabbed the man's arm again. "Fedder," he said, still struck by an uneasy feeling as he tried to figure what it was about the smell that worried him, "wait, there's something—"

"He hurt the girl, Butcher," the mage said in a gravelly voice. "He'll have to pay for that."

"Of course," Dannen began, "but—"

But it was too late. Firemaker broke away from him, moving to stand in front of Historial who was still wearing a small smile, apparently no more afraid of the giant mage than he had been of Mariana. That, of course, added to Dannen's growing sense of unease, and he felt the hairs on the back of his neck stand up.

"Shouldn'ta hurt the girl," Fedder said. "We were goin' to hurt you before, true, but you've gone and made it personal now, threatenin' Clare, hurtin' the girl."

"Well, then," Historial said, spreading his lips and revealing too-white teeth, "I guess I ought to be punished, hadn't I?"

Suddenly, the smell of sickness and death grew stronger, crowding into Dannen's mouth and nose, seeming to coat the inside of his throat and nostrils. And that was not the only thing. Something, some *force,* seemed to be building all around them, though he could see nothing. The force crowded the air and made it difficult to breathe, pushed against him the way the wind might but from all directions at once. It was an oppressive, sickening feeling, and he felt as if he were being crushed.

"Fedder..." he said slowly, but if the mage felt anything amiss, he showed no sign.

Instead, Fedder took a step forward and sent a haymaker flying at the Tribune's face which carried such force Dannen didn't doubt it would easily knock the man's head from his shoulders if it connected. But Dannen somehow knew it would not, that Historial would once again demonstrate that impossible speed, easily dodging the blow and turning to flee before the mage could recover.

But Historial did not dodge, and he did not flee. The mage's blow struck him in the face with shocking force. There was a *crack* as the man's jaw broke, and he was flung into the wall, slamming against it before collapsing in a heap on the ground.

Fedder turned back to Dannen, grunting. "I'm gonna go check on the girl, make sure she's alright."

"Fedder," Dannen began, then hesitated, not sure what he meant to say, only that something felt wrong.

The mage turned back, glancing at him, and after a moment, Dannen grunted. "Be...careful."

Fedder grinned. "Yes, Mommy," he said.

Maybe Dannen should have been relieved that the mage had dealt with Historial so easily, but he was not. He was sweating despite the chill of the tunnels, and his hands felt clammy. The oppressive feeling was so terrible that Dannen was amazed to see the mage continue as if he felt nothing. But then, suddenly, Fedder stopped.

The Firemaker turned back to Dannen, a curious expression on his face. "What is—" But his words abruptly turned to a grunt of surprise as his feet flew out from under him, and he landed on his back with a *crash*. Dannen glanced down and saw that the mage's foot had gotten tangled up in the Tribune's arm, for the unconscious man's hand seemed to be wrapped around Fedder's ankle. But no, that didn't make sense either. After all, Fedder had been standing still when he'd fallen, and it hadn't looked like he'd tripped. It looked like someone had pulled one of his legs out from under him.

Impossible, Dannen thought. *The man is unconscious, he has to be. Shit, after the hit he took, it's just as likely he's dead.*

But just then, there came a croaking, dry laughter, and Tribune Historial rose to his feet. He studied Dannen with malevolent eyes that had certainly turned completely black. His jaw hung at an impossible angle, proof that Fedder's blow had struck as hard as Dannen had thought, but if it pained him, the Tribune gave no sign.

Suddenly, Dannen understood many things at once. He had asked himself, when chasing Historial through the subterranean tunnels, how a man in his fifties could outpace him so easily, had asked himself, too, why Historial had appeared more annoyed than afraid when his soldiers had either died or fled by turns, leaving him alone to face three opponents. He had wondered at how such an old and overweight man could throw Mariana as if she were nothing and go on to shrug off a blow from Fedder powerful enough to have ruined not just the day but the life of anyone Dannen had ever met.

Now, he understood. What sort of man could shrug off the kind of blows he'd taken and demonstrate such speed and strength? The answer was none. The only way a man could do such a thing was if he were more than just a man. Dannen understood all of this in an instant, just as he understood what the smell of decay which he'd detected meant. "Shit," he breathed.

Fedder, though, was privy to none of Dannen's inner thoughts or outside fears, for he was facing the Tribune again, and before Dannen could warn him, the mage charged once more, swinging his meaty fists in several powerful blows that were surprisingly quick, any of which, had they landed, would have made sure that the Tribune's ribs spent some quality time with his spine. But none of the blows *did* land, because the old man dodged and weaved around them with unnatural, jerking movements which were eerie in their own right until he finally seemed to tire of the game.

Fedder swung again at the man's face, but Historial caught the fist as if it were a child's. The mage's bushy eyebrows drew down in a confused frown, then Historial twisted and Fedder flew through the air, hitting the wall with a resounding *thud* before collapsing in a groaning heap.

Historial did not seem out of breath or tired at all from the brief exchange as he turned to regard Dannen. "Ah," he said, seeing something in Dannen's face—probably the sweat and blatant fear a blind person would surely have noted—"it seems you begin to understand, Butcher, who you face."

"Not who," Dannen breathed. "What. You're...you're a ghoul."

Historial rolled his eyes. "Oh, do not look so disgusted," he said, each word muffled and unclear thanks to his broken jaw. "I will not be judged by a man known throughout the world as the Butcher."

Dannen was shaking his head before the creature had finished, for it *was* a creature, of that much he was certain. He had run into a few ghouls in his time—run *from* them mostly—and whatever else he might have once been, Tribune Historial was a man no longer. He was a monster. A creature who sustained itself by consuming the flesh and blood of the living. Thankfully, such creatures were rare, for they could only be made by the most powerful of curses, ones only the world's most gifted necromancers could perform.

"Shit," he said again as yet another realization dawned. "You're helping them. That's why you are voting to refuse King Ufrith aid. You're working for the necromancer and his brother."

"I don't work for *anyone*," Historial hissed, showing far more emotion at the thought than he had at the reality of his jaw coming unhinged. "The brothers and I have a mutually beneficial arrangement, one that as you see"—he paused, holding his hands up to the side—"has proven most useful."

"You don't get it," Dannen said softly, "you don't understand what they've done to you. Ghouls are not men, not any longer."

"Yes," the man hissed, seeming impatient now, "they are *more* than men. I'm sure your unconscious friends would testify to that."

"More," Dannen agreed, "and less. Ghouls, you see, are the subjects of their masters, formed by their master's powers, and should that master take that power away, you will..." He hesitated. Die wasn't exactly right, since, technically speaking, Historial was no longer alive, had died whenever he'd allowed the necromancer to cast his spell. "You'll be destroyed," he finished.

Historial snorted. "Lies told in the hopes of saving your skin," he said, but Dannen could see some glimmer of knowing, of understanding in his eyes. He knew something wasn't right, perhaps had known for some time, but though he was no longer strictly a man, it seemed that he still possessed a man's ability, unparalleled among all other creatures of the earth, to delude himself. "But you are far past being saved, Dannen Ateran. You should never have come here, should never have placed yourself against me. Now—"

"Ah, excuse me."

They both spun to look behind Dannen where a newcomer had arrived, and Dannen was shocked to see that it was none other than the prisoner he'd abandoned in the cells only moments ago. Suddenly, he felt a warmth in his pocket, one that was growing exponentially, but he ignored it for the moment.

"How the...look, lad, I don't know how you managed to get out of the cell, but you need to run."

The thought occurred to him to push the unfortunate prisoner in front of himself, making Historial go through him to get to Dannen and thereby buying him a few more seconds, but he did not. For one, the Firemaker was close to unconscious but not quite there, and despite everything, the man still believed Dannen a hero, a belief he was surprised to find, he wasn't prepared to shatter just yet. But even more importantly, if Historial was indeed a ghoul it wouldn't take him long to finish with the prisoner and take after Dannen. At best, he'd be buying himself a couple of seconds more of life.

So instead, he gave the prisoner a gentle shove. "Go, now. While you can."

"I can't," the man said simply, glancing at the squirrel on his shoulder. "She wouldn't approve. Anyway, sorry it took us so long to get here. There was something I had to do first."

Dannen blinked, deciding the crazy bastard must have no clue of where he was or what was about to happen to him. Well, he supposed that wasn't the worst of things. He'd seen the remnants ghouls left on more than one occasion, and they were never pleasant, little more than bits and pieces of unidentifiable, bloody gristle and bone. Probably better the man didn't know.

"Look," Dannen said, turning back to Historial, "just let this one go, alright? He's got nothing to do with this, and you can see he's crazy as a loon."

Historial said nothing, seemed to be done talking for now, and his mouth twitched into what he might have meant to be a smile. With his broken jaw, it was a gruesome sight, and he started toward Dannen and the prisoner.

Shit. There were only a few ways to kill a ghoul, the things being notoriously hardy. Perhaps Fedder, had he been conscious, might have been able to do the trick with some of his fire magic, but the mage was still lying half-senseless on the ground, groaning incoherently. Dannen could expect no help from that quarter. As for the girl Mariana, he could not see her except for an unmoving clump of shadow in the darkness, a clump of shadow that, as it happened, wasn't moving. He was on his own then. Just him and the prisoner and the ghoul in a tunnel, trying desperately to think of some way not to get killed in the next few seconds.

He came up empty. The problem was that ghouls were infamous for shrugging off wounds that would kill a normal man—wounds like a sword to the gut or heart. Not that Dannen *had* a sword. They could not be choked or suffocated, could not die of old age—though the old ones were really ugly bastards—or sickness, as technically speaking, they were already dead. Dannen had once heard of a ghoul being chopped up into small pieces, but he had nothing with which to chop and, even if he had, he doubted Histarial would be kind enough to stand still while he went about it.

"Just go," he murmured to the prisoner as he watched the Tribune creep closer. "I'll buy you as much time as I can. And if you make it out, look for Tribune Clarissa. Tell her that they're coming for her and...tell her...Dannen said he's sorry. She'll know what it means."

"I'm sorry," the prisoner said, "but I must stay." He glanced at the squirrel perched on his shoulder who seemed to watch Dannen with eyes far too intelligent for what was little more than a furry rat. "She is adamant about that."

"*Listen, damnit,*" Dannen hissed, "this, this *thing* is a ghoul. A *ghoul,* do you understand? And that thing on your shoulder is a fucking squirrel. So unless that little bastard knows magic or happens to have this *other* bastard's life gem, then we're pretty well—"

"Life gem?" the man asked.

Dannen let out a growl. "It's what gives the ghoul his power, alright? It's invested with some of the necromancer's magi...you know what? It doesn't matter because ghouls don't just leave those things lying arou—" He cut off as the prisoner withdrew something from his pocket.

"A gem like this?" the man asked.

Dannen was no expert on the undead—maybe on the dead, the gods knew he'd seen enough—but he knew the item on sight, and he felt his breath catch in his throat. The gem was about the size of a child's fist. It was a pale, bone-white, but shadows writhed within. "How did you—"

"She told me," the man said, gesturing to the squirrel. "Anyway, am I supposed to just—"

"*Nooo!*" came a roar. Histarial's eyes were wild with fear and anger. "*Impossible,*" the ghoul growled, "you couldn't have—"

Dannen never knew what the creature meant to say, for even as it was speaking it had begun to bound forward in a lurching, leaping run ending abruptly when the stranger threw the gem on the ground.

The foggy white surface shattered, and smoke as black as pitch poured out, more smoke than could ever have been contained in so small a space, filling the air around them. Unlike real smoke, it did not make Dannen cough or cause his eyes to water, yet where it touched his skin it left a greasy, somehow sickly feeling. Dannen held his breath, knowing it was ridiculous, that with the shattering of the gem what magic had been invested in it was gone, the spell broken, yet the thought of any of that smoke getting into his mouth left him feeling faint.

The smoke shifted and writhed like a thing alive, and for a brief moment, Dannen fancied that he could see a form within it, one twisting in pain and fear and rage, thought that, perhaps, it might have even been Histarial. But a moment later, the smoke dissipated, fading as if it had never been, and he was left thinking—not believing, but certainly *wishing*—he had only imagined it.

A powerful stink of decomposition arose from where the Tribune had collapsed when the gem shattered. Through the necromancer's spell, the Tribune had cheated death, had accepted it while rejecting it at the same time. Now the enchantment was broken, it seemed that death was intent on taking its share as quickly as possible. Histarial's body was decomposing at an incredible rate, his flesh blackening and withering, his face sinking in and becoming more and more cadaverous with each moment.

In less than a minute, Dannen and the prisoner were left staring at no more than a skeleton. "Well," Dannen said, nudging the Tribune's remains with a toe. "I'd say that pretty well did for him."

"Yes," the prisoner said, his tone casual as if the sight of a murderous ghoul or its swift decomposition after the breaking of a magical spell was something that he experienced every day. "Yes, I do believe you are correct."

Dannen glanced sideways at the man. "Thanks. I reckon if you hadn't shown up, I'd be dead right now."

"Doubtful," the young man said seriously. "As I understand it, ghouls prefer eating their victims while they are alive. Anyway, it is not me you have to thank but her." He tilted his head to indicate the squirrel still sitting on his shoulder.

Dannen blinked, clearing his throat. "Well...thanks anyway, I guess. To...to both of you."

The young man frowned, glancing at the squirrel. "Oh, would you just relax?" he muttered. "Everything isn't all about you." He paused for a moment, and Dannen stood uncomfortably as the man seemed to listen to the chittering squirrel. "That's not fair and you know it," the man said angrily. "And don't talk to me about destiny, I—" He froze as if only now realizing he'd been speaking out loud—yelling really—and glanced at Dannen. "I...um...apologize, for that. She can be...difficult. Sometimes."

Dannen glanced between the man and the squirrel. "Sure...sure, no problem."

Just then, a groan that sounded like the sort of sound a bear might make when it rouses itself from hibernation reminded him that Fedder was still lying on the ground a short distance away. Dannen knelt beside him. "Hey, Fedder. You alive?"

The mage grunted, rolling onto his back. "Hey, Dannen. Sort of," he said, blinking.

Hearing the mage use his first name instead of that damned nickname made Dannen wonder if the poor giant hadn't hit his head. "You wounded?"

The mage winced. "Just my pride."

"Well," Dannen said. "Pride heals."

Fedder grunted. "Never all the way."

"No," Dannen agreed. "Never all the way." He offered his hand. The mage took it and after a lot of grunting and hissing, Dannen managed to lever the man to his feet.

Fedder blinked, wavering uncertainly for a moment, but finally seemed to catch his balance. He regarded the Tribune's remains. "Ghoul?"

"Ghoul," Dannen agreed.

"Strong bastard."

"Well," Dannen said. "He was."

"You broke his life gem?"

Dannen shook his head, nodding his head at the young madman. "He did."

Fedder stared at the man with a frown, the prisoner staring back while feeding something from his pocket to the squirrel on his shoulder. "Who are you?" he demanded.

"Tesler," he said, smiling pleasantly and offering Fedder his hand as if they were strangers having a conversation in some well-lit tavern instead of standing in dark tunnels surrounded by several corpses and in more than a little danger of joining them. "Nice to meet you."

Fedder stared at the man in disbelief then turned to Dannen who sighed, shrugging. "Ah, shit," Fedder said abruptly, "the girl." He turned and hurried down the tunnel, Dannen following.

By the time they reached her, she was sitting with her back propped against the wall, her arms draped over her knees. "'Bout time, was beginning to think you all had forgotten about me. Ah," she said, glancing past them to the prisoner who was standing behind. "Who's that?"

"Tesler," the man said, flashing her a smile similar to the one he'd shown the Firemaker as he offered her his hand, "nice to meet you."

The girl blinked then turned to stare at Dannen who, just then, wanted to shout that the man wasn't *his* responsibility just because he'd happened to be the one who'd found him in a cage. After all, he'd *left* the bastard there, hadn't he?

"Oh, dear," Fedder said in the sort of fussy, worried tone a grandmother might use, a tone Dannen had never thought to hear from the man, "you're hurt." He levered his bulk down beside

Mariana, and for the first time, Dannen saw what the fire mage meant. Somehow, when he'd thrown her, the ghoul had managed to tear a scratch into Mariana's leather trousers, starting at her knee and went about halfway up her thigh. The tear revealed a cut that, while not deep, was plenty long and bleeding. "I'll help," Firemaker said, reaching his hands out, "though I may have to tear the pants a bit mo—"

"Don't even think about it, old man," Mariana said, slapping his hands away.

Fedder grinned like a child caught at mischief.

"Still," the girl said, "does seem it needs seein' to. What about you?" she asked Dannen. "You good at bandaging wounds?"

Fedder barked a laugh. "The Butcher's good with wounds, but he's about makin' 'em, lass, not patchin' 'em up."

Dannen was about to argue that while he was certainly no healer, he'd learned enough over the years to clean and bandage a wound, but the girl was already turning away to look at the young man. "What about you? Fester, was it?"

"Um...Tesler," the young man answered, fidgeting and avoiding her eyes. Dannen blinked. He'd seen the man seem perfectly at home in a cell awaiting torture, but Mariana's regard was enough to make him clearly uncomfortable. "And yes. That is, yes, I know some about healing. It—"

"Well?" she interrupted. "Come on before I bleed out, why don't you?"

Dannen had seen a lot of wounds in his day, and he knew the girl's wound was far from life-threatening, and if bandaged would heal up nicely. True, it might leave a pretty nice scar on a pretty nice leg—maybe Dannen was old, but he wasn't blind—but there were worse things than scars.

The boy—Dannen thought of him then as a boy, for faced with the young woman, he certainly acted like one—leapt forward, kneeling beside her as if she were going to expire at any moment without his care. Dannen sighed quietly. Women had many powers, like ghouls or necromancers, but the greatest of those was that, with a single word, with a single *look*, a woman could turn the bravest, wisest of men into fawning fools.

While the young man worked at the girl's leg, Dannen turned to Fedder. "How'd you find out I came here, anyway?"

The mage snorted. "Seemed obvious enough when Clare met us in the street somethin' was wrong, what with her bein' escorted by a small army. While you two chatted, I did a little bit of investigatin', talked to some of her staff. My opinion, if you ever want the truth of a thing and to know what's goin' on, ask the servants. Folks got a habit of treatin' 'em like furniture, sayin' things in front of them they wouldn't say to their closest friends."

"Investigating," Dannen repeated dryly. "When she said she had a private bar, I thought you'd be drinking."

Fedder wiggled his bushy eyebrows, making them look like two caterpillars preparing to fight. "Who's to say I can't do both?"

Dannen nodded. "Well, I'm glad you came. I'd be dead otherwise."

The mage shrugged. "The ale tasted like piss," he said, clearly a lie as Dannen knew Clarissa enough to be sure she would only stock the finest, but Fedder, a man who Dannen had personally seen fight a manticore singlehandedly and wrestle an ogre to a draw, was uncomfortable with gratitude, so he let it slide.

An idea struck him then. "Anyway, I hope you came in quiet. Clarissa said to be subtle. True, we killed the master of the house, but if we're lucky, we might be able to make it out of here without anyone knowing who we were or who sent us."

Fedder winced, avoiding his eyes, and Mariana let out a snort as she rose, her wound bandaged. "We're not," she said.

"What's that?" Dannen asked.

"Lucky," she said. "We're not lucky. When the old giant and I learned where you'd gone, we figured you'd need help. Turns out we weren't wrong. Anyway, seems I recall recommending we sneak in. Ought not to have been that hard a thing to do as I've got a bit of training in that area and your friend here is a mage, well, I thought that'd help out nicely. I was wrong."

Dannen had a sinking feeling in his stomach, one that the embarrassed expression on Firemaker's face did nothing to assuage. And was that faint smell he detected smoke? "What happened?" he asked, looking at the mage.

Fedder cleared his throat, avoiding Dannen's gaze, opening his mouth as if he were about to speak before closing it again. "Oh, please," the girl said, rolling her eyes, "allow me. See, thing is, I was still trying to explain why we ought to be subtle, why sneaking was the best policy, when your pal here decided to burn the front gate down after knocking both the gate guards decidedly unconscious and realizing that he couldn't rip it off with his bare hands." She snorted. "Men."

"You can't be serious," Dannen breathed.

"Oh, that's not all," Mariana went on. "Your friend here might think magic is for sissies—though if I've ever heard anything more foolish in my life, I don't remember it—but once he got started, he got a taste for it, throwin' fire every which-a-way, showin' off."

"Wasn't showing off," Fedder mumbled. "Anyway, it kept the guards off our backs."

"Suppose that's true," Mariana admitted. "Hard for them to focus on protectin' the house, when half of 'em were on fire and the other half startin' to catch."

Dannen grunted. "So you made your way through the gardens..."

Mariana rolled her eyes. "What gardens? Ain't nothin' but fire and ash up there now, but that's not the worst of it. What *is* is that your friend here apparently decided the best thing was to let everyone within a city block know who was responsible, shoutin' about how folks were gonna suffer the wrath of Fedder the Firemaker. And what was that other bit you said?" she asked, glancing at Fedder. "Somethin' about the world, wasn't it?"

Fedder winced again. "Might have said something about burning the whole world...I was pissed-off," he said to Dannen, "thought maybe you were hurt or..."

"Sure, that's it," Mariana interrupted, "burning the whole world. I would have thought it ridiculous, but even though I think it was a damn fool thing to do, I can't help but admit he got a good start on it anyway. Speakin' of, we'd best be going. Some of the walls were startin' to flame up when we found the tunnel entrance, and I don't imagine we've too long before the whole damn building's burnt to a crisp."

Dannen glanced at Fedder, who still refused to meet his eyes. He thought of saying something, rebuking the mage, but he knew Fedder enough to know it wouldn't do any good. He was just built that way, that was all. Besides, considering the fact that him deciding to take the most direct approach might well have been the only reason why Dannen was still breathing, he thought he'd let this one pass. He was just about to say they should head out when he felt an uncomfortable heat in his pocket again and since, this time, he didn't have an insane ghoul preparing to rip his face off and was instead only risking burning to death, he spared a moment to investigate, digging into his pocket and retrieving the Divining Stone. No sooner had he touched it than all the heat he'd felt seemed to surge into his hand, spreading through the rest of his body and bringing with it knowledge of the identity of the fourth hero Perandius wished for him to work with.

Dannen's eyes went wide at the revelation and the strange feeling, then he turned to stare at the man who had been Histarial's prisoner. Tesler didn't notice, however, for he seemed to be occupied in having a murmured conversation, not with Fedder or Mariana but with the squirrel perched on his shoulder. If it wasn't enough that he'd been paired with a battle-hungry mage and a suicidal assassin, now it seemed that the final member of his team was a man who spent his time chatting with rodents. "You've got to be kidding me," Dannen said.

Tesler turned at that and gave him a small smile, as if he knew exactly what he was thinking. "Destiny," he said softly.

Destiny, Dannen decided, was a real bitch. "Come on," he said wearily, "let's get out of here."

By the time they reached the tunnel entrance, Dannen could smell smoke. And he didn't *just* smell it but saw it too. It curled down in wispy tendrils from the roof of the tunnel, tickling his nose and throat. He paused, only for a moment, with his hand on the door, hoping Mariana had been exaggerating about what Fedder had done. When he opened the door, it was clear that his worst expectations came nowhere close to the mark.

Fire raged in every direction, billowing great towers of dark gray smoke into the night air. Indeed, it seemed that Mariana had been right—Fedder had gotten a good start on burning the world down. "Huh," Dannen said, because he couldn't manage much else. He turned to the mage who had grace enough to look embarrassed, then gestured at a small bush that, miraculously was currently untouched by the blaze. "Seems you missed a spot."

"Was in a bit of a hurry," Fedder muttered, still refusing to meet Dannen's eyes and staring at the burning gardens like they were an enemy he could slay. Which, of course, he already had. All the many plants and bushes Dannen had observed when sneaking into the manse were nothing but blackened roots and ash. What wasn't burned was burning, and if they stuck around much longer, they'd burn right along with them. Already, the smoke created a dark gray curtain in the air everywhere he looked, making it nearly impossible for him to see anything.

The guards seemed to be having the same problem. They were screaming and running—one or two of them on fire as well—with no idea where to go or how to escape the burning inferno. But the guards would have to live or die by themselves. Dannen and his companions had their own problems, and he scanned the gardens, desperate for a path through the seemingly uninterrupted flames.

"Damn it," he coughed. "I don't see any way out." He turned to Fedder. "Hey, is there any way—"

"Sorry, Butcher," Fedder said, shaking his head, his brows drawn down in a frown. "It's too much, now. If it were only the magic flames, sure, but they've been fed, you know, and—"

"It's alright," Dannen said, interrupting the giant. "It's alright."

Fedder winced. "Sorry, Dannen."

Dannen knew what people were supposed to say in such situations: it's not your fault, or it's okay, but he couldn't stomach the first, not just then. After all, Fedder had been the one who'd sat the gardens on fire, hadn't he? To be fair to the mage, Dannen thought it only right to admit he'd seemed to have courted death for nearly his entire life, and all the responsibility for it finally catching up to him couldn't be placed at Fedder's feet no matter how convenient it might have been. So he only gave a single nod, trying on a smile immediately ruined by a bout of coughing as more of the smoke got in his throat and lungs. "It's alright," he said finally.

"Well," Mariana said, sniffing and rubbing a finger at a soot stain on her cheek with almost dainty affectation. "Not the death I'd have picked, maybe—always had my heart set on drowning in money—but then I guess there's worse ways to go." Dannen turned and scowled at her, and she cleared her throat. "Though," she went on as she gazed out at the flames which were growing by the second now, towering over them like great specters wreathed in flame, "to be fair, none come to mind."

Dannen figured if he hurried and tried not to breathe in too much smoke, he could probably kill the girl before the flames did. The problem, though, was he was fairly certain she'd kick the shit out of him, if he tried, and the last thing he needed was to die to the sound of Fedder's bellowing laughter at *that* little gem.

"You wish to escape?"

Dannen turned and stared at the prisoner, the man who'd given his name as Tesler, wondering if maybe they were having a contest to see who could say the dumbest shit and hadn't let him know the rules. "Well, you know," he said, then paused to cough as more of the smoke filled his lungs, "I hadn't thought about it, but come to think of it, escaping might not be too bad of a damn idea."

"I see," Tesler said slowly, nodding. "Well, in that case, this way." Then, without another word, the man turned and started into the flaming gardens.

Dannen stared after him, thinking the odds were good that if he followed the man, he'd be dead in the next few minutes. But what alternatives did he have? He could go back into the tunnels, could spend his last few moments watching the smoke billow into them like some creeping, living thing intent on taking everything within its vapory grasp, the air getting to be a little less air and a little more smoke with each moment. Each breath would be shorter than the last until he went to take one and found that there wasn't any to take, wasn't anything to do at all but lie there, gasp for a bit, then die.

No, that didn't sound good to him, not good at all, that slow, creeping death. Better to get it done quickly. He glanced at Fedder who met his eyes and shrugged, clearly having similar thoughts.

"Alright, then," Dannen said, "come on."

Tesler was waiting on them, standing without any fear or concern on his face. He nodded as Dannen and the others came to stand with him. "Are you ready?"

About a dozen smart-ass responses popped into Dannen's head then, but considering that the flames were growing, and breathing was beginning to feel like trying to draw water from a dry well, he went with brevity. "Yes."

"Very well. We mu—" Tesler began, cutting off and listening intently as the squirrel—still perched on his shoulder, though only the gods knew how the damned wild thing hadn't scampered away in fear by now—began to chitter. Dannen was trying to decide who was crazier—a man who talked to squirrels or a man who followed such a man into a blazing inferno—and, truth be told, wasn't much caring for the answer he was coming up with when Tesler finally raised his head. "No," the man said, incredulous, "I won't say. They don't, I mean, they wouldn't get it…" He paused as if listening again then sighed. "Fine, later." He huffed, turning back to Dannen.

"Sorry about that. She can be quite a…challenge, sometimes. Anyway, it's this way," he said, taking a deep breath and stepping into a thick wall of smoke.

Dannen glanced at Fedder and the girl, noted grim expressions on their faces to match his own, then with a fatalistic shrug, took a deep breath and followed. It was all he could do to make out Tesler's vague form in the thick, choking smoke, but Dannen stumbled after him. A moment later, Tesler turned left and seemed to step directly into the flames. Dannen stared, dumbfounded and would have shouted had he the breath to shout. Instead, he staggered forward, his eyes squinted nearly shut and watering anyway, one hand up in front of him.

In seconds, they reached the place where he'd lost sight of Tesler and was surprised to find a break in the flames, one in which the man stood, patiently waiting. The break continued as far as Dannen could see—admittedly not far, considering the billowing smoke obscuring his vision. He glanced back and saw Fedder and Mariana both looking as surprised as he felt to still be alive, then he nodded at Tesler and the man started forward again.

The bastard was still crazy—Dannen wasn't ready to give that up, not yet—but he seemed to have some talent for finding his way through the maze of smoke and flame. But if any of it gave the man any trouble, he showed no sign, walking on unerringly and finding openings in the flames where Dannen never would have guessed any existed. The man was so good at it Dannen began to get the strange feeling he wasn't finding the gaps in the fire, after all, but was *making* them somehow, as if the fire sensed where he wanted to go, and was moving out of his way.

It seemed as if they walked forever, stumbling through the roiling smoke, the heat of the flames on his skin, all of them hacking and coughing. Then, finally, Tesler stopped, glancing back at them. "There are people in the street."

Dannen hacked and spat, trying and failing to rid his throat of the smoke coating it. "It's...what the street's...for," he wheezed.

The young man nodded slowly, thoughtfully, as if Dannen had just said something profound. "They are armed," he added as if it was an afterthought.

Dannen frowned. There was no way the man could have known people were waiting in the street. For one, the smoke and the flames obscured nearly everything around them, but more pointedly, even if they *could* have seen, they would have seen only the wall Dannen had climbed when gaining entry, a wall which blocked the street from view entirely. But there wasn't much point arguing with the man, and if they took the time to do it, the argument would be ended definitively when they both died from fire and foolishness, so he nodded. "Lead on, Tesler."

The young man smiled pleasantly, still seemingly oblivious of the danger they were in. "That's the first time, I believe, that you've called me by name," he said, and thankfully didn't wait on a response from Dannen—who had none that wasn't a curse for the lad's decided inattention to the fire and death all around them—before turning and heading into the flames once more, finding a gap as if by magic where none had been a moment before.

Dannen glanced back at Fedder and Mariana, both covered in soot and ash and looking just about as miserable as he felt, and gave a tiny shrug, the most of which he was capable, before following Tesler once more. Each step was a trial, the journey one of the hardest things he'd ever done, and that was saying something for a man who had spent the majority of his life as a would-be victim of one terrible creature or another.

His vision was blurry from the smoke, and his thoughts were muddled and foggy, buried as they were in the soft downy blanket of approaching unconsciousness. Placing each foot in front of the other was no longer a physical act but instead an act of pure will, the foot and leg to which it was attached driven onward not by muscles and tendons but by a desire, a *need* to live. Stopping and letting the fire and smoke do their work would have been far easier, but the only men who had it easy were dead ones, so Dannen struggled on, knowing that life was hard and that struggle, that pain and fear and anger, was how a man knew he was alive in the first place.

Yet for all his efforts and all his will, he felt himself flagging, thought his next step would be his last, when suddenly Tesler came to such an abrupt halt, making Dannen stumble into him. "'Scuse me," Dannen wheezed, and immediately thought it a stupid thing to waste breath on.

Tesler turned, glancing at him. "You're sure?"

Too tired to speak, Dannen only waved the man on, and to his shock and amazement, they stepped from the hallway of fire to find themselves standing directly in front of the gate.

"Damn," Dannen rasped, immediately breaking into a coughing fit. He had all but convinced himself that Tesler had only been leading them on a death walk, their trudging steps only able to carry them from fire to more fire until sooner or later they collapsed, but here, the gate stood open and beyond was the street, a street that was, Dannen saw with a giddy wash of relief, not aflame.

On one side of the gate lay a guard, his face decidedly misshapen from—judging by the blood stains—several impacts with the wall, as good a signature as Fedder had ever had. There was another lump on the other side which might have been a second guard, though it was difficult to tell as this one was covered in flame. "Let's get...out....of here," Dannen wheezed, and soon he and the others were stumbling out into the street.

For several minutes, they said nothing, only hacked and coughed and retched, Dannen, Fedder, and Mariana all collapsing to their knees. Only Tesler remained standing, seemingly unaffected as if he could breathe smoke as easily as another might breathe air. "H-how," Dannen said after he finally caught some semblance of his breath, "how did...you know the way out?"

A sad look came over Tesler's face at that, and he gazed back through the gate at the burning gardens. "The plants told me," he said softly. "In their screams and their cries for help."

Dannen grunted a laugh, one that he cut short when the man's face didn't change, and he realized he wasn't kidding, after all. "Well," he managed, "'course, they did. Why wouldn't they?"

The man's brows drew down as if considering what any fool ought to have taken as a rhetorical question. "Hate. Probably, they might not have said because, by and large, they hate us."

Dannen blinked, thought about asking a question and decided against it. The man was insane, he'd already decided as much, and there was just as much point being surprised by an insane man saying insane shit as there was stabbing yourself to see if you'd bleed. And since it would be pretty damned rude to kill the man who just saved his life, he chose to check on Fedder and Mariana instead. They were both alive, but that was about as much as could be said.

They were covered in greasy residue from the smoke, and Fedder's right eyebrow was gone, burned off by the heat. The missing eyebrow did nothing to decrease his already considerably menacing appearance. Mariana had a sickly look that was reinforced by how she was currently hacking the remnants of what appeared to be a meager dinner of mostly ale onto the cobblestones.

All of them dirty and in poor shape, their clothes well and truly ruined, but that was fine by Dannen who was shocked to still be counted among the living. He took a slow, deep breath, savoring the air passing into his lungs as he did, thinking he'd never tasted anything so fine. He felt a powerful euphoria then, one he'd felt before when overcoming incredible odds. The euphoria lasted right up until he noticed the ten guardsmen standing a short distance away, eyeing him and his companions warily.

Their swords were drawn which was bad, but they hadn't started at hacking him and his companions down yet, and Dannen took that as a good sign. His gaze traveled to the man standing at their front. He was older, appearing to be in his mid-to-late fifties, with long hair that was silver instead of gray, and a long, distinguished beard. An older man, but not elderly, a man who wore his age like a badge of honor, and instead of making him look frail or run-down, his silver hair made him appear vigorous, and he had an air of authority, a magnetism that Dannen had seen in only the world's most powerful men and women.

Dannen realized he did not need to be told who this newcomer was, would not have needed it even had the man not been accompanied by ten guards who, judging by their stances and gazes which seemed to miss nothing, Dannen expected were well-versed in the use of the swords they now held bare.

"Hello," the man said, gazing at their beleaguered, soot-stained party without any sign of disdain or disgust. Without, in fact, any expression at all, his features giving nothing away as to how he felt or why he'd come. "I am—"

"The High Justice of Talinseh," Dannen finished for him, and this, at least, did get a reaction, a small almost imperceptible smile which crept its way onto the man's face.

"Just so," he said, inclining his head, and though his demeanor was casual, Dannen's survival instinct—honed to an edge, if poorly treated over the years—warned him in no uncertain terms that they were in very real danger. "I am Valarius Stendar, High Justice of Talinseh," the man went on, "and you, unless I am mistaken, are Dannen Ateran, the famous Bloody Butcher. And unless my information is lacking, your hulking companion there is one Fedder the Firemaker, a fire mage of no small renown, and..." He paused, squinting as he gazed at the girl, "Mariana Vanderia, a recent graduate from the Guild." He frowned at Tesler. "You, on the other hand, I do not know."

Dannen got the impression that there was very little the High Justice didn't know. Still, he was annoyed that the man was aware of their identities. "You're well-informed," he managed.

A slight smile again. "Yes, well, your entrance into Talinseh was, let us say, slightly less than subtle."

Dannen frowned at Fedder, but the mage refused to meet his eyes. "A pleasure to meet you all," the High Justice went on, "two very famous personages. Still, I regret that my position—and your current situation—requires me to ask what you have been about. This house—you see"—he gestured at the flaming gardens—"belongs to Tribune Histarial, a member of Talinseh's ruling body. I do not wish to make accusations out of turn, of course, but it seems you have chosen to burn it down, a regrettable act, I'm afraid, for as a member of the city and even more so the Tribunal, Histarial is under my protection."

The man seemed reasonable enough, calm, and intelligent, and Dannen had no problem understanding how such a one might rule the Assassin City. *Be careful here, Dannen,* he told himself, *be so very careful.*

The man studied him with eyes that missed nothing, seeming to see right through any lie he might tell to excuse their presence. Dannen felt at once that he was outmatched, like a swordsman who has shown up for a duel only to realize that he has no sword, that he is not even a man, in truth, but a target of the kind used in tilting practice. Clare had told him, only hours ago, that he was not so clever as he thought, and Dannen knew at once that he was nowhere near clever enough to trick the High Justice. Still, given a choice between trying or ending up in a dungeon at best and, far more likely, being executed in the city square, he thought he didn't see that he had much to lose. "Well, you see, High Justice, we were just happening down the street here when we saw the house on fire and..."

"I wonder," the man interrupted, his voice still calm, collected, "do you always go out on the town in such a...state?" He stared pointedly at their filthy clothes.

Dannen frowned down at himself. "Been a tough day."

"Thing is," Mariana said, jumping in, "we were just walking along when we saw the fires, right? So we thought, well, might ought to help, if we can. But the flames were too much, so..."

The High Justice nodded slowly. "I see. So you are just concerned citizens, then?"

"Oh, very concerned," Dannen agreed, and that much, at least, was true, though what it probably wouldn't be useful to say he was mostly concerned about keeping his head attached to his shoulders.

"Kind of you," the High Justice said in an almost bored tone. "I wonder, might Tribune Histarial be here to verify your claim?"

"Fucker had it comin'."

Dannen turned to see that for better or worse—no doubt worse—Fedder seemed to have gotten his breath back, and the mage was staring challengingly at the most powerful man in the city as if he meant to challenge him to a fight.

"I'm sorry?" the High Justice asked.

Ah, screw it, Dannen thought. He was confident that his lie wouldn't have fooled a child anyway, and certainly stood no chance of convincing such a man as the High Justice, so he grunted. "Histarial was a ghoul."

"A ghoul?" the Justice asked, and this time his expression did show a reaction, though it was no more than the raising of an eyebrow.

"That's right," Dannen said. "A ghoul, created by a necromancer. He attacked us, and we destroyed his gem, so he's dead. Or, well, he was already dead, but..." He trailed off, being painfully reminded how talking his way *out* of trouble had never been his strong suit.

"I see," the High Justice said. "And do you have proof of this claim? Perhaps the broken gem—I believe they call it a life gem, do they not?"

Although knew they were likely heading down a conversational road that ended with their hanging, Dannen couldn't help but be impressed. He had expected the ruler of Talinseh's Tribunal to be well-informed, but few people—living people, anyway—knew what a ghoul was, let alone about the magic-infused gems which maintained their pseudo-lives. The man watched him, that slight smile on his face again as if he knew full well Dannen didn't have it, and there was something in that expression that made Dannen angry, an arrogance, like he knew that he was the cleverest person here. And, if anything, Dannen was all the more angry that the man was almost certainly right. "No, we don't have it," he said, "we were a little busy trying not to become human torches, if you want to know the truth."

"I see," the High Justice said again, nodding slowly once more. "So, then, am I to believe that you heard Histarial was a ghoul and chose—one can only assume out of the goodness of your hearts— to come here and save our city from the threat he presented?"

Dannen grunted. "Something like that," he said, knowing the man would shortly give the order for those ten swordsmen to step forward. The only thing left in question would be if they would kill Dannen and his companions now, or perhaps torture them first.

"I sent them."

Clarissa stood in an alleyway, soldiers, some of whom she recognized as the guards which had accompanied her before, pouring out around her.

"Ah, Tribune Clarissa," the High Justice said, and if he was surprised at Clarissa's appearance, he hid it well. "What an unexpected pleasure. Now, forgive me, but do you mean to say that these men—and woman—came here under your orders?"

Clarissa glanced at Dannen, a world of meaning in her gaze, her eyes roaming over the beleaguered group and resting for a moment on Tesler, a vague look of confusion on her face that she banished in an instant. "Yes."

"And by what authority did you give such an order?" the High Justice asked, and though his voice was casual enough, Dannen could feel the trap in his words, a trap which, since he was the ranking authority in Talinseh and any such order would have had to have come from him, seemed unavoidable.

"By my own," Clarissa said, not even attempting to avoid the trap but stepping directly in it as if daring it to bite.

"Your own?" the High Justice asked, and for the first time the man looked genuinely surprised, and there was a flicker of what might have been concern in his eyes. He glanced around at the forty or more soldiers surrounding him and his own men in the street, seeming to notice them for the first time. He did not hurry but swept them with his gaze slowly, meaningfully, before turning back to Clarissa. "You have come, then, to be Talinseh's new High Justice, is that it, Tribune Clarissa?"

Clarissa only hesitated for a moment, but in that moment Dannen saw the ambition, the lust for power and respect which had driven her to such great heights twist her face. Here, then, was the driving force behind her success, the grasping, almost frantic side of her which was like a beast possessed of an insatiable hunger. She normally kept that side of herself well-hidden, and until now, Dannen had caught only hints of its existence, usually in the late hours of the morning when they, in the past, had lain in bed together talking of their dreams, their hopes and needs. Dreaming had always seemed like such a friendly thing, an easy, pleasant way to pass the time, but not for Clarissa. For her, dreams were only proof that she had not yet obtained those things which she wanted, proof of her failure.

It was a side of herself she usually kept well-hidden, but when Valerius mentioned her becoming High Justice, there was no hiding the greed, the *need* that twisted Clarissa's expression. Only for a moment, but it was there, then she cleared her throat, giving herself a visible shake as if waking from a dream. "I...have not come for that," she said slowly as if it was difficult to get the words out.

"Oh?" the High Justice asked.

"I've come for them," Clarissa answered, inclining her head at Dannen and his companions.

"I see," the High Justice said slowly. "Kind of you, I suppose, to have come to gather your employees and ensure their safety. There are many—some might even have believed you among them—who would have happily left them to take the blame themselves."

He was baiting her, looking for a reaction, that much Dannen could see, though what reaction he had in mind, Dannen couldn't guess. Clarissa, though, chose to say nothing, only watched the High Justice silently. She shot a quick glance at Dannen, meeting his eye. Only for a second, but he saw the caring there, the worry, and he immediately felt ashamed of his earlier thoughts. The High Justice was right. Clare could have easily left them to fend for themselves. Certainly, most would have, would have, at the least, denied knowledge of their doings. Clare, though, said nothing.

"Very well," the High Justice said, smiling as if he had earned a point by Clare's silence, "either way, I am afraid you are bound to be disappointed. These men are to be questioned regarding the attack on Tribune Histarial and the burning of his property. It is, you understand, quite impossible for me to allow you to take them from this place. I am sorry, Clarissa."

"You misunderstand me," she said, and though she spoke confidently, Dannen knew her well enough to see the undercurrent of fear thrumming through her, to hear it in her voice. "I am not asking you. These men are under my protection, and they will not be harmed."

"I see," Valerius said. "And tell me, Tribune, if I should refuse your...suggestion? If I should, now, order my men, soldiers in the service of keeping Talinseh safe from those who would destroy it, to step forward and gather up these men, then what would you do?"

"I would feel terrible," she said, "and no doubt I would have guilt, later. But I would order my men to cut them—and you—down."

For the first time, a genuine, inarguable emotion showed on the High Justice's face. Annoyance. And when he spoke, his voice was no longer calm and placid as it had been. "Think about what you're doing, Clarissa," he warned. "I know you had your issues with Histarial. I, too, had some serious questions even after the investigation's conclusion, but blood spilled in the streets is not the way. You, better than anyone else, perhaps even better than myself, know the precarious situation of our city, how easily it might all fall apart. And you would risk all of that, all that you, that *we* have worked to build, for these four?"

Dannen had to admit the man had a point, had damn near talked him into cutting his own throat and saving him the trouble. He glanced over at Clarissa. Their eyes met, and she gave him a small, sad smile. "Yes." She answered simply, and Dannen realized how much of a fool he had been, staring at her, powerful and vulnerable all at the same time. He did not regret the years he had spent with Val, for they had been the most wonderful years of his life. But he understood now that Clarissa had been right, he had always looked at her as an object or an alien species, beyond understanding, powerful and far above him, but he had never seen her as the person, the woman she truly was.

"Clare," the High Justice said, and there was an almost desperate quality to his voice, "please, don't do this. They have been caught in the act, stumbling from the flames they set. If you should aid them in escape...well, justice must be done, there is no way around it. Even I, the High Justice, cannot change that." He said the last sadly, but Dannen barely heard it. He was too busy hearing what the man had called her over and over again in his mind. *Clare.* Dannen had thought only he and the Firemaker called her that, but that wasn't all. The man's voice practically thrummed with feeling, with emotion, and Dannen saw Clare returning the man's stare with an emotion-packed look of her own.

It was clear there had been something between them, perhaps still was. "I know, Valerius," she said softly. "Do what you must— I'll do the same."

The High Justice gave a small, sad smile of his own. "Like always."

She nodded her head. "Like always."

To this point, Dannen had been shocked and sure he and the others were in immediate danger of death, and so was hardly able to make his brain work. Now, though, he found that something pulled him out of his smoke and fear-induced stupor. Jealousy. He saw the way Clarissa and the High Justice were looking at each other, and he did not like it. Ridiculous, of course, to be jealous when he ought to be worried about getting his head caved in by one of the swords pointed in his general direction. Stupid to be thinking about the way the two were looking at each other instead of thinking on what he was going to say—and how quickly he was going to say it—when the torturers started asking questions about why he'd come to Histarial's in the first place.

Ridiculous and stupid, sure, but that didn't change anything. He was jealous. He had no right to be, but the words came out of his mouth before he could stop them. "Well?" he said. "I mean this is sweet and all, two old lovers rekindling their feelings, but if it's all the same to you, I think we'll be leaving—don't suppose you need an audience to get on with this. Just a bed, maybe."

"You're not going anywhere," the High Justice said.

"Yes, Valerius," she said. "They are."

The older man sighed. "Are you sure you want to do this, Clare? You've worked hard to get where you are in Talinseh. Are you really going to throw it all away for...for *them*?" he finished, gesturing at Dannen and his companions with obvious disgust and disbelief.

"Yes."

The High Justice said nothing else, perhaps there was nothing *to* say, and Clarissa turned and walked toward Dannen and the others. "This is subtle, is it?" she asked, raising an eyebrow at the great pillar of smoking rubble which had once been Histarial's home.

Dannen grunted, glancing at Fedder. "Just about as subtle as some people get, I reckon. Come to it," he said, turning back to her, that jealous feeling—ridiculous or not—still close to the surface, "about as subtle as you and the old man's relationship, anyway."

She recoiled as if he'd struck her, a hurt look on her face, but in another moment it was gone as if it had never been. "You all should leave quickly," she said in a soft, hurt voice which made Dannen feel guilty. "I should be able to hold Valarius here for a

194

time, but sooner or later someone is going to carry word of what's happening to his other men, and he has *far* more than I."

Seeing the pain his words had caused, Dannen felt ashamed. Clarissa has risked her life for him, was doing so even now, and as thanks he had put her in a position where, at best, it seemed she was going to lose the power she'd worked so hard to get in Talinseh. And here he was, while she was quite literally saving his life, poking at her. "Clare..." he began, "I didn't mean—"

"No, Dannen," she said, and there was a hard edge to her voice. "No. You don't get to apologize and make it okay. What happened between me and Valerius, *when* it happened, that's none of your business. You were gone with your wife and...and I don't have to explain myself to you." There were tears in her eyes, and Dannen nodded, feeling like the world's biggest ass.

"You're right, Clare," he said. "I...you're right."

She opened her mouth as if she might say more, though whether it would be an angry rebuke or something else, Dannen did not know and never found out. Instead, she took a slow, deep breath, visibly gathering herself. "Get out of here, Dannen." She glanced at the High Justice standing calmly. "I'll deal with Valerius." She did her best to sound confident, but Dannen didn't miss the uncertainty in her eyes.

"Clare—"

But she was already turning away, looking at the Firemaker. She reached out to shake his hand, but Fedder's mouth spread into a wide grin, and a second later, he was scooping her off the ground in a big embrace, surprising Clarissa and Dannen both. But while she might have been surprised, Clarissa didn't look displeased in the slightest, and when the giant mage sat her down she was smiling. "Fedder," she said, "it's been good seeing you again."

The mage smiled. "You too, Clare. You...you sure you don't need our help with this?" he asked, gesturing vaguely at the High Justice's guards as if taking care of it would be no more trouble than chopping firewood or cooking dinner.

"I'm sure," she answered. "Just, do me a favor? Take care of him, will you?" she asked, glancing sideways at Dannen. "I'd hate to go through all this trouble just for him to end up getting himself killed anyway."

Dannen might have argued that Fedder was responsible for the vast majority of the recent threats against his life, but he remained silent, and the red-haired giant grinned widely. "I'll do what I can, but you know the Butcher—he doesn't make it easy."

"No," she said softly, "no, he doesn't." She glanced at Tesler and Mariana and gave them a single nod. "Good luck."

She turned away then, and Dannen was struck again by her beauty, by her grace and, more than that, by the vulnerability she kept hidden beneath her hard exterior. A vulnerability which, when it showed itself, was one of the most beautiful things Dannen had ever seen. "Clare..." he began, but she shook her head sadly, turning back.

"Don't, Dannen. It won't do any good for you to say it, will just hurt us both. We've had our chance, I think, had our time, and it was good. Sometimes, it was even great. But the past is the past and neither priests nor gods nor mages can bring it back, and that's probably for the best anyway. Now, go."

There was a lot Dannen wanted to say then, but he had never been good with words. Besides, she was right. The past was the past and no amount of wishing could bring it back—if so, Val would still be alive. "Goodbye, Clare," he said finally, "and thank you."

She smiled. "Goodbye." He turned and started away but stopped as she spoke again. "And Danny?"

"Yes, Clare?" he said, his heart racing, suddenly thinking that perhaps their time wasn't gone, after all, and if it were, perhaps they could find it again, together.

Her smile turned sad. "Don't come back to Talinseh. Ever."

And just like that, the tower of vain hopes he'd built in moments collapsed even quicker into ruin. *If there is any skill at which men excel,* he thought, *it is in telling ourselves the world is how we want it to be. But the world is and can only be the way it is.* "Goodbye, Clare," he said softly.

He said nothing else, for there was nothing to be said. He turned and headed down the streets, his three companions following, silent as funeral attendants showing respect for the dead. Perhaps, Dannen thought, that was exactly what they were doing. He wanted to turn, to tell Clarissa something of the way he felt, to try to make her understand, but the truth was, he didn't understand it himself, so he walked on, and he did not turn back. After all, there was nothing to turn back for—he had seen to that himself.

CHAPTER EIGHT

They were not attacked when leaving the city, though everyone they passed stared with suspicion. Dannen could not blame them. He, too, would have been bothered by the sight of such an odd group walking down the city's main street in bloody clothes with soot-stained faces and hands.

Still, the others weathered the stares without complaint—likely too shocked to still be among the living to care—and Dannen hardly noticed. He was too busy thinking of Clare, and of all the wrong a man could do without ever meaning it. He always set out to do good—or at least to do nothing at all—but it seemed he always ended up doing bad anyway. Certainly he'd done so with Clare, first breaking her heart without knowing it and now leaving her in the ill graces of the most powerful man in the city.

"She'll be okay," Fedder said after an hour of walking, as if he could read Dannen's mind.

Dannen glanced at him. "Will she?" It wasn't a challenge, not really, and what he wanted more than anything was for Fedder to tell him she would be, to lie, if he needed to. But the mage said nothing, only walked on in uncharacteristic silence.

Perhaps aware of his dark mood, Mariana and Tesler also did not speak. It was a somber party which finally arrived at the northern gate of the city. Four guards were stationed there, and when they saw Dannen and the others approach, they went for their weapons. "Ho, there," one said, "just what in—"

Fedder wasn't a patient man at the best of times, and these were far from the best of times. He raised his massive fist above his head and suddenly it was wreathed in flame. "Get out of our way," he growled in a voice which promised violent and permanent retribution should the guards refuse him.

The men were paid well to be guards in such a dangerous city, made even more money, Dannen suspected, by the many bribes they were paid, but it didn't take any of them long to mark Fedder as a mage and not much longer than that to decide that, however much they were paid, it wasn't enough to get set on fire. They got out of the way, and Dannen and the others walked through the gate. No doubt, the guards would run and tell those who paid them to keep tabs about the incident as soon as Dannen and the others were past, but he didn't care. The only thing they would be able to tell was that the group was going north, and it was a big world, after all.

A big bitch of a world.

***

They walked for over an hour before Mariana finally spoke, breaking the silence. "So uh...you don't mind my askin', where are we goin'?"

Dannen started at the sound of her voice in the stillness, pulled from his thoughts, thoughts of Clarissa, yes, but thoughts of Val, too, of how much he missed her. He always did, of course, but sometimes, that feeling of loss, of *being* lost, was a distant thing. Still there—it was always there—but something he could almost forget about. Now, though, it was close, that feeling, pressing around on all sides, and he cleared his throat, giving his head a shake. "North."

Silence again for another few moments before Mariana answered. "North. Well, that narrows it down a bit, doesn't it?"

Fedder coughed what might have been a laugh but said nothing, and Dannen sighed. He didn't feel much like talking. Didn't feel much like walking, either. Come to think about it, he didn't feel like doing anything at all. He'd been this way before, especially in the days following Val's death. He felt empty, like a wineskin turned up. In the past, he'd sought to banish that feeling—or failing that, to drown it—by visiting the nearest tavern. The ale helped—it hurt, too, of course, putting him into situations like the one he was currently facing—but it did help him to forget, at least for a time. But a man couldn't be drunk forever—the gods knew he'd given it a few honest tries—and whenever he sobered up, the past was always there waiting. And he was always left to understand that the drink hadn't banished it after all, that it had always been there, latched onto him like a tick, fat with his blood.

He would have liked to have been drunk then, loved it, really, but even if they'd had anything to drink, it would have been foolish to stop. Clarissa might be able to hold off the High Justice, but not forever. Sooner or later, he would send men after them, *had* to. After all, if people found out a Tribune had been murdered—hard to keep it quiet since Fedder had seen fit to burn the man's estate down—and nothing had been done, it would set a dangerous precedent.

No, men would come for them, might even be coming already, and so they walked on. They walked until the fields outside Talinseh gave way to thick forests, the road flanked on either side by towering trees, some with trunks wider than a man was tall, massive specters in the darkness. They walked until the lights of Talinseh vanished somewhere behind them, and the need to rest, to catch their breath, began to overshadow their need to put as much distance between themselves and the city as possible. After all, a man could not sustain terror forever. Eventually, no matter how reasonable a reaction it might be, terror would fade into the background, as it was now doing for Dannen, leaving him feeling only tired and wrung out, all too aware of the soreness in his feet and legs.

"We'd best make camp," he said finally, his voice the first noise aside from their shuffling footsteps and panting breaths for over an hour. No one argued. No one said anything at all, in fact, simply followed as he led them away from the road. Not too far, of course, for the woods here were deep and dark, and it would be easy to become lost. No point in getting lost in the woods, starving to death or being eaten by its creatures and saving the High Justice the trouble.

"Best forego a fire tonight," he said. "They might see the light." No one argued and it looked like they'd had no intention of making a fire anyway. No sooner had he stopped in a clearing—from which the road was still barely visible through the trees—than his companions silently unrolled their bedrolls and collapsed into them.

Dannen sighed, laying out his bedroll near the others. He didn't lie down though, not yet, for he had seen other clearings like this over the years, other faces pinched with weariness and fear. He'd seen them, and he knew enough about himself to know he would be unable to sleep, not for a while, at least. Instead, he only stared down at their three shadowy forms. They had all turned on their sides so that they faced away from him, faced away from each other, choosing instead to gaze out into the darkness of the forest. Only a reasonable precaution to help them react faster if those who were no doubt searching for them found them...or was it something else, something more? Some subconscious attempt to forget about each other for a little while, to forget about their plight, and forget about the soldiers chasing them, and the fact that those companions with whom they found themselves were strangers.

Oh yes, Dannen had seen this clearing before, had been in it, had *lived* it, too many times to count. He knew well this empty feeling of loss when one for whom he had cared was lost, and though he had not seen the executioner's blade do its work, was spared that much, at least, it seemed to him that there could be no other outcome for Clarissa, for doing what she had done. Clarissa was clever, the cleverest person he had ever met, and if anybody could make it out of such a predicament, surely she could, but that gave him little solace. After all, he'd known other clever people over the years, and by and large, their cleverness bought them nothing but an early grave. The world didn't care for cleverness, after all, seemed to take it, like so many other things—like the living, come to it—as a personal affront.

He knew this place. Though the shadows were everywhere, huddled around them, though the faint moonlight did nothing to drive away the darkness, served instead only to accentuate it, to give it lines, to define it and thereby give it power, he recognized this place. Perhaps he recognized it *because* of the darkness, that darkness not just without, huddled among the trees and crouched in their canopies, but that darkness which lay within him as well. Clarissa would not be the first he had lost. In truth, she would be only one among many of that long list that trailing back seemingly to his birth. He had watched one person after the other, each his better by far die, while he somehow lingered. It made no sense, but then only a fool looked for the world to make sense.

Something landed on his shoulder. Felt like maybe a dinner plate or a bear paw. Turned out, it was Fedder's hand. The mage stood beside him, a mass and height that under normal circumstances would intimidate any man, as if a mountain came up to stand beside him, one that was liable, at any moment, to take it in mind to crush him. Just now, though, the Firemaker wasn't laughing maniacally, bellowing a war cry, or smashing someone's something into a *new*, unrecognizable something. Instead, he looked different than normal—he looked tired. His thick shoulders were slumped, and there was a haggard look to his face. He gave Dannen a small smile that obviously cost him.

"How's it going, Butcher?" he asked quietly in a compassionate voice that was as strange coming from the man as a cat's meow from the mouth of a dog.

Dannen didn't dare answer that, didn't even dare search within himself to find the answer, for he knew enough about himself to know it was better to just keep moving forward, especially when only pain lay behind any man who took it in mind to glance back. "Thought you'd be asleep," he said finally.

The Firemaker nodded his head almost imperceptibly, acknowledging Dannen's evasion of the question. "Don't sleep much, not anymore." He glanced back as if to make sure the other two were still asleep then leaned in close. "Don't say nothin' to the girl, but in the last few years, seems to me I spend all my nights jumpin' out of bed and racin' to the privy to see if I can make it before wettin' myself like some child." He shook his head as if in wonder then hocked and spat. "Damnest thing of it is that, sometimes, it's a close-run thing."

"It's a bitch," Dannen said.

"What's that?"

"Getting older."

"Yeah," Fedder agreed. "It's a bitch. When I ain't havin' to run and take a piss, I'm lyin' awake for fear I'll have to in another moment. Still, guess I ought to be thankful. After all, there's plenty of others ain't been so lucky, aye? Plenty we've spent time with, maybe, friends and enemies, too. And you know the funny thing? I find I miss 'em both just about the same."

Dannen had known Fedder for years but had never known him to be the kind of man who stood around talking about his feelings. Unless, of course, he was feeling like putting someone's head through a wall. Not exactly a sensitive type, and he knew it cost the man to have this conversation. Just as he knew that it was as close as Fedder would come to talking about Clarissa. Though the moonlight was poor, it was good enough to illuminate the tears in the giant's eyes. It made him wonder why there were none in his own. He thought, perhaps, he'd cried all his tears out when Val died and there just weren't any left. Still, it was a wonder to see Fedder in such a way. *Sometimes,* he thought, *the strongest of us can also be the most vulnerable.*

"All of them dead and gone," Dannen said, "yet, here we are, lingering."

Fedder shrugged, staring out into the darkness thoughtfully. "Guess that's what winnin' feels like. After all, we've beat everythin' we come up against, hadn't we?"

Dannen watched the man, watched him until he felt his eyes on him and turned to meet his gaze. "You feeling like a winner right now, Fedder?"

The giant winced, scratching at his thick beard. "Naw. Naw, I don't guess I do. You?"

Dannen sighed. "I just feel tired."

"Best get some rest, then. Busy few weeks ahead, you know, what with the undead and the necromancer and his asshole swordsman brother and all that."

"I didn't mean that kind of tired," Dannen said.

"I know."

They said nothing else for a time, for there was nothing they could say, nothing to answer the emptiness all "heroes" felt when the fighting was done, in those moments of quiet when the princess was saved, the villain vanquished, and they were heroes no more but only people once again. People with aches and pains, with scars that made each step a little harder, burdened with the weight of regret and loss, a weight that grew heavier over the years until a man could barely walk for it, until his back, his *soul,* were bowed beneath the weight of it.

It was the part the storybooks didn't talk about. What was left of a man's soul once the vanquishing was done, a bent, twisted thing that, could a man have seen it, he might have thought it formed by some cruel, malevolent god, an inside to match the beaten, battered outside that being a "hero" left a man. It was a damned joke, being a hero. Life in general, come to that. A man walked through his life while the world threw punches at him, knocking him down over and over just for him to stand back up and do it all over again. At least, that was, until he was no longer *able* to stand. Then those who loved him—if he were lucky enough to have any—said some words, threw some dirt on him, and the whole thing kept right on going, a mad carnival where the rides never stop, kept getting faster and faster the older a man gets, and he can't get off if he wants to.

"Well," Fedder said after a time, "Guess I'll go lie down, think about pissin'."

"I wish you the best of it," Dannen said.

Fedder grunted, moving away, and Dannen sighed, staring out at the darkness and the shadowed forms of the trees. There were ghosts out there, watching him. Thousands of ghosts, men and women he had known once, ghosts who followed him everywhere he went, a trail of the dead that always dogged his heels. He wondered if he looked close enough, if he would see Clarissa among them. They never smiled or laughed or spoke, those faces. But though they said no words, their empty, slack faces and their empty, dead eyes spoke volumes, showing Dannen their hopelessness, gazing at him with accusation. "I'm sorry, Clare," he whispered. "I'm sorry."

"Dannen?"

He turned to see Firemaker staring at him. The mage studied him with calm eyes that were not angry or threatening, only sad, and Dannen was acutely aware that in all the years since he had met him, Fedder had rarely ever called him by name. "I was just remembering," Fedder said softly, "years ago, when we first met Clare. You remember?"

Dannen couldn't help but give a small smile. "I remember. As I recall, you tried to hit on her, and she threatened to tear you apart limb from limb."

Fedder's mouths split into a wide grin. "And I all too keen to let her—there are far worse ways for a man to go. Anyway, I remember bein' impressed myself. Not too many folks would come back at me like that, you know? It was brave...fearless. *She* was fearless."

"Yes," Dannen agreed, "she was. Just like when you didn't stop, despite her warnings, and as I recall she gave you a black eye for your trouble."

Fedder barked a laugh. "Like I said, fearless. But not just that—plenty men thought they were fearless are rotting in some unmarked grave just now or bein' digested in some monster's stomach. No, not just fearless—*clever*. Why, over the years, I guess she must have saved our lives half a dozen times, always doing research and learning more about any job we got than the man who gave it to us, outthinkin' everybody else."

"Yeah," Dannen agreed, remembering the way Clarissa had, seemingly effortlessly, always been there to help. "She was something."

"She *is* something," Fedder said, and Dannen winced, recoiling as if he'd been struck as he met the big man's eyes. "She'll be alright, Dannen. If anybody in the world is capable of coming out of this thing not just alive but smellin' like roses, it's her. You know that, don't you?"

Dannen hesitated, then finally gave a nod. "I know."

"She'll be fine," Fedder said again, then he glanced over at the sleeping forms of Tesler and Mariana. "And so will they."

Dannen grunted. He had been worried about the two, worried they would just become others on the long list of people who had died trying to help him, but he thought he'd hidden it well. Despite Fedder's rough exterior, the man possessed more than a little cleverness of his own. Dannen shrugged as if it didn't matter either way, trying for casual nonchalance. "I'm sure you're right."

The giant mage gave a small smile as if he knew good and well how Dannen felt, and likely he did. "I *am* right," he said, then he winked and started back toward his bedroll, leaving Dannen alone once more. Alone, but he was surprised to find, that he was not as lonely. For all the aggravation Fedder caused him, for all those times when the man seemed bent on getting them killed, he was a good friend. Maybe even a good man, though Dannen wasn't sure he would know one if he saw him. And to his surprise, he felt better after their talk.

The clearing was still the clearing, the darkness still dark, and the shadows still waited, capering around in the edges of the circle cast by the moonlight. But somehow, the clearing did not seem so full of menace, the darkness not quite as dark as it had been. And as for the shadows, well, true, their caperings might have been strange or threatening, fey and otherworldly, but then he had felt much the same about Val, had he not? Before he'd married her? And those few years he'd had with her had been good years—maybe the only truly good years of his life.

He shook his head, staring at the big form of the mage in his bedroll in something like wonder. A mage, that much was certain, a wielder of magic, and not all magic was flame and death. Some, Dannen thought, was subtle. He felt better, then, good enough that he didn't even mind that the others had gone to sleep and left the first watch to him.

CHAPTER NINE

Sloan glided through the dark woods like a shadow, flitting from tree trunk to tree trunk, making use of the skills the Guild had taught him, how to blend in, how to move silently even over the eaves and twigs littering the forest floor. Everyone in the Guild was taught as much, of course, but Sloan had moved beyond even the teachings of the Guild, had become better than any other, had become the *best* assassin in all Talinseh. He had used those same skills—and others—to make sure any who might have challenged his claim to the title of the world's greatest assassin were instead too busy decorating some of the city's back alleys—their throats irrevocably and terminally slashed—to waste any time challenging Sloan.

Admittedly, the title of the world's greatest assassin didn't come with any trophy or plaque, and there were no celebratory applause as there might have been for a man being knighted after some great feat of arms. The applause for the success of an assassin were always silent, given, as they were, by dead men and women who could neither shout nor cheer, who could do nothing but serve as mute testament to Sloan's talents.

Yet, he had never begrudged his relative obscurity. After all, obscurity was vital for an assassin to do his work. It was enough for his peers to fear him, to know to stay out of his way. Peers who would look away when he entered a room, refusing to meet his gaze, who never competed with him for a particularly lucrative contract as they had when he'd first started out.

Not sporting, perhaps, not exactly something to foster the spirit of competition, but that suited Sloan just fine. He cared nothing for sport or competition. He killed because there was money in it, good money, money that he would not allow others to take from him. Of course, that was not the only reason. There was good money in whoring too—he should know, as he spent a fair bit of coin on it himself—just so long as a woman or man was willing to accept a few black eyes, maybe a bit worse now and then. He was an assassin because he enjoyed it.

When he first started out, there had been those among the Guild—mostly of the old guard, men and women who had long since given up on the business of killing or, more likely, had it give up on them and were content to sit around saying menacing things and thinking menacing thoughts—who'd questioned Sloan's methods. Methods not just about his dealings with other Guild members, though that was a large part of it, but also with his marks. Every assassin of the Guild had his or her signature, a mark or method they left to let others, particularly other members of the Guild, know who had completed a contract without letting the guards know as well. In truth, of course, the guards often did know, but a little coin made sure they forgot quickly enough.

Some assassins enjoyed leaving trinkets—dolls or small blades or a dozen other fool things. Others loved to gain their fame and infamy from simple marks they left etched into a wall or bedpost. Alternatively, there were always those who preferred to use a unique method for their kills, a patterned garrote, exsanguination, there had been many over the years, and if the members of the Guild were anything, they were inventive. Sloan, though, did not care about leaving anything behind, thought it was only a fool who did. Nor did he care about taking the time to leave a mark for those who discovered the body. None of those things were enjoyable to him, and he most definitely wouldn't have enjoyed the thought of having to stick to a particular method of killing, making his job more difficult, for any fool knew each job lent itself best to a different method.

Sloan had no hobbies, did not care to go drinking or carousing like so many others. Even his visits to the whores of Talinseh from time to time felt to him like no more than a necessary thing, a release of pressure like turning a valve. Neither was he a man who enjoyed gorging himself on food or losing himself in drink. What he *did* enjoy, however, was killing.

He had started with small animals, had been at it for over a year before his mother and father caught him at it. It had not stopped him, of course, for the urge to kill, to spill the blood of another living thing, had been strong—still was—far too strong to repress. What it *had* done, however, was to make him better at hiding those urges, those wants and *needs*. But when he was on a job, he allowed his true urges to take hold, and only in those moments did he truly enjoy himself. And when given free rein, his urges, his wants, were without fail, quite...bloody. Quite...brutal.

A ferocity, a brutality that sometimes even sickened *him* when he'd finished, when that beast within him had finally vented its fury for the moment, leaving nothing behind but blood and glistening bone...and the screams, of course, screams the echoes of which lingered long after the one who made them was dead. What he felt, following those first moments of sickness, was not shame as some might have expected. Instead, it was contentment, elation, the pleasure a blacksmith might feel after crafting his masterpiece, the satisfaction of a job well done. In short, he felt...happy.

He loved to kill, loved to do it savagely and brutally and to make his victim an object, to, by some trick of magic normally reserved for the greatest of magicians, transform a living, breathing man or woman into a pile of blood and flesh and bone.

And few jobs were offered to him which he did not take, for it had never mattered to him who those men and women were that he killed, just so long as they died by *his* doing. But this time, on this mission, he was not at work for the Guild, or some individual seeking to hire him without the inevitable records requesting a job at the Guild produced. Instead, tonight, he worked for himself.

He had heard, of course, of the woman known as Mariana, just as he knew of all the Guild's assassins and, just like with the others, he had cared to know nothing more. She had been largely irrelevant, a woman who, assuming she never got in his way and became an obstacle in his path, in the sating of his desires, did not warrant his attention. Still, she *had* found herself in his path, and not stumbled into it blindly out of unfortunate incident, but had stepped boldly into it, giving away his identity to all those gathered in the town square of Talinseh.

A few dozen people, no more than that, but in less than a week everyone in the city would know his identity. After all, the remains of Sloan's victims, once found, always produced somewhat of a spectacle, even in a place where assassinations and crimes were commonplace, and his identity had long been a topic of speculation and rumor among the city's citizens, whispered in quiet voices in taverns throughout the city as if even saying it aloud might act as some spell to draw his attention. Sloan had heard the whispers, had enjoyed them too, enjoyed the fear in the eyes of those who whispered it. It had amused him, on such occasions, to imagine going over to the speakers' table, of telling them who he was, smiling and seeing what came of it.

But it had always been an idle fantasy, one he never would have acted on, for he knew a killer's greatest strength was his anonymity. And somehow—he did not yet know how, but he would find out—the girl, Mariana, had discovered his carefully guarded secret and proceeded to casually reveal it to the mob, tossing it out like a man might toss meat to a pack of dogs. Even Sloan could not imagine the full extent of the damage she'd caused in doing so. Some of it, of course, could be fixed, could be paid for either in coin or blood, but there was some, he knew, which would be irreparable.

No, Sloan did not know all the consequences of her careless act, but he at least knew one of them—she, and those with her, would die. They would die badly, and their collective deaths would go some way toward paying him back for the trouble she'd caused. She would not volunteer to do so, of course, but it did not matter. There was no assassin in Talinseh, in all the world, who was Sloan's equal, and whether she wanted it or not, he would carve the price of her mistake, of her audacity, from her flesh and the flesh of those with whom she traveled.

She had destroyed years of work in a casual moment, clearly not understanding what she gambled in doing so, but Sloan would make her understand. He would enjoy it. So, even though there was no monetary reward in it for him, he had followed at a distance as the girl and her companions left the square where she had been accosted by a mob. He had followed them as they'd been escorted to the house of Tribune Clarissa, a woman that was, among the Guild, known for being notoriously difficult to kill no matter the large number of contracts put on her life, had even followed them to Tribune Hastrial's dwelling. He had watched the havoc they'd wreaked, particularly the giant who Sloan now knew to be a mage. And not just any mage, that one, but a mage of incredible skill, one Sloan suspected few in the world could match.

Him, Sloan would kill first. The others—a young assassin, an out-of-shape swordsman who was clearly past his prime, and what appeared to be a madman with a pet squirrel—would cause him little trouble. The mage, though, could prove difficult, if he was not careful, but Sloan had learned at a young age to *always* be careful. He crept into the woods in the direction the group had gone, gliding from shadow to shadow as silently, as stealthily, as if he were a shadow himself, no more than a patch of darkness in the night.

It was a slow process to move silently, rolling his feet with exaggerated care to keep from breaking any twig underfoot or stepping on a dead leaf that might alert his prey of his coming, but he did not mind. Now, as always, when the killing was close, he felt eager and anxious, full of excited energy. He knew his satisfaction was close at hand. It would not fix all the damage the girl had done. But it would go a long way toward it.

Blundering through the woods as they had, he doubted if the group had taken more than ten or fifteen minutes to reach what could only sneeringly be called a campsite, as they had lit no fire, had only collapsed from weariness where they now lay in a rough circle in the clearing. It was understandable, given the last few days they'd had, to be exhausted, but that understanding would do nothing to keep them from suffering.

Sloan crouched low, surveying the campsite, and froze when he noted a figure seated with its back propped against a tree, seeming to stare directly at him. But after a tense moment, he realized it was the young madman, and he was asleep. A slow smile crept on Sloan's face. Not an easy thing, keeping watch, far harder than most thought even for those with experience in such things. It was difficult to stay awake while everyone around you slept, when the night pressed close and sleep tempted you with soft whispers like a lover beckoning you into her embrace. It was understandable, then, that the man had fallen asleep, but that would do nothing to change what his mistake would cost him and his companions.

Sloan carefully examined the other figures lying in their bedrolls. The darkness and their bedrolls hid their identities, but each showed the telltale bulge—the mage's far larger than any other—that indicated without doubt they were fast asleep. The only member of the party he did not see was the madman's squirrel, but that mattered little to Sloan. Likely, the beast had run away, choosing to be with its forest kin.

An inexperienced assassin might have rushed forward then, allowing his eagerness to outweigh his caution, but Sloan had not become the greatest of Talinseh's assassins by being careless. So, instead of charging forward, he waited. A minute, then another, until he was confident they were all truly asleep. At least, they were all turned away from him, as if even in slumber they did not wish to acknowledge the death that came upon them, so that even should their eyes happen to flutter open, they would see nothing of his movements.

Silently, Sloan drew the two knives sheathed at his sides, one a long, cruel blade, sharp as a razor, and another, shorter one, curved and notched. The smaller one was his favorite, a tool technically not for killing but torture. The big knife might extract blood, might cut away flesh, but the smaller one extracted pain, cut away hope. Sloan lived for that moment when he saw the last remnants of hope of salvation leave his victim's gaze. His grin widened as he promised himself he would leave the girl for last, so he might take his time with her, might make her understand, before the end, the true nature of her mistake.

Slowly, so slowly that even *had* someone been watching, they would have thought him no more than the shifting of a shadow cast by the swaying branches overhead, Sloan began to creep forward. He called on all his years of experience, on skills unsurpassed in the entire world, to move stealthily, so stealthily he began to believe he was no more than a shadow, no more than a blur of darkness in a world of it. *Surely,* he thought as he glided toward them, *even the air itself cannot go so undetected.*

That was when he felt the tap on his shoulder.

Sloan was not a man often surprised. After all, it was he who surprised others, who ambushed them when they least expected it. He was not often surprised and so had little practice at it. So when he spun to stare at the giant looming over him, a mad grin on the man's face, he froze. Only for an instant, only for the space of a single breath, but it was enough, for in that instant the giant moved, struck with a speed which should have been impossible in one of his size. The last thought that went through Sloan's head before a fist the size of a dinner plate crashed into it was that it was impossible. He had seen the man's sleeping form, had *seen* it.

But then the mage's blow struck home, driving all thought and consciousness out with it, and Sloan was spinning, spinning through the air and the darkness both. *Impossible.*

***

Fedder grunted, scratching at his thick beard as he studied the unconscious form at his feet. The figure had dropped his blades when he struck the tree, maybe before then—not that it mattered much either way. Fedder knelt, studying the man, trying to see if he recognized him, a task made more difficult by the way the stranger's face was all twisted up, his nose seeming to have decided that, having spent a lifetime on the front of his face, it might give the side a go. The blood—copious amounts that looked black in the moonlight—didn't help. After a moment, though, Fedder thought he did recognize him after all, as the man the girl had called an assassin, the city's best, as he recalled. He shook his head. Seemed that standards were dropping everywhere, and wasn't that a shame? Time was, a man took pride in what he did.

The assassin's eyes were open, staring blankly up at Fedder as if in question of where he had come from. "Had to take a piss," Fedder explained, figuring maybe he owed the man that much after rearranging his face as he had.

He heard a rustling and turned, expecting—hoping, if he were honest—that the man had come with others, for the fight had been far too short to entertain him. Instead, he was surprised to see the little squirrel which was normally propped on Tesler's shoulder skitter out from his own bedroll. It paused, looking at him, then at the stranger, and had Fedder not known better, he would have thought the creature was having some very humanlike thoughts, for there seemed to be an intelligence in its gaze. Then it skittered up to the madman's shoulder and peered at him in an expression that, had it been a man, Fedder would have thought smug.

Fedder hocked and spat, promising himself that he'd be sure to wipe that smug look off the furry little bastard's face if it had taken it in mind to shit in his bedroll. Then, because there didn't seem to be anything else going on and he was experiencing one of those rare moments when he didn't feel the immediate need to take a piss, Fedder walked to his own bedroll and fell asleep.

***

Dannen woke slowly, gently, with none of the jerking, brief surges of panic he often felt when waking—remnants, perhaps, of his years spent playing at being a hero. The forest breeze was gentle on his face, and he stared at the tree limbs swaying overhead, a rhythmic, peaceful quality to their movements. Birds chirped in the air, and the sun filtering through the trees was warm. Dannen knew he needed to get up, knew there was still some distance between them and their objective, and that it would be wise to get as far away from the city of Talinseh as possible. Instead, though, he chose to lie there, to enjoy that moment of calm, of peace, for he knew such moments were incredibly rare, and when they came, incredibly brief.

But it was not just his surroundings which gave him calm. His conversation with Fedder the night before had done it, too, had taken the worst of the edge off his worry for Clare. The man had been right, after all—if there was a more capable woman, or *person* for that matter, in all the world than Clare, Dannen had never met them. If anyone could survive the High Justice's displeasure, it was Clare. Dannen wouldn't at all be surprised if, the next time he saw her, he discovered that she had somehow managed to turn the whole incident to her advantage.

He was so full of peace, of a quiet joy he couldn't remember having felt in years, that he reveled in it, lay drifting on its currents the way a man who'd been dying of thirst might float upon the eddies of a chanced-upon lake or river. It seemed to him, in that moment, that perhaps the stories and fables with their chivalrous knights where monsters were always vanquished and everything set to right again—stories he'd always thought ridiculous, if not outright dangerous—might be true after all, that he might have somehow found himself within one of their pages.

It was a feeling that remained with him as he finally rose to his feet, stretching and glorying in the pleasant numbness in his mind and body. A feeling that lasted for another moment, right up until he saw the dead man. At least, he thought the man *must* be dead. His face was a mask of blood, his arm bent at an unnatural angle.

"What the fuck?" he said, not sure who he was talking to, not sure of much of anything, really, as the peace which had filled him a moment before slowly faded to be replaced with confusion and panic.

"Ah, you're up."

Dannen turned as Fedder walked up beside him, his hand held out to offer a piece of hard traveling bread, a pleasant smile on his face.

"Who the fuck is that?" Dannen demanded, taking the bread and thrusting it in the direction of the body crumpled at the base of a nearby tree.

"Oh," Fedder said, looking embarrassed, "that. Well, we had an unwelcome visitor in the night."

"An unwelcome visitor," Dannen repeated.

"That's right," Fedder agreed. "I took care of it."

Said casually, the way a husband might inform his wife he'd shooed away some traveling merchant come knocking at their door. "What do you mean you took care of it?" Dannen demanded.

Fedder blinked. "Well...seems obvious, don't it?"

Dannen gritted his teeth, telling himself that it would be unwise to attack the mage with a sword—particularly since he didn't have one—and even more unwise to attempt to do so barehanded. "Well?" he snapped. "Is he dead?"

Fedder's face screwed up in thought, and he turned to gaze at the body, scratching at his beard and, by all appearances, giving it a good think. "You know? It's hard to say."

On that much, at least, Dannen had to agree. Though he tended toward thinking the poor bastard was dead. If he wasn't, he was in for a wakening substantially less pleasant than Dannen's had been. "So what did he want?" he asked, scared of what the mage might say, thinking it likely as not that the man could have been some traveling merchant and Fedder taken it in mind to have a good row.

The mage's eyebrows drew down in thought. "No way to know for sure, I guess," he said. "But with the blades he was carryin' and the way he was creepin' up with 'em like he aimed to use 'em, I'd say he likely wanted to kill us."

The realization that Dannen had been sleeping soundly while a man intent on his murder crept toward him in the darkness sent a shiver of fear crawl up his spine. The mage, however, seemed wholly unconcerned. Of course, Dannen had been in some tight spots with Fedder over the years and knew it would take more than a single assassin—indeed, a raging manticore hadn't been enough to do the trick—to make the mage uncomfortable.

"Someone tries to kill us in the middle of the night," he said sharply, "and you didn't think to *wake* me?"

Fedder appeared surprised by his anger. "Well, it was just the one, wasn't it? Seemed like a bit of a waste, wakin' everyone up, makin' a big to do. Besides, you all looked so peaceful, sleepin' like you were."

"Probably would have looked less so with a knife sticking out of me," Dannen managed through gritted teeth.

Fedder nodded. "Probably."

"So what then?" Dannen asked. "You heard him, is that it, or was it your watch?"

"Nah," Fedder agreed, smiling pleasantly as if they were having a relaxed conversation about the weather instead of their attempted murders. "It was the lad's watch—fell asleep, but don't worry, I already had a word with him. Anyway, I just had to take a piss. 'Bout tripped over the bastard comin' back to camp."

Dannen felt another shiver of fear in understanding that the only reason they weren't all dead was because Fedder had needed to piss. He spun, looking for Tesler, intent on giving the young man a piece of his mind, but when he saw the man, sitting a short distance away with his back propped against a tree, a dejected look on his face, he decided to let it go. After all, they were alive—against all odds—and judging by the man's expression, and the way the girl, Mariana who was currently busy packing her bedroll, scowled at him, he'd been punished enough already.

Mostly, Dannen was just glad the girl wasn't looking at him like that, the type of look capable of drawing blood. It was funny—not in a laughing sort of way—how women all seemed born with that scowl, while he'd had to work at his own for years and still wasn't close to theirs. Seemed that the gods just handed the scowls out to them along with all their woman bits. Men might conquer kingdoms—and take swords and horses and arrows and blood to do it—but women could conquer those same men with nothing but a look. No, he'd say nothing to the boy, but he damned sure didn't envy him.

"Well," he said with a sigh as he turned back to Fedder, "maybe we should search him, find out—"

"We're not *all* fools," the girl said, making sure to scowl at Tesler in case there was any doubt who she meant. "I already did." She glanced at the body. "It's Sloan. From Talinseh."

Sloan...Sloan. Something about the name was familiar to Dannen, and he grunted as he remembered where he'd heard it. "You mean Sloan as in the man you said was the best assassin in a city full of assassins?"

"That's the one," she said, nodding before going about packing her bedroll, seemingly as unperturbed as Fedder.

What were the chances, Dannen wondered, of a man surviving when all of his companions seemed to be competing to see who could get them killed in the most brutal fashion? No. Probably, it was better not to think of it. He still had Perandius's impossible task to be about, and running away from his companions and screaming like a stark-raving madman—something he was likely to do if he spent more than a few seconds contemplating his odds of living through the month—wouldn't help him get it done.

"Do you think others will come?"

He turned to glance at Tesler who'd spoken and was more than a little gratified to see that he, at least, seemed uncomfortable. The problem, though, was his discomfort had less to do with the assassin on the ground and more to do with the way Mariana was still staring daggers at him.

"Like flies to shit," Dannen said, hocking and spitting. "Come on—let's get moving. We need to put more distance between us and the city."

Everyone set about packing and in less than five minutes they were on their way again, leaving the dead—or unconscious—man lying crumpled against a tree behind them.

***

They made good time—few things motivated one to exercise as much as the threat of imminent death. By midday, they were considerably farther from Talinseh and Dannen, at least, was considerably out of breath.

"No sign of anyone yet."

Panting from their exertions, Dannen glanced over at Tesler. The man was barely even breathing hard. Mariana, likewise, seemed to be suffering no ill-effects from their exercise, the only indications she'd done more than wake up were her rosy cheeks and a slight sheen of sweat.

Dannen scowled as best he could while struggling to suck in ragged breaths—not his best scowl, he was certain—and tried, failed but tried, at least, not to hate the two for their youth. Even Fedder, a man near his own age, seemed relatively unaffected by their brisk pace, though the mage had a grim expression like someone who had undertaken a difficult task and just wanted to get it done. *Not really a fair comparison,* Dannen thought, *considering the bastard takes one step for every three of mine.*

He glanced at his paunch—or what was left of it, the last few weeks not having erased it, not yet, but certainly having made a dent—and decided for at least the thousandth time that he would ease off the drink from here on out. It was a decision he was quite confident would hold up, at least until they passed a tavern and had a moment where no one was trying to kill them. Which likely meant for the rest of his life.

"No," he agreed finally, looking back at Tesler and the squirrel propped on his shoulder, "no sign yet."

The woods around them had grown deep and thick, the trees seeming to crowd in on each other as if fighting for space, something somehow malevolent about the way they loomed overhead, the way their branches seemed to reach toward the path as if eager to scoop up travelers. Dannen realized he knew exactly where they were.

"The Dead Forest," Fedder said, as if reading his thoughts.

Even the words made Dannen uneasy, for he had been here before, had nearly died—something that could be said, sadly, of almost any place on the continent—here. And not just died but died horribly, as he had been attacked by a wild unicorn who, as it turned out, was far from the lovable, mystical creature the storybooks made out and were instead vicious beasts who, when not standing around looking majestic and cropping grass, loved nothing more than skewering unwary travelers on their horns.

Dannen rubbed idly at his side where one of his many scars was, this one made by just such a beast. He consoled himself with the fact that it was unlikely such an incident would be repeated, for while the storybooks painted a very inaccurate picture of unicorns and their temperament, they did, at least, come close to accuracy on the rarity of the beasts.

"Dead Forest?" Mariana said doubtfully, looking around at the massive trees, these far taller and thicker at the trunk than those they had seen outside Talinseh. "Kind of a stupid name, isn't it? Don't know that I've ever seen a forest look so...alive."

"You've seriously never heard of it?" Dannen asked, surprised that the girl, having lived so close to the place all her life, would not know of its existence.

"An angry place," Tesler said, seemingly speaking more to himself than his companions. "The trees here are very old, and they hold very old grudges."

Mariana grunted. "Been busy, what with working my way up in the Guild and all. Don't have a lot of time to read about old forests. Still, it seems like a stupid name. I mean, I don't even see a single dead bush."

"The woods aren't named for the plants but for the people who disappear in them," Dannen said. He did not like these woods, this place. He had heard over the years, of travelers on the path losing their way and disappearing into the forest never to be seen or heard from again. It made a man wonder how, if that were true, the stories ever came about in the first place, but not so much he wanted to walk into them to find out. And whether the stories were true or not, Dannen could not deny the feeling of unease, the feeling of being watched settling in him. "Come on," he said, doing his best to ignore the stitch in his side, "let's step up the pace."

They moved on more quickly and for a time no one spoke. Dannen tried to coax the heavy air into his lungs. His back was hunched not just out of weariness but because of that feeling that someone—or some*thing*—marked their progress. Fedder seemed to share some of his anxiety, for he scowled at the trees around them as if considering setting them on fire. That would have suited Dannen fine except that he got the feeling that unlike other forests, these trees would not sit back and let themselves be burned.

So, Dannen walked on, praying for restraint from the fire mage, an effort he suspected was as hopeless as praying for it to rain ale, and he was more than a little surprised when Fedder only trudged on, scowling still but not setting anything on fire, at least.

The sun was low on the horizon, casting shadows along their path, when Dannen came to a panting halt. "Best rest for a minute, keep our strength," he said. None of his companions argued—which was just as well as he didn't have the energy for it. In a few moments, they were all sitting on the path, Mariana examining one of the thin iron poles she used as weapons and Tesler engaged in an intense, whispered conversation with his pet squirrel. Dannen couldn't hear what the man said, and didn't care much in any case, his concentration taken up by his struggle to remember how to breathe.

"Well," Mariana said, glancing between Dannen and Fedder, "you two sure know how to show a girl a good time."

"What...can I say?" Dannen gasped. "It's a gift."

Fedder barked a laugh at that, and Mariana shrugged. "At least it seems like the High Justice didn't send anyone after us."

Dannen was going to tell her to shut up and not tempt fate with such comments, fate, after all, being a massive bitch, but before he got a chance he heard what sounded like distant, rumbling thunder. The problem was that there wasn't a cloud in the sky. He frowned, concentrating on it. The sound was barely audible, so low that he thought he might have imagined it, but a few seconds listening confirmed it was growing louder. Not much point in looking, he figured, not much need to, the world being what it was, but he rose to do so anyway.

The last bit of their trek had led them up a steep hill—an answer to the question of why his shins felt like someone had taken a hammer to them, and his knees felt hollowed out—and so it was an easy enough thing to look back and see the trail stretching miles back toward Talinseh. Easy, but not enjoyable. For on that trail, in the far distance, he could make out a long, thick dust cloud, writhing like a serpent. Not much point in wondering what might cause such a cloud, and not much need to as he'd seen its like before, often in similar circumstances.

"How many, do you think?" Fedder's deep voice asked from beside him, and it was all Dannen could do to keep from screaming in surprise, so quietly had the mage approached.

When his heart decided it wasn't going to burst from his chest after all, he frowned at the distant dust cloud, trying to get an idea of the soldiers' numbers and not liking what he was coming up with. "Too many."

Fedder grunted. "Reckon they mean to talk?"

"No," Dannen said. "No, I don't reckon they do."

"What is it, what's the—" Mariana paused, coming to stand beside them and following their gazes. "Well...fuck me."

Fedder made a sound in his throat. "How old did you say you were agai—"

"Don't even think of it, old man," she said, but the words were half-hearted, as she, like the rest of them, was far too intent on the cloud of dust advancing up the valley. Far away now, too far to get any eyes on what was making it, but Dannen knew well enough. Men on horses—lots of them.

"What do you want to do?"

Dannen turned to see that they were watching him, waiting for what he would say. Fools, then, to think he would know, to think he was worth following. Others had believed so, in the past, and most had died for their mistake. Fools, and he the biggest fool of all.

He hesitated, glancing between the dust cloud and the menacing forest around them. How many times did a normal person find himself in such situations, Dannen wondered. Once, maybe twice? While Dannen had been in this spot—or others close enough as to make no difference—seemingly his entire life. This might have made some people feel better, would have helped them be confident because they had faced such odds before and survived. But Dannen was not one of those people. In his mind he had made it out of those other situations on luck more than anything else, luck and running fast—he hadn't had the paunch then. And, sooner or later, luck, like time or a woman's patience, ran out.

No good answer, no answer that probably didn't end in death, but they were still watching him, waiting. Finally, he took a slow, deep breath. "We go into the forest."

"What about our trail?" Mariana asked.

Dannen was amazed—and more than a little frightened—that following his suggestion seemed, for all of them, to be a foregone conclusion.

"What about our trail?" he asked, feeling suddenly very tired, very old.

"Well…" She hesitated. "Shouldn't we, I don't know, cover it or something?"

"You know how to do such a thing?"

She cleared her throat. "No."

"Me neither," Dannen said, "but it doesn't matter in any case—there's no time."

"Thought you said there were bad things in the forest, though," she said, as close to arguing as anyone seemed ready to be, and that was too bad. Mostly, Dannen wished they would argue, wished one of them would come up with a better idea, any idea really.

"There are," he agreed.

They looked at each other then but said nothing. There was really nothing to be said. They headed into the forest.

***

Dannen understood, at once, why the forest was called the Dead Forest. There was nothing that he could put his finger on, though. Everywhere he looked, plants and bushes and trees grew in thick, green profusion, what, in another place, might have been the very symbol of life. Here, though, it felt different, somehow. Wrong. The blooming wildflowers and reaching tree limbs might, in another place, have seemed beautiful, but here they seemed menacing, as if their growth was not a proof of life, but instead proof of a desire to swallow the world or, circumstances permitting, anyone foolish enough to seek passage through them.

But even the twisting vines and grasping limbs were not the worst of it. Instead, it was a feeling. A feeling similar to the kind he experienced when entering an old temple or venturing into ruins hundreds, perhaps thousands, of years old. It was a feeling of walking through an ancient place, one that made him feel small and insignificant. But there was more to it than that. This place was not just old—it was angry. Filled with a fury far too old and far too alien to ever be understood. He could feel that anger radiating from every leaf and stem. Even the flowers that might have been beautiful were filled with it. The very air he breathed felt choked with it.

The breath was thick in his lungs as they pushed their way farther in, each of them, by unwritten accord, doing their best to touch nothing, to disturb nothing, a task made impossible by how thick the forest growth was.

They walked in single file—anything else would have been impossible—with Dannen granted the dubious honor of leading the party. And though they were forced to make their way slowly due to the undergrowth, Dannen's breath came in shallow gasps, and he felt far more tired than he had walking the trail. His companions' faces were pinched, their jaws clenched, and they gazed about them carefully as if they expected an ambush at any moment, as if they expected the trees themselves to come alive and attack. It was a thought that might have been funny in another place, another time. But not here, not now.

It was a terrible walk, perhaps the worst Dannen had ever taken, so bad, in fact, that he almost wished the soldiers the High Justice had sent would catch them up if for no other reason than to draw some of the forest's attention away from him and his companions.

Something else bothered him, tickling the back of his mind, and it took him some time to realize what it was—the forest was silent.

There was no sound of animals scampering through the tree branches that nearly choked out all sunlight before it reached them. There was no call of birds, no leaves or limbs rustling or swaying in the breeze, for there was no breeze. There was only a terrible, suffocating stillness, as if time had frozen in this place, and a deep, brooding silence from the forest around them.

The plants, so tightly crammed together, didn't seem like individual plants but one great organism, as if he and the others traveled through some sprawled beast, slumbering perhaps, but if so dreaming hateful, angry dreams, and one that, should it wake, would not hesitate in swallowing them whole.

Under this oppressive feeling, they traveled on in silence, the only sounds those of their ragged breaths. Suddenly, there was a flicker of movement ahead of them, and Dannen froze, only just managing to hold back the scream that wanted to come. He held up a hand, and the others stopped behind him.

"What is i—" Mariana began, but cut off at a harsh hiss from Dannen.

"*Wait,*" he hissed. At first, he saw nothing but the never-ending wall of green expanding before them. He was just beginning to think the movement he'd glimpsed no more than a figment of his anxiety-ridden mind when a glimmer of something off to their left drew his attention.

He turned slowly and his breath caught in his throat as he saw someone standing no more than thirty strides away. The undergrowth covered much of the figure who appeared to be no more than four feet tall, but luckily it did not seem to have noticed him and his companions. Dannen was still trying to decide what it was—he thought he knew but was hoping to all the gods that he was wrong—when half a dozen more appeared next to the first, also, thankfully, paying him and his companions no attention. Now there was no denying what they were, no matter how much he might wish it, and Dannen decided that they should have stayed on the trail after all.

There was the slightest rustle behind him as the others pushed their way forward to stand as near to him as the undergrowth would allow. Dannen tensed, sure they would be overheard, but when he looked back at the figures, he was relieved to note that none of them seemed to have taken any notice. He was less relieved, however, when he saw that more had arrived out of the underbrush and walked into the clearing, bringing their numbers to over twenty, with more appearing every second.

The figures began to move into a rough circle in the clearing as if by some ritual. Some, therefore ended up facing Dannen and the others. For the first time since they'd entered the forest, Dannen found himself glad of the thick undergrowth which concealed them from view.

"What *are* they?" Mariana whispered from beside him, so quietly he could barely hear her though they crouched side by side.

"Welves," Fedder said, a tone of disgust in his voice.

"Welves?" Mariana asked. "You mean, like elves but—"

"But worse," Dannen hissed back. "Now, keep quiet before they hear us. Welves have good ears."

"And not much else," Mariana muttered, but Dannen gave her a sharp, warning look, and she said no more. Still, though she might not have spoken, the expression on her face—matched by the expressions on the faces of the others—spoke her thoughts about the welves clearly enough. It was partially a look of awe, of disbelief, but mostly, it was a look of disgust.

The creatures in the clearing, cousins of the elves, were ugly. But the truth was the word went nowhere near far enough. They were short and squat and what little hair was left on their heads was snarled and thin and filthy, but that was far from the worst of it. Where their scalps showed, so, too, did great boils which spread all over their entire bodies and which wept yellow-white milky pus. It was nearly impossible to tell the men from the women. All were squat with bellies protruding over their pants—if a mish-mash of twigs and leaves which, unfortunately, left little to the imagination could be called pants. Their emaciated arms and legs seemed disproportionately short relative to their bodies.

Yet, the welves seemed entirely unaware of their ugliness and they stood in the circle staring at each other proudly with smiles that were perhaps meant to be demure, inviting, but which were ruined by the rotten teeth they put on display.

"What do we do?" Tesler asked quietly, and Dannen grunted.

"We wait. The last thing we want is—"

"Have you come for the dance?" a new voice interjected, one which managed to be both guttural and piping at the same time with a definite phlegmatic quality.

Dannen spun with the others to see six more of the welves, just as ugly as their counterparts, standing behind them. The one who had spoken was a female—at least he thought it was, he damned sure didn't want to look close enough to be certain—and she smiled as he and the others fumbled for words. A smile that, judging by her manner, she meant to be alluring, as she slowly ran a hand through her thin, tangled hair. "Ah, you are speechless. Do not fret, mortals, for many experience such a reaction when face to face with the Sidhe, for ours is elder blood, and beyond mortal ken."

Dannen swallowed hard, praying to the gods the others would keep their mouths shut. The welves might have appeared friendly enough—though their smiles could be considered weapons in themselves—but he knew from personal and thankfully brief experience that they could grow angry quickly.

So, keeping in mind that he didn't want to end the day in a welf's belly, Dannen forced a sickly smile onto his face, bowing his head low. "It, uh...it is an honor to meet you."

"And your other companions?" the welf asked, and though her voice was pleasant, Dannen could hear the warning in it. "Are they not, likewise, honored?"

The others hesitated—perhaps doing their best not to be sick at the sight and smell of the creatures before them—then finally bowed.

"Ah," the welf gurgled. "That is better. Still, do not be overcome with wonderment, mortals, and do not be afraid. You have come at a most opportune time, for it is the hour of drawing, when day draws into night and the shadows caper and so we, too, shall dance with them. Will you join us?"

Dannen cleared his throat. "We would love to, of course, but...see, the thing is...well we'd hate to intrude and—"

"Nonsense," the welf interrupted, waving a hand in what he imagined she thought a graceful, dismissive gesture which was somewhat diminished by the way she gracefully—and accidentally—struck one of her companions who stumbled away. "You have come during the time of drawing, and whether by design or chance it matters not. Come, and I will show you a sight few mortals have been so privileged to see in hundreds of years. Come, witness the Dance of the Welves."

"Look, we really don't—" Fedder began, but Dannen gripped his shoulder with a smile, tightening his grip, and the mage grunted. "That is, we really don't believe the uh...honor. You know, that you're doin' us."

This was, perhaps predictably, cause for some more posing and preening among the welves as they showed off their sidhe—

and nauseating—virtues to the best advantage. "Come," she said after over a minute spent at it, her tone making it clear she thought she had done them some great favor, "night draws near, and we must greet it."

The six welves spread out around Dannen and his party. Though they drew no weapons, they stood in the formation of a guard escort. The female welf nodded then turned and led the procession toward the undergrowth. She waved the fingers of her short, stubby hand and the plants blocking the way shrank away from her to reveal an open avenue. Dannen blinked, open-mouthed. An impressive trick, that, one which would have saved him and the others hours' worth of walking as well as the many thorn pricks he had accumulated while working his way through the forest.

Their escort led them to the clearing. The other welves who were already there turned to regard them as one, and while they might have been ugly—incredibly, impossibly so, each one seeming worse than the last as if they made a game of it and, if so, they were all winning so far as Dannen was concerned—there was something strange, something alien in their eyes that sent a chill up his spine.

"They come for the drawing," his escort said simply in an undeniably eager tone. "They wish to witness the Dance of the Welves."

The others did not speak, only bowed in exaggerated gestures usually reserved for ostentatious castle audience rooms or graceful balls. Not that the welves were either and, on them, the courtly bows and curtseys looked ridiculous, a mockery. A few of the more unskilled—even here, it seemed, there were degrees of terrible—fell into the dirt, failing at the attempt, but Dannen did his best not to notice.

The welves who had escorted them spread out among the others, taking their place in the rough circle while the female who had spoken to them moved to its center, raising her arms to the moon. "The night comes," she said.

"The night comes," the other welves repeated in unison, the one nearest Dannen picking its nose as if it had a grudge against it. Others were scratching at the sores on their flesh, scratching other places too, yet they all seemed oblivious of this, and the looks they

cast around themselves were smug and arrogant. This, if nothing else, they shared with their cousins, for Dannen had met elves before—beautiful, graceful, pompous, arrogant bastards, in his experience. He remembered thinking it was a good thing they lived so long as they took several times longer than a human to get anything done, so focused were they on how they looked while doing it. To conquer them, Dannen had always thought a man need only bring enough mirrors for each, and they'd all still be celebrating their magnificence while he walked away with everything they owned.

The welves also seemed arrogant and pompous, but more than that, possessed of what must be an extremely large blind spot regarding their own appearances.

"The Lady of Darkness visits; she is at the door," the female intoned in what seemed to be the beginning words of some ritual.

"*She is at the door,*" the others intoned. It was a lot of intoning all around for Dannen, but while he might not have been a big fan of it, it was better they did that than start carving pieces out of him and his companions.

As if suddenly reminded of their presence, the female elf turned to face them, smiling that smile which Dannen thought was meant to be sultry, perhaps even tempting, "She knocks. Shall we let her in?"

"*Yes,*" those in the clearing answered, their excitement clear in their voices, some even going so far as to leave off scratching at their boils and picking their noses to say it.

"Very well," the female welf said, turning away, her hands raised high in the sky. "Then we shall let her in."

As one, the welves began to dance. Or, at least, Dannen thought it was meant to be a dance, though a man might have been forgiven for thinking they were all having fits. The welves threw themselves about the clearing in wild, gesticulating jerks displaying no rhythm and very little muscle control. Dannen had never seen elves dance, but he doubted if such a spectacle as this shared anything in common with that of their cousins at play.

The welves jumped and flopped around like fish left on the bank by some cruel fisherman, undulating wildly, their swinging arms more than once catching another of their number in the face hard enough they would doubtlessly have bruises the following day. But despite their obvious lack of skill and poise, Dannen couldn't fault the welves' enthusiasm. They hurled themselves into the effort with alacrity, shaking and bobbing and writhing as if their very lives depended on it.

Something about the whole thing seemed perverse and sickening. When the female welf who had spoken to them paused in her seizure-like jerking to beckon him into the circle, Dannen pretended not to notice.

Finally, after half an hour of frenzy, the welves tired themselves out, and Dannen and the others stared in disbelief and more than a little disgust as the small, sweaty figures rose, all coming to stand behind the female who had first spoken to them. The small figures were covered in mud and leaves and at least half sported fresh bruises on their faces and arms where they had been struck. They stared at Dannen and the others expectantly, as if waiting on something, but Dannen and his companions were at a loss for words.

The female leader smiled, panting as she did, a snot bubble rising and shrinking again from one nostril. "Aah, mortals, but it is a fine thing, the Dance of the welves, the Dance of Drawing. I see it has left you quite speechless, but do not fear that we might be offended, for we understand. Few are as privileged and honored as to witness the welves at play, and you might now count yourselves among them."

"What the fu—" Fedder began, but Dannen cut him off.

"Thank you," he managed past the rising bile in his throat. "It was...spectacular." A spectacular horror show, perhaps, but he thought it more politic—and far less life-threatening—to leave out that last.

The welf smiled as if it were no more than her due, and the others smiled too. Dannen and his companions did not smile— were not capable of it, just then—but they at least managed to hide the worst of their disgust and horror, so that was something.

"Now that the dance is done, tell me, travelers, what brings you to the realm of the welves?"

Dannen wanted nothing more than to be away from this place as quickly as possible, but the welf was looking at him expectantly. Though they were smiling now, the wrong word on his part could make those smiles turn to snarls easily enough, so he bowed his head again. "We seek to go north."

"To what purpose?"

Dannen didn't like the idea of sharing their plans with these strange creatures, didn't, in fact, like the idea of standing here for one moment longer, not trusting his companions to restrain themselves from saying or doing something that would get them all killed. "Forgive me, ma'am, but if it's all the same to you, I'd prefer we kept our business to ourselves."

The welf studied him carefully, her face a blank mask—save for the boils and the snot bubble—and there was no way to know what she might be thinking. Under her scrutiny, Dannen began to think he had gone too far and would be punished, was wondering if he'd have enough time to push the crazy squirrel man in the way and make a run for it, when the female spoke again.

"So formal," she said, smiling tightly. "There is no need to call me, 'ma'am,' stranger. 'Your Highness' will do."

Dannen blinked. "Your...Highness?"

She inclined her head. "It is so, for you see I am Grallia Estarian, princess of the welves."

"It...it's an honor," Dannen said, because if his life had taught him anything, it was that it rarely hurt to be polite and often hurt not to be.

The princess smiled wider. "And your name, sir?"

"Dannen Ateran, Your Highness."

She hesitated, watching him for several seconds, and finally nodded, seeming to come to a decision. "Very well. You and your companions will follow us back to Riverlan, Dannen Ateran. You will be our guests."

"Bullshi—"

"It would be our pleasure, Your Highness," Dannen said hurriedly, speaking over Fedder, "but, if you'll forgive us, I was not exaggerating before. We are under a bit of a time constraint and if you allowed us to pass through your lands—"

"Impossible, I'm afraid," the princess said, a regretful tone in her phlegmatic voice. "No matter how polite you may be, Dannen Ateran and company, you have all ventured into the land of the welves uninvited and, what's more, have witnessed the sacred Dance of Drawing."

As if any man would choose *to see such a thing,* Dannen thought.

"As such," the welf continued, "you must be brought before the queen so that you may make your case to my mother who will determine if your need for doing so is worthy."

Dannen considered pointing out that he hadn't *wanted* to watch the dance—had seen things in the last hour that he was certain would haunt his nightmares for some time to come—and that neither had he wished to come into the forest in the first place, but he saw that there was no point. "And...if we are unable to convince the queen that it is?"

The princess shrugged casually. "Death, I imagine. Yet, do not despair, for even such a death at the hands of the welves would be a greater distinction than any mortal can expect in their brief lives. Besides which, you will be allowed to look upon Riverlan, the home of the welves, a truly prestigious and unprecedented honor."

Dannen wished he'd lived a life that would have left him surprised that he was likely to die in the next few hours, but it was more or less just another day. Fedder tensed beside him, and Dannen put a hand on the mage's shoulder, quieting him before he could do anything stupid. "The trees, Fedder," he whispered.

Fedder frowned then glanced at the trees around them, grunting as he noticed the tell-tale glimmer of arrow points aimed in their direction from at least a dozen spots in the undergrowth. "As you wish, Your Highness," Dannen said, trying for a smile before he gave it up as a lost cause.

***

Dannen and his companions were led through the forest, making far better time escorted by the welves than they had on their own, as roots and branches, bushes and thorns, retracted to clear a path for the welves only to close again the moment the party was past.

The welves muttered amongst themselves in whispered conversation, but Dannen didn't bother listening to what they had to say, was too busy trying to formulate an argument to give the queen, one that might not see him and the others killed. He'd gotten as far as, "Please, Your Highness," when the princess came to a halt, raising her hand and turning back. "From here, we proceed in reverent silence to show Riverlan the respect it deserves. You come now, mortals, to a place beyond your understanding. Look upon the work of the welves in wonder."

The princess paused with her hand on the thick bushes in front of her and turned to Dannen and the others. "Welcome, mortals," she said in a breathless voice, "to Riverlan."

At the last word, the bushes which had blocked their view slid aside like a curtain, revealing the home of the welves. Fedder grunted beside him, and Mariana gave a sharp intake of breath, but Dannen barely noticed. He was too busy focusing on what lay before him.

The princess had spoken of Riverlan almost as if it were a sacred place, a place of great, profound beauty and despite everything, Dannen realized that some small part of him had been excited to see it. After all, while the welves were vastly different from their elven cousins, the elves were known throughout the land for their entrancing cities, beautiful and hidden away deep in the recesses of the world.

But Riverlan, like its inhabitants, was a far cry from the graceful architecture of elven cities. Here were none of the sweeping vistas or ornamented buildings said to populate the cities of the elves. No sweet meadows with quaint bridges leading across flowing rivers. Riverlan was, by all measures, a shithole— and Dannen should know considering some of the places he'd gotten drunk in over the years. And this shithole, it had to be said, was one of the best...or worst, depending on how a man looked at it.

The "road" leading through Riverlan was no better than a dirt trail and was crowded with small, crude huts, each with a decided slump as if it might collapse at any moment. Indeed, from where he stood, Dannen could see three piles of wood and wattle where it appeared that was exactly what had happened.

The princess came to stand beside him, and she must have noticed his look, for she nodded sadly. "Yes, Dannen Ateran, it is a sad truth that not even the great works of the elder races can forever withstand the test of time."

Dannen would have answered her, *meant* to, but he had no words. At least, he told himself, there was a stream of sorts, though creek might have been more accurate as it was no more than ten feet across. Then one of the welves who'd escorted them, hunkered over and unceremoniously began to take a shit in the nearly-still water.

A shithole then, and no mistake. Not much different, really, than a thousand others Dannen had found himself in over the years, usually after a night of far too many drinks and far too little sense. Except, of course, for the welves standing around, filthy and stinking. Whatever blindness kept them from noticing their own grotesqueness also applied to the city—"city," of course, giving the dump far more credit than it deserved. The welves stared at the rundown buildings and the creek as if it were the land of the gods. It wasn't—Dannen could attest to that, having so recently visited the place—and, in fact, was just about as far from it as a place *could* be.

But the welves weren't just staring, they were *gazing* with adoring eyes. Dannen had seen such looks before, when a man gazed on something inspiring, like a tall mountain or a beautiful woman. In fact, he thought he'd had a similar expression on his own face when he'd seen his first unicorn. Of course, that was before the mad bastard had taken it in mind to try to eat him, had been so insane with rage that it hadn't seemed to understand that its teeth—pretty much the same as any mundane horse's teeth—were nowhere near as sharp as a sword.

Following the incident, Dannen knew two things for certain: unicorns were dicks, and they tasted like dirt. The bards and poets, when they spoke of the beasts, never seemed to make it around to those two simple facts—the most important ones, to his mind—but he supposed people might be a bit less inclined to pay for tales of majestic creatures if they knew said creatures usually stank like a pig sty and would have found nothing more pleasing than giving their many admirers a good chew.

But the welves, with their apparent blindness, seemed to see only Riverlan's beauty and none of its flaws—not that there was much beauty to be found, at least to Dannen's mind. He supposed that, in many ways, that might be both a gift and a curse. After all, if every woman you ever met appeared gorgeous to you, then did it really matter if she had all her teeth or that she only bathed on full moons? Besides, for all Dannen knew, the blindness might well have be a survival mechanism. For if they knew their own ugliness, he doubted there'd be many welf babies running around—likely, the race would have died out eons ago and the world no poorer for it.

"Ah, Riverlan," the princess said in a tone that he supposed was meant to be soft and respectful but which came out in a gurgling croak. "No matter how often my eyes look upon it, each time is like the first. Oh, but to be as lucky as you are now, Dannen of Ateran."

"Lucky?" Dannen asked, doing his best to hide his incredulity. He had been called many things in his life, most of them bad and, as it happened, most of them true, but he couldn't remember ever being accused of being lucky before and with good reason.

"Oh, yes," she said, nodding and running an arm across her nose, not wiping the snot that had leaked onto her upper lip away but smearing it anyhow. "Don't you see? You and your companions get to experience the gift of seeing Riverlan for the very first time while I have seen it many times myself, and so its beauty is, for me, diminished. For me, it has become like a much-beloved epistle, worn and faded from years of handling. So I say it again, Dannen of Ateran—you are lucky. You and your companions are receiving a gift. A very special gift."

"Rather have a beer," Fedder said. "Probably need one before we're done here anywa—" he grunted as Dannen backhanded him in the stomach.

He turned back to the princess, expecting her to be enraged. Instead, she was smiling, giving Fedder the type of look one might give a child. One of the other welves, this one younger, Dannen thought, if for no other reason than that he had fewer of the characteristic boils of his people dotting his skin than most, growled and started forward only to freeze when the princess laid a hand on his shoulder. The welf blurted something in the guttural, croaking language of the welves. Dannen didn't understand the newcomer's words, but from the welf's tone and the glare he was giving Dannen and his companions it wasn't hard to guess what he was saying. After all, he'd listened to enough people debating how to kill him over the years to know it when he heard it, and he tensed, trying to decide whether to run or push Fedder into the welves *then* run.

The princess, though, shook her head, responding to the welf in the same language he had used, but in a far calmer, slightly less frog-like voice. Whatever she said didn't seem to pacify the welf who scowled at them, pointing angrily and started to say something else. The princess beat him to it, however, snapping something else.

Whatever she said, it was brief, and had an immediate effect. The young welf recoiled as if he had been struck and wilted under the princess's scowl. Dannen had seen a lot of scowls in his time—most of them aimed in his direction and most of them, truth be told, more than deserved. Val, for instance, had had a fine scowl when she wanted to, but she had nothing on the princess. Hard to know for sure, but Dannen suspected it had something to do with the boils and the missing teeth and the breath which made his stomach lurch even though she stood several feet away and was turned in the other direction.

The princess's glare followed the welf as he slunk toward the back of the gathered welves, his punishment, it seemed, to no longer be able to stand near the princess, a punishment Dannen would have accepted gladly if he'd known they were handing them out. He opened his mouth to apologize, to try to explain that Fedder was a fool—easy enough since it was nothing less than the truth—and to tell her he thought both Riverlan and the welves were beautiful. That one, he suspected might be a bit tougher.

"I would be careful, strangers," she said, "of what you say here. Unlike many of my brothers and sisters, I know some small bit about mortals, pity you your short lifespans, your...forgive me, inelegance. Many of my people do not understand mortal humor, as it is far cruder and...humbler than our own."

"Of course, Princess," Dannen said through gritted teeth, sparing a moment to scowl at Fedder, though if it landed, the mage did a good job of ignoring it. "We will be sure to keep our jokes in check, for the last thing we want to do is offend such...wondrous people."

She seemed appeased by that—at least, Dannen thought so, and the fact that all their heads were still in their proper places seemed to indicate as much. After a moment, she nodded. "Come," she said, "scouts were sent ahead. Her Majesty will be waiting."

"The Beautiful...does not wait on *men*," said a voice in a poorly enunciated version of human speech. The angry welf had eased closer, but he retreated quickly, disappearing behind the others at a look from the princess.

"I apologize for Elster's behavior. He is young and rash and *foolish*," she finished, saying the last loud enough there was no way the welf could not hear.

"It's fine," Dannen said, meaning it. He didn't care if the welf hated him—it was a long list, one grown over the years to such a degree that he'd long since bothered keeping track. He could keep right on doing it as long as that hate didn't manifest itself into murderous rage. Dannen was far more curious about the queen being called "the Beautiful" than about any angry welf child.

"Come," the princess said, "walk with me. You will see another wonder, it seems, for I shall lead you across the Arch of Evarandril."

Dannen and the others followed, and he was just about to ask the welf what arch she referred to when she led him to the small bridge that went across the brown, murky creek. A few semi-rotten logs had been lashed together with twine and laid across the ten-foot distance from one bank to the other. Dannen cleared his throat. "Is this...?"

"The Arch of Evarandril," the princess remarked in a voice filled with pride. "Built by Evarandril himself, perhaps the most famous poet and crafter of our generation and a welf whose presence only serves to magnify Riverlan's greatness even further." She held out a hand in invitation. "Please, as you are guests, it would be proper if you crossed first."

Dannen frowned at the rickety logs and twine, a child's idea of a bridge. Then he turned his gaze to the murky brown water, noticing the floating pieces within it and confirming his earlier suspicions of what they might be. He didn't love the idea of crossing that bridge, not at all. It seemed all too likely it would give way as soon as he put his full weight upon it, spilling him into the foul water. Likely, he would rise from such a spill looking as bad as the welves themselves. "This Evarandril," he said, stalling, "he uh...he's your best craftsman?"

She gave a laugh he might have called a 'titter' on a human but, on the welf, sounded like a liquid gurgle. "Not just *our* best, Dannen of Ateran, but the best of the world."

Dannen cleared his throat. "I see. And, your craftsmen, I mean, those of your people, they test their work?"

"Of course," she said, a slight frown on her face now.

"I was only asking," Dannen said hurriedly, "because my friends and I are a bit bigger, you know, than welves."

"Yes," she said slowly, "I have not failed to notice your unfortunate proportions. And while I understand you, being mortal, are no doubt accustomed to a poor quality of craft and your doubt that anything so beautiful could be functional which stems from a deeply-ingrained cynicism which is no doubt rightly earned by most, if not all, human craftsman. But you need not fret. For this Arch, Dannen of Ateran, this bridge, was built by Evarandril, the greatest crafter of his generation. It is no haphazard construct built only to last a day or two as humans are, but a making of the sidhe, of Evarandril himself. I say again, you need not fret."

But Dannen stared at the few wooden planks strapped together over the murky brown span of water, and he did fret. He fretted deeply. As far as he was concerned, "haphazard" would have been a drastic improvement from how the bridge now stood, but he didn't say so. He'd been through a lot in his life, had long since lost count of the number of men and beasts which had tried to kill him. In some ways, he'd grown accustomed to it, at least as much as any man could. But getting killed and taking a shit bath were two very different things. He swallowed hard, nodding, and doing his best to put a brave face on his fear. For this, at least, his life had given him ample practice.

The princess smiled. "I will proceed first to allay your fears. Follow, but see that you traverse the arch one at a time, for the journey across is meant to be one of contemplation and serenity, one a welf—or mortal—might only take alone." With that, the welf turned and started across the bridge.

Fedder snorted. "A journey a man has to take alone unless he fancies the idea of the bridge collapsing and dropping him into that shit pit," he muttered.

Although Dannen suspected, somewhere not so very deep down at all, that this was all Fedder's fault, he couldn't disagree. "Best go across," he said. They all looked at the bridge with dubious expressions he knew he shared, and he grunted. "At least it's short."

"So's a dagger," Mariana said doubtfully.

Dannen opened his mouth but then decided not to respond to that. Instead, he started toward the bridge. Whatever he'd thought of the shape of it from a distance, it looked even worse close up, and he could see that the few ragged planks were covered in some sort of slippery substance. Moss or grime, that was the best-case scenario. The worst, of course, being that it was an accumulation of the filth from the creek beneath it, a coating of toxicity that would likely cause a man's finger to rot off if he touched it.

Dannen stood there wondering what grand, unforgivable mistake he had made in his life which had led him here, to this moment. Certainly, being covered in that water—sludge might have been closer to the truth—would be the crowning of a lifetime's bad luck and bad choices. Dannen didn't have much pride left. In his experience, either a man killed his pride or his pride killed him, but he didn't like the idea of being covered in that stuff, not at all. Thought, maybe, he'd rather die. But his survival instinct, honed over the years, disagreed. Moments later, he surprised himself by stepping gingerly onto the logs.

The wood groaned and creaked in protest but held. Still, Dannen didn't think he imagined the way the bridge bowed beneath his weight when he stepped onto it. He considered turning around, but the princess was waiting on the other side, watching him. Left with no choice, Dannen held his breath and took a second step. Another groan, another creak, another stab of pure terror. Then a third step. Far enough out now that should the bridge choose to give way beneath him, there was no hope of being able to leap back to solid ground.

A terrible predicament, one no one might have envied. But then, Dannen had been in a lot of such predicaments before, and while some men might have frozen with fear, he had always been able to act under pressure. Not necessarily doing the right thing or the smart thing, but at least doing *something*. So he walked, putting no more pressure on his feet than necessary. Might have taken a few seconds, or a year, but soon he was at the other end of the bridge, and he let go a ragged, shaking sigh of relief when his foot struck solid earth once more.

His knees weak, Dannen moved toward the princess and despite her assurances of the bridge's safety, Dannen thought he detected a flush to her cheeks and a bit of sweat on her grimy brow. "Ah yes," she said, trying a smile, "I can see by your face that you were deeply affected by the Arch. Do not worry over that, Dannen of Ateran, for all who pass across it are. The Arch spoke to you, didn't it?"

Dannen blinked, trying to figure out how to answer that. He opened his mouth, intent on asking if she referred to the creaks and groans it gave off with each step, to tell her that the only thing they had told him was that he had to get his shit together and soon, but the princess held up a hand. "What words the Arch spoke to you were for you and you alone, Dannen of Ateran," she said. "I will advise you only to heed its wisdom."

Dannen was struggling for a proper response when the princess pointed past him. "It seems your friends prepare to cross."

Mariana had already taken her first step onto the bridge. Unlike Dannen's tortured progress, she was across in a moment, flitting so quickly and dexterously over the rotting logs it almost seemed her feet never touched. He stared at her, impressed despite himself, but she shrugged as she came to stand with them. "That wasn't so bad."

Dannen thought about telling her he would have done much the same if *he* were a hundred pounds lighter, but knew it wasn't true, for the girl had displayed a grace and athleticism that, at any age, was simply beyond him. "Good job," he said instead.

She grinned, clearly pleased with the compliment, and Dannen turned back to see that it was now Tesler's turn. When Dannen had met him, the crazy man had been locked in the dungeon of a crime boss—what Talinseh called a Tribune—and hadn't seemed anxious in the slightest, not even at the torture tools laid out in clear view outside his cell. But he seemed nervous now, and not *just* that. He was staring at Mariana—who pointedly avoided his gaze—in unconcealed amazement and awe. Dannen noted the ever-present squirrel was not adorning the young man's shoulder.

Not a squirrel god, surely, but not, it seemed, a completely stupid beast, for it was clever enough to not risk the bridge. He wondered, for a moment, what that said about him and his companions when a squirrel seemed to know better than they did.

Tesler shuffled forward slowly, his eyes wide and locked on the river of sludge beneath his feet and the rotten logs which were the only thing separating him from taking an impromptu bath in it. He slipped halfway across, flailing, and Dannen thought for sure the poor bastard was going in. But then, just at the last minute, he managed to regain his balance. There was a strangled sound from beside him, and Dannen was surprised to see Mariana take an urgent step forward as if meaning to catch the young man before freezing. Dannen glanced at her, raising an eyebrow, and her face turned a deep red.

"Wouldn't wish that on anybody," she said, pointedly looking away.

"'Course not," he agreed, frowning thoughtfully. Just genuine concern for a companion she'd only met a few days ago or something more? *No,* he thought, glancing between the two of them, *can't be.* For one, the only time he had seen any interaction between the two at all it had been for Mariana to scowl at a nervous-looking Tesler. More importantly, the man was crazy— the girl, too, as far as that went...Dannen's frown deepened. Both of them crazy, how could a man guess what they might do? Still, he hoped perhaps he was just imagining the look she'd given the man, imagined that she had jumped forward far more quickly than she would have for him or Fedder. And if his hopes ended up being wrong and the two did wind up being interested in each other, he would have a talk with them. His group had enough on their plates already without romance being involved.

Yes, he would talk with them, if he decided it was becoming a problem. Which, of course, went nowhere toward saying they'd listen. Mariana breathed an audible sigh of relief, and Dannen winced, turning back to the bridge, unsurprised to find that Tesler had made it across and was now staggering toward them.

Tesler gave Dannen and Mariana a sickly smile then turned away as Mariana scowled at him more viciously than ever. Dannen couldn't blame the man—it was a mean look, alright, one that made it seem like she hated the him. The problem, of course, was that often, men and women *did* hate the things they loved. Ridiculous, maybe, but true nonetheless and one of the main reasons why he'd decided some time ago that the world was a cruel joke and death the punchline.

As Tesler reached them, his legs gave way and he collapsed to his knees, breathing deeply.

"Some," the princess said smugly, "become overcome with awe by the words the Arch speaks to them."

Likely the fumes, Dannen thought as he glanced at the brown creek but thought it better not to say. He turned back to Tesler, noted his pale, sweat-drenched face. The man was overcome with something, alright, but Dannen would have bet that something wasn't awe. Likely it was the knowledge of how close he'd come to bathing in shit.

"Sure, a thing like that," Dannen said louder than he needed to, "well, a man can't help but be affected." Tesler glanced up from where he'd been studying his trembling hands, a brief look of gratitude on his face before he looked away once more.

And then there was only one left. Fedder scowled at the bundle of logs lying across the creek like he was considering ripping them up, maybe breaking them apart for good measure. Finally, the Firemaker sighed, met Dannen's eyes, and gave a fatalistic shrug.

Dannen held his breath, hoping the logs would hold while, at the same time, sort of hoping they wouldn't. After all, considering all the misery and sheer terror Fedder had caused him over the years, the bastard deserved it—he'd gotten Dannen in enough shit it would serve him right if some of it got on him this time.

At first, it looked as if Dannen would get his wish. The boards gave a tortured groan, and if the bridge had been "speaking" to Dannen and the others before, then it was screaming at Fedder, creaking as if it might give way at any minute. Dannen had seen Fedder stare down angry trolls, raging manticores, assassins and a thousand other dangers without ever blinking an eye, but there was no mistaking the tense set of his jaw as he took his time across the rickety bridge.

As he neared the end, it seemed the rotten logs would hold after all, when Fedder began to shake. Only, on closer inspection, it wasn't the mage who was shaking, but the bridge itself. Fedder raised his head and met Dannen's eyes, a look of unmistakable fear in his gaze as he did, then, a moment later, there was a great, splintering sound and one of the logs bucked and began to split down its center. Just one log out of a half a dozen, but it was enough to send the whole thing tearing apart and a moment later the air was filled with the sound of the other logs cracking and breaking.

Fedder roared, taking a desperate step forward and turning it into a powerful leap which sent him hurtling toward the bank. Dannen saw at once that the man wasn't going to make it—he was simply too far away. Dannen leapt forward, landing stomach-first on the ground, knocking the wind out of himself in the process.

He reached out and just when he thought Fedder was going to disappear beneath the rim of the overhang, the mage caught his wrist. Dannen felt as if his arm would be ripped from its socket as the man's full weight fell on it. The mage's weight began dragging him across the ground immediately. Dannen grunted and hissed, spat and strained, trying to decide how long he could stand before letting go. Friend or not, he refused to follow the mage into that fetid liquid.

Suddenly, his forward slide stopped, and he became aware of hands grasping his ankles. Dannen peered over one shoulder and saw Tesler and Mariana bent, one grabbing each of his legs. The squirrel, too, had reappeared, and by all the gods it looked as if the little creature also had a handful of his trouser leg. It might have been cute if Dannen wasn't in immediate danger and also, perversely aware that he hadn't had a decent meal in quite a while and had always liked the taste of squirrel.

With their combined efforts the man and woman—plus one rodent—managed to stop his forward progress which was good. But Dannen's hand, slick with sweat or something worse—the logs falling into the water had caused quite a spray—was beginning to lose its grip.

He could only see the mage's face now above the rim of the bank, the rest of him dangling out of sight, somewhere above the creek, but what he saw was enough. Fedder's eyes were wide with terror, his face twisted in a rictus of concentration as he tried to hold on. Then, a sort of peace overcame his face as fear gave way to the reality of his situation, the inevitability of it, and he met Dannen's eyes. "Dannen—" he began, but Dannen interrupted him.

"Just shut up and hold on, you bastard," he growled, trying to catch the mage's wrist with his other hand, but it was too far away, the angle wrong, and he kept coming up empty. Then, just like that, his grip was no longer slipping, but gone altogether, and he watched the mage disappear beneath the bank, plummeting out of sight. "*Nooo!*" he shouted, but words could not help them, nothing could, and moments later there was a great *splash* as the Firemaker struck the water.

Dannen and the others rushed to the edge of the bank staring down the ten feet or so at the brown water. Ripples spread through it but Fedder was nowhere in sight. Then, suddenly, the water erupted in a fountain as the giant tore his way to the surface. Dannen let out a decidedly unmanly screech as he and the others leapt backward, narrowly avoiding the spray.

Fedder pawed at the bank, and Dannen had enough time to think that he should help—enough time, too, to dismiss the idea immediately—before the mage heaved himself onto the bank with a gasp, clambering forward before falling on his knees.

"Gods be good," Tesler breathed, and Dannen wanted to tell the man that, as a general rule, the gods were anything but good. Proof of it, after all, was crouched only a few feet away.

The Firemaker was always an intimidating sight, a giant of a man whose hulking figure could strike fear in the heart of enemies and—if they weren't complete and utter fools—friends alike, but Dannen had never seen the man look so terrifying as he did now, covered as he was in the filth of the creek.

There was silence for several seconds, a silence of awe, disbelief, and more than a little disgust as Dannen and the others struggled to keep down their rising gorges. Finally, Dannen cleared his throat. "Fedder?"

The mage, who had been sitting with his elbows draped over his knees, his head hanging, looked up at him. "Well," he grunted. "We gonna see this queen or what?"

Dannen grinned. He wouldn't have thought it possible given the circumstances, particularly since it looked as if he was likely to die at the hands of the welves in the next few minutes, but he couldn't help himself. "Yeah," he said. "Let's." He turned to the princess only to see her staring in disbelief as the others had been, but she wasn't looking at Fedder. Instead, she was staring at the bridge. Or, at least, what remained of it. Which was nothing. Say this for Fedder Firemaker—the man was damned thorough. There were dead men that would have agreed with that much for certain, had they been able.

"Princess?" Dannen asked, half-convinced the welf had been struck dumb, so stunned did she appear.

"It...it fell," she said, her voice low and filled with disbelief. Others welves had begun to gather on both sides of the creek, tears streaking down the grime and dirt and pus on their faces.

"The Arch of Evarandril," the princess said, still in that breathy voice as she turned to him, "it has fallen, Dannen Ateran."

"All things fall, sooner or later, Highness" Dannen said, and then, because he'd always been a bit of an asshole, and had grown tired of the welves constant attitude of superiority, "take it from a lowly mortal like myself—all things fall."

"Yes," the princess said slowly, "even those great manifestations of elder skill must give way to the ravages of time sooner or later. It is only poor luck for your friend that time's decay showed itself now."

Dannen could have told her that time's decay had nothing to do with it, that the "bridge" the welves had so grandiosely named hadn't been a bridge at all and would have been just as likely to be knocked down by a strong breeze as an unlucky mage, but he chose to let it go. The welves, after all, had a talent for only seeing what they wanted to see.

"We will rebuild it," the princess said with finality, "or, at least, Evarandril will, for he alone among us has the skill, though I do not doubt it will take him some years in the doing. Still," she went on, drawing herself upright with obvious effort, "the welves will make do until then."

"Brave of you," Mariana muttered, but thankfully the princess seemed too distracted by her thoughts to catch the sarcasm in the woman's voice.

"We will rebuild," she said again, "and I do not doubt that what replaces the Arch of Evarandril will be even more magnificent."

"Wouldn't take mu—" Mariana began, but cut off at a sharp look from Dannen. The welf might have been distracted, but only a fool poked a lion a second time just because he hadn't gotten his face bitten off on the first.

"Come," the princess said, oblivious of the assassin girl's jibe, "we will hurry to the queen to see what will become of you and your company, Dannen of Ateran." She turned to another of the welves. "Find Evarandril and tell him of what has occurred—he will wish to begin making plans."

"Of course, Highness," the welf answered, bowing his head before jogging away.

The princess turned to Dannen and the others. "This way, if you please."

She led them past one ramshackle house after the other, recounting, as she did, an unending litany of the Arch of Evarandril's greatness. Dannen nodded, keeping his true feelings from his expression as best he could. He might well not have bothered as the princess was consumed by her own stories—mostly of prominent welves walking across the bridge, which seemed to Dannen not to be that magnificent at all but the whole damned point of the thing.

Eventually, they were shown to a dwelling which, unlike the others, didn't look in immediate danger of collapse. The walls still had a distinct lean to them, but one not so noticeable as many of the others. Likewise, it shared a distinct coating of grime and moss but one that was not as thick as that covering the other dwellings.

A figure sat in a chair outside the house, attended by half a dozen welves. One was busily trying to serve her food, another to refill a wine cup she held, and two more were fussing at her long gray hair, or at least trying to. They were all getting in each others' way and getting nothing accomplished except giving each other a few new bruises.

The princess led Dannen and the others to within twenty feet of the seated welf, then she and the rest of their escort dropped to their knees, bowing their heads.

"Prostrate yourself before the Beautiful and her throne," one welf hissed, and Dannen and the others knelt.

After a moment, a voice spoke. "Rise." An older voice which possessed none of the phlegmatic quality of the other welves, sounding, instead, much like a human's might. If, that was, the human in question was very old and very tired.

Dannen waited until the welves with him rose, then followed suit, taking the opportunity to look closer at the one called "the Beautiful." He was unsurprised, of course, to discover she wasn't. She was far less ugly than the rest of the welves he'd seen with none of the red, rashy scabs or boils common in her kin. She looked, more than anything, plain, with dull, lusterless gray hair and a nose that was too big for her otherwise small, pinched face. Still, he thought he understood why she might be called such just as he understood why the simple wooden chair she sat in might be called a throne. Relative, after all, to the rest of the welves, the woman was indeed beautiful and the chair, looking to Dannen like a simple wooden tavern chair, was of far sturdier make than anything he'd seen in the village thus far.

"Tell me, daughter," the queen said in a formal, though not unkind tone, "who is this you have brought before me?"

The princess bowed deeply. "Strangers, Beautiful, ones we discovered while preparing to perform the Dance of Drawing. They seek passage through the village."

The older woman sighed. "How many times, daughter, have I asked you to call me 'Mother?' 'Mom,' even, as the mortals do, would be better."

"Forgive me, Beautiful, but you know I cannot. Your daughter I may be, but that matters little. You are the Beautiful, the queen, and I am only a welf who does not deserve any special treatment." Her words might have been respectful enough, but Dannen detected a hint of resentment in her tone.

The queen winced, "Ally, that's not..." She glanced around at the other welves, each of them doing their best to appear not to listen, and each of them also doing their best to hear every word, then sighed. She cleared her throat and sat up straight in her chair, waving away those welves who had been fussing over her in frustration. "We will discuss this later," she said to her daughter in a formal voice, the voice of a queen. Then, she turned to Dannen and the others, and he hoped the anger he saw in her pinched face, and heard in her authoritative tone, wouldn't transfer to them. Likely, it would. In Dannen's experience, anger rarely came down on the one who'd roused it but on those poor, unsuspecting fools who happened to be close by.

"Now, strangers," the queen went on, "tell me, why it is that you have come to Riverlan?'

Threat of being killed if we refused, mostly, Dannen thought. He glanced at the others, hoping one of them would speak up, but they were all staring at him, once again waiting for him to lead. He held back the sigh that wanted to come and bowed his head again. "Forgive me, Your Majesty, but we were only passing through. We are heading north."

The old lady nodded thoughtfully, and while the princess—and all the other welves, for that matter—appeared foolish and arrogant, the queen, at least, had a glimmer of intelligence in her eyes. "The north, I see. There are not many who choose that path just now, for it is said that there are troubles there."

"There are troubles everywhere, Highness."

The old welf sighed. "You have no idea just how right you are, stranger," she said quietly, glancing over the crowd of some thirty or forty elves that had gathered to watch. "Now, tell me more of what calls you nor—"

"*Your Majesty!*" someone shouted from behind them, and Dannen thought he saw what might have been disgust, maybe even hatred pass across the queen's face, only for a moment, to be replaced once more by a placid, unreadable expression. Frowning thoughtfully, he turned along with the others to see the growing crowd of welves part, creating a lane through which walked the ugliest welf Dannen had ever seen.

He was shorter than his brethren, topping no more than three feet, and while the other welves all had boils, this one's face and hands where they showed at the end of his robe's sleeves were positively covered in the things. His eyes, instead of the usual brown or hazel that most welves seemed to have, looked like an almost dim red and were bloodshot with red lines radiating out from them. What little skin showed past the boils covering him was yellow and jaundiced in appearance, and Dannen realized his own upper lip had curled away from his teeth in disgust at the mere sight of the hideous creature.

If the other welves noticed the newcomer's ugliness, though, they did not show it. They all hurried to move out of the small one's way, bowing low as he passed, the male welves sneaking looks of what Dannen could only describe as jealousy and admiration while the females cast furtive, flirtatious glances in his direction. Unlike the poor clothes most of the welves wore, this one wore a dark silk brocade robe with golden accents. Dannen didn't know much of clothing or fashion, but he knew the robe would have cost a fortune, though considering its wearer's diminutive stature, perhaps a small one. Surely, the tailors would have given the welf a discount.

Yet, for all his ugliness, the welf strode through the opening confidently, glancing down his nose at those on either side as if their obeisance were no more than his due. He came to stand beside Dannen and the others then tilted his head the smallest fraction toward the queen in what *might* have been considered a bow if a man squinted hard enough. "I apologize for my tardiness, Majesty," the welf said in a voice that sounded far more accusatory than apologetic. "I have no doubt you sent a messenger to inform me of the arrival of strangers to our fair land, but it seems he has neglected his duties. It would be my humble recommendation as your advisor he be whipped and thereby taught a lesson in the importance of following orders."

Dannen was stunned the welf would be so brazen as to speak to the ruler of their people in such a way. He turned to the queen expecting her to at the least cut the man down with her words or, more likely given the temperament that seemed common in rulers, to order the obnoxious welf's beating or execution, either of which Dannen would be fine with as he had taken an instant disliking to the welf himself.

But the queen did not order the welf be beaten, nor did she order his execution. Instead, a look that almost appeared guilty passed across her face. "My apologies, Oofen," she said, each word obviously costing her, "but in all the excitement, I must have forgotten to send a messenger."

"Ah," the welf said, nodding slowly and studying the queen with a look that hardly could have been more threatening had he been holding a blade and screaming bloody murder. "I see. Well, I understand, of course, that your position as our *queen* keeps Your Royal Highness quite busy. It is no surprise, then, that one of your *infirmity* would find it difficult to keep track of all which requires your attention."

Dannen blinked. The welf had as much as called the queen an old fool, yet still no one moved to rebuke him, including the queen herself who only sighed. "Perhaps you are right, Oofen."

The welf, though, barely seemed to pay the queen any mind, turning to regard the princess. "Alliandra, Princess, the day finds you as beautiful as always."

The princess in question blushed in a decidedly *un*beautiful way, her skin going a splotchy, angry red, though whether it was in anger at her mother's treatment or in pleasure at the man's compliment, Dannen couldn't tell. At least, that was, until she spoke, giving a smile. "I thank you, Advisor Oofen, for your kind words. And you, of course, are as noble and wise in bearing as ever."

Dannen thought he'd seen slugs that looked nobler than the welf, but Oofen took the compliment—some might have said outrageous lie and been right to do so—as no more than his due. Then he turned to Dannen and the others, dismissing the queen and the princess as easily as a king might his servants. "So you are the mortals, then."

"Last I checked," Dannen said, immediately regretting the sarcasm, but he didn't like the little welf, not at all.

The welf gave him a small, humorless smile. "I see. And tell me, then, what has brought you here to our fair Riverlan?"

"None of your damned business, whelp," Fedder growled, and despite his obvious arrogance, the welf took an involuntary step back at the menace in the giant's voice, one which Dannen was glad to see. He was less glad, of course, that the Firemaker seemed intent on getting them killed, but his dislike for the welf made it worth it...almost.

"Watch your tongue, *mortal,* you speak to the voice of the Divine," said a young welf—Dannen thought it was the same who'd accosted them earlier with the princess, though it was hard to tell with all the boils and dirt—as he stepped forward, his hand going for a blade sheathed at his side, which was worrying. What was more worrying, to Dannen, at least, was that half a dozen other welves had stepped forward as well, also reaching for weapons, but they all froze as if struck by a spell as Oofen raised his hand.

"All is well," Oofen said, giving Dannen a knowing smile as if he were a swordsman who had just shown some masterful

249

flourish of his weapon. "The Divine has not called for the deaths of these mortals, not yet," he finished, studying Dannen and the others for several seconds, giving the not-so-subtle threat a chance to sink in, before turning back to the welves. "After all, we would not want to displease the Divine, would we?"

"O-of course not, sir," the welf said, his eyes going wide as he and the others quickly retreated to their places among the crowd.

"Now then," the advisor said, still grinning in a way that made Dannen want to punch him in the face, "I apologize for their...*eagerness*. Welves, you see, are kind and clever, full of wisdom and honor, chock-full. Yet they can be terrible enemies when angered."

Another threat in case they were somehow too deaf or too dumb to have missed the first one, and it was all Dannen could do to keep from sighing with boredom. He had been threatened plenty of times in his life, after all, and by far more intimidating people and creatures than a three-foot-tall welf. "No problem at all," he said, shrugging. And then, because he really *did* dislike the little bastard, "Or, if it is, then it's a damned *small* problem."

The breath caught in the short welf's throat, and Dannen thought maybe he'd pushed him too far after all, and that they were about to die. But after a moment, the welf took a slow, long breath and seemed to master himself. "Yes. Though sometimes, it is the problems we thought small and of little consequence which cause us the greatest grief. Like a small scratch which becomes infected and, thereby, kills. Do you understand?"

Fedder grunted. "Be pretty hard not to, you little ba—"

"We understand," Dannen blurted hurriedly, thinking they had already pushed their luck quite enough as far as the welf was concerned.

Oofen scowled at the giant for a moment, showing no fear, not now, but finally nodded. "Very well. Take these mortals to the dungeons." The welves stepped forward eagerly, and the advisor held up a hand bedecked in sparkling rings. "They are not to be harmed. The Divine must be consulted first."

Dannen noted obvious disappointment in the eyes of the welves—not exactly a vote of confidence in the surviving the day tally—but they bowed their heads. "Yes, sir."

"Come and try," Fedder said, "I ain't goin' in no dungeon of yours, 'less there's bloodlettin' first."

"I'm with you, old man," Mariana said, the two lengths of steel appearing in her hands with a speed that made it seem almost like magic.

The crazy man, meanwhile, continued to look crazy, chattering back and forth with his squirrel before turning back to the advisor and, since he had no weapon to brandish, chose to brandish an angry scowl instead.

"Put your damned weapons up, you fools," Dannen snapped, and they all three looked at him in surprise. A dumb thing to say, maybe, since only one of them actually *had* a weapon, but they seemed to understand well enough. A moment later, Mariana's weapons were back in their sheaths, Fedder's massive fists were no longer clenched, and the crazy man went back to appearing just crazy and no longer demented.

Not much of an improvement all around, truth be told, but Dannen would take what he could get. The ambassador smiled slowly at Dannen, as if they both shared a secret and gave the welves a nod. "Take them."

"No," the queen said in an almost pleading voice, "these are our guests, Oofen, and should be treated as such."

Oofen, turned to regard the queen who paled under his attention. "Forgive me, Majesty, but are you saying that we should no longer follow the will of the Divine?"

The queen said nothing and, after a moment, Oofen gave a smug smile before turning his back on the queen, dismissing her as if she were of no consequence before motioning to the welves. They moved forward, surrounding Dannen and his companions, and a moment later he and the others were being marched through the village at the end of pointy sticks.

They passed shitty hut after shitty hut—with a few heaps of rubble mixed in for variety—until eventually their escort led them to the biggest building they'd seen so far, one that looked about the size of a tavern. Dannen had a moment, while their escort spoke with another welf at the door with a sharp pointy stick of his own—what must have served as a guard in this backward place—to wonder what it said about him that he thought of everything in terms of taverns and drink, decided it was probably nothing good, and let it go.

Having concluded their brief conversation, the welf leading their escort turned back to Dannen and the others. "You come."

Dannen glanced at his companions and shrugged. "Well. Seen one dungeon, you seen 'em all."

Which wasn't exactly true, of course. This dungeon, in particular, had some of its own eccentricities. The walls were so slanted that he and the others had to walk in leaning to one side, crouching to make it under the five-foot-tall door frame.

The inside of the dungeon wasn't an improvement. The floor was hard-packed earth and the cell—of which there was only one—took up most of the room. Its bars weren't fashioned from steel—because who worried about things like durability and security for a dungeon?—but wood. Wood which, like the rest of the wood Dannen had seen in the village, was rotten and looked ready to collapse under the pressure of no more than a harsh word. Not really a command to stay in place so much as a whispered suggestion, one a man could ignore, if he had a mind to break down the "bars." Not that he would need to. The bars were spaced so widely apart that all but Fedder with his great bulk could have walked through them sideways.

A damn terrible place to keep prisoners, but being that Dannen looked to *be* one of those prisoners, he thought it best to keep such thoughts to himself, even tried for a look of quiet terror he didn't think quite came off as he followed his companions into the cell.

"Stay here," the guard barked.

With that, he departed, and Dannen and the others were left alone. There were no windows, of course, such niceties being far above the level of craftsmanship of which the welves were capable, but there were plenty of holes in the walls and ceiling—proof of that same craftsmanship—for pale moonlight to filter in, keeping them from total darkness. Enough light for him to see the scowl on Fedder's face.

"Don't much like this, Butcher. Feel like an animal in a cage."

"Oh, come on, Fedder," Dannen said, finding a likely piece of ground and having a seat, propping his back against a wooden wall which creaked dangerously until he took his weight off. "Ain't like this is the first dungeon you've been in, that I know for a fact."

"Not the first," Fedder admitted, "but can't say I've ever been too keen on it."

"Well, neither am I," Dannen said, raising his hands to the sides, "yet here we are. In the lap of luxury."

"Don't have to be," Mariana said. "Not exactly high security in this place, is it? Reckon we could break out sure enough."

"And then?" Tesler asked quietly in a reluctant voice that made it clear he didn't like the idea of contradicting the girl any more than he did wrestling a lion, maybe less so, in fact. Crazy was crazy, sure, but all men felt the bite of love, sooner or later, and Dannen thought love had sank its teeth deep into the poor bastard sure enough.

"And then we would be broke out, wouldn't we?" the girl snapped, scowling at him. Maybe it was the moonlight, or maybe she'd been practicing, but Dannen thought it an even better scowl than she'd given him a day before.

"He's right," Dannen said. "Sure, we could break out, but what then? Then we'd be faced with an army of angry little bastards with sharp sticks that seemed pretty damned keen on using them. We'd take some of them down with us, sure, but all?" He shook his head. "Not likely. Besides, I'd just as soon get some rest anyway. It's unlikely any men the High Justice sent after us will make it this far and, even if they do, they'll face the same sort of welcome." He shifted uncomfortably. He'd slept on dirt before, but it seemed the welves, either intentionally or, more likely based on what he'd seen of their skills in...well, anything really, completely unintentionally, had left the dungeon floors bumpy and uneven.

In the end, he decided to lie down, resting his hands behind his head. "Anyway, suicide by a village of angry welves is an option that'll remain on the table. For now, why not just relax and see what happens?"

Fedder grunted. "Never been much good at waitin', Butcher, but if you say so, I'll do it."

Dannen might have been touched by that in other circumstances, but just then he was too tired and too uncomfortable. "I do say," he agreed, "and as for waitin', as I recall, you've never much of a problem with it, just so long as you've an ale in your hand."

Fedder nodded thoughtfully, then glanced at him hopefully. "Reckon they've got some ale?"

"If they did," Dannen said slowly, "would you drink it?"

Fedder sighed, sitting down. "Probably I wouldn't."

Mariana laughed, then paused to scowl at Tesler, just in case the poor bastard had somehow forgotten where he stood in the last few seconds. "Maybe you're not a total old fool after all," she said to Fedder before she, too, sat down.

"What do you figure they meant by this 'Divine'?" Fedder asked.

Dannen sighed. "The gods alone know. Probably something bad, likely something that'll want to kill us."

"Why do you say that?" Mariana asked.

Dannen met her eyes. "Well, there's a bit of a precedent, ain't there?"

"It's that ugly little shit, one they called Goofen," Fedder said.

"Fairly sure it was Oofen," Dannen corrected.

"'Smug bastard'll be good enough to be gettin' on with," the mage said. Then, his eyes widened. "Hey, here's an idea. That fucker's the one wants us dead, right? And any fool can see he's got somethin' over on the queen, maybe the only reasonable person here."

"Not people, strictly speaking," Tesler ventured, then carefully studied his feet at a fresh scowl from Mariana.

"Anyway," Fedder said, apparently deciding the girl's scowl was a good enough rebuke, and on that Dannen couldn't disagree, "seems to me, that's the kind of fella ought to fall on an assassin's blade. Bound to, sooner or later. And just so happens, we've got an assassin with us. Wouldn't be any great thing to take a blade and slit that smug bastard a second smile in his throat."

Dannen grunted thoughtfully and they all turned to study Mariana who shifted uncomfortably. "That idea does have some things to recommend it," he said.

"No," Mariana said.

Dannen raised his eyebrows in surprise, but it was Fedder who spoke. "What'ya mean, 'no'?"

"Give it a think," the girl said, "I'm sure you'll come up with it, old or not. It's the opposite of yes, that helps you any."

"Can we ask why?" Dannen ventured.

"Well," she hedged, "there isn't any money in it, is there? Bad example to set as an assassin, going around killing folks for free."

Dannen frowned. It was obvious the girl was hiding something, and whatever it was, it made her decidedly uncomfortable. "Even if doing so saves your life?" he asked. "What is it really, Mariana? What's the problem?"

"Just don't like goin' around knifin' folks, that's all," she said quietly, avoiding their gazes.

"Might be," Dannen said slowly, "that you took up the wrong profession."

"I'm just not slitting anyone's throat and that's the end of it, alright?" the girl demanded.

Dannen shrugged. "It's alright with me, but—"

"Out with it, girly," Fedder said. "It don't do for teammates to hide stuff from one another, not at all. Folks end up dead that way."

Dannen expected some sort of angry rejoinder, but the girl just sighed. "Suppose I ought to tell you now as you'll likely find out sooner or later but..."

"But what?" Dannen prompted, overcome with curiosity which was a nice change from the fear which had been overcoming him recently.

She winced. "Thing is, I don't like blood. Like, you know, the sight of it."

Dannen frowned slowly. "Can't say I much like the sight of my own, but I've never been all that averse to that of others. What uh...what bothers you about it?"

"Makes me sick," Mariana said.

"I understand," Tesler agreed, nodding sagely. The movement sent the squirrel dancing desperately to maintain its perch. "War is a terrible thing and it is no small matter to spill another's blood even in the defense of—"

"It's not that, you damned fool," Mariana said, but she didn't seem angry as she usually did when speaking to the crazy man. Instead, she sounded embarrassed. "It literally makes me sick. I mean, just the sight of blood, and I'll start spewin' my dinner all over the place."

Dannen found himself thinking of the fight they'd had before meeting Clarissa when Mariana had gotten sick all over his boots. At the time, he had taken it as just one more sign that the world was a bitch, but now he realized it was more than that, remembered her pointing out that he was bleeding before she got sick. He remembered, too, the way Clarissa had seemed to be poking fun at him when she'd found out he was traveling with the girl. Now it made sense.

"Don't like blood..." Fedder said slowly as if she'd just posed some great riddle, one he was having a damn hard time solving.

"It makes me *sick,*" she repeated. "Don't you get it, you old fool?"

Fedder blinked, realization finally dawning, and he barked a laugh. "You get sick at the sight of blood? But you're a bloody *assassin.*" he said in disbelief.

"Not if I can help it, I ain't!" Mariana snapped.

"That's the reason then," Dannen said. "For the rods."

"What's that?" Fedder asked, glancing at him.

Mariana didn't answer, so Dannen did. "The weapons she uses, the steel rods. Most assassins prefer cutting weapons, and it's hard to argue with their efficiency once you've seen what a knife across the throat can do to a man. I've been wondering why it is that our Mariana here foregoes the use of blades and chooses to use steel rods instead. But now, it makes sense. Rods don't cut, don't slice or stab. Rods, they maim, they break."

Fedder barked an incredulous laugh, the sound like a lion coughing. Then he broke into howling laughter, and Dannen didn't think he imagined the walls shaking, not this time, so he was more than a little thankful when Fedder's laughter finally died out. The giant shook his head slowly, still grinning. "An assassin scared of blood and a man with a pet squirrel thinks he can talk to animals. Tell me, Butcher, just how pissed-off did you make this god of yours?"

Dannen noted the vulnerable look in the girl's eyes, expecting to be judged, waiting for it. He turned back to the Firemaker. "Well, finish it, if you're gonna start it, Fedder. We also have a mage— maybe one of the world's greatest—who for reasons unknown believes magic's for sissies, and a swordsman," he gestured at his paunch, "who's vowed never to use a sword and who's fat besides. Not a recipe for success, maybe, but it's what we got."

Some of the shame seemed to leave Marina's expression at that, and she gave a small smile. Dannen was surprised by how good it felt to see that smile, just as good as it had to see other similar ones years ago when he and Fedder had found themselves partnered up with one person or another for a job. It felt good, but he tried not to consider what had happened to a lot of those smiling faces, tried not to think of the last expression he'd seen on many of them—not a smile, not that. Men being tortured and killed rarely smiled, but oh how they screamed.

"So what then?" Fedder asked simply. "You mean to just stay here?"

Dannen nodded muzzily, closing his eyes. "I mean to just stay here."

"But...what if they plan to kill us?" Tesler asked.

Dannen opened one eye, peering at the man. "If they show up plannin' to kill us, I'd probably just as soon not be awake for it. Now, get some rest, everyone. From what I understand, dyin's hard work—you'll want a good night's sleep." Not that any of them were likely to get a good night's sleep, not on the world's most uncomfortable dirt, but near-imminent failure didn't excuse a man from trying. After all, he'd been in similar situations before and by luck more than design, he was still breathing and walking around and getting his life threatened.

***

A few hours had passed when they came. The door creaked and groaned, announcing its opening as effectively as if there had been a man standing by with a bell, and Dannen opened his eyes. He did not waken, for to do that a man first had to fall asleep, and no matter what he'd said to the others, Dannen had spent the last hour fretting and worrying over what would become of them.

Oofen was studying him from outside the cage bars, flanked by two welves with crude blades in their hand.

"Ah, mortals," Oofen said, looking even smugger than he had before, "I see you are awake."

"Suppose we're just a bit too picky about the accommodations is all," Dannen said, thinking he had a pretty good idea of what was coming now. The welf was making a power grab—the how of it didn't really matter. Such a welf, ambitious and greedy, like similar men Dannen had met, would eliminate anyone, would stoop to any crime or act, to get what they wanted. They would destroy any person—or, in this case, persons—who happened to get in their way. Persons like Dannen and his companions. The fact that they were still alive meant only one thing—the welf had some sort of job he wanted them to do, the type of job he couldn't rely on the other welves to do for him. As for the job itself, Dannen thought he had a pretty good idea about that too.

"You make more jokes," the welf said. "I am impressed. After all, some in your position would be afraid of the inevitable torture awaiting you, should the Divine choose to deal harshly with you."

Trying to scare him and the others, to let them know without doubt where they stood so that whatever shitty offer he planned on making in the next few minutes would sound a little less shitty. Dannen shrugged. "Seen one torture chamber, you seen 'em all. Anyway, there's worse things than being tortured." He couldn't think of a single one, but better not to let the welf see their fear and lose what little bargaining power they had. "Anyway, what is this 'Divine,' exactly?"

Oofen glanced at the two welves with a smile as if Dannen had just asked something foolish. "The Divine, mortal, is a being of unsurpassed beauty and wisdom, one which your meager mind could not fathom. Know only that it is the queen which guides the welves, and the Divine, the will of the gods made flesh, which guides the queen."

It didn't seem like the queen had been guiding the welves to Dannen, not at all. Seemed more like the welves were a runaway chariot, and she was being dragged behind them. As for the one steering the cart, well, that seemed obvious enough. Still, he didn't bother saying so. He knew who was steering just as he knew the welf *knew* that he knew. Just as well, in fact, as he knew what was coming next, just as soon as the man got around to saying it. "Sounds fancy," he said, mostly because the welf was watching him, clearly expecting something.

"Fancy?" the welf asked, pretending to be offended. "Mortal, we do not speak of some fine necklace or dining set which women in face paint and expensive silk might preen over. We speak of the *will of the gods,* a being as far above the welves in wisdom and understanding as we are above your kind. One which has chosen to reside among us."

"Must be tough," Dannen said, "havin' your god living next door."

"The Divine is not a *god,* mortal, only a mouthpiece through which the gods make their will known to me."

Dannen nodded slowly, the coin finally dropping. "I see. And, let me guess, you're the only one among the welves capable of understanding it?"

The welf shared a look of amusement with his guard escort. "The Divine does not speak to me, mortal, any more than I might converse with a mouse, so far above us is it. Yet, it makes its will known well enough."

"Oh?" Dannen asked. "How's that?"

A soft laugh. "Perhaps you will find out, mortal, in time. But that is not why I have come to speak with you." He turned to the two guards who'd escorted him. "I will speak with the prisoners alone."

"But, sir," one said, looking confused, "the queen would want—"

"It is the will of the Divine," Oofen interrupted in an imperious tone, and the guards stiffened, their faces going pale.

"O-of course, sir," the one who'd spoken said, and then they were both hurrying away.

Oofen waited, watching the door, until it shut behind the guards, then he turned back to Dannen and the others. "Now then, I have a proposition for all of you, one that might garner you favor with the Divine who will determine your fate. Such an offer—"

"You want us to kill the queen," Dannen interrupted.

"What?" the welf said, his eyes going wide, the smug arrogance vanishing from his face, giving way to confusion and more than a little fear. "How did you know—I mean, wait, no, that's...it's not what *I* want, not at all."

"Of course not," Dannen said dryly. "The Divine wants it, right? You're just the mouthpiece."

For a mouthpiece of the gods, the man was awfully silent for several seconds as he stared at Dannen, all his authority and confidence stripped from him to be replaced at first by shock at Dannen's guess, then an undisguised eagerness. He glanced nervously at the door, as if expecting the guards to barge inside, their weapons drawn. When none did, he turned back to Dannen, finally mastering himself. "I am loyal to my queen, of course, and only a fool and a liar would claim otherwise. Yet, I am more loyal still to the gods, and the Divine has spoken on this matter."

"Loyal to your own interests too, eh?" Fedder asked. "And this Divine, I got a feelin' this Divine spoke to you only, that it?"

The welf sneered. "You would be wise to keep this dog of yours quiet," he said to Dannen. "Anyway, I can assure you..." He paused, clearing his throat. "That is, the *Divine* can assure you safe passage out of welven lands if you should perform this one simple task for it. A dark, grim task, it is true, but necessary. The queen might wish to help the welves, she is not the one to lead us."

Fedder grunted a humorless laugh. "Don't take a genius to figure out who you'd pick for the job."

The welf hissed. "It is not *I* who have chosen, *fool,* but—"

"The Divine, sure," Mariana said. "We get it. You don't *want* to be the ruler of all the welves, don't want all the power and money, 'course not. You just got to do it, huh? For the good of the welves."

The welf studied her carefully as if trying to decide whether or not he was being mocked, but finally seemed to settle on taking her words at face value. "That's right."

Dannen grunted. "You don't mind my askin', what're the queen's crimes? Or—and this is just a guess—what sorts of things are you, I mean the *Divine,* wanting to do that she's standing in the way of? Doesn't have nothing to do with a certain princess, does it?"

The welf had a guilty expression for a moment, looked like nothing so much as a child caught out. A particularly ugly child but a child nonetheless. Then, the guilt and shame that had flitted across the welf's features changed to anger. "*Enough,*" he snapped. "You have your choice. Either obey and find your way safely out of welven lands, or refuse me, and die terrible deaths. And they *will be* terrible, that much I promise you." He watched them for a moment, trying to look intimidating but failing, not that it was all his fault. Dannen figured it was a hard thing looking intimidating when you were less than half as tall as those you meant to threaten.

Finally, Oofen gave a single, sharp nod. "I will return in the morning to hear your answer."

With that, the welf turned and strode for the door, and Dannen and the others were left looking at each other. From what he'd seen of her, Dannen had liked the queen, at least more than he had any of the other welves. He had met cruel rulers in the past, and she didn't seem like one of those, had seemed, mostly, just tired, maybe even scared. Didn't seem like she deserved killing, but then Dannen hadn't deserved Val. Deserving, as always, had nothing to do with it.

The glances of the others were troubled, worried, and he thought he knew why, for no matter how much of a fool the welf was, he had them in a tight spot. Dannen didn't like the idea of hurting the queen, but then neither did he much care for the idea of dying horribly. Though nearly everything Oofen had said was a lie, Dannen believed that much.

"What do we do, Butcher?" asked Firemaker. The mage had a troubled expression on his face, an expression Dannen hadn't seen the slightest hint of when their deaths seemed a near-certainty, or when he was forced to butcher men in a fight. A strange man, Fedder Firemaker, with his own particular morals, ones either too complex to understand or, and Dannen thought this more likely, ones the big bastard made up as he went along.

Dannen considered his answer carefully. He was no assassin, and whatever the "Divine" was, it was clear Oofen was just using it as an excuse to get the queen out of his way so he could make a grab for power. He tried to think of all the angles, to be rational and logical and make a plan. Mostly, though, he was just pissed. He didn't want to do what the welf asked, not because it was wrong to kill the queen but simply because Oofen was a rude, arrogant little shit. Dannen knew the type, had seen it plenty of times, folks walking around with a face might as well have "Punch Me" painted on it. And one of Dannen's problems—at least when it came to finding himself in life-or-death situations—was that he could rarely resist such an invitation. But then, he wasn't alone. The others were with him, counting on him, and if he decided to tell the little bastard to get fucked, it wasn't just his life he'd be gambling with.

Finally, he sighed heavily, turning to Fedder. "I don't know," he said softly. He felt their eyes on him as he made his way toward the corner of the room and lay down again. He really was tired, that was true, but mostly he didn't want to see their eyes watching him, searching for an answer he didn't have, for some sort of comfort or reassurance he couldn't give. Turning away didn't help. He could feel their eyes on him, their need, a need he could not answer, so he said nothing, only lay there, and eventually he heard the soft rustlings of his companions as they did the same.

They would learn if they didn't know it already. Sooner or later, they would learn. There wasn't any use looking for answers to life's questions, no use trying to win the game because life was a bitch and never played fair. The truth was that, most times, there were no lights in the darkness. Sometimes the knights never found the princesses in their towers, and when someone finally *did* show up there was nothing left to save but a skeleton in a faded dress. And sometimes, just sometimes, the knights weren't knights at all—they were the dragons.

***

Dannen had always been a light sleeper—in fact, most men and women adventurers were. Not that they trained for it exactly. The truth was far simpler and, as was usually the case, far more brutal—heavy-sleeping adventurers didn't last long. So he heard a muffled *whumpf* from outside, a sound like something being struck or someone falling, heard it through his sleep and he rose, staring around him at the darkness.

It was still night then, the deadline Oofen had given them still some hours away, that much he could tell by the moonlight filtering in through the many ragged holes in the dungeon's walls and ceilings. Seemed the power-hungry welf had not been able to resist and had come back early for his answer. That was too bad, for Dannen had none to give him, none that sat well, anyway. He glanced at his companions, still sleeping. Much easier to get along with when they were unconscious, that much had to be admitted, but good people, deep down, good men, a good woman. And if they were not, then at least they were *his* people, those who had put their faith in him not to lead them astray, just like those men and women in the old days.

Some had made it, and some hadn't. A lot hadn't. Dannen thought he had made his peace with that, but standing there, he felt a fury spark to life inside him, rising and rising, a fury he would not have expected. It was what he thought of as a young man's anger, and he too old to feel it, but he felt it anyway. An anger at the injustices of the world, an anger at mortals and creatures and gods who all seemed content only if they were ruining—or often taking—the lives of someone or something else.

Dannen could not change the world, could not make it better than it was, and even had he been gifted the authority, he knew enough of himself to realize that he would have been a shit choice for the job, one of the worst, probably. If a man couldn't change the world, then all he could do was do his best to live within it. To *live*. And if they didn't agree to the welf's terms, if Dannen did what his pride and his anger wanted him to do—namely, tell the welf in no uncertain terms what he could do with his offer—then he and the others would die. True, there'd be the torture first, but they'd die eventually. Didn't sound all that bad to Dannen, sounded a lot, in fact, like an opportunity to rest. But the others would die too, die like those in the past had, and he didn't like that, not at all.

Suddenly, the door creaked open, and Dannen was pulled from his thoughts as a cloaked, hooded figure stepped into the dungeon, a furtive, stealthy quality to its movements.

He moved toward the cell, as close as he could without bumping into one of the bars and sending the whole structure crashing down on their heads. "I'll do it. But me alone—you leave the others out of this, you understand?"

The figure froze at the sound of his voice, tensing, and for a moment, he thought he would flee, perhaps Oofen was finally considering what would happen to him if the queen realized what he was about. But when the hooded figure raised its head, Dannen was shocked to see that it wasn't Oofen staring back at him. Instead, it was the welven queen. Not a face he would have called "the Beautiful" under normal circumstances, but considering he'd been expecting to be speaking to the ugly bastard Oofen and agreeing to be an assassin, he could have been convinced.

"Quiet," the queen said, glancing back over her shoulder. The door had not closed completely but had caught on its crooked frame, and Dannen thought he could make out the vague form of someone—the guard, unless he missed his guest—lying in a heap on the ground. Either the man had decided, quite abruptly, to take a nap or, and this was a touch more likely, the sound that had woken him had been the queen insisting he take one. "Welves have good ears, you know. Now," she went on, eyeing him with a knowing look, "what is it you'll do, hmm? What is it we must leave the others out of?"

He thought, judging by the look in her face, not the vacant, stupid expression on so many of the welves, but a discerning, wise look, that the queen already knew the answer to her own question, so he shook his head slowly, deciding to ignore it. "Seems we're popular today. Should I be bowing?"

"Save it," the queen said, glancing at the door again, "and quiet, will you? It wouldn't do for me to be caught sneaking around like some thief in the night."

Dannen grunted softly. "First a visit from the *royal advisor*, now a visit from the queen. Should I be expecting the Divine himself next?" He glanced around at the crooked walls and dirt floors. "If so, might be I ought to tidy up a bit first."

"Herself."

He frowned. "What's that?"

"The *Divine*," she said, scowling, "the creature that bastard Oofen is using to supplant me, it's female. Though I have no idea why that would make any difference any more than I know why a griffin would follow the orders of that smug little shit."

Dannen raised an eyebrow. "Wait a minute, are you saying that the Divine, that this 'voice of the gods,' is a griffin?"

"That's right," the queen said sourly. "It lives in the forest not far away. Except, that is, when it decides to come *into* the village and prance around all majestically or, as sometimes happens, decides to eat someone. Someone who is, inevitably a rival of Oofen's, either as one of my advisors or as a rival suitor for my daughter's attentions."

Dannen blinked, struggling to keep up with the steady stream of information. "Why is it you're trusting me with all this?" he asked. "I mean, don't you think it's dangerous?"

She snorted, as if he was a fool. "More dangerous than my 'closest advisor' plotting for my assassination? Oh yes, Dannen Ateran, only a fool wouldn't be able to guess what reason Oofen would have had to visit you here, and though I am old, I am not so old I cannot see that which is right in front of my face. Not yet, at least. I must admit, though, to some curiosity about what you were agreeing to, when I entered?"

She did a good job of hiding it, of being brave, but he could see the fear lurking in her eyes. Welves were said to be long-lived creatures, perhaps even as long-lived as their elven cousins, so for her to appear aged as she did, the queen must have been old indeed. Yet, it was the paradox of the mortal races that however much time they have on the face of the world, and however terribly that time was spent, they were never prepared to let it go. "He said he would grant us safe passage," Dannen said quietly.

"Ah," the queen said slowly, following his gaze to the sleeping figures of his companions. "I see. You care for them."

It was not a question, not really, and so Dannen chose not to answer it.

"I understand," she said. "Gods, but how could I not?"

"But...why have you stayed?" Dannen asked. "I mean, if you know Oofen is trying to kill you, why stay? Or, failing that, why not have him arrested or put to death?"

She shook her head. "Why stay?" she asked. "That's simple. I stay here, among my people, for the same reason you will do what Oofen asks. You will not like it, but you will do it, and when you do, it will not be for selfish reasons, Dannen Ateran, for my welven eyes see that much. It will be for love."

Dannen tried to grunt a laugh, but it came out weak. "I don't, I mean, that is—"

"Relax, mortal," she said, laughing softly, "I will not make you say it. And as for having him arrested or put to death, I fear that time has passed. I might have, in the beginning, when the griffin first showed up, for then it seemed Oofen, like the rest of us, feared it and exercised none of the power over the creature he now seems to. Should I order him arrested or put to death, Oofen would call on the creature to obey his commands, and many of my people would die, but even then I am not sure he would need to. For there would be those—many, perhaps most—who would refuse my order, who would choose Oofen. Not all, though, and then there would be war. Or, perhaps, it is more right to say a massacre and not just because 'war' sounds far too grandiose for our poor little village, but also because I have a sneaking suspicion Oofen's supporters would far outnumber my own."

"Poor village?" Dannen said, more surprised by this than nearly anything yet, for since they'd been taken by the welves, he had grown accustomed to their shared arrogance regarding anything they made or did, an arrogance which didn't bother itself with little inconveniences like reality and truth.

She gave him a small smile. "I told you, Dannen Ateran, I am not so old that I cannot see, not yet."

"But the other welves...your daughter..."

The queen sighed. "Are fools. Oh, do not look so surprised. I love my daughter, mortal. I love my people also, yet loving a thing does not change the truth, no matter how much we might wish it. They are fools, but they are *my* fools, do you understand?"

Dannen glanced back at his three slumbering companions. "Yes," he said.

"I see that you do. Then you know that, for my love of my people, I refuse to create a situation in which war will take their lives."

"Even if that means you die?" Dannen pressed. "Even if we refuse him, Oofen will only try another way, won't stop trying until either he's succeeded, or he's *made* to stop."

"Even if I die," she said, slowly, meeting his eyes. "And whoever ends up doing it, I would only ask, Dannen Ateran, that they do it quickly, for though I should not be, I find that I am afraid not so much of an ending, for I am very tired, but of the pain which will accompany that end. Better a blade across the throat than to be eaten by that little shit's trained beast."

Dannen frowned. "I've seen a few griffins in my time—always from a distance, it's why I'm still alive, probably—but I've never known anyone to train one. In fact, I hear that's why people gave up trying to tame them in hopes of riding them like a flying horse. But griffins aren't horses, not at all, and eventually enough would-be griffin-riders were killed that the thing was given up. Now, you expect me to believe a three-foot-tall welf has somehow made one his...what, his *pet?*"

The queen shrugged. "I don't expect you to believe anything, Dannen Ateran, and I would understand if you did not. Yet, the truth remains unchanged whether we choose to see it or not."

Dannen found that he liked the queen as naturally as he had disliked Oofen. Unlike the rest of her people, the queen of the welves was no fool, and there was something noble, perhaps even *beautiful* about her—a grace, a sort of dignity that did not exist in any of the welves he'd met and in very few people for that matter. "But...what about your daughter?" he asked. "She seemed to command the respect of the welves. Perhaps, if she would—"

"No," the queen said, shaking her head before he could finish. "I will leave my daughter out of this. At least, as much as she can be left out. Besides, it is just as likely that she will choose Oofen as me, anyway."

Dannen grunted. "Surely she wouldn't. Not her own mother—"

"My daughter is a fool, Dannen Ateran," the queen said simply. "I do not say so with any cruelty or malice, simply because it is the truth. She, like the rest of my people, is a fool. You have no doubt seen enough to know that the welves and reality are like distant relatives who visit only on days of celebration. For this reason they believe themselves beautiful and graceful. They are as arrogant, perhaps even more so, gods watch over us, than our elven kin."

"But...but *how?*" Dannen asked in disbelief, knowing they were running out of time, for the unconscious guard would wake or be discovered sooner or later, but unable to quiet his curiosity.

The queen tilted her head at him. "Why do they believe themselves beautiful, or why are they so ugly?"

"Uh...both," Dannen said.

"They are arrogant, Dannen Ateran, because they are welves—which, like all of the elder races, are predisposed to it—and, more importantly, because they are spoiled children who have always been told by their mother, a mother who had feared that, in their ugliness, they would grow to hate each other, to hate themselves, that they are beautiful and worthy and fine."

"Their mother?" Dannen asked.

She shrugged. "A figure of speech, though great, great grandmother might be closer to the truth—except for Gabriella, my daughter, one who I birthed far later in my life than is normal for my people. As for their ugliness, for *our* ugliness, it is perhaps just that the gods have made us as we are."

Dannen frowned. "But you don't look like they do."

She gave him a small, sad smile. "An unfortunate side effect of me trying to instill confidence in my people—a confidence which, as you've seen, turned to arrogance—is that they believe themselves perfect. And what need does perfection have of things such as baths or ointments for rashes and boils? And so they grow uglier as the years pass, thinking themselves and their appearances beyond reproach. As for why we came here, to this place in the wilderness, it is because a group of our elven cousins moved in near us. They have always despised us, thought us less than they, mocked us as well, and I did not wish for my children and grandchildren to suffer their taunts. So under my order, we left the city of my people—a true city, Dannen Ateran, not like this heap of rubble you see before you—and brought my family here, to this place, so that they might not feel the hatred and disgust their ugliness would inevitably cause. That was hundreds of years ago now, nearing a thousand, in fact, and since then my family has grown."

Dannen respected the queen even more. What strength, what courage did it take to leave the only place you ever knew, so that your children might not suffer? To protect them, she had given up everything and had come here, to this place. A thought struck him then, and he grunted softly. "But if what you're saying is true, then Oofen—"

"Is my blood," she agreed. "Though so far removed by hundreds of years that, by a mortal's reckoning, you might not consider it so. Still, that makes no difference and yes, before you ask, it is another reason I do not wish to go to war with Oofen. No matter how power-hungry and cruel he is, he is still of my blood. I would not see him suffer, if I could help it. I would not see any of them suffer."

Dannen didn't understand that, not really, but he decided to let it go, for time was growing short for him and his companions. "But if it's just a griffin, then why are your people convinced it's divine? And how can they not see that Oofen's up to something? I mean, I just met the bastard and already I can't stand him."

The queen sighed heavily. "Do you have children, Dannen Ateran?"

A twinge of grief ran through him. Val had wanted kids, and he had too. Or, at least, he had told her so. But every time she brought it up, he had put it off, had given her one excuse or another, saying, *believing* that they still had plenty of time. Believing it right up until they didn't. "No," he managed, forcing the word out.

The queen studied him, the compassion in her gaze indicating that she had some small inkling of the pain her simple question had caused. "I see. Well, to answer your question regarding why Oofen's deception has been so accepted by the welves, you must understand, that my children are fools. You have seen, already, that they believe themselves beautiful, have grown vain in this belief as so many of the races of elder do. Only, they have taken it one step further, becoming blind to their own flaws. Fools, then, and it is no great matter to trick a fool. Particularly," she said quietly, "an angry one." She waved that thought away, taking a slow, deep breath. "Yet, they are my children just the same, and I love them. I would not see harm come to them, not if I could help it."

Dannen nodded. "So how does Oofen do it? How does he get the griffin to obey his commands, I mean?"

She shook her head, frustrated. "I do not know. I have tried to investigate the matter, but so far, at least, have come up empty and time, as you have seen, grows short. Oofen is impatient for my throne, and I fear that soon he will have it, one way or the other. I do not know why the beast obeys him. Whenever he is challenged, the beast appears. Already, all who openly opposed his thirst for power have been taken by the beast, and Oofen explains this only by saying their deaths were the will of the Divine. Now," she went on, "that is enough talk. I dare not linger here any longer. I knocked the guard unconscious, but I am old now, and I fear I do not hit as hard as I once did. Soon, he will awaken, and he is Oofen's man, through and through."

Dannen nodded. "Thank you, Beautiful. Your title, as extravagant as I first thought it, does not do you justice."

She smiled. "I am old, Dannen Ateran, and not so blind that I cannot see my own ugliness, even if my children fail to do so. Once,

269

I might have been reckoned beautiful, but that was many years ago, in a faraway place."

"There are many types of beauty, Majesty."

She beamed at that, and the smile transformed her plain, wrinkled face so that, in that moment, she was truly beautiful. "I came here, thinking to ask you to refuse Oofen, but I will not, not now. I know that your decision is no easy one, Dannen Ateran, and I wish you to know that I will hold you blameless, whatever you decide." Her gaze traveled to his sleeping companions. "The world can, betimes, become a place of darkness, and in the long nights, a person must do what they can to protect those they love."

"As you did," he said softly.

She inclined her head. "That, too, was many years ago, and in a faraway place. Goodbye, Dannen Ateran. Whatever comes, I wish you and your friends well."

"Goodbye, Majesty."

With that, she turned and headed for the door. Dannen watched her go, his mind whirling with a thousand different thoughts, a thousand different regrets. He waited, silently, afraid someone would raise the alarm as she left, wondering, too, what he would do if they did. Would he break through the flimsy bars and rush to the queen's rescue though it would almost certainly mean his death? He thought maybe he would, thought, too, that there were far worse ways for a man to die, and far less deserving causes in which he might give his life.

No alarm came, however, and after several tense minutes, he turned to regard his companions. The queen had asked him what he would do, and he had told her nothing. But the simple truth was—he did not know. He liked the queen, thought she was far better than the welves deserved. A queen, a mother, who would sacrifice her own happiness, her own *life* to protect those she cared about. Yet, it seemed to him that for all her wisdom and kindness, it was Oofen who held all the cards, Oofen who could, if he so chose, have Dannen and the others murdered either by welves who would jump at the chance to obey him or by a griffin who seemed to have decided, against its very nature, to become the welf's pet.

One option would leave him and his companions with a guilt, a shame that would likely follow them, follow *him* for the rest of his days. More blood on his hands to mix with that he already saw every time he looked at them. The other option, though, meant they would not live long enough to regret much of anything. How could he then, in good conscience, make either choice? Yet, a choice had to be made, and it was clear the others would only wait to see what he had decided, would follow him, the fools, in whatever course he deemed best.

Perhaps, they would hate him, if he chose to take Oofen up on his offer. Perhaps, he would even hate himself. Yet, they would all be alive to do so at their leisure, and the dead could never seek to make amends for the wrongs of their past. That was a gift, a curse reserved only for those who still drew breath. He should kill the queen. It was the only real choice. She had known it, had as much forgiven him for doing it in advance, understanding well the situation he and the others were in. And while he would not have trusted that bastard Oofen with something as simple as watching his cat while he went to the market, he thought he could trust him to let them go unharmed. After all, the welf had nothing against them, and by showing that the Divine chose to spare them, he would at once undermine the queen's authority further and reinforce the belief of the welves that the griffin—and, thereby, *he*—was the only one capable of communicating with the gods and understanding their will.

He should kill the queen. It was the only thing to do, really. The wise thing. But then, Dannen had long thought himself a fool, had survived if not in thanks to, then certainly in spite of, his own foolishness for more years than a man who'd faced the sort of dangers he had had any right to expect. So he decided he would not kill the queen, would tell Oofen, that smug little shit, that he could do what he would to him, he would not help him destroy the finest thing among the welves. He knew without doubt that he would do as much, that he would refuse the welf's offer, knew it without really even understanding the why of it.

Certainly, he had been selfish before, had acted in his own interests before and often to the detriment of others. And yet, he would not do this. There were some bridges which when, once crossed, a man found that he could never return, no matter how hard he might try. But even that wasn't the real reason. The real reason was...

"Because fuck him, that's why," Dannen whispered, and as soon as the words were out of his mouth, he felt better, stronger. The decision had been made, now, and it would not be changed. He would suffer what he would suffer, and should he die, at least he would do so with some small bit of the shame he had accumulated over the years sloughing away behind him.

"Thank the gods for that."

Dannen jumped at the sound and turned to see Fedder rising from where he had lain on the floor, not looking sleepy at all.

"You bastard—" Dannen began, but was interrupted by Mariana's voice.

"I liked her."

Dannen grunted. "How...you were awake? Why didn't you bastards say something?"

"Seemed rude," Tesler said, rising with a smile, "interrupting the two of you while you were having a conversation."

Dannen shook his head in wonder as they all smiled at him sheepishly, as if they thought he might be angry, might start any minute with the screaming and shouting and carrying on. Maybe he should have been angry. It was hard to tell, what with his mind feeling like it had been stuffed to the brim with wool, his thoughts fuzzy and, though he wouldn't have thought it possible, exhausted. Certainly, they had each lain there silently of some separate, silent accord, while he struggled with an impossible decision, one which they might have helped to make. But the truth was, he was not mad, and he had nothing bad to say any more than a drowning man, when rescued, might have been able to criticize his rescuers for taking too long. Such a thing would have been ridiculous, and while he often *was* ridiculous, he did not make an effort at it.

He didn't feel angry or cheated or resentful. What he felt, really, was relief. Relief that they had heard his decision, relief that they each seemed not only to understand it but to be happy with it. Relief, too, that they were no longer asleep, and he was no longer alone.

"Thanks," he said to all of them, meaning it.

Fedder shifted, obviously uncomfortable with the gratitude. "So, what now? I'm all for tellin' that short little fucker to go...well, anyway, I'm glad we're doin' it, but can't say as I'd mind havin' a plan which accounts for the wild impossibility of us survivin' the next few hours."

"Easy enough if we could figure out how that Oofen bastard is getting that griffin to do what he wants," Mariana said.

"Right," Dannen said, then sighed. "Anyone got any ideas?"

Judging by the looks on Mariana and Fedder's faces neither of the two had anything to contribute. Tesler, though, was frowning thoughtfully. Dannen had hope, for a brief moment, that the man had an answer, had seen something he himself had not, had that hope right up until the man spoke and that hope died a quick death. "Griffins don't like people."

It was Mariana who spoke next, the scowl that always seemed in place when she spoke to the young man appearing out of nowhere. "Well, genius, *this* one seems not to mind 'em all that much, he's willin' to kill for 'em."

"She," Tesler muttered, too distracted by his own thoughts to notice the threatening look Mariana gave him. "The queen," he went on, clearly talking to himself, "said it was a she."

"What damn difference does that make?" Mariana demanded. "Look, we don't have time to stand around while you say crazy shit—it's almost daylight. Any minute now that ugly little welf will come back and have us all executed."

"Rich?" Tesler asked, frowning.

She rolled her eyes. "Blind as well as crazy, are you? The bastard was wearing so many rings on his fingers, it looked like he was wearing a rainbow for gloves. And that robe, too, was worth a fortune, though I doubt it will be once it's touched that skin of his."

"Rich," Tesler repeated, nodding slowly, "the griffin a she..." He trailed off into inaudible murmuring.

"Repeat me one more time, you crazy bastard and—"

"Wait," Dannen said, holding up a hand to silence her.

"*Wait?*" Mariana said. "We're running out of time and he—"

"*Quiet,*" Dannen hissed, and to his relief she subsided into silence, a scowl on her face. Probably, Dannen would regret that later. In his experience, hired killers—and women, come to that— tallied personal affronts more accurately and carefully than any banker might a loan. Still, he thought he saw something in the young man's face, his eyes. Might have been just pure craziness, but then again he might have been on to something,

But several seconds passed, and the man said nothing, his mouth moving as if he were muttering to himself but far too low for Dannen or the others to hear. Then he turned to the squirrel on his shoulder, and began speaking to it, though Dannen couldn't make out the words. He sighed. No great insight or revelation after all, just a madman being a madman, and Dannen the fool for thinking it might have been anything else.

A fool, yes, but not so much he didn't notice the way sunlight had began to filter in through the holes in the roof while they talked. Night had given way to day at last, and they were out of time. "Come on," he said finally, "we have to get out of here before that bastard comes back with his guards."

"Get out and do *what,* exactly?" Mariana asked. "Don't get me wrong, I'm all for not getting killed, but seems to me whether we get killed here or trying to escape from the city, we'll be dead either way."

Dannen winced. She was right, of course, but all in all, he decided he'd rather die fighting than sitting in this shitty little jail in this shitty little town. He was just about to say as much, but Tesler spoke. "We need to find the griffin."

Dannen grunted, not much liking that suggestion. After all, seemed they had enough ways they could die just now that they hardly needed to go searching for another. He looked at the others to see what they thought of it, and Mariana scoffed as if she'd never heard anything so foolish. Fedder, though, only met Dannen's eyes and gave a shrug. "Better that thing kills us than these damned welves."

"You can't be serious," Mariana said. "Obviously this bastard"—she waved a hand at Tesler—"is batshit crazy. Who knows, maybe if we run straight into the forest, the welves won't be able to find us. Might be, we can survive the day, but I don't like our chances if we go messing around with a mythical creature that, from what I hear, isn't all that bothered by eating people."

Dannen was tempted to agree with her. True, he didn't think there was any chance of them escaping really, not after having seen the way the plants of the forest seemed to obey the welves, moving at their commands, but neither was he much interested in seeing what the inside of a griffin's stomach looked like. But Tesler was studying him with pleading eyes, saying nothing and not needing to, for his gaze said enough. *Asked* enough. "Ah, screw it," Dannen said finally. "We find the griffin."

"Gods, you can't be serious," Mariana said. "We'll be regretting this, the griffin starts to have its dinner, and that's even assuming we manage to find it. The gods alone know how you plan on figuring out where the damn thing is." She scowled at Tesler. "Griffins can *fly*, after all."

"I've enough regrets that one more isn't likely to make any difference," Dannen said. "And how will we find it?" He paused, glancing at the door then at Fedder before slowly smiling. "Well, we'll just ask nicely, won't we?"

***

They charged through the village of Riverlan, following the directions the guard had told them led to the griffin's hunting grounds. The sun was just peeking over the horizon, chasing away the shadows. A nice pretty sunrise, the last Dannen was ever likely to see, but he didn't have the time to stop and enjoy it now. The welves of the village watched the group of sprinting humans with disbelief and suspicion, some with outright hatred. It was only a matter of time before Oofen and his lackeys heard of their escape, and then Dannen didn't doubt their lives would get a whole lot more interesting. Likely a whole lot shorter, too.

Gasping for breath, he turned sharply around the corner of a welven hut, so sharply, in fact, that he would have fallen had Fedder not steadied him. Dannen nodded his thanks and ran on. At least they knew where the griffin was. The guard outside the decrepit building the welves called a dungeon had not wanted to give them the information up, but proved no more an obstacle than the rotten wooden bars of their cell had been. They *had* tried asking nicely, just as he'd told Mariana, but the guard had refused, claiming that they weren't holy enough to see the Divine. He'd seemed real convicted about it too, at least, that was, until Fedder lifted him off the ground and gave him a good shake. Imminent death, in Dannen's experience, had a way of wreaking havoc on a man's convictions, and the guard, when his teeth stopped chattering, had been more than happy to tell them anything they wanted to know.

That had been no more than ten minutes ago and since then they'd been charging madly through Riverlan, Dannen doing his best to look friendly and unthreatening to the welves they passed, not an easy thing considering that Mariana had drawn her weapons and Fedder was still covered in the river filth. All in all, Dannen supposed they looked just about as desperate as any four humans could.

As they reached the edge of the village, nearing the forest, he glanced back and saw that a crowd of welves was following them. Though they were still some distance away, there were a lot of them, so many it appeared as if the entire village was on the move. Hundreds of welves, yet even from this distance, Dannen couldn't mistake the angry scowls they had or, and perhaps this was a bit more pressing, the weapons they held ready, torches too, even though it was daytime. Not a crowd at all then, but a mob, and what self-respecting mob would track their victims down without torches to wave about while they killed them?

"Shit," he breathed and turned back to see that the others were watching him. "Well? What, are you all waiting around to see how sharp those blades they're carrying are? Let's go, damnit."

And go they did, with Fedder in the lead, pushing through the thick undergrowth. But despite the mage's strength and size, it was slow going as he had to stop constantly to shove aside a new branch or to step over a fallen log, and it began to seem as if the forest itself had turned against them. They were still pushing their way through when he began to make out the sound of the mob behind them, unmistakable shouts of anger, and while they spoke in the language of the welves, he didn't need a translator to know what it was those shouts were meant to communicate or to figure out where they were directed.

"I hope you know what you're doing," Dannen hissed at Tesler as he narrowly avoided tripping over a thick root. The crazy man glanced up from where he appeared to be in a quiet but fierce conversation with his pet squirrel but said nothing before continuing. No reassurance there then, so Dannen consoled himself with the fact that, should they die in the next few minutes, at least there would be no more running. Nobody called the dead lazy, after all, never mind that they just lay around all day and night.

By the time they reached the outskirts of the large clearing the guard had told them about, the sound of the welves was louder still, so Dannen kept glancing back, expecting to see them right behind. But so far, they remained out of sight, not much of a comfort since the thick undergrowth and trees blocked from view anything more than a few feet away, but he'd take what he could get.

Save the sound of the approaching welves, the clearing was silent, almost eerily so, and he might have thought they had taken a wrong turn somewhere except for one small detail. Namely, the dozens of bones scattered about the area. Skulls and shin bones and all other sorts—enough, he imagined to piece together quite a few skeletons, if a man had the time and inclination. The bones were small, obviously belonging to welves, and he wondered grimly if the next time someone happened on the clearing they'd chance upon a few human bones as well, maybe remark on the fate of the poor bastards before traveling on their way.

The griffin was nowhere in sight, and despite what they had come to do, he was okay with that. Hard to be upset about it, staring at all those bones. He glanced back the way they had come, wondering just how close that shouting mob was, as the forest did strange things with sounds, made it seem as if the bastards were all around them, coming from all directions. Which, he supposed, was more than possible considering the way they could move through the forest. "What now?" he asked Tesler. "Do we, I don't know, make an offering or—"

"I will walk into the clearing," the man answered.

"By the gods, no you won't!" Mariana demanded. "Any fool can see this griffin, wherever it is, doesn't much care for visitors." She gestured widely at the expanse of scattered bones as if anyone with eyes could have missed them.

Dannen bit back a curse. He'd wanted to believe the man's plan didn't involve an elaborate suicide. Turned out he'd been wrong. And whose fault, really? A madman for being mad, or the fool that trusted him to be anything else? "We push on through the forest," he said, turning to Fedder. "With luck, maybe we can make it back to the path before the welves catch us. On the road, we should be able to outdistance them."

"Sound plan, Butcher," Fedder said, "only"—he paused, gesturing at the thick forest surrounding them—"I've no idea which way the path is."

Dannen realized that he, too, had no idea. On their mad charge through the woods, he'd become hopelessly lost. In fact, he had been lost even before they'd made it to the welven village when their escorts had brought them there. "Shit," he said, his mind racing, trying to find some way out of the situation they'd found themselves in, or rather, walked in blindly the way some adventurers he'd seen had charged blindly into a monster's lair. It hadn't ended well for the adventurers. "Okay," he said hurriedly, all too aware of the shouts of the pursuing mob growing louder by the moment, "just pick a damn direction. Anywhere is better than here."

Fedder grunted, peering at something over Dannen's shoulder but not moving.

"Well?" Dannen demanded. "Let's go befo—"

"Might want to take a look, Butcher."

Dannen frowned, turning and following the mage's gaze. This time, he did not bite back his curse but let it come. "What are you doing, you mad bastard!?" he shouted.

But Tesler, the mad bastard in question, ignored him, continuing to walk into the clearing, having to step over the bones of dead welves as he did so, which ought to have served far better than a "Keep Out" sign for anyone that wasn't completely insane. Which, of course, he was.

"Get back here, fool!" Mariana said, the panic in her voice indicating she cared more for the crazy man than her scowling made it appear. A moment later she charged into the clearing, apparently willing to risk becoming a bone donor to save him.

She didn't get far, though, before Fedder reached out almost casually, grabbing the back of her shirt as she passed and lifting her off the ground as if she weighed no more than a kitten.

"Let me go, son of a bitch!" she shouted, fighting furiously, though with no more effect than the kitten might have had.

Fedder only held her calmly. "Leave it, lass," he said softly. "He's made his choice."

"But he'll *die!*" she yelled.

Fedder continued to hold her as she struggled, saying nothing. Dannen didn't say anything either. After all, seemed to him that she'd said nothing but the truth. He risked a glance back at the young man and saw that he was halfway to the center of the clearing now. When he turned back to Fedder and Mariana, a glint of something caught his eye in the distant undergrowth. He peered at it, narrowing his eyes, then grunted. "Best put her down, Fedder."

"Butcher?" he asked, confused. "But she'll go after the lad, and they'll both—"

"No," Dannen said, still staring at the spot where he'd seen that glint of steel, noticing other such glints now, and what could only be the flickering orange light of torches, "she won't. After all," he said as he caught sight of the first welf emerging from the undergrowth, "we've got our own problems."

***

Tesler could hear Mariana shouting behind him, calling him a fool and other worse things. He winced, doing his best to tell himself the lie that her opinion didn't matter, did his best to believe it. She called him crazy, too, but at least he was used to such names, had heard them all his life and worse besides. "Demon" had been a favorite of many of those in his village. "Monster," too. "Cursed," and "Evil," and "Devilspawn," and on and on it went. Few things, he'd found, made a man or woman as creative as hatred.

Mariana's voice grew louder, with anger or desperation there was no way to know, getting louder just the way the voices of the villagers had gotten louder until his father finally had had enough of him and his strange ways, of this child who claimed he could hear animals talk, and had decided the best way to have such a child was to not have him at all. And so he had done what any man might do, if he finds himself with trash he does not want—he threw him away.

Tesler hadn't thought of his father in a long while, his face no more than a vague blur, slowly erased by the passage of time, but he thought of him now, standing in the clearing with Mariana shouting behind him. And he was surprised to find the memory of his childhood, which he had thought scabbed over like a scar on the mend, was still tender to the touch, after all.

No easy thing, living in a world when everyone thought you were crazy. He had fought such thoughts, once, when he was young, argued with his father and the villagers and so many others, but he'd long since given it up. If the whole world thought he was crazy, after all, then who was he to disagree?

He thought of the world and his father, thought of his childhood come and gone and of Mariana shouting behind him, but mostly he thought of the griffin, wherever it was, wondering if his theory was right. At least if he was wrong, he would have little time to mourn his mistake—he did not doubt the creature would make sure of that.

No sooner did he have the thought than he reached the center of the clearing, and there was a heavy gust of wind that flattened the grass. He looked up to see a great white beast with its wings flapping, in the sky no more than fifty feet above him. The creature gave its wings another gusting flap then landed gracefully in the grass in front of him, no more than ten feet away.

Mariana's shouts intensified, but Tesler met the creature's golden eyes and did not look away, did not *dare* look away. He had never met a griffin before, but he knew such creatures took a refusal to meet their gaze as a sign of insult or weakness. He could afford neither, not if he wanted to go on living life undigested.

He knew he probably should be afraid, but he wasn't. That might mean that the villagers—that his father—had been right after all. But what Tesler felt, in that moment, as he gazed at the creature, was not fear. It was awe.

Griffins, it was said, were rare beasts, a cross between a lion and an eagle, but although the beast shared characteristics with both, Tesler would have had to disagree. He had met lions—even called a few friends, after convincing them not to eat him. He had met eagles too, though he had found them largely aloof, as if they considered themselves as high above every other creature on the face of the world as they could fly above them. This creature, though, shared only a passing resemblance with either. There was something grand, something magnificent in its form, in the pure white feathers covering it, and the intelligent, golden eyes studying Tesler as if they could see through him into the depths of his soul.

Its claws were large and sharp, but they were not threatening so much as majestic, and while some, in their foolishness, believed griffins a corruption of the natural order of things, he knew in that moment they were not a corruption of any form, but a perfection of it. He understood, too, why the welves might have taken the creature as some sort of god. It had a weighty, profound presence, and as its great feathered wings unfurled behind it in what appeared to be a stretch, Tesler thought he had never seen anything so beautiful. The beast studied him for several seconds, its golden pupils shining in the early morning light, then it tilted back its head and let out a great roar that seemed to shake the very ground beneath Tesler's feet, drowning out the sounds of Mariana's shouts, and driving all thoughts of his father or the villagers from his mind.

"I can hear you," Tesler said, as calmly as he could under the circumstances, "there's no need to shout."

Finally, the deafening thunder of its cry faded, and the creature folded its great white wings against its sides, lowering its gaze to regard Tesler, a quizzical tilt of what appeared to be surprise to its face. After a moment, it reared back on its powerful, lionlike haunches, and puffed out its feathered chest, lifting its massive paws, bigger even than Fedder's hands, into the air and revealing long, dagger-sharp claws.

"Very impressive," Tesler said, telling himself it would be the exact worse time to wet his trousers. "Your claws look...they look quite sharp."

The creature made a sound that might have sounded like a menacing growl to any normal person. Tesler, though, was no normal person, and there was a lifetime of people's opinions that assured him of as much, so for him, the growl, though still inarguably menacing, came out as words.

"You will learn just how sharp soon enough, human."

"Tesler," he said.

Another growl. *"What?"*

"My name," Tesler said, unable to pull his eyes away from the creature's flexing talons. "It's Tesler. Not human. What's your name?"

"*My name is Shegateriac. What manner of creature are you, that you can speak the language of the griffins?*" the beast demanded in, perhaps unsurprisingly, a growl.

Tesler thought of the many things he'd been called by his father, of the many names and labels the villagers had given him, the kids, too, as they threw rocks—one of their favorite pastimes, as it happened, then he finally shrugged. "Honestly? I don't know what I am."

The creature studied him for several seconds, then slowly settled back down onto all fours, and while its extended claws, like the rest of it, were majestic, Tesler had to admit he wasn't disappointed to see them go. "It is a sad thing for one not to know what one is. You have my pity...Tesler."

"Thank you," Tesler said, meaning it. He cleared his throat, forcing the voices of the villagers' shouts, remnants of a past that refused to stop haunting him no matter how far he traveled, back into the recesses of his mind. They would return, he knew, but he could not afford to be distracted, not now.

The creature stared at him with its luminous eyes, its head cocked again as if it, too, could hear the sounds of those shouts, as if it could hear the names he had been called, the curses which had been hurled at him along with the stones. "You have been sorely used, mortal named Tesler," it said, and this time its words came out in a low rumble instead of a threatening growl. "No creature should be treated so. Perhaps it is good that I will eat you, for the dead may feel no pain, no hate or the fear which drives all creatures to hate."

"If it's all the same to you, I'd rather not be eaten. There is no pain in death," Tesler agreed, for he had thought much of just such a solution when he was younger, before he had come to peace with who he was, with *what* he was. "But there is also no joy, no hope, or love, for these things are for the living and them alone."

The creature leaned forward slowly, craning its neck toward him as if to see him more clearly. "You, Man Tesler, possess much wisdom for one of your kind. I regret that I must eat you."

Tesler frowned. "You could *not* eat me."

"Alas," the creature said, "it is not my choice to make. Only know that I take no joy in it. Now, if you will close your eyes..."

"Your master—it's Oofen, isn't it?"

A low, rumbling growl came from the griffin's throat. "I have no master, mortal. Griffins are not dogs to scrape and bow at a man's feet in hope of being tossed a bone."

"And yet," Tesler said, "you are a slave."

The griffin did not speak, but its golden eyes seemed to shine more intensely as it stood on its four feet, stretching out its wings and arching its back to regard him. "It is time." It started toward him slowly, and while Tesler could see a look of unmistakable regret on its face, he doubted he'd prefer being regretfully eaten to just regular eaten.

"He has your egg, doesn't he?" he asked softly.

The griffin froze, its whole body seeming to tense as if it might, at any second, launch into the air or, alternatively, pounce some unwitting fool who had prodded at a particular sore spot. "What do you know of it?" the griffin said, and a man didn't need to be able to talk to animals to hear the pain and desperation in its voice.

"So he does," Tesler said nodding. "And is it he, then, who made you kill these welves?" he asked, motioning at the bones scattered about the clearing.

The creature drew itself up on its hind legs, looming over him. "No mortal might make—" it began, then paused and seemed to deflate. "This Oofen has declared that I must kill anyone who enters the clearing or risks drawing near. I believe he fears that they will make some sort of deal with me and surpass his own influence. Foolish, of course, as you are the only mortal I have ever conversed with and so long as the welf has my egg, I dare not risk his ire for my youngling's sake."

"And if he did not have your egg, this Oofen," Tesler said, glad to see that much of his theory confirmed, at least, "what would you do?"

"I would leave this place, mortal Tesler. There is something wrong about this wood, about the creatures within it. Something here warps and twists those living things, plant and animal both, who call it home. A mild evil, all told, but one I would not subject my egg to, had it not been necessary. I was traveling to find a nest in the mountains when the birth pangs took hold, and I knew I did not have time to seek my refuge and was forced to alight here. When it was finished, I was weary, exhausted from the long flight and the birthing, and I slumbered. The one you call Oofen came

283

upon me while I rested. When I awoke, he held my egg in one hand and, with the other, was rooting about my nest and this clearing, collecting my droppings."

Tesler blinked. "Your...droppings?"

The griffin shook its head in obvious disgust. "I do not know what he might want with them, and when I asked, he refused to answer, using my egg as a weapon against me and threatening to crack it prematurely should I accost him further."

Tesler glanced around the clearing. The grass was knee-high, and obscured much of the ground itself. "May I see your nest, Griffin Shegateriac?"

"Why, mortal Tesler?" the creature asked, tilting its head, and there was something undeniably suspicious about its gaze.

"I wish only to understand, Shegateriac," he answered. "I believe I know much of what happened, but there are still a few questions which remain unanswered."

The griffin's muscular shoulders shifted in what might have been a shrug. "Very well. I like you, mortal Tesler, and so I will grant you this boon, but then I am afraid I must eat you, for should the creature, Oofen, find you here unharmed, and I speaking with you, he will destroy my egg. He has told me it is so."

"I understand."

The griffin stalked through the grass, brushing it aside in great sweeping swathes which made walking through it far easier for Tesler. In a few moments, they came to the nest which resembled in nearly every way the nest of any bird of the sky, though it had to be said this example was considerably larger. There was, however, one noticeable distinction which separated the griffin's nest from the nest of any common bird, and that distinction came in the form of more than a dozen sparkling points of golden, shining light. Here and there were piles of the griffin's droppings, and it seemed to Tesler that the golden shine seemed to be most often in the same area as the droppings, around or inside of them. He walked over to the nearest shimmering pile and knelt down, looking at it without touching. Tesler had grown up in a poor village, been chased out of even that, and had spent the majority of his life wandering alone and afraid from place to place. Yet he, like every living mortal, knew well the look of gold. "Griffin Shegateriac," he said.

"Please," the griffin answered, moving up beside him, "call me Shega. All my friends and family do, and I think that I would call you friend, mortal Tesler. Before I eat you."

Tesler bowed his head, flattered. And terrified. "Tell me, Shega," he said, "are these your...droppings?" he asked.

The griffin shifted uncomfortably. "It is not normal behavior, among my kind, to speak of one's leavings with others, mortal Tesler. It would be thought crass and uncouth."

"It is much the same among my people," Tesler agreed. "And yet, I'm afraid I must ask the question nevertheless."

"Yes," the griffin said. "They are mine."

He glanced at the golden chunks, not refined or turned to coins like most gold he had seen, but the metal just the same. "And the pieces of gold within those droppings?"

The griffin stared past him. "It is all droppings, mortal," it said, sounding curious.

Tesler nodded as a suspicion was confirmed. What would make a welf—or a man, for that matter—risk his life picking through the leavings of a beast such as the griffin? Well, if those leavings, by some natural process within the creature's digestion, were partly made of gold, then that would do the trick sure enough. "Shega, do you see the golden streaks among the droppings?"

"Of course, I see them," the griffin said slowly, as if he were talking to a madman. Which, according to the majority vote, he undoubtedly was. "Are not all droppings the same?"

"They are not," Tesler said, everything finally clicking into place. When he'd come up with his theory, he'd asked himself how a welf living in the forest with his people could possibly manage to amass the sort of wealth that the rings and robes he wore made it obvious Oofen had. Certainly the welves themselves seemed to have little need of money, so Oofen himself would hardly have come into contact with it except for on those rare occasions where the welves might have traded with humans. No way at all, really, for such a welf to make a fortune. Unless, that was, a mystical beast found itself in dire straits and was forced to land nearby where any lucky—and opportunistic—welf might see. And had there been a vulnerable, injured path to Shega's flight? Tesler thought that likely there had been. He doubted, of course, that Oofen had

285

tracked the beast then already knowing his plan, but instead had done so perhaps to kill it for its meat—seemingly a rarity in this wood, for Tesler had seen or heard no animals—or for some other purpose. But instead of finding a beast dead, as he might have expected, Oofen had stumbled on a slumbering griffin, beside which lay an egg. And as his eyes alighted upon that egg, he hatched a plan.

"Why do you laugh?" the griffin asked.

Tesler cleared his throat. "No reason."

"I still do not see what difference that my...droppings are different than a mortal's."

"All the difference in the world, Shega," Tesler answered. "You see, that golden material among your droppings? That, among the race of men—and other races besides—is highly valued. People spend most of their lives working for it. It has been the cause of marriage and war, of more bloodshed than perhaps any one other single thing in the history of men."

The griffin blinked, craning its neck close to look at him in wonder before peering at its droppings. "Surely, friend Tesler, you jest. It is only griffin leavings, the same as any other kind."

"I'm afraid I don't, Shega. The welf, Oofen, has been using that material, as well as holding you ransom against his kin, to attain power with the welves, planning soon to supplant their rightful queen, one of the few just and kind rulers I've ever seen, one who has given up her entire life to protect her people. In fact, he seeks to blackmail me and my companions to kill her, holding our lives as ransom."

The griffin let out a sound that might have been a sigh. "Life, Tesler, is full of much pain, but that, I think, is a truth you already know. I will mourn the queen's passing, and if it helps, you and your companions only did what you had to protect yourselves and the ones you love. Any manner of creature or beast would do the same," it finished quietly, glancing at its nest with a look of profound sadness. "We must do what we can to protect those we care about."

"We did not kill the queen."

The griffin turned to gaze at him in surprise. "She lives still? But then your lives will be forfeit, and the welf, Oofen, will come with his men for you and your companions." The griffin's luminous eyes grew wider. "He will track you here, to this place."

"I hope so," Tesler said. "After all, I'm counting on it."

The griffin's head suddenly jerked its head up as if sensing something, and it turned sharply. Tesler followed its gaze to Dannen and the others who were no longer facing the clearing but now looking into the forest or, more specifically, at the army of welves who stood a short distance away, an 'army' he thought specifically because of all the weapons and the undeniably violent quality of them as they stood there. And at their center stood Oofen.

"He has followed you here," the griffin said, a panic in its voice that did not suit the words of such a majestic and noble beast. "He will see that I have not slain you, and he will harm my egg. He has said as much."

"He has told you a lie, Shega," Tesler said sadly.

The griffin cocked its head again. "A lie?"

Tesler blinked as he realized the creature did not understand what such a word meant, wondered, idly, what it would be like to live in a world where lying did not exist. He wasn't sure what consequences such a thing might have, but it was hard to imagine the world being worse off for it. "It...it's saying something that's wrong on purpose. Telling...an untruth."

"Why would any creature wish to say a thing that is wrong on purpose?"

"To trick," Tesler said. "To deceive. Mortals are masters of such deception, an art they practice on each other for their own gain, but not just that...more, it is that they simply enjoy it, I think."

"And this...'lying,' you believe that Oofen, the welf, is doing it?"

"I *know* he's doing it," Tesler said. "Look, Shega, I believe he has your egg, and I believe he has threatened to break that egg if you refuse to obey his wishes. But you are a great and powerful creature, and he a small welf. What would you do, do you think, should he harm your egg?"

"I would slay him," the creature growled immediately, rearing up as if it meant to search for Oofen and kill the power-hungry welf right then.

"Of course you would," Tesler said, "that much is obvious. Obvious even to a fool, and while he is many things, this Oofen has

287

not struck me as foolish. You see, Shega, he must understand that his threat to you is idle. He dares not harm the egg, for fear of what you will do once his leverage is gone. Do you understand?"

The creature shifted, flexing its massive claws, something like anticipation dancing in its golden eyes. "I begin to, friend Tesler." Then the griffin seemed to deflate again. "Yet, whether the welf tells truths or untruths matters not—I cannot, I *will not* risk my youngling. Griffins do not often produce children, Tesler. Such a thing may not occur in the space of two or three mortal lifetimes, if not more. Most griffins go their entire lives without the opportunity. It would be a crime, then, to risk my egg, not just for my youngling's sake or my own but for all griffins throughout the land. Do you understand?"

Tesler winced, nodding slowly, thinking that it was looking more and more like he'd end the day as a piece of gold. "I begin to," he said.

He wracked his brain then, looking for some solution. Then an idea occurred to him, and he looked up at the griffin. "Listen, Shega, if you'll continue to hold off eating me, at least for another few minutes, I'd like to try to help you to get your egg back."

"You would help me?" the creature asked in a surprised voice. "Knowing full well that I am to eat you?"

"Yes, Shega," he answered. "Yes, I would."

"Why?"

Tesler considered that, glancing back at his friends, still in what appeared to be a stand-off between the two groups. "Because the world would be a fine place if lies did not exist, Shega. Because all men should strive to create things of beauty. And should they not be able to do so themselves, they should at least try to help beauty along where they find it, for the world is ugly enough already."

The griffin regarded him for several seconds. "You are a good man, mortal Tesler. Your people were wrong to exile you, but you should know it was their loss, not your own. They could have allowed you to remain, should have thanked you for doing so. After all, everyone should try to help beauty along where they find it."

Tesler gave a small smile, surprised at the tears gathered in his eyes, not just at the old hurts, but at the magnificent beast's words, words which acted like a salve on those painful memories. When he trusted himself to speak again, he looked up at the creature, meeting its eyes. "Will you trust me, Shega? Trust I will do everything I can to get your egg returned safely to you?"

Not an easy decision to make, not an easy thing he was asking. After all, the creature had only just met him, one way or the other, and its egg was at risk, but it inclined its head in a nod. "I trust you, mortal Tesler," it said.

Tesler took a deep breath and nodded, only wishing that he trusted himself. He glanced around at the field around them, the grass nearly as tall as his waist in places and concealing rocks of various shapes and sizes such as the ones he had nearly tripped over on his walk into the clearing. "I'll need your help."

***

Dannen had been in a lot of life-or-death situations over the years, had managed to slip out each time. This time, though, there did not seem much slipping to be done. They were surrounded by an army of welves, creatures who, should he and his companions try to run, would be able to pursue them through the dense underbrush with ease thanks to their magic.

So far, the welves, armed with weapons as ugly and crude as they were themselves, had not attacked. This, Dannen didn't doubt, was in large part due to the fact that Mariana had drawn her steel rod weapons and even more to the fact that Fedder—with a visage to give a man or welf nightmares even at the best of times—was standing with his massive fists raised, both of which were wreathed in flames.

Still, Dannen knew the stalemate would not last forever. After all, while the welf weapons looked pathetic—sticks with rusty blades tied to the end, mostly, and a few crossbows that looked like a good burning would only improve them—the welves outnumbered them at least twenty to one with more appearing out of the underbrush all the time. He didn't doubt they'd take a lot of the welves with them—or, at least, that Mariana and Fedder would—but it would only take one lucky strike or for one crossbow to stay intact long enough to fire a well-aimed shot to put Fedder out of commission. And once that happened, it was only a matter of time—likely a very brief, very painful amount of time—before it was over.

Some of the welves began to creep closer, and Dannen reached down and picked up a tree branch from the ground. Unwieldy, the balance all wrong, but he figured that if death had finally caught up with him after all these years, he was going to make sure at least one of the little bastards had a bad day.

"*Come on, you fuckers*," Fedder bellowed, raising his flaming hands into the air and nearly catching Dannen—who did a quick sidestep—on fire as he did. "*Who dies first?*"

Silence followed as the two groups considered each other. Dannen was thankful for the extra few seconds of life—how else would he get to feel the bowel-clenching terror now gripping him?—but he knew they would not, *could* not last. Sooner or later, one of the welves, most likely one of those wielding what looked like crossbows if a man squinted hard enough would grow tired of waiting. When that happened, he was confident that his life as well as those of his companions would be measured in seconds.

There was silence following the mage's shout, a tense, pregnant silence, one in which Dannen—who'd been in far too many of these situations in his life—could *feel* the moment progressing toward its inevitable, bloody climax. He stared at the welf, Oofen, who stood at the front of the welven force, scowling dangerously but, it had to be noted, not quite so arrogant or dangerous to risk being the first to piss off an already pissed off fire mage. Still, the bastard had an ugly exterior to match the ugly, power-hungry inside of him, and Dannen promised himself that whatever happened, he would make sure he took Oofen with him into the afterlife.

Just as Dannen felt the tension building to a crescendo, the silence was broken by the sound of a voice. "It's over."

Everyone gathered, including Dannen, spun to see Tesler walking up, which was surprising. What was a touch more surprising—outright terrifying, in fact—was that he was not alone but was accompanied by a very angry-looking griffin. Though, to be fair, Dannen couldn't imagine anything so large or with quite so sharp claws looking friendly.

"What's that?" Dannen managed, and maybe there was a bit of a squeak to his voice, no way to know for sure, and nobody called him on it at any rate, probably trying to decide how to avoid being dinner for a massive bird lion that looked like it could swallow a welf—or a human—whole.

Tesler did not turn to look at the sound of his voice. Instead, he gazed steadily at Oofen, the welf whose eyes were wide and terrified—forgivable under the circumstances—and more than a little guilty, which, to Dannen's mind at least, wasn't. The first thing Dannen noticed was how uncomfortable the welf appeared, the second was there seemed to be a bundle underneath Tesler's shirt. Either the man had gained twenty pounds—all in his stomach—in the last five minutes, or he was holding something, though whatever it was remained hidden beneath the fabric of his shirt, held in place carefully, almost gently by both of Tesler's arms which were wrapped around the bottom. No way to tell what it was, but to Dannen it looked like it might have been about the size of Fedder's head.

Not so threatening, really, when compared to the army of welves facing them or, for that matter, the flaming fists of Fedder beside him, at least not to Dannen. Seemed plenty enough threatening to Oofen, though, whose blotchy, rashy skin went a deathly white.

"W-what are you doing?" the welf demanded in a terrified voice.

"I think you know," Tesler said, for once not sounding crazy at all—looking it, sure, standing beside a griffin like they were best friends, but not *sounding* it—as he met the welf's eyes. "But this isn't about what I'm doing. This is about what you've *been* doing."

"I-I don't know what you mean," the welf said, swallowing hard. "B-but you should get away from the Divine, it, it should not be, you shouldn't..." He floundered there, then seemed to come up with an idea. "Y-you you do not deserve to be near it. T-that it's sacrilegious!" he snapped, then nodded, getting warmed up to the idea now. "That's right, sacrilegious. H-he, *they* are profaning the Divine. Seize them!"

But the other welves did not look ready to seize anybody. Most had dropped to their knees, prostrating themselves before the creature, ironically too busy averting their eyes from what Oofen himself had convinced them was a godlike being. What few hadn't fallen to their knees had their heads bowed, shifting as if unsure what they ought to be doing, some of them looking like maybe all they *wanted* to be doing was getting their asses out of there as quickly as possible. Dannen understood that sentiment—felt it himself at that moment—but that feeling must have been doubly strong for them as these welves believed themselves to be face-to-face with their god. It was one thing, after all, to sacrifice and pray to a being one believes all-powerful, asking for favors, for more money or more women, just *more,* really. It was quite another to be only feet away, to realize that the hands that had been expected to give—talons, in this instance—could also easily take away, if they so chose, with the welves themselves unable to do anything about it.

Some prayed, some begged, some even cried, but none moved to obey Oofen's command, and Oofen, noticing this, began to falter, glancing around nervously as if looking for help. "Y-you blaspheme—" he began, but Tesler spoke over him, cutting him off.

"You stole its egg," he said, not in an accusatory way, just a man simply stating a fact, "you stole it, along with gold from its nest which you turned, by the dubious magic of commerce, into the robe and rings you now wear." The welves began to glance curiously at Oofen then, but Tesler wasn't finished. He spoke on, each word seeming to slam into the flinching Oofen like a blow. "No doubt, you have other treasures at your house, paintings or sculptures, perhaps. But none of those are your greatest treasure. Or should I say *were.*" Tesler smiled, and Dannen frowned, having no idea what was going on but taking some solace in how little the welf seemed to be enjoying it.

***

Tesler forced himself to remain calm, doing his best to conceal his doubt, his worry, for here was the gamble, the part where, if he was wrong, everything would fall apart. "Still," he pressed, pinning the squirming welf with his eyes, "those were not the greatest of your treasures, were they? Not the most important, the most *vital* piece of your particular collection. That," he said, hefting the large rock which he'd hidden under his shirt, "is this."

Now, he knew, was where things would go wrong if they were going to. It would not take much that, too, he knew. For while the foundation of his accusation might have been built on fact, the walls and ceilings of the increasingly tall tower were built of fabrication and supposition, of the truth bent so much as to be almost unrecognizable. Lies, then. Lies that could unravel in an instant, if the nervous welf had the presence of mind to demand to see what Tesler hid under his shirt or, alternatively, if he'd not hidden the egg, his bargaining piece with the griffin, in his house at all. They were in the forest, after all, with a thousand nooks and crannies, hollowed-out trees or holes, that he could have stashed it in, and Tesler was gambling that the ambitious welf would have wanted to keep the key to his power secure but also close, in case he needed to use it or, more likely, threaten to. A gamble that was far preferable than being eaten outright by a griffin and being majestically gobbled down its majestic gullet, but one that could easily come undone, too.

Tesler held his breath, waiting for the welf's reaction. Finally, Oofen's eyes went wide. "Seize him!" he demanded of his fellow welves. "He's a liar!" But the welves were past listening. Instead, they were instead staring at their erstwhile leader with looks of increasing hostility.

"You," Tesler went on, "have been blackmailing this wonderful creature, threatening the destruction of its offspring should it not aid you in the killing of any—welf or mortal—who opposed your desperate grasp for power. A grasping which even led you to attempt to enlist me and my companions to assassinate your queen, the rightful ruler of your people."

"T-that's ridiculous," the welf wheezed in a choked voice, sounding as if he'd just had the wind knocked out of him. He was not scowling at Tesler, not anymore. Instead, he was looking around him at the other welves, most having overcome their initial shock and fear as they seemed to have decided that their deity didn't plan on eating them, at least at the moment. Those who had knelt had now risen, and they were all eyeing Oofen with suspicion and disbelief. A moment later, there was movement in the crowd and the welves began to part, making way for the princess who marched through them, her jaw set, her fists clenched tightly at her sides.

When they had first been introduced to the queen and Oofen, the princess had been among those welves who had looked at Oofen with undisguised attraction and admiration. She did not do so now. Now, the look on her face was one of pure fury. Oofen seemed to notice the princess's anger—he would have been blind not to and deaf, too, considering the growl coming from her throat—and he backed away. Either by blind chance or because the forest itself was disgusted with the welf, a root seemed to appear as if by magic behind Oofen's foot, and he let out a squeak as he toppled head over heels.

***

Everyone was focused on the scene playing out before them as the princess stalked toward the ambassador, the welf looking neither powerful nor threatening now but pitiful as he slid backward on his butt, dragging desperately at the ground, his eyes studying the approaching princess in obvious terror. The crowd was so focused on the spectacle that it would have been an easy enough thing for Dannen and his friends to slip into the forest without anyone noticing. The problem, though, was that his friends were just as absorbed in the drama unfolding before them as the welves.

Dannen risked a glance at Tesler and frowned, studying the man. He, like the others, was watching the princess approaching the desperate Oofen, but the man did not look victorious for pointing out the welf's betrayal. Instead, he looked nervous, licking his lips anxiously as he watched the two. Dannen studied the bulge in the man's shirt again. Hidden, so he couldn't make out any specifics, but there was something about it that struck Dannen as wrong, that made him think something wasn't matching up with the story the man had told.

After a few seconds' thought, he realized what it was. The "egg" possessed jagged edges which were visible beneath Tesler's shirt. Dannen wasn't a griffin expert—wasn't an expert in anything except killing, maybe, the gods knew he'd had the experience—but he'd never seen an egg with sharp, angular edges to it. Seeming to notice his attention on him, Tesler glanced at him and winced, shifting the bundle underneath his shirt with obvious effort. In doing so, his shirt rode up the slightest bit. Only for a brief moment, but enough to show what Dannen had begun to suspect—not an egg at all, but a rock. One not dissimilar to the many lying in plain sight around the field, scattered among the bones.

Tesler hurriedly covered the rock once more and met Dannen's eyes, his own wide with fear. Dannen looked around hurriedly, already preparing an excuse—or more accurately, trying to and failing miserably—but he needn't have bothered. The welves, as well as Fedder and Mariana, were far too busy studying the princess and the ambassador to have noticed Tesler's slip.

Oofen's desperate scrambling across the ground had been brought up short by the thick trunk of a tree, and he whimpered, bringing up his hands as if to ward off a blow as the princess came to stand above him. "Is it true?" she said. "Did you lie? About the Divine? About...everything?"

Oofen cast a frantic look around him as if searching for help, but no one moved forward. Seeing that he was alone, that those erstwhile allies of his, those welves who would have jumped at the opportunity to do his bidding half an hour ago, now stood unmoving, Oofen went paler still. Then, as Dannen had seen so often before, his fear began to turn to anger. With a growl, he shot to his feet, forcing the princess back a step. "Yes, I *lied!*" he screamed, staring at her and all the other welves too. "But they were lies easily told, weren't they?" he demanded. "Lies easily *heard*. Easily *believed*."

The princess seemed taken aback by the welf's anger. "What do you—"

"Oh, come off it," the welf snapped. "You know well enough what I mean. *All* of you do. You believed my lies about the Divine because you *wanted* to believe them! And why, I wonder? Because all of you, like me, were looking for something, for *anything* to drive back the incredible boredom that assails us every day as we hide away in these woods, exiled from the outside world. As we are *made* to hide away by the *queen,* your *mother!*" he finished, turning his petulant scowl on the princess who winced as if physically pained.

"She...my mother, the Beautiful," the princess said defensively in a quiet voice, "she...she means well. She only wants—"

"To *protect* us?" Oofen interrupted with a sneer. "No, to keep us prisoners, more like, prisoners who have nothing to do all day but bow and scrape and jump to obey her every whim! We *all* looked for ways to drive back that boredom, that lethargy which the exile she forces on us creates, and am I to blame for being the one to find it? Am I to be blamed for being the only one to see this beast?" He waved a casual hand at the griffin, but as far as Dannen was concerned, a man shouldn't do *anything* casual around such an imposing creature—"first? And tell me, would it really have been so terrible to have me lead? I would not have kept you all locked away here, this much I can promise you, watching whole generations grow old and die without ever seeing what's outside of this accursed forest!"

"Oofen—" the princess began, but the angry welf had hit his stride now, and blurted over her.

"Yes, I took the beast's egg!" he shouted. "And yes, I used it to attempt to seize control from *your* queen, so that we might be free! Oh, do not look so betrayed, *Princess,*" he sneered. "After all, you have had these same thoughts, have you not? You have whispered them to me in the darkness after we have made love, about how your mother is too old to be queen anymore, how she is timid when boldness is needed and how she lets us all stay here and waste away while the world moves on without us!"

"Is this true, daughter?" Everyone, man and welf alike spun to see that the queen had approached from the other side of the forest without anyone noticing. She stood there now, not beautiful physically, at least, Dannen thought, but beautiful just the same, a beauty that did not exist because of her choice to send herself into exile to protect her family, but a beauty that was only reflected in that choice. "Do you so chafe at my rule?" the queen finished, studying her daughter carefully, and although Dannen could see that the thought of her daughter whispering behind her back to *Oofen* of all people, pained and saddened her, she kept her back straight and her face neutral, accepting the news with dignity few others could have.

"Mother," the princess said, her eyes going wide with surprise. "It...that is...I love you, mother, but yes, it is true. No matter how I ask, no matter the reason, you have never let us venture out of our home. You have seen the world once, when you were young, but we have not," she went on, gesturing at the welves around her. "I know that you are doing it to protect us, to protect me," she said, wincing, "but we are not children anymore, mother. We are welves grown."

"You are *my* child," the queen said, but there was a weariness to her voice, to her face, as she turned to regard the gathered welves. "Are there others among you who feel this way?"

About half of the gathered welves nodded, refusing to meet their queen's gaze, pointedly studying their feet, but nodding just the same. "Mother," the princess said, "it is not that we are ungrateful for all that you've done for us, for all that you've protected us against. Without you..." She shook her head, seeming close to tears. "I am sorry, Beautiful," she said finally. "It was wrong of me to speak so."

"No," the queen said, studying her daughter, "it is I who was wrong. It is I who am sorry. I am old and have had my fill of the world, am content to sit here in the safety of the woods and have nothing more to do with it, hoping it only forgets me and those I love as I have striven to forget it. For the world, in my mind, is a cruel place, one to be feared and avoided whenever possible." She sighed. "But," she went on reluctantly, "it is also a place of wonder, of beauty." She paused, glancing at Dannen and the others. "Of courage and sacrifice found in the most unexpected of places. I realize now that I have done you all a disservice and for that I am sorry."

There was no doubting the tears leaking from the princess's face now, and a moment later she dropped to her knees. "Praise to the Beautiful who in her wisdom protects us." The other welves dropped to their knees a moment later. *"Praise to the Beautiful,"* they said in unison, and unlike the last time they had said it, this time, their voices rang with conviction, *"who in her wisdom protects us."*

The queen studied the welves bowed before her, obviously moved by their affection, then inclined her head. "Rise," she said, "my people, for I have made my decision. You have been trapped here, in this place, but no longer. My daughter—all of you—have shown me your strength, and I only regret that I did not see it sooner. So, my daughter, your princess, will lead an expedition out

297

into the world for any of those among you who wish to go. The rest of you will, of course, be allowed to stay here if you so choose."

"Mother," the princess said, her voice sad, "we don't need...it's fine if—"

"No, daughter," the queen said with a loving smile, "it is not. I have kept you prisoner here long enough, all of you. Only know that, should you ever wish to return, Riverlan will always be here waiting for you. *I* will be here."

A touching moment as mother and daughter stared at each other, both with tears in their eyes, one looking through the lens of centuries of life, the wisdom—and cynicism—that such time brought, the other staring back with the eyes of a youth, little more than a child, but, like a child's, full of hope and excitement.

A touching moment, one where Dannen felt a lump in his own throat, but one that was broken a moment later by Fedder's menacing growl.

"No you don't, you little fucker."

They all turned to see that Fedder was standing on one side of the clearing, though how he had left Dannen's side without him noticing he couldn't imagine. But it wasn't the giant mage which drew everyone's eye but instead the small welf he held off the ground in one hand with ease. Oofen struggled and fought, but it made little difference, and Fedder held him casually, only wincing when he noticed that he had drawn the attention of every man, woman, and welf in the clearing. He cleared his throat. "He was tryin' to make a break for the forest."

"Ah yes," the queen said, staring at the small welf who finally gave up his struggles to hang sullenly like a kitten from Fedder's paw, "Oofen. Were you trying to leave us so soon?"

The welf said nothing, only glared about the clearing with a scowl the effect of which was somewhat dampened by the way his lower lip trembled.

"Please, mage," the queen said, "bring him before me."

Fedder did so—after a fashion. Instead of walking the welf to her, he decided to haul back and hurl him the twenty or so feet which separated them. Maybe not the most politic way of doing things, but Dannen couldn't deny the surge of satisfaction he felt as Oofen struck the ground at the queen's feet, groaning in pain.

Dannen thought that many, in a similar situation as the queen, would have felt no small amount of vindictive satisfaction to see such a traitor brought low before them, would have gloried in it. But the queen only looked sad, showing her wisdom, her dignity, even in that moment. "You have behaved poorly, Oofen of Riverlan," she said. "But even the most foolish, the cruelest, might be made whole again." She considered, then finally spoke on. "We will have a trial for you to determine the full extent of your crimes and to determine, also, what is to be done."

Some of the welves looked uneasy at that, the angry looks they shot in the welf's direction making it clear they would have preferred to see the puny welf strung up or killed outright. Still, they would not disobey their queen.

The griffin, though, was not a welf and therefore not subject to the Beautiful's rule, and it seemed to have a different idea. It moved forward with incredible speed, snapping up the puny welf in its great maw. There was a sharp intake of breath from the crowd and, in another moment, Oofen disappeared down the creature's gullet.

"Damn," Fedder grunted.

Silence followed as everyone looked on in shock at the griffin who gave a swallow and regarded them with a placid expression, before turning to Tesler and growling something. The man cleared his throat, wiping a completely forgivable sheen of sweat from his forehead before looking around, clearly uncomfortable being the center of attention. "It uh...that is, the griffin says Oofen threatened its youngling. Its egg. I promised we would find it."

Fedder frowned. "I thought you had its egg?"

Tesler gave a guilty look as he withdrew the large stone from underneath his shirt and allowed it to drop to the ground. Another disbelieving silence followed as everyone began to understand that the man had been faking all along, a silence that was broken by Fedder's roaring laughter.

Mariana stepped forward, looking at the stone as if it were magic. "You...all this time, you were *faking?*"

Tesler winced. "Um...yes?"

She stared at him in disbelief, and Tesler fidgeted uncomfortably. "I...that is, I thought it—" He gave a grunt, cutting off as Mariana threw herself at him, pulling him into an embrace so tight it seemed to knock the air from his lungs.

Tesler stood as if stunned before finally hugging her back, awkwardly. Then, just when Dannen was thinking that one more sweet scene would be enough to drive him over the edge and have him blubbering like a baby, the assassin withdrew her embrace and slapped Tesler ringingly across the face, the sound of it echoing in the clearing. The griffin let out a low growl at that, but Mariana didn't seem to notice, too busy scowling at Tesler. "You could have been killed! By the gods, you're a crazy bastard."

"Yeah," Fedder grunted, walking up and giving the man a pat on the back which, to his credit, Tesler managed to endure without being knocked from his feet, though it was a near thing. "Crazy clever. Damn fine show, boy. Damn fine."

Tesler, though, didn't seem aware of the Firemaker or of the slap, was busy staring at Mariana, a stupid grin on his face like a child who'd just been given an unexpected treat. *Gods help us,* Dannen thought. He walked forward, offering the stunned man his hand. After a moment, Tesler became aware of him and took it.

"Well done, lad," Dannen said, meaning it. "Well done."

Tesler grinned again. "Thank you, sir."

Dannen hid a wince at being called "sir," and gave him a single nod. Crazy as a loon, that much was certain, but also the only reason they weren't all figuring out what decomposing felt like firsthand.

"Dannen Ateran and companions."

Dannen and the others turned to see that the queen had walked forward, her daughter beside her, the two welves leaning on each other, not out of any need, but simply out of a wish to be close. Dannen had never been one of those bowing and scraping sycophants seeking a king or queen's favor, but he bowed now, not for any desire to gain favor, but because he wanted to. The queen of the welves was the only ruler he had ever met who didn't seem more concerned with her own wardrobe than her people's wishes, and he thought she deserved that much, at least. A moment later, Fedder and the others followed suit.

"Please, rise," the queen said, "it is I, it is *we* who should bow to you. After all, it is thanks to you and your companions' bravery that Oofen's lies were brought to light."

In his youth, Dannen had never been good at dealing with the praise of those grateful for his services, and he found that he was even worse now. He didn't think he would have rather wrestled a troll than dealt with the awkwardness of such a situation, but it was a close-run thing. "I...you're welcome."

The queen smiled, obviously aware of his discomfort. "I fear we welves live simply, and I do not have coin to repay the great debt I owe you. But please, tell me what it is that we can do for you. If it is within my ability, you need but ask."

"If you've any ale—" Fedder began, but Dannen interrupted him.

"Thank you, Your Majesty, for your kind words and offer," he said, giving a sidelong scowl at the mage before returning his attention to the queen, "but we ask only that we be allowed to travel north. There are matters there that demand our attention."

She raised an eyebrow. "More heroics, I suspect?"

"Gods, I hope not," Dannen answered honestly.

She studied him for a moment then gave a single nod. "Very well. You are, of course, more than welcome to stay among us if you so wish. However, if your desire is still to travel north to the frostlands, I will not stop you. And, in fact," she said, smiling in a way that caused a knot of foreboding to grow in Dannen's stomach, "we may even be able to do one better, if you will tarry with us for a little while longer."

Considering that Dannen had absolutely no idea of where they were or how to get where they were going, it wasn't a decision long in the making. He gave her the best smile of which he was capable. "We'd be honored."

CHAPTER TEN

The next week among the welves passed relatively uneventfully, which was to say that no one tried to kill them. A depressingly novel experience for Dannen, but one he enjoyed immensely. The welves who were going to leave with the princess—over half the population of Riverlan—spent the time preparing for the journey, while he and his companions were left with little to do. Something that, on the first day, was a pleasant change, but that by the end of the week was beginning to make him itch.

Dannen had never done well with boredom, an enemy who couldn't be slain with a sword or threatened into giving way, and he thought many of the mistakes he'd made in his life—of which there were a considerable number—were due to that simple fact. But as restless as he was, Fedder was even worse, likely because the welves had no tavern among them and, in fact, seemed to have no ale or beer at all.

This meant Fedder spent the week stomping around the village, scowling at any who came too close while Dannen grew increasingly worried that the mage would decide to light one of the friendly welves on fire if for no other reason than to have something to do.

As for their other companions, Mariana and Tesler were far more pleasant company. At least separately. If anything, the brief show of affection between them seemed to have made tensions even higher, so Mariana spent the majority of the week scowling at the man while pointedly avoiding speaking to him. Tesler, on the other hand, spent his time doing his best not to notice the woman's angry looks and speaking with his squirrel pet.

Dannen had to admit the man had saved all of their lives, that maybe he actually *had* found some way of communicating with the griffin—which had departed swiftly after recovering its egg which had indeed been hidden in the late Oofen's home—but he still found something unnatural about a man talking to animals. Though, it had to be said, crazy was preferable to the building tension of Fedder himself.

But whatever means Tesler had used to communicate with the griffin or discern what the problem was, Dannen still could not bring himself to believe the man could actually converse with animals. After all, he didn't know much about druids—still more than he'd like, in truth—who were known to keep to themselves, spending their time in the wilds, but he knew only the most powerful druids claimed the ability of communicating with animals. The most powerful being, without fail, old men with long beards and wrinkled faces, not men who appeared to barely have reached their twentieth year.

Between Fedder's sullenness, Mariana's scowls, and Tesler's insanity, the itch to be moving, to be doing *something* grew worse and worse. By the time the week finally came to an end Dannen was anxious and fidgety. A clear sign he was getting ready to do something particularly stupid. Val had often told him that he was as fidgety, when bored, as a young man asking a father for his daughter's hand in marriage. He'd never really believed it but he did now.

Still, despite his lingering suspicions it would never come, the end of the week had arrived after all, and Dannen woke in the small hut—shack, really—the welves had lent him to someone gently nudging his shoulder. He yawned, opening his eyes to find the queen staring down at him, smiling pleasantly.

"Sometimes I wonder, Dannen Ateran," she said, "that, if given the opportunity, you would spend your entire life sleeping. For me, one who has lived for centuries and might well live for one or two more before I pass from this place, it is strange to see from one such as you, a mortal who, if you will forgive me, lives but a fraction of that time."

Dannen grunted, rising and giving his head a brisk shake to knock off the remnants of drowsiness. "Val once told me it didn't matter how long a person lived but that it was how well they lived that counted."

She did not ask who Val was, for she knew well enough. In fact, over the last week, the most pleasant time Dannen'd had—perhaps the *only* pleasant time—had been during his daily conversations with the queen, and while Riverlan itself was a shithole he could take or leave, he knew that he would miss their talks.

The queen nodded as if in acquiescence. "As always, it seems Val possessed far more wisdom in her short time in this realm than I have gained in my own many years. And, as always," she went on, giving him a small smile, "it makes one wonder why she would choose to spend her life with you."

Dannen shrugged. "The gods only know. Tell you what? Why don't you come back in say, a few hours, let me get a bit more shut-eye? Might be I'll have the answer for you."

She rolled her eyes, snorting in a very unqueenlike manner. "With each day that passes, Dannen Ateran, I find myself impressed with your Val—not just for her wisdom but for her patience as well. You are aware, aren't you, that there are things happening in the world, things a man will miss, if he sleeps through them?"

"Bad things mostly," he said, sighing as he accepted the fact that he wasn't going to get any more sleep, not today at least.

She shook her head sadly, and when she spoke she did so in an admonishing tone. "You are far too young, Dannen, to be so cynical. Besides, anything good that happens in sleep is not real, and even the best of dreams vanish on waking as if they had never been."

"Maybe," Dannen agreed. He had learned on their first day of conversing that he couldn't hold a candle to the queen in debate or discourse or knowledge or...well, pretty much anything. Still, he wasn't quite prepared to let this one go, fool that he was. "But in my experience, it's hard to provoke someone to want to kill you while you're sleeping."

"Oh?" she asked, raising an eyebrow. "As I recall, you told me almost exactly that regarding your friend, the mage, and his...snoring, was it?"

Dannen grunted sourly. "If that's snoring, everyone else is doing it wrong. Except maybe bears—they're the closest, anyway."

The queen laughed at that. She had a good laugh, pleasant and warm with none of the self-consciousness of the young who seemed far too focused on how their laughter sounded and none of the bitterness of the old who had seen far too much for their laughter to be anything but cynical. After a moment, she sobered. "I will miss our talks, Dannen Ateran. I do love my daughter, my people, but none of them are your equal for diverting conversation."

He gave a laugh of his own, rising. "Not for lack of trying," he said, and that much, at least, was the truth, for since the idea of leaving Riverlan had been broached, it seemed the welves were all in a contest to see who could get the most words in before it was time to leave.

"Perhaps," she admitted, "but though they talk and have their opinions, they have, because of my own doing, experienced little of what life has to offer and so their words, their opinions are, I'm afraid, as insubstantial as mist. Now, are you prepared?"

Dannen had spent the last week wishing time would move faster, itching for it, but now that it was time to leave, he was reluctant. Still, time waited on no man no matter how strong or how foolish—another favorite of Val's, usually told to him when he was being a fool—and the queen was watching him, so he nodded. "I guess I have to be."

She smiled. "Your companions are already ready and gathered with the other welves. It would be an honor if you would walk with me."

"The honor, Majesty, is all mine," he said, meaning it.

"Very well," she said. "Then, if it suits you, I will wait outside for you to prepare your belongings, and we might be off."

Dannen scooped up his traveling pack, the one that included his bedroll and his rations—increased now thanks to the queen's kindness. "I'm ready." He wondered what it said about him that he could be ready in an instant, that everything he owned and counted of any value could fit into a pack he could easily carry across his back. Probably nothing good, but if the queen thought as much, she was too dignified to say so, and she inclined her head.

"Let us go, then. The others await."

As they stepped outside, he noticed that Riverlan appeared deserted. In the last week, Dannen had, on more than one occasion, cursed the noise of the welves as they sang or danced— or, at least, their approximations of each—but now he missed it. He had grunted and complained to himself while they had sung and danced on through the night, but now the silence was a sad one. He wondered, staring at the empty homes, many of which might never be lived in again as their occupants ventured into the world, if those occupants would come to regret their choice. He wondered, too, what it was in men—and welves—that so often yearned for peace only to grow bored with it once they'd found it.

"Are you ready?" the queen asked, and in her voice there was a world of meaning, a world of understanding, and he knew that however much sadness he must be feeling, hers was greater still, for today she lost her daughter and many of her loved ones. Some, perhaps, would come back in time, but many would not. That was something they both knew. And would he ever find his way back here, to this refuge in the forest? He did not think it likely.

It was something they both understood, but saying it would change nothing, so he bowed. "Lead the way, Your Majesty."

They walked in silence past the ramshackle huts and debris where others had collapsed, past the muddy creek and the spot where the bridge once stood. Up ahead, in the distance, he was able to make out his companions standing in a group next to the welves who had elected to leave Riverlan.

"Forgive me, Dannen Ateran," the queen said quietly, staring at the group of welves among which her daughter stood. "Might I have a moment?"

"As long as you need, Majesty," he said.

"Is it the wrong choice, do you think? To let her go?"

Dannen considered that. He was not a wise man, nor was he a man known for his ability to comfort those who needed comforting. He was a warrior or, at least, had been once, and what little wisdom he had was the cutting kind. Still, she was watching him, waiting for what he would say, and though, as always, she maintained her composure, he thought he detected a hint of desperation in her gaze.

"Maybe," he said finally, "but it's not your choice to make—it's hers."

She nodded. "I am being foolish, aren't I?"

"No, Majesty," Dannen said. "Never foolish."

She stared back at her daughter and the other welves, as ugly as they had ever been, the excitement and anxiety on their faces like that of children learning that troupers were coming to town to perform a show.

"The world will be cruel to her," the queen said softly, and he followed her gaze to her daughter. "It will see only the surface of her—the boils and the rough skin. It will not take the time to see what's beneath, the beauty which lies there."

"The world is cruel to us all," Dannen said. "It's what it does. For what it's worth, if you ask me, it's not your daughter to be pitied but those who cannot see past her face. Rainbows, sunrises, they exist, their *beauty* exists, and that does not change whether or not we choose to look at them."

Not great words of comfort, maybe—probably, not even good—but it was the best he could do. The queen studied him for several seconds, thinking he was a fool, probably, thinking about a dignified way of saying so, then, to his surprise, she smiled. "Thank you, Dannen," she said. "I feel better...I believe you."

Dannen saw she did, wished that only he could believe it too, but the queen was satisfied, and she offered him her arm. "Shall we go?"

"Of course, Majesty."

Dannen expected a big speech, some tearful goodbye between mother and daughter, between several mothers and daughters. Indeed, it seemed to be building to that. The two groups, those who were staying and those welves who were leaving, faced each other across a space of only a few feet, nothing separating them but blades of grass, still damp with morning dew. Yet, there was a *feeling* of distance, as if they were separated now by some great chasm, one which could only be crossed, if it could be crossed at all, with the greatest of effort.

In the end, there was no great speech, no words of farewell said through tears. The queen simply encompassed all those welves leaving with her gaze and forced a smile Dannen knew she did not feel. "Be well," she said, "and should you ever wish to return, Riverlan will always be here for you. May the Green guide you always, sheltering you beneath the bows of its trees and providing you with what you will need upon your journey."

There were tears shed then, looks of anxiety and near-panic on the faces of many of those departing welves, looks Dannen understood. After all, it was easy enough, while being safe and secure, to dream of adventure. But adventure, in Dannen's experience, usually meant being hungry, cold, wet, and more often than not, under immediate risk to one's life. Fun enough for a short time, maybe, something new if nothing else, but the problem with adventures was that, once began, they rarely stopped when or how a person wanted them to.

The queen turned to Dannen and the others. "Thank you again, all of you, for helping my people."

"Our pleasure, ma'am," Fedder grunted, shifting uncomfortably. Dannen regarded the mage in surprise, for he had never heard the man sound so respectful before in all the years he'd known him. Tesler and Mariana's eyes were full of tears, and they both eschewed a verbal answer for nods and the most miserable looking smiles Dannen had ever seen.

Ridiculous, of course, for them to be so upset about leaving. After all, they had only been in Riverlan for little over a week, it was an inarguable shithole and their time here had begun with the threat of being executed or eaten by a griffin. Ridiculous for them to feel anything but glad about leaving, about getting back to the mortal world away from plants that moved at the welves' command and "bridges" which fell apart beneath one's feet. But ridiculous or not, Dannen felt a lump in his throat as he bowed to the queen. "It has been a pleasure, Majesty."

She smiled. "The pleasure was all mine, Dannen Ateran. May the world be kind to you and yours."

Dannen might have told her that would be a first, that the world was many things, but kind was never one of them, but he saw that she meant it. He thought, too, that if the world might change to suit the wishes of anyone, it would surely be the welven queen. "Thank you," he said.

The queen nodded and raised her hand. Suddenly, it was enveloped in a vibrant green glow, and she turned to the forest surrounding Riverlan. "The Green will guide you and show you the way," she said in a strained voice, then suddenly the plants retracted, and a large path, one wide enough that two or three could comfortably walk abreast, opened in the undergrowth, traveling deep into the forest as far as Dannen could see.

He had seen such magic from the welves already but never on so great a scale and, judging by the whispers of astonishment among the gathered welves, he was not the only one. And that was all. The welves with whom he and his companions would travel for the next several days until their paths split started toward the opening, and Dannen and his companions followed in silence. He paused at the edge of the village before he stepped into the woods, turning and looking back.

An ugly place, Riverlan. Ugly buildings and ugly people, even an ugly stream. Ugly but beautiful too, and Dannen knew he would miss this place, knew he might want to come back one day and knew, too, that the world being what it was, he probably never would. So he only tried to hold on to the moment as best he could, to grasp the feeling of contentment he felt and to store it away, to hoard it like a miser his treasure, so he could look over it later, and be pleased. But he had lived enough years to know that the feeling, the memory, would fade with each time he drew it out to examine it, like a letter's text which fades over time until the memory becomes no more than the ghost of a dream, until it is something that happened to another man, in another life.

He did not want to leave, then, wanted to stay and talk more with the queen, for here, far from civilization, a man could almost trick himself into thinking everything was alright. But the north lay ahead of him as did Perandius's quest, so he waved, turned and followed the departing welves into the forest.

CHAPTER ELEVEN

They traveled for a week, the queen's magic guiding their way, opening up a path in the undergrowth feet in front of them as they traveled as if they were walking into a ballroom and servants were stepping back to let them pass. They did not have to worry over food and drink, for while the welves might have many flaws, they were attuned to the forest in a way mortals never could be, finding food and fresh water easily.

Yet for all that they were fed and watered, Dannen's companions, who'd first been excited at the prospect of finally leaving Riverlan, were sullen and quiet, the way men or women became when they were forced to face some trial and had no choice but to endure it until it was over. Dannen understood, of course. After all, they had been traveling in the forest for a week already, not to mention over a week spent with the welves. Two weeks then, two weeks without sleeping in a proper bed, without a drink of ale for Fedder or a bath for any of them. He supposed they could have taken a bath in the welven river, but a man would have to be pretty damned filthy not to come out of it dirtier than he went in.

Even Dannen, who thought most people were assholes best avoided and, at worst, endured, was beginning to miss human settlements. Such places would have a room for rent—even if the price was exorbitant. They would also have ale to drink and food to eat other than berries or bark. The trade-off, of course, was that while it would have both of those things, it would also have humans. Still, Dannen was excited to finally get out of the forest and find a human town, thought an ale and a chance to rest his weary legs and aching feet would be a damn fine thing.

The welves were nice enough, of course, but after the princess and the others had decided not to kill them, they'd had little to say, choosing instead to keep to themselves. Not surprising, really. After all, they had seen nothing in their lives, experienced nothing, and therefore had nothing to talk about even—judging by the common silences when they stopped—to each other.

"Damned woods. Damned trees."

Dannen glanced over at Fedder who was scowling at the lush green around him like a man looking for a face to punch. His clothes were covered in burrs and stained green from walking through the forest, much like Dannen knew his own were, and the man's hair and beard looked like a tangled mess. A tangled mess which, since they had woken up only a few minutes ago, was covered in a thin layer of frost. The weather had cooled considerably as they traveled north, and Dannen's breath plumed in front of him in great clouds.

"Not long now," he said, because it was the type of thing a man said. Truth was, he had no idea where they were, hadn't for days and had given up trying to figure it out, choosing instead to carry on in weary ignorance, sure that, as always, knowledge would only bring more misery.

Fedder let out a low growl, the kind of growl a bear might make if it were considering making someone a snack, but said nothing further as they pressed on, following the welves.

Dannen glanced over at his other companions. Mariana, who apparently had never experienced cold before, seemed to be wearing a mish-mash of all the traveling clothes she'd brought layered on top of each other, but was shivering anyway, her arms wrapped tightly about herself as if they journeyed in the middle of a blizzard, even bent at an angle as if to lean into a wind that did not, strictly speaking, exist.

Tesler, on the other hand, seemed largely unfazed by their predicament, walking on much as he always did with a distracted, vaguely confused expression on his face as he spoke to his pet squirrel in a whispered voice. Dannen supposed a benefit of being batshit crazy was a man didn't have to deal with the little inconveniences which often afflicted those sane enough to notice.

He thought maybe he ought to say something, something to make their feet not hurt quite so bad, but as so often was the case, he could think of nothing, so he let it pass, walking on in silence.

It was nearing midday when the welves abruptly stopped, forcing Dannen and his companions to do the same. He took his pack off his back, assuming that they were making camp, but instead of retrieving their packs, the welves only stood in a group, whispering excitedly, while the princess walked over to Dannen and the others. "The time has come, Dannen Ateran."

"The time?"

"The time of the welves," she said. "The time when we will leave our home behind and travel forth into the lands of man and beast to see what we might find there."

Misery, likelier than not, Dannen thought. The princess, though, gazed off into the distance, her chin raised slightly, like some great conquering warrior standing for a portrait, the effect dampened somewhat by the fact that she was less than four feet tall, covered in boils and that dry flaking skin which seemed to afflict all the welves except for the queen. She seemed almost to be unaware, in her posing, that Dannen and the others still existed at all, and he shared a confused look with his companions. "I..."

"It is time, Dannen Ateran," the princess said apparently satisfied that she'd spent enough time gazing knowingly off into the distance. "For our leaf-taking."

Dannen frowned. "I'm pretty sure you mean—" But he cut off as the welf stepped forward, extending her hand toward him. Three other welves did the same, and Dannen blinked down at the leaf in the princess's hand. A dead leaf, this one, part of it missing where it had dried and flaked away. He glanced at Fedder. "What this?" he muttered.

"It's a leaf," the mage said, missing his point. "Think we're meant to take it."

Dannen fought back the urge to sigh and offered the princess the best smile he could as he took the leaf. "Thank you, Your Highness. For the...leaf."

She smiled in a benevolent way as if she had just bestowed some great gift upon him. "It is I who should be thanking you, Dannen Ateran, for without you and your companions my people would have been lost."

Dannen shifted uncomfortably. "It was nothing rea—" He cut off as she withdrew something from her satchel and offered it up with both hands with unmistakable reverence. Dannen blinked at the object.

"Ah, yes," she said, smiling knowingly, "I see that you are overcome with amazement, and I understand well, for the works of the welves are of the finest make, with magical qualities fashioned into them by their creators. Here, then, Dannen Ateran, is a gift, a token to express my gratitude for the service of you and your friends better than words ever could, a boon to match the boon you granted us."

Dannen continued to stare at the offered item in disbelief. The "token" looked like nothing so much as a mildly sharp rock— naturally sharpened by its formation, it appeared, and not by any effort of the welves themselves—which had been lashed to a piece of lumpy wood that he thought must have been meant as a handle. Though words like "handle," and even "lashed," gave the thing far more credit than it deserved as the weapon looked like it had been crafted by a child who had never actually seen a knife but only had it described to him.

"Take it, Dannen Ateran," the princess said in a voice that seemed to indicate that she stood in awe of the thing she held, "for it is of sidhe-make. May the Green grant that it serves you well."

From what Dannen could see, the pitiful attempt at craftsmanship would most likely serve to give him a splinter or to fall apart and, in doing so, become nothing more but a stick and a rock again. But he'd already nearly been killed by the welves once and was in no particular hurry to repeat the experience, so he nodded. "Thank you, Princess," he said gravely, "for your kindness. I wish you and your people well in your travels."

The princess gave him the dubious honor of a smile—one which put her crooked teeth on display—then turned and walked back to the welves. "A human settlement lies half a day's travel north of here," she said, glancing back at Dannen and the others and gesturing to the forest. "The Green will show you the way there. I and those with me travel a different path. We wish you luck, all of you. And if you ever need anything, you need only search for the welves."

With that, the princess turned and stepped into the forest. The other welves followed and in moments they vanished into the trees, leaving Dannen alone with his companions, all of whom were holding the leaves the welves had given them awkwardly, unsure of what to do with them. Dannen felt much the same but finally he decided to stuff it into his pocket, and the others followed his example. They were all silent for several seconds, staring off after the welves. Dannen truly did wish the princess and the other welves the best of luck, hoped that they would find a place that made them happy. But the world being what it was, he doubted that they would.

A strange, ugly people, maybe, but they had their beauty, too. "Come," he said finally, "you heard her. If we hurry, we can make this settlement she spoke of before nightfall and sleep in a real bed." That got them moving easily enough, and they walked on through the path the queen's magic made for them, a path which led to only the gods knew where.

***

The sun was low on the horizon by the time they shuffled wearily from the forest. Dannen was in a bad mood. Partly it was because he had spent the last several days listening to Fedder's grumblings, watching Mariana's scowls, and Tesler talking to his damned squirrel. Partly, it was that he felt bad for the welves, the ones who had remained in Riverlan, as well as the ones who had traveled into the world. Mostly, though, his feet hurt—there was a pebble in his shoe which contrived to evade his increasingly desperate attempts to dislodge it—and his back ached from nights spent sleeping on the hard ground. Also, he was hungry. The welves had provided them with food on their travels, at least of a sort, but berries and bark could only take a man so far.

He needed real food, needed a real bed to lie down in, maybe even one that came equipped with a pillow—which seemed almost too great a luxury to hope for—and an ale to wash the food down. Maybe a few ales.

They stood atop a rise outside the forest. Beyond them, fields dipped into a valley at the bottom of which, an hour or two's walk away, stood a village. Smoke rose from some chimneys—

necessary, so far as he was concerned, as the cold was getting more intense as the day wore on and Dannen had stopped being able to feel his toes and fingers hours ago. Could still feel the damned pebble though, shifting around beneath his foot.

The settlement was small, looked like fewer than a thousand people might have lived there. The buildings, from this distance, appeared to be made of stone, functional rather than pretty, the "street" running through the center no more than hard-packed earth. But after weeks spent in the forest, Dannen felt as if he and the others had just stumbled onto the Land of the Gods, an image heightened by the mountains towering at the other end of the valley, and he grinned. "Well," he said, glancing at his companions who all wore hopeful expressions—even Mariana had taken a break from scowling at Tesler to grin at the distant village—"let's go."

They moved onto the trail leading into the village and hurried past fields where men and women were picking corn. As they walked, he noticed something strange. Here and there among the workers were armed men, guardsmen that much was certain, for he'd seen plenty enough to know. Strange to see them there, standing over the workers as they were, but then he supposed it might have been a necessary precaution considering that here, in the north, the dead were said to be rising from their graves to attack the living.

The guardsmen nearest them watched their progress with suspicion, but none accosted them, and Dannen paid them little mind. After all, considering the state their stay among the welves and journey through the forest had left them and their clothes in, he would have been far more shocked had the guards not frowned at their appearance.

In time, they reached the village. More guards stood along the road and what few normal citizens were out seemed skittish, scared. Dannen wondered at that but not for long. He guessed if there was ever a recipe to make a man skittish, it was the dead coming back to life. If things were even half as bad as Perandius and the queen of the welves had claimed, then he figured these people had every right to be scared. No point in him bothering them about it. Besides, there was the ale and the bed to think of.

They walked on, but none of the buildings were marked as inns, and Dannen decided to use the expedient of asking directions for the nearest one. He walked up to a merchant at a stall, nodding in greeting.

"I-I don't want no trouble, stranger," the man said, avoiding his eyes.

Dannen frowned. In his travels, he had seen all manner of merchants with all sorts of strategies to part a man from his coin, but this was new. "Me neither, but my friends and I have been on the road for a while, and a drink would do me fine. Where's the nearest inn around this place?"

The merchant looked around nervously, as if he expected ghouls to pop up and attack at any moment. Ridiculous, of course, considering that even if ghouls *did* show up, the village seemed to have far more guards than a place of its size normally would to deal with it, guards which the man couldn't help but notice. "Palden's got several inns, stranger. Closest one is just there," he said, pointing then jerking his hand back as if he'd been burned. "Y-you can't miss it."

"Thanks."

Dannen led the way down the path to the building the man had indicated, then stepped inside. He was surprised to find it empty except a barkeep that seemed far too thin who was busily cleaning an empty mug with a rag. The man shot a nervous look up as they entered, then tried a smile that looked sickly on his face as they moved to the bar.

Dannen took a seat, breathing a sigh of relief to be off his feet for the first time in what felt like an age. The welves had possessed chairs, of course—or at least, their own approximations of chairs—but he'd rarely sat in them, thinking each time he did that there were plenty enough ways for a man to die without him going and looking for more. "How's it going, friend?" he asked.

"I-it's g-good," the innkeeper said, licking his lips anxiously. "A-are you lot new t-to town?"

Dannen frowned. Something was definitely wrong here, but it would take more than a nervous barkeep to ruin his mood just now. He grinned. "We are. You don't mind my sayin' so, everyone in town seems a bit nervous. Is it on account of I've heard the north's been having trouble with undead and the like?"

The man swallowed, glancing at the door. "Troubles, anyway." There was the creak of a door opening, and the innkeeper jumped in startlement, fumbling and nearly dropping the mug he held. He looked over to the door beside the bar and breathed a heavy sigh of relief as a short, plump woman walked through holding a broom. Then glanced back at Dannen and the others and gave a sickly laugh. "Sorry about that, friends. Just...been a bit jumpy lately."

Dannen thought that calling the man "a bit jumpy" was like calling fire "a bit hot" but he didn't bother saying so. "Four ales, for me and my companions, please," he said.

"O-of course," the barkeep said, nodding his head so frantically it was a wonder it didn't come off. "L-look, Liddy," he said, turning a weak smile on the woman, "we've got visitors."

The woman looked up from where she'd set about sweeping the floor, her eyes going wide. "What in the name of all the gods for?"

Dannen was beginning to see why the inn didn't have any customers, but he'd be damned if an odd innkeeper and an even odder serving maid were going to put him off after all he'd been through. "You can just bring our drinks to that table over there," he said, motioning to one, and the innkeeper nodded again, setting about the task as Dannen and the others made their way toward it.

Once they were all seated, Mariana frowned around them. "Something seem strange to you?" she asked quietly.

"Maybe," Dannen agreed, "but whatever it is, it'll keep 'til mornin'. I'm exhausted, and right now I can't be bothered with anything but a drink and a bed."

Less than a minute later, the woman, Liddy, appeared with four mugs of ale on a tray, still holding the broom she'd been using to sweep in the other hand. She set the mugs down hurriedly and left without saying a word.

Dannen stared at the drink before him. Not foaming over the rim of the glass, not like he'd imagined, and when he touched the cup it wasn't cold, but instead was room temperature. Probably it wouldn't have the crisp, refreshing taste he'd imagined either, but that was okay. He leaned back in his chair, a smile on his face as he raised the mug to his companions. "To not being dead."

Fedder lifted his mug quickly in response to the toast, but then again the mage never needed much of an excuse to drink, knocking it back with fervor. Dannen stared at him, blinking, and was just about to take a slightly-more controlled drink of his own when Mariana spoke. "Might be you spoke too soon."

"What do you mean—" Dannen began, but then he glanced over Fedder's shoulder toward the door and got his answer. Town guardsmen filed into the tavern, their faces grim. Dannen counted four in all. He was glad that at least they had not drawn the swords at their sides, though judging by the way they fingered the handles, they weren't far from doing so.

"Y-you know these men?" Tesler asked in response to Mariana's statement.

She snorted. "How in the name of the gods am I to know people live in this freezing climate? No, I don't *know* them," she went on, "but I know the type."

"What ty—" Tesler began, but Dannen held up a hand, silencing him.

"Quiet."

Mariana was right, of course. The men might wear guard uniforms—in his experience, such men often did—but he knew them just the same. Power-hungry men out to take what they could and more than willing to cause pain or hurt in the doing of it. Men looking for trouble the way a cruel child might look for bugs to squash or mongrels to throw rocks at. And considering that he and his companions were the only people in the tavern save the barkeep and the serving maid, and they were arriving only minutes after Dannen and the others, it didn't take a genius to riddle out what had brought them here.

Indeed, the man in front—obviously the leader, for he looked like the biggest asshole of the lot, the one with the best scowl, and Dannen figured that was the usual way such things were decided—swept Dannen and the others with an imperious gaze, his nose lifted in the air. But just when Dannen was thinking the man was going to speak, was going to issue some challenge or another, he turned to the barkeep instead. "Looks like you've got customers, Meckam. How exciting."

318

The innkeeper nodded. "T-thank you, Guardsman Lauder," he stammered, his eyes seeming to roam everywhere around the room except for on the armed men.

Lauder, though, didn't appear to be offended by the innkeeper refusing to meet his gaze. In fact, he seemed pleased by it, taking the fear as only his due, and Dannen didn't think he imagined the way the man's chest puffed out a little more, or how his back grew a little straighter. He looked around the room again, making a show of it, before his gaze finally settled on Dannen and the others. "Huh," he said thoughtfully. "Looks to me, Meckam, like each of them ordered an ale, that it?"

Meckam licked his lips nervously. "I—um, that is, yes, sir, Guardsman Lauder."

The man studied them for several seconds, his eyes settling on Dannen who stared back at him, thinking he had a pretty good idea of what was coming. It didn't matter much where a man went, the north, the south, a forest deep in the wilderness—the world was full of assholes, enough you had to expect to bump into them from time to time. But to his surprise, the man turned back to the innkeeper.

"Happy for you, Meckam, damn happy, though not so happy for them considering your ale tastes like piss." Some laughter from the other guards at that, not genuine, really, but the sort of obligatory laughter common among those who chose to follow the assholes of the world. "Still," he said, heaving maybe the world's biggest sigh of regret—though certainly not its most genuine— "happy as I am, I'm afraid I got to collect your taxes."

Someone at their table snorted in disgust, and Dannen started to scowl at Fedder before realizing that everyone was staring at him, and that he'd been the one who'd snorted. A stupid thing to do, but he was tired, irritable from days and weeks spent in the woods, and angry, too. Angry that the moment he'd finally been able to relax had been interrupted by this bastard.

"Sorry," the guard said, staring at Dannen like he'd finally found his bug and was just getting ready to squish it, "you got somethin' you want to say, friend?"

Just leave it, Dannen thought. *You've got plenty enough problems already, no need to go looking for more.* Sure, the guard was an asshole, but what of it? If a man wanted to start picking a fight with every asshole in the world, he was going to have a damned busy time of it. "Sorry," he said, "had something in my throat."

The guard gave him a small smile, no doubt pleased with himself for making Dannen back down, then turned to the innkeeper once more. "Now then, Meckam, I'll take your taxes and be on my way."

The innkeeper swallowed guiltily. "I...I didn't make them pay them."

The guard put on a feigned expression of surprise, as if before now, he could not have imagined anyone ever doing such a thing, overdoing the act a bit, at least to Dannen's mind. "My, my," he said, shaking his head. "Well, that's quite alright, Meckam. Mistakes will be made, of course." He considered. "How about this—it seems unfair, now, to ask your guests to pay extra, you being the one that forgot and all. I guess the only thing to do is to take the taxes out of your own coin. The fair thing, wouldn't you say?" he asked, a challenge in his voice.

Meckam's face was pale, but he finally gathered the courage to meet the man's eyes. "No," he said, trying to sound confident, his efforts undermined by the way his voice trembled as he spoke.

The guard, Lauder, cocked his head as if he had never heard the word before and had no idea what it meant. "Forgive me, Meckam, but I must have misunderstood you," he said, stepping toward the bar, the other three guardsmen following behind. "It almost sounded as if you said you didn't intend to pay your taxes, the taxes which are required by every man and woman living in Palden. Which, of course, can't be right. After all," he went on, the confused tone leaving his voice to be replaced with a menacing one, "its those taxes that Duke Navierd uses to keep you and every other citizen of Palden safe, to protect you from the many dangers which might do you harm."

"Y-you'd take all the money I have," the innkeeper managed. "A-already I've had to let everyone go, 'cept Liddy," he said, gesturing at the older woman who stood near Dannen and the others' table, seemingly frozen, her broom gripped tightly in her hands as if it were a shield. "My wife and I can barely afford to eat as it is and—"

"*Enough*," the guard growled. "Times are tough all around, Meckam, for everyone."

Though now, as was often the case in Dannen's experience, times looked far less tough for the guardsmen who appeared well-fed and well-equipped, while the innkeeper wore little better than rags and had a shrunken look to his face as if he'd recently lost a significant amount of weight.

"Surely," the guard went on, "you can't mean to say that you are so selfish you would refuse to pay for the protection the Duke provides while others in Palden do so without complaint?"

The innkeeper opened his mouth as if to say more, but apparently his courage had run out, and no words came, his face screwing up as if he were about to cry.

"Now, Meckam," the guard said in a falsely soothing voice, "it seems to me that, considering what you were trying to do, it's only fair you pay double the taxes. I'm sure the coin will not be unappreciated—"

"*Enough.*" Dannen wasn't aware he'd spoken until everyone in the common room turned to look at him, just as he only then became aware that he'd risen from his chair.

The false kindness left the guard's face to be replaced by an angry sneer. "Look, stranger," he said, "maybe you don't know how things are done here in Palden, but if you know what's good for you, you'll sit down and enjoy your ale while my friend Meckam and I have a little chat. Otherwise..." He glanced at the guards around him then back at Dannen. "Well. Don't be foolish."

Dannen stood there, his chest heaving for no reason, feeling the mood which sometimes swept through him moving forward in his mind like a heavy bank of fog rolling in, fighting it. He told himself they had their own problems, more than enough, and that the last thing he needed was to borrow trouble. He didn't respond, *couldn't* respond, so focused was he on fighting that urge—the one which had gotten him into so much trouble in the past.

The guard stared at him for another moment then smiled, apparently taking his silence as agreement, before he turned back to Meckam. "Now then," he said, no kindness—feigned or otherwise—in his voice now, "I don't want your damned excuses, old man. I want your coin, and that's—" The man cut off, turning back, and Dannen realized the low rumble he'd taken for distant thunder was coming from his own throat, not thunder at all but a growl, one growing in intensity by the moment.

He felt the urge coming stronger now, rushing over him. He turned to the woman, Liddy, where she stood nearby. He reached out his hand. "Can I borrow that broom?" he said, his voice sounding distant and hollow to his own ears. "Seems there's a bit more cleaning needs doing." The woman's eyes were wide with terror, though whether at Dannen or the guards he couldn't have said, but she handed him the broom.

Dannen took it, thinking that he really needed to stop going into taverns, then thinking nothing else, for the urge surged forward, *charged* forward, overcoming what meager defenses he tried to erect before it, washing over them as if they weren't even there. "Come on, then," he said, turning back to the guard and his three companions, "let's get this over with."

***

Mariana stared at Dannen, feeling as if she were seeing him for the first time. Since meeting the two men a few weeks ago, she'd long since decided Dannen was the reasonable one. Now, though, as she watched him walking calmly toward the four guardsmen—all of whom had drawn their swords—his face plastered with a macabre grin even though they wielded sharp steel while he held nothing but a broom, she realized just how wrong she'd been. The man was crazy, alright, crazier even than Fedder and Tesler combined. He just hid it better.

He was hiding nothing now. His eyes were wild, like some mad beast, and there was something feral, something animalistic about the way he stalked forward, still growling. *He's going to get himself killed and us along with him,* she thought. She rose, not sure what she meant to do, only knowing she needed to stop him somehow, but a hand as thick as a dinner platter gripped her arm, halting her as well as a brick wall might have.

"I wouldn't, lass."

She turned to see Fedder regarding her seriously.

"He's going to get killed, can't you see that?" she demanded.

"Ain't the Butcher you got to worry about, not now," Fedder said, giving a small, humorless smile. "Have a seat—finish your ale."

Mariana stared at Tesler, looking to him for help, but the crazy man was listening to his squirrel chattering at him. She frowned in disgust, turning back to the mage. "I have to stop him."

"I wouldn't," the mage repeated. "Last person tried to stop him when the mood was on him died, and in a bad way."

She blinked. Sure, something had come over Dannen, that much was clear, but she couldn't believe what she was hearing. "You don't mean...that is, he killed someone for trying to stop him?"

The mage frowned as if she'd just spoken in gibberish. "Gods, no. No, as I recall, the poor bastard died a year later, trampled by a team of horses and a runaway carriage." He shook his head. "Damn messy way to go."

Mariana suddenly wanted to scream. "Then what are we supposed to do?"

"Just sit down and relax," Fedder said, motioning to her chair, "take a load off. If I know the Butcher, this won't take long."

Mariana looked to Tesler again, but the man was still in deep conversation with his pet squirrel and so no help at all. She wanted to shout, to scream at him that he was a fool, that they were *all* fools. Had they really just traveled as far as they had only to be killed barely an hour before setting foot in the north? It was ridiculous, it was—

Her train of thought cut off at the sounds of angry shouts and Dannen broke into a loping run directly at the four waiting guardsmen. A moment later, he was among them, moving with a shocking speed she wouldn't have credited him with, pouncing and lunging like some wild beast. And when the screaming started in earnest, it came not from Mariana, but from the four guardsmen. Too stunned to do anything else, Mariana sat. And watched.

***

When Dannen came to, he was standing, his chest heaving, the coppery taste of blood in his mouth. He had a brief moment in which he hoped that he'd managed to beat the urge back after all, a moment that lasted until he realized he held the broom—or what was left of it—in one hand. Not much remained but a two-foot-long stake where the handle had broken off, a stake coated in blood.

He blinked dazedly, looking around him and, at first, his mind felt fuzzy, unsure. Then, slowly, reality asserted itself, and he saw the four guardsmen lay at his feet, scattered like broken dolls and surrounded by the shattered remnants of tables and chairs. And judging by the blood covering them as if someone had upended several buckets of red paint on them—not to mention the gaping wounds—they were quite dead.

"Shit," he croaked, running a crimson-speckled arm across his suddenly dry mouth. He turned back to look at the table where his companions had been to see that they were still sitting there, watched Fedder nod his head and raise his glass.

"Damn fine show as always, Butcher," the mage called.

Dannen blinked, fighting back the urge to vomit. "Shit," he repeated.

Mariana was standing, her face looking green and sickly as she stared at the bodies. "I...I can't—" Suddenly, she clapped a hand to her mouth and ran out of the common room and into the street.

Fedder grunted, finishing his ale in one long gulp then slamming it on the table before standing. "Fine ale, barkeep." He tossed some coins on the table. "Might be, we'll have to forego rooms just now."

Dannen, as always following one of his spells, felt exhausted and confused, and he turned to the tavernkeeper to see the man staring at him, looking even more terrified than he had by the guards.

"W-what are you?" the man said, his voice shaking with fear.

It was a question Dannen had been asking himself all his life, or at least ever since he'd first been overcome with rage at the age of eight or nine, not killing anyone, thank the gods, but making sure the three or four older kids who'd chosen him as a target had a pretty shitty week. "What am I?" Dannen asked, his words little more than a rasp. "Mostly, Meckam, I'm tired."

"Y-you need to leave," the man stammered, then he paled further as if Dannen would attack him for his insolence. "P-please. I-I don't need any trouble."

Dannen sighed. How many times had he been asked to leave such a place? Too many, and many of those at the point of a sword. He walked to where the woman, Liddy, still stood as if frozen, but not so frozen that she didn't recoil at his approach. He reached out, offering the remains of the broom. "Sorry," he said. "About..." He paused, glancing around at the carnage, broken tables and chairs, broken bodies, too. "About everything."

The woman reached out, tentatively taking the broken handle before deciding she'd had enough and fleeing into the backroom at a run. Dannen couldn't blame her. He'd run too, if he could, but then how did a man run from himself?

"Best we go see to the girl," Fedder said, stretching and tipping his head to the tavernkeeper as if nothing untoward had occurred, before lifting a stunned-looking Tesler to his feet as easily as a mother cat might lift her kitten. "Come on, lad. Daylight burning and all that."

He walked the dazed young man across the room, picking his way among the bodies and frowning as if they were no more than an inconvenience. He paused beside Dannen, glancing at him. "You comin', Butcher?" He looked at the bodies. "Seems like you're pretty well done here."

Dannen swallowed, unable to decide, at that moment, if he loved or hated the man, thinking that, most times, the line between the two was a pretty damn fine one. "Yeah. I'm coming."

Wasn't an easy thing, leaving the inn, leaving the dead behind him. He had done it a thousand times before, far too many, but it wasn't the sort of thing a man got used to. He was feeling pretty low then, as always after succumbing to the urge, to that ever-present anger always threatening to rise to the surface, feeling just about as low as he imagined a man *could* feel.

Then he walked out the door and saw the few dozen guardsmen—many toting crossbows—arrayed in the street, all facing him and the others, including Mariana who'd stopped short outside the doors—couldn't blame her, for a street full of crossbows, all pointed in your direction generally had that effect on a person. A man, he decided, had to be very careful with what he thought, particularly when he was thinking about how miserable his life was, for the world had a way of taking such thoughts as a challenge.

Dannen figured that he and his companions were about to get filled with crossbow bolts, so he was more than a little surprised when a few of the guards stepped aside to allow a man to walk through. The newcomer was dressed in fine, expensive clothes that looked as if they'd cost a small fortune. Not that unusual to see in the bigger cities but here, in this frontier village where most people were far too concerned with survival to think of fashion, they were odd to say the least, and Dannen thought he knew who the man must be even before he introduced himself.

"*I*," the man proclaimed—he had the sort of pompous voice that made Dannen think he never just said anything but always proclaimed it, "am Duke Navierd, ruler and protector of Palden and its outlying areas, keeper of—"

"And I'm tired," Dannen said, figuring that if he was going to get killed, he'd just as soon get it over with. At least that way, he could get some rest.

Fedder snorted a laugh beside him, but the duke and his guardsmen looked decidedly less amused, scowling deeply. "Tell me, strangers," the Duke said, "so that I might know before your hanging: what has brought you here, to my lands?"

"Your lands?" Dannen asked. "I always thought that was strange, men claiming to own land. How does a man own a field or a forest? What claim can he lay to it? What right does he have to it over the people and animals who call it home?"

The duke sneered. "What right?" he asked. "I, fool, have the right of Divine mandate, for my blood comes from a long line of—"

"Wait," Dannen interrupted, knowing he should shut up but too weary to care, "so because your family line is about as straight as the bolts your lads there have loaded in their crossbows, I'm supposed to bow and pay you tribute?" The duke sputtered, his anger making him momentarily lost for words, and Dannen pressed on. "To answer your question, we came because we heard there was trouble in the north, the undead kind, and thought we might be of some service."

The duke laughed this time, a sharp, piercing laugh that drove into Dannen's head like daggers. "There are no undead in Palden, fool. "Why," he went on, "any undead, should they wish to trouble us, would have to travel miles and miles through the mountains.

Mountains which, with winter coming on, are covered in snow and ice and largely impassable."

"I see," Dannen said, "so it sounds like the only danger the folks of Palden have to worry about's you, then."

The duke's face colored a deep, ugly crimson. "The citizens of Palden have *nothing* to be afraid of, for I protect them from all dangers. Except, undead, of course," he said, then paused to allow the guardsmen a moment to snicker, "for to make it here to Palden, they would have to fly. Perhaps," he went on, grinning, "were they undead birds or manticores—" He froze as a great roar split the air like thunder. It sounded distant, that roar, but loud and terrifying.

"Or dragons," Fedder said into the stillness.

The duke swallowed. *"Dragons,"* he mocked. "Everyone knows dragons aren't real. Why, such a thought is ridic—" He cut off, scowling angrily as one of the guardsmen frantically grasped him by the arm, turning to point into the sky.

Dannen and everyone gathered followed the man's gesture, staring off at the distance near the mountain peak outside the village. A great, hulking form flew in the air, far away now, but even from this distance, Dannen thought it looked as if all of it, even its great, massive wings which were as long as several carriages sat abreast, was nothing but bone and tattered remnants of flesh that flapped in the wind like great banners.

"Shit," he said, once again thinking that the world had a way of taking a man's confidence and making the worst out of it. Not a bird, that was sure, not a manticore either, not that massive form filling the sky. Could only be one thing, no matter how much Dannen might have wished otherwise. The air was suddenly filled with terrified screams as guards and duke and peasants alike scrambled for cover.

"Thought you said there weren't any dragons in this story," Fedder said, the shock in his voice—so unusual—enough to terrify any man who knew him, if it was needed, which, with an undead dragon flying in the sky, it most certainly was not.

"Didn't think there were," Dannen said. An undead dragon which was bad, but what was worse was that, though it was still distant, there was no denying that it was flying directly at the village of Palden.

Fedder hocked and spat. "Be a damn shame to end it this way after all we been through."

Dannen glanced at Tesler and Mariana, both of them looking pale and terrified, then back to his friend. "Yes. Yes, it would."

THE END
of
BOOK ONE
of
THE
ANTIHEROES

Now we have come to the end of *The Antiheroes.* Thanks for sticking around to the end. Book two in the series will be coming soon, and we'll see what becomes of our heroes…that is, our antiheroes. While you wait, check out *A Sellsword's Compassion*, book one of the bestselling and complete Seven Virtues series.

If you've enjoyed *The Antiheroes*, I'd appreciate you taking a minute to leave an honest review. They make a tremendous difference as any author can tell you and there are few things better than hearing someone's thoughts on your book. As long as they're good. Otherwise, feel free to lie to me.

If you'd like to reach out and chat, you can email me at JacobPeppersAuthor@gmail.com or visit my website. You can also give me a shout on Facebook or on Twitter.

I'm looking forward to hearing from you!

Sign up for my new releases mailing list to hear about promotions, launches, and, for a limited time, get a FREE copy of *The Silent Blade,* the prequel book to the bestselling epic fantasy series, The Seven Virtues.

Go to JacobPeppersAuthor.com to claim your free book!

Note from the Author

Well, fellow adventurers, we've reached the end of the Antiheroes...or have we? Dannen and his companions have come far, but they will go further still. Though, whether that journey will take place inside the gullet of an undead dragon, or on their own feet is anyone's guess.

I hope you have enjoyed this book half as much as I enjoyed writing it—if not, lie to me, won't you? I'm easily fooled. Now, let's let Dannen and the others rest there, for a bit—I doubt they'll mind considering what they face. I'd like to take a moment to thank all of those who have worked to turn the steaming pile of which I was so proud into something people might enjoy reading. Again, if you didn't enjoy it, just lie—I'll believe you the same way I believe my wife every time she claims to have "accidentally" locked me in the basement.

Now, on to the thank-you's. I'd first like to thank my wife who spends her time and energy trying (sometimes even successfully) to keep our two-year-old tornado from destroying the house while I sit around and make stuff up. I'd also like to thank my family and friends. Look, guys, a bit of gratitude isn't exactly going to give you back all the time you lost listening to me prattle on about this plot point or that, but it's the best I've got, alright?

Thank you, also, to all the beta readers who have not only been brave enough to face the tangled mess of my writing, cutting away misspellings and grammatical errors like they're blazing a trail through the jungle with a machete, but have also managed to avoid calling me an incompetent fraud in the process.

Thank you, finally, to you, dear reader. I cannot thank you enough for spending your time with me and Dannen and Fedder and all the rest.

Some writers are so skilled at their craft, their work often seems to me like some great ocean, one I could lose myself in, one whose currents I could float on for hours, lulled to contentment by crashing waves of poetic prose and perfect dialogue.

In case you've made it this far without realizing it—if so, you are to be commended, though it may be time for a visit to the eye doctor—I, I'm afraid, am not one of those writers. This book—and the books that follow—might be more akin to a pool than an ocean. And not one of those fancy inground numbers with the steps made specifically for tripping either, an image that is somehow never captured in the catalogue pictures.

No, I'm thinking more of the blow-up kind that last until you look at them for too long and then inevitably wind up with a hole. That's right—this, then, is my kiddy pool. Or should I say *our* kiddy pool? After all, you're here, aren't you? S...yeah. Here it is. Splash around a little, if you like—it's yours. It's not as deep as the ocean, maybe, but that's okay. The ocean, after all, has sharks. Which, as far as I'm concerned, are far worse than undead dragons. After all, dragons aren't real...

Right?

Happy Reading and until next time,

Jacob Peppers

About the Author

Jacob Peppers lives in Georgia with his wife, his son, Gabriel, and three dogs. He is an avid reader and writer and when he's not exploring the worlds of others, he's creating his own. His short fiction has been published in various markets, and his short story, "The Lies of Autumn," was a finalist for the 2013 Eric Hoffer Award for Short Prose. He is also the author of *A Sellsword's Compassion* and *The Silent Blade*.